The voice was hauntingly familiar

Blinking furiously, Linnet made out a figure hunched over her. "Sweet Mary, I have died," she whispered. Dimly she was aware of gentle pokes and prods as he examined her arms and legs.

"I do not think anything is broken." The man sat back on his haunches. "Can you move your limbs?"

"Simon?" Linnet murmured.

He cocked his head. "You know who I am?"

"But…you perished…."

"Nay, though I came close on a few occasions."

Joy pulsed through her, so intense it brought fresh tears to eyes that had already cried a river for him.

He leaned closer, his jaw stubbled, his eyes shadowed by their sockets. "Do I know you?"

A laugh bubbled in her throat, wild and a bit hysterical. She cut it off with a sob. She had been right. He did not even remember her or their wondrous moment together….

Dear Reader,

What a perfect time to celebrate history—the eve of a new century. This month we're featuring four terrific romances with awe-inspiring heroes and heroines from days gone by that you'll want to take with you into the *next* century.

Simon of Blackstone, a knight returning from the Crusades, is one of those characters. He's the valiant hero in Suzanne Barclay's latest medieval novel, *The Champion.* This is the first book in our new connected miniseries, KNIGHTS OF THE BLACK ROSE, about a handful of English knights who come home from the horrors of the battlefield to new lives and new loves. Simon returns to confront the father he never knew…and finds himself and his lady love the prime suspects in a chilling murder. Don't miss this reunion romance with unparalleled twists!

Wolf Heart is the fascinating, timeless hero from *Shawnee Bride,* an emotion-filled Native American romance by Elizabeth Lane. It's about a white Shawnee warrior who falls in love with the young woman he rescues from river pirates. In *By Queen's Grace* by Shari Anton, Saxon knight Corwin of Lenvil heroically wins the hand and heart of his longtime love, a royal maiden.

Antoinette Huntington is the unforgettable heroine in *The Lady and the Outlaw,* a new Western by DeLoras Scott. After her husband's murder, Antoinette flees England and has a romantic run-in with an outlaw on a train headed for the Arizona Territory.

Enjoy! And come back again next month for four more choices of the best in historical romance.

Happy holidays,

Tracy Farrell
Senior Editor

SUZANNE BARCLAY

THE CHAMPION

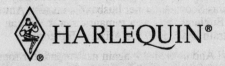

HARLEQUIN®

TORONTO • NEW YORK • LONDON
AMSTERDAM • PARIS • SYDNEY • HAMBURG
STOCKHOLM • ATHENS • TOKYO • MILAN • MADRID
PRAGUE • WARSAW • BUDAPEST • AUCKLAND

ISBN 0-373-29091-8

THE CHAMPION

Visit us at www.romance.net

Printed in U.S.A.

Available from Harlequin Historicals and
SUZANNE BARCLAY

* The Sommerville Brothers
† The Sutherland Series
‡ Knights of the Black Rose

Please address questions and book requests to:
Harlequin Reader Service
U.S.: 3010 Walden Ave., P.O. Box 1325, Buffalo, NY 14269
Canadian: P.O. Box 609, Fort Erie, Ont. L2A 5X3

To the talented ladies who created the
Knights of the Black Rose:
Shari Anton, Laurie Grant, Sharon Schulze,
Ana Seymour and Lyn Stone.
What fun we had brainstorming this terrific series.
Let's do it again sometime.

Prologue

England, May 10, 1222

They rode north on the road from York to Durleigh, six Crusader knights in worn gray tabards with a black rose stitched over the heart, a babe scarce a year old and Odetta, a goat that was more trouble than the Saracens they had faced in the East.

Thick gray clouds obscured the noonday sun. The raw breeze that harried their backs carried a hint of rain that discouraged lingering on the trail.

Not that Simon of Blackstone was inclined to linger. He'd set a brisk pace since rousting his comrades from their blanket rolls in the darkness of predawn, and he meant to be in Durleigh by midafternoon. Ignoring the discomfort, as he had so many other unpleasant things life had flung at him, he concentrated on the muddy track ahead. His thoughts, his entire being, were focused on reaching the town a half day's journey north.

Durleigh, where he'd been fostered and knighted in the household of Lord Edmund de Meresden. Durleigh, seat of the great cathedral presided over by Bishop Thurstan de Lyndhurst.

The man who had sired him.

Simon's jaw set tighter, and the heat of anger rose to counter the damp chill. Three long years he had waited to confront the priest who had given him life, but never bothered to acknowledge him. Three years of living with the bitter knowledge that his whole life had been a lie.

"We need to call a halt," muttered Guy de Meresden, riding at Simon's right.

Stop then, but I will not. Not till I've seen the mighty bishop and extracted a penance for his sins.

The words stuck in Simon's throat. Two hundred men had ridden out from Durleigh four years ago bound for the East. Only six had come back alive, and Simon's five comrades were as precious to him as the family he never had.

Sighing, Simon glanced back over his shoulder at the rest of the troop. Hugh, Bernard, Gervase and Nicholas were veterans of long marches and short rations, but their mounts were beginning to droop and Odetta was wobbling. If the damn thing keeled over, there'd be no milk for wee Maudie's supper. "I had hope to reach Durleigh today," Simon muttered.

"As do I, my friend." Guy smiled, teeth white against bronzed skin that betrayed his mixed heritage. According to Guy's Saracen mother, he was the legitimate son of Lord Edmund de Meresden, born after his lordship had left Acre for England. "We are equally anxious to confront our sires, if for different reasons. But our horses need rest and water."

Simon grunted in reluctant agreement and looked over his shoulder again. "We will halt in yon meadow for a bit."

Nicholas of Hendry grinned. "Better yet, I know of an inn up ahead where the ale's sweet—"

"And the lasses sweeter, I wager," Simon grumbled.

Nicholas's easy smile, the one that charmed every woman he met, faded. "I have put aside the wild ways of my youth."

"Forgive my sharp tongue," Simon said, though privately

he thought, *once a rogue, always a rogue.* Living side by side for four years had forged a bond between them, but Simon disliked Nicholas's easy morals. Who knew how many bastards Nick had spread about the country—and abandoned? Just as Bishop Thurstan had abandoned Simon. "Lead the way to this inn, then."

"I have changed," Nicholas said crisply before taking Simon's customary place at the head of the column.

"He understands why you feel as you do," said Guy.

"Nay, I do not think anyone does, even you." Simon cast his mind back three years to when Brother Martin, confessor to their band of Crusaders, had fallen ill. As he lay dying, the priest had revealed a startling secret. Simon was Bishop Thurstan's son. "At least your father was wed to your mother."

"Aye, but Lord Edmund vowed he'd return for my mother. He never did," Guy said softly. "Perhaps he wished to forget he'd wed an infidel...even if she did become a Christian."

"You knew your mother. She raised you, loved you, and you saw to her welfare when you were older. I do not know what became of my mother." The pain ripped at Simon's insides. "He abandoned her and ignored me, though we lived in the same town."

"Perhaps he had a good reason."

"Bah! He sought to preserve his reputation, did Bishop Thurstan," Simon growled. "But I will confront him with his dark deed, and I will have my mother's name that I may find her." The thought of her, alone and likely destitute, was nigh intolerable.

"There is the inn," Nicholas called as they rounded a bend in the road and came upon a small hamlet. They caused quite a stir as they dismounted in the yard of the inn, the horses snorting and tossing their heads, Odetta bleating for all she was worth. Baby Maud awoke with a start and wailed.

"Shh. We'll be getting some milk." Hugh of Halewell jiggled Maud. The black-haired imp looked incongruous in his massive arms, but there she had ridden from Acre to England, though she was not Hugh's child. Maud was the daughter of a prisoner held in the same compound from which the knights had rescued Hugh. With her dying breath, the woman had begged Hugh to save her daughter. It was a charge the knight took most seriously.

"I think she needs to be changed again," Simon murmured.

Hugh stared ruefully at the wet spot on his tabard, blue eyes twinkling. "'Tis no wonder my mail is constantly rusty."

"And we've more wash than a whole Crusader camp." Simon glanced at the nappy tied onto Hugh's lance tip to dry.

The door to the tavern opened and a burly man peered out. "See here, what is—" His eyes rounded. "Sir...Sir Nicholas?"

"Aye. I'm pleased you remembered me, Master—"

"Ye're dead." The innkeeper crossed himself and backed up.

"Dead?" Simon exclaimed. "What do you mean?"

"Killed. Dead." The innkeeper eyed them warily. "King's messenger brought word last autumn ye were butchered by the infidels. Bishop Thurstan held a special mass in Durleigh."

Simon's lip curled. "Likely he was celebrating my demise."

"What a thing to say!" the innkeeper exclaimed.

"Thanks to my stupidity we were away when our comrades were attacked," Hugh grumbled. "If I hadn't gotten myself captured—"

"We would not have gone to Acre to rescue you." Simon looked at Hugh's back, remembering the Saracen arrow that had lodged there as they fled. If not for Gervase's special healing skills, he'd have died in that alley. "I had no idea we had all been reported dead." He glanced around at his comrades and saw his own speculation mirrored in their faces. What had those they'd left behind thought when they had heard the news? Would the knights be welcomed with rejoicing when each reached his home? Or would there be more challenges to face?

"Well, praise be to God for saving ye." All smiles, the innkeeper hustled them inside to a table by the hearth and brought a round of ale. A pretty maidservant offered to take Maud above stairs for a change of nappy and a bit of Odetta's milk. Used to the company of men, Maud clung to Hugh.

"Shh, here, lovey." Hugh gave her a cup of milk.

Simon settled back in his chair, the cup of ale resting on his lean belly, as he watched the five men who had unexpectedly become his friends. How much they had all changed in four years.

Bernard FitzGibbons had grown the most, under Hugh's expert guidance, from a bumbling knightling to a seasoned warrior. Fair-haired Gervase of Palgrave had discovered he had a healing touch that defied explanation. Torn between two worlds, Guy had found a haven with the knights of Durleigh and grown especially close to Simon.

"How far we have come," Simon murmured. "We are different men from when we set out together."

"Aye." Nicholas scowled. "I hope I can convince my sire I am now worthy to be his heir, else he'll make good his threat to cut off that part of me he blames for my mischief."

Hugh laughed. "Gervase may be able to make it whole again."

"My healing is not a thing to be used lightly."

"Oh, I'd not take it lightly," Nicholas teased.

They grinned at that, but beneath their banter lurked a

tension Simon finally put into words. "Being reported dead may have consequences when we reach home."

Silence fell over the table, each one recalling the troubling circumstances that had led to their taking the cross in the first place. Simon had gone with lofty hopes of saving the Holy Land, but the Crusade had been a bitter, dismal failure. Nicholas had gone to escape a horde of amorous women. Bernard to atone for his overlord's sins. Gervase because of a vow made on his father's grave. Hugh as a penance for killing a friend on the tiltyard. In each case, their going had been demanded by Bishop Thurstan as payment for a sin. To Simon, such manipulation was but another crime the bishop had committed.

"No one will be pleased to see me return," Simon said.

"You may be surprised," Guy said quietly. "We do not always know whose lives we have touched."

Simon grunted, drained his cup and stood. "Well, we shall soon find out. I'm for Durleigh." He turned to Hugh. "Are you certain your brother will welcome wee Maud in his household?"

"Aye. He should be wed by now, and he has a soft heart. If for some reason that is not so, I will raise her myself."

Simon nodded. "If you cannot, send her to me. I will not stay in Durleigh after I confront the bishop, but I will leave word at the Royal Oak Inn where I have gone. I would not like to think of her raised without love and caring." *As he had been.*

"Rest assured that will not happen," Hugh replied.

The sun was making a valiant effort to fight off the clouds when they emerged from the tavern. Rested and watered, the horses picked up the pace. Not long now until they parted company, Simon thought unhappily. Nicholas and Guy would ride with him as far as Durleigh. The others would take different paths. Who knew if they would meet again?

The sense of loss that filled him was unexpected. He had learned not to need anyone.

Fighting to regain his composure, Simon looked up and noted a flock of birds rising from the trees ahead. *"En garde,"* he said softly. "It may be someone waits around yon bend." He gave the orders that sent Bernard and Nicholas off the road and through the trees in a flanking action.

Hugh handed the dozing Maud to Gervase. "Guard her."

"With my life." Gervase withdrew into the brush.

Simon pulled the sword from his scabbard, laid it across his thighs and lowered his visor. "Ready?"

"Aye," Hugh and Guy replied as one. They cut in behind Simon and rode warily down the road.

The forest seemed to close in on the trail, dark and sinister. Senses alert, Simon scanned the area ahead, probing each leaf and branch for some sign. "There! To the right," he whispered, muscles tensing. "Behind the rocks."

Just as they came abreast of the rocks, the woods were suddenly alive with men. Screaming like banshees, they streamed onto the road, led by a slender man with a mask over his face.

Simon counted ten bandits as he brought his sword up to counter a stinging attack from the largest of the men. They were armed with swords and axes but wore only leather vests and caps for armor. Nor were they battle trained, Simon thought as he made short work of his first opponent. He had no time to savor the victory, for two more men challenged him.

Behind him, Hugh roared his battle cry, wielding his great sword like a Viking berserker while Guy swung his own wicked blade in a deadly, killing arch. But what they lacked in fighting finesse, the men made up for in sheer numbers. Simon could feel himself faltering under the withering attack of three men. *Dieu,* where the hell was Nicholas?

"For the Black Rose!" Nicholas shouted, charging out of the woods with Bernard at his side.

"Just like old times!" Hugh screamed, and fought harder.

Simon grinned grimly and took one opponent down with a single stroke and turned on the other two, dimly conscious of other battles raging around him. The clash of steel, the grunts of straining men and the screams of the vanquished ones.

In minutes, it was over.

Breathing harshly, Simon turned away from his last opponent and scanned the road. The only men left standing were his and they were clustered around a rock where Bernard sat. Simon sprinted to them. "Is anyone hurt?"

"My leg." Bernard grimaced. "We killed all except for that cur." He glared at a man sprawled on the ground a few feet away. "I disarmed him, but he picked up a boulder and mashed my leg."

"The leader." Simon hunkered down and tugged off the mask.

The outlaw's eyes flew open, then widened with shock and horror. "Simon of Blackstone? Ye're dead."

As Simon stared at the narrow face with its sly eyes and grim mouth, a memory stirred. "I have seen you before...."

The villain shot up from the ground as though launched from a catapult and dashed into the trees with Simon in swift pursuit. But he was not quick enough, and the brigand obviously knew these woods, for he disappeared as though swallowed up.

Simon gave up and stalked back to the battlefield.

"Find him?" Nicholas asked.

"Nay." Simon kicked at a clump of dirt. "Bernard?"

"Gervase thinks his leg is broken," said Hugh. "He knows of an abbey close by and wants to take him there. I will go, too."

Simon nodded and stared at the woods. "I have seen that man before. At Durleigh Cathedral."

"Simon, do not leap to conclusions," Nicholas said. "The bishop could not have sent this thug to kill you. He did not know we were alive, much less likely to come this way."

"Perhaps, but it makes me wonder what evils I will find in Durleigh," Simon murmured.

Rob FitzHugh kept running until he reached the little hut where he and his band had sheltered. Panting, one hand pressed to the burning wound in his shoulder, he pushed open the flimsy door and halted. "What are you doing here?"

Jevan le Coyte rose from the stool by the hearth. The coarse clerical robe he wore emphasized his lean, lanky frame. "I need money." His handsome features twisted with distaste. "Though from the looks of you, the raid did not prosper."

"Prosper!" Rob cried. Kicking the door shut, he stumbled to the hearth and drank from the flagon beside it. The sour ale eased his parched throat but did not wash away the taste of defeat. "We were routed. Everyone's dead but me!"

"You took no coin, then?" Jevan asked coolly.

"Nay, what we took was steel." Rob moved his bloody hand to display the nasty wound, but the youth who was the mastermind behind their little scheme merely shrugged. "They were knights, dammit, five of them, not helpless merchants."

"Five against your ten." Jevan snorted derisively.

"Five Knights of the Black Rose. Led by Simon of Blackstone."

Jevan's jaw dropped. "He is dead."

"It was him...no mistaking. And he recognized me."

"Nay!" The usually cool Jevan shoved both hands into his silky black hair and screamed, "Not now! Not when

Thurstan's fortune is within my grasp. I will not lose. I will not.'' His eyes were as wild as a mad dog's.

Rob backed toward the door. ''What will you do?''

''I will not lose.'' Teeth set in a furious grimace, Jevan pushed past Rob and out of the hut. ''Come, we've work to do.''

Chapter One

Durleigh Cathedral, May 10, 1222

He was dying.

The malaise of spirit he could attribute to the loss of his son. But the weakness in his limbs that grew steadily worse, the pain that had built from a grinding ache this winter to a sharp burning, these he could no longer ignore. Impossible as it seemed, given his wealth, his power and his divine connections, he, Thurstan de Lyndhurst, Bishop of Durleigh, was dying.

"Nay." His anguished cry of anger and denial echoed the length of his withdrawing room. It bounced off the intricately carved wooden beams, slid down the wall hangings embroidered with scenes from the Bible and was swallowed up by the thick carpet covering the floor of his second-story sanctuary.

Fear drove him to clutch the edge of his writing table so hard the knuckles of his long, soft hands turned white. It was an emotion he had felt only once before in his one and fifty years, on the day he'd realized that the love he and the lady Rosalynd had shared would bear fruit.

Simon. A son he could never claim. Dead now, was Simon,

a bright, promising light extinguished before it had had a chance to shine. And soon Thurstan would follow the son he'd loved but had never even been allowed to hold.

Thurstan sighed. Little as he wanted to quit this life, at least when he and Simon were reunited in the Promised Land, he could explain why he had done what he had.

A wry smile lifted Thurstan's lips. That was supposing he went to heaven, which was by no means a sure thing, given the sins he had committed—some in the name of profit, others in retribution. Sins nonetheless, he thought as he slowly stood and crossed to the window. The richly embroidered tunic he had donned in honor of tonight's dinner weighed down his body as surely as Simon's death preyed on his conscience.

If only things could have been different.

But it was too late to make reparation, had been since that grim day last autumn when a messenger arrived with news that Simon and the other Crusaders of Durleigh had perished.

The sharp pain in Thurstan's chest was not borne of his illness, but of an anguish too deep for words. He and Rosalynd had been denied a life together, but he had taken solace in providing the best for their child. Though he could never claim Simon, Thurstan had cleverly schemed to have him fostered with Lord Edmund and raised here in Durleigh at Wolfsmount Castle so he could watch Simon grow. His chest had swelled with pride when he'd officiated at Simon's knighting ceremony, for the boy had become a man of unswerving loyalty, courage and honor.

Heartsick, Thurstan unlatched the shutters and opened the two sections of the oiled parchment windows. Fresh damp air poured in, momentarily chasing the scent of death from his chamber. Below him lay the green bailey that surrounded the cathedral, and beyond it, the rooftops of the bustling, prosperous town of Durleigh, all of it lorded over by Wolfsmount Castle on its rocky hillside. Durleigh had been a small town when he'd come here five and twenty years ago. Now it was a center of commerce and trade to rival the great city of York to the south. Much of Durleigh's growth had come as a result of Thurstan's scheming and his family's connections at court. As Durleigh had swelled with tradesmen and laborers, so had Thurstan's coffers.

All that gold was small comfort now. His love was lost to him, his son was dead, and he was dying.

Thurstan sighed, his thoughts growing more morose as his gaze skimmed the roof of the apothecary. Ah, he would miss his golden-haired Linnet with her quicksilver wit and boundless zest for life. He had had plans for the young apothecary, but with Simon dead, they would never come to fruition.

A sharp pain cramped his gut, doubling him over. When the wave of agony passed, Thurstan grabbed hold of the windowsill and straightened. What was this sickness that tormented him so? Over the years of bringing absolution to the stricken, he had seen death in many guises, but never one that weakened the victim yet brought no fever, no wasting of the flesh. Even Brother Anselme, the infirmarer, was at a loss to identify this ague, nor did any of the tonics Anselme and Linnet had concocted bring Thurstan any relief.

This disease was like a poison invading his—

"Poison…" The word slipped from Thurstan's lips with a hiss. He recalled with dawning horror the insidiousness with which this illness had crept up upon him.

Could it be that someone was poisoning him?

Who? And why?

Thurstan's narrowed gaze swept over the town he'd ruled for so long. Ruled it like a despot, his detractors whispered. But they spoke softly and behind his back, for Bishop Thurstan's wealth and power exceeded even the dreams of the manipulative sire who had bought for him the Bishopric of Durleigh so many years ago. Was there one among his flock who chafed under a heavy penance? Or did the culprit lay closer at hand?

Crispin Norville, Durleigh Cathedral's archdeacon, had made no secret of the fact that he heartily disapproved of Thurstan's methods. The cold and grimly pious archdeacon coveted the bishopric. He made a great show of contrasting his behavior with Thurstan's, spending more time on his knees in the chapel than he did in the administration of his duties. Crispin wore coarse robes and styled himself after St. Benedictine, while Thurstan wore embroidered silk and superfine wool.

But murder…?

Though Crispin's hatred was plain to see, Thurstan had trouble casting the archdeacon in the role of murderer. Why, the man was known to flog himself every Saturday for those sins he might inadvertently have committed. Nay, not Crispin.

Prior Walter, then? He had been a frequent visitor this winter and had, in fact, arrived this very day, ostensibly to bring greetings from His Grace, the Archbishop of York, and to inquire into Thurstan's health. Walter de Folke was a sly, slippery man whose rise to power within the church had been swift and unexpected, given his humble origins.

Thurstan tried to think if his illness had been worse after Walter visited. But his mind was bogged by shock. Shuddering, he turned from the window, his eyes darting wildly about the richly appointed chamber. How had it been done? Food? Drink?

He stumbled across the room to the massive writing table. The tray on one corner held a silver flagon filled with his favorite Bordeaux wine. Nay, it could not be that, for he served the wine to guests, to his sister, Odeline, to whom he'd given temporary rooms upstairs, and even to Walter. Aye, Walter had drunk a cup only this noon.

Thurstan relaxed until he looked through the open door to

his bedchamber. On the bedside table stood the bottle of herbal brandy. He sipped a wee dram of the strongly flavored liquor each night while he wrote in his journal. Could it be poisoned?

Thurstan stared at the little bottle, too weak to walk so far. And smelling it would tell him nothing, for he'd been drinking it with ease these past months. How could he judge when he knew not what had been used? Belladonna? Hemlock? Monkshood?

Monkshood.

The air caught in Thurstan's throat, along with a sob. He had gotten some of that poisonous herb from Linnet to kill off the voles that had been eating the roots of his prized roses. Had he touched the powder? Nay, he had handed the small jar to Olf, the gardener, who had mixed the powder with the grain to be set out in the garden. If anyone was poisoned by contact with the monkshood, it should be Olf.

What then, was killing him? And who?

Thurstan glanced down at the slender black ledger lying on the table. The first three pages contained his favorite prayers, the rest his personal journal, an accounting of how he spent his days. But recorded there, also, were the sins of Durleigh's citizens as told to him in the confessional. And next to each name, the penance Thurstan had extracted for that slip.

For the poor, the price had been a prayer or a good deed. From the wealthy, he had taken coins to fill the church's coffers. And sometimes his own. For those whose crimes were evil or cruel, the penalties had been stiffer. Had one of them decided to exact his own form of revenge?

The horn sounded, heralding the dinner hour.

Thurstan grimaced. The last thing he wanted to do was break bread with his nag of a sister and two men he found tedious, and, possibly, murderous. He wanted to seek out Brother Anselme, discuss these suspicions and see if the good brother could find an antidote before it was too late. If it was not already. He wanted to study the journal and see if he could determine who—

The door from the hallway suddenly flew open.

A man paused on the threshold. He was clad in a faded gray tabard. And on the left shoulder was embroidered a black rose.

The emblem of Durleigh's Crusaders. But they were dead.

Thurstan gaped at the intruder, a tall, broad-chested man with shoulder-length black hair. His face was partially hidden in the shadows, but Thurstan knew that face.

Simon. *Dieu!*

Now he was hallucinating. Thurstan sank into his chair and covered his face with his hands. "Go away, specter," he pleaded.

"Not till I know the truth. Are you my sire?" growled the apparition. The floor seemed to shake as he advanced.

I must be dead, Thurstan thought. *Dead and gone straight to hell.* "Aye. I did sire you," he muttered.

"Why did you never tell me what I was to you?"

"I had no choice," Thurstan whispered.

"Was my mother so foul a creature?"

"Nay. Never that." Thurstan looked up and found the creature standing across the table from him. He looked so real, the stubble on his cheeks, the anguish in his eyes. They were green, like Rosalynd's, but with a hint of his own gray, and ablaze with emotions too painful to endure. Thurstan looked away. "She was an angel, your mother."

"Then why?" A fist struck the table, rattling writing implements and making the candlelight dance.

Gasping, Thurstan sat bolt upright. "What manner of visitation is this?" he asked brokenly.

"A long overdue one, I should say." The eyes went cold and hard. "Brother Martin contracted a fever and died in Damietta. I sat with him during his last hours, and he did confess to me that you were my sire.'' He leaned closer, his breath warming Thurstan's icy flesh. ''Why was the truth kept from me?''

Thurstan blinked. ''You are alive.''

''Aye. A fact that no doubt displeases you. Were you hoping that your mistake would be lost in the Holy Land?''

''It is a miracle.'' Thurstan had never put much faith in them. Nor in prayers either, for his own had gone unanswered until now, but this was surely a miracle.

''A strong sword arm saved me, not divine intervention.'' Simon's lip curled. ''I survived with but one thought, to return here and accuse you of these crimes to your face. Perhaps you sent Brother Martin to make certain I did not return.''

''Why would I want you dead?'' Thurstan cried.

''Obviously I am an embarrassment to you, else you would have acknowledged me years ago.''

''There were reasons.''

''So you say.''

''It is the truth.''

Simon waved the declaration away. ''You would not know the truth if it bit you in your holy arse. For years I watched you manipulate others to your will. Half the men who went on Crusade did so because you blackmailed them into going so you could swell the ranks you sent in answer to the Pope's cry for help. A stepping-stone on your way to becoming archbishop, perhaps. You walk in their blood,'' Simon growled. ''For that and for what you did to me, I despise you.''

''You do not understand.''

''I understand that I hate you, above all men.'' Simon's eyes narrowed. ''You wanted to keep our relationship secret, and I agree. I have no wish for anyone to know that your blood flows in my veins. There is but one thing I want from you. I would know who my mother was.''

"I cannot tell you," Thurstan mumbled, bound by a vow that had been forced upon him long ago.

"Then I will find out for myself."

"Nay." Desperation propelled Thurstan to his feet. He swayed, gripped the desk as white-hot pain lanced through his belly. A reminder he was dying. Terror gripped him even as the pain receded. Whoever was killing him might transfer his hatred or greed or whatever drove him to Simon. Until he knew who the murderer was, Simon was not safe. Thurstan studied the dear face he had not expected to see again in this life. *Dieu,* he wanted to hold the boy, if only for a moment. Instead, he steeled himself for the task ahead. "You must leave, for I am expecting an important visitor." The lie was a small smudge on his already blackened soul. What mattered was getting rid of Simon before someone saw him, or worse, overheard.

Simon straightened. "I want her name. Doubtless you have left the poor woman destitute."

"She is dead," Thurstan said quickly, desperately.

"You lie. She lives, and I will know where."

"I cannot tell you. Go," he cried. "We will speak of this another time." He had much to do, a killer to unmask, an inheritance charter to amend, and little time remaining.

Simon stiffened as though the words had been a sharp slap. "If I go, I will not return."

"That is your choice," Thurstan said, his heart aching.

Simon turned toward the door, his black woolen cape swirling softly. Then he paused and looked back. His rigid stance and unrelenting expression reminded Thurstan of his own father. Aye, there was much of Robert de Lyndhurst in his grandson. Simon would not forget a slight or forgive an injury. "I am staying at the Royal Oak Inn. Send word to me there of my mother's name and whereabouts. If I have not heard from you by this time tomorrow, I will investigate on my own."

The slamming of the door echoed through the room with dreadful finality.

Thurstan sank into his chair, the ache in his heart sharper than the pain in his gut and limbs. Simon hated him. It was the final, cruel irony.

Dimly Thurstan heard the horn sounding the second call to sup. Brother Oliver would come looking for him if he did not appear soon. Indeed, a slight creak signaled the opening of the door into his secretary's small chamber.

"Oh, Thurstan."

Thurstan opened his eyes to see Linnet rushing toward him across the room. "My dear." He managed to sit forward, though it cost him dearly. "You should not be here."

"I know." She knelt at his feet and took his cold hands in her warm ones. "I know it will cause you problems if the archdeacon finds I've been here."

"It is your reputation I fear for." He squeezed her hands and looked into unusual whiskey-colored eyes. So warm, so filled with compassion a man could get lost in them.

"Your color seems better this evening," she said, smiling.

Simon is alive. The words hovered on Thurstan's tongue, but he held them back. It wasn't safe. "The warmer weather helps."

Her smile faded; her grip on him tightened. "Thurstan, I fear this is no ordinary sickness. I think it is poison."

"Poison?" He forced a laugh. She must not suspect, must not voice her suspicions until he knew who the poisoner was.

"Aconite. Monkshood—you will remember I gave you some for your rose gardens. I read about it in an old herbal, and the symptoms of monkshood poisoning are similar to yours."

So, at least he knew what was killing him. "I've heard it kills, not sickens."

"In small quantities, it would bring pain such as yours."

"No one is poisoning me, my dear. You must not think—"

The corridor door opened, and Oliver peered around it. "My lord, your guests await in the—" His plain-as-pudding face twisted into a frown. "What is *she* doing here, my lord?"

Linnet stood and shook out her skirts. "I had to come and see how my lord bishop fared."

Oliver sniffed. "He has myself and Brother Anselme to look after his health." Of Thurstan, he asked, "Are you well enough to go below and dine?"

Nay, he was not. But Robert de Lyndhurst had raised no weaklings. *Never let your enemies see you are vulnerable.* "Tell them I will be down directly." But for how long could he continue? As the door closed behind Oliver, Thurstan's eyes fell on the journal. What if he collapsed, and it fell into the wrong hands? Partly his concern was for the townsfolk whose sins he had sinned in recording…and in using against them. Mostly, it was for the document concealed behind the front cover of the journal. The charter, granting Simon the manor of Blackstone Heath. Thurstan had purchased the estate to give to Simon after his knighting, but the boy had promptly pledged himself to the Crusade. And died.

Thurstan had still been reeling from the horrible news when his youngest half sister, Odeline, and her son had arrived. Her scandalous antics had resulted in her being exiled from court. If Thurstan did not provide for her, Odeline had cried, she and Jevan would starve. Not wanting that on his conscience, too, Thurstan had taken them both in. He'd also amended the charter, granting Blackstone to Jevan, provided he completed his studies at the cathedral school. The boy was as vain and spoiled as his mother and no student, but Thurstan had hoped that the discipline would turn Jevan into a capable overlord.

Now that Simon was back, the charter must be changed

again so that Blackstone would go to him. Another bit of land could be found for Jevan, or perhaps coin so he could buy—

"Thurstan…" Linnet's eyes were filled with tears.

"Do not fret, my dear." He managed to stand and found his legs steadier than expected. "I am feeling better." Simon was alive, and Thurstan thought he knew what, if not who, was killing him. Hope fluttered in his chest for the first time in months. Directly after dinner, he would take the herbal brandy to Brother Anselme for examination. Perhaps ceasing to drink the stuff would be enough to save him. But the sense of impending doom did not lift. It moved over his skin like chilling fog—or a draft from the grave—making him tremble.

"Thurstan?" Her hand closed over his on the journal.

That damned journal with its dark secrets. "I want you to have this, my dear." What better person to guard his secrets than the woman whose own transgression he had meticulously recorded within? After all, her life was intricately connected with Simon's. With luck, the two of them might find the happiness that had eluded him and Rosalynd. "My favorite prayers are within."

"Thank you." She clasped the book to her breast. "But I am afraid for you. For your soul. I would help you."

"You have helped, more than you know, but you must leave now, before Archdeacon Crispin comes looking for me and finds you here. Will you close the window on your way out?"

She nodded, her expression still troubled, and hurried over to the window. "It is because I love you that I am worried, Thurstan," she said as she drew the window shut.

"Do not fret, my dear Linnet. I am feeling stronger by the moment. In a few days, I will send for you." By then, he might know who had planned this vile deed. "We will sit together in the garden." He would extract the charter from its hiding place in the journal and make the critical changes that would shift Blackstone Heath from Jevan's grasp into Simon's.

Simon flung out of the bishop's palace, barely hanging on to the temper that had plagued him all his days. He kicked stones from his path, imagining each was Bishop Thurstan.

Dieu, the man was even more of a coldhearted, unfeeling monster than Simon had remembered.

"It is because I love you that I am worried, Thurstan." A choked female voice carried in the still air.

Simon stopped in his tracks. He turned, looked over his shoulder and scanned the bishop's palace, four stories of impressive stonework, broken at regular intervals by small windows. A lit one on the second story was just closing. A moment's calculation told him it was the room he had just left. The bishop's withdrawing room.

Thurstan's important visitor was a woman. A woman who openly professed her love for him. For an instant, Simon was sickened. *Dieu,* was there no limit to the man's crimes?

What if it was his mother?

The notion hit Simon so hard he trembled. Then he crept up beneath the window and cocked his ear, but heard no more. Still shaking, he leaned against the building for support. The voice had been soft and so choked with emotion as to be ageless.

Did she live here?

On the chance that even Thurstan would not be so brazen as to keep his mistress within the cathedral, Simon ducked around the side of the building and hid in the bushes. The scent of roses from the nearby garden assailed his senses, temporarily piercing his turmoil. There had been nights in the desert when he'd lain awake, pining for England, for the damp air, the lush smell of grass and roses.

He knew why.

That last night in England he had dreamed of a woman, a

woman whose skin smelled of roses, and whose touch had ruined him for all other women. Four years he'd spent searching in vain for a woman who completed him as she had.

The crunch of footsteps on the gravel walkway shattered Simon's reverie. Peering out, he saw a cloaked figure hurry away from the palace. The cowl hid face and hair, but the person was small and moved like a woman.

His mother?

His heart atangle with hope and dread, Simon emerged from hiding and followed.

Thurstan stood with his hands braced on the table, his head bowed as he sought the strength to negotiate the winding stairs to the ground floor and endure the six-course meal. Hearing the door open, he lifted his head, hoping that Simon had returned.

Odeline entered in a whisper of bright silk, gems winking like stars in the crispinette that held her hair back. She was the image of her mother, a clever, sensuous beauty who had caught Robert de Lyndhurst's eye when he was fifty and she twenty, luring him to the altar, much to the disgust of Robert's children. "Are you coming down to sup?"

"Aye." Thurstan rounded the desk, his slow, shuffling gait in marked contrast to Odeline's catlike glide as she closed the distance between them. It was then, as she moved from shadow into the golden circle cast by the candles on the table, that he saw the fury in her emerald eyes. "You are upset."

"Upset?" She spat the word. Her hands came up, fingers curled into talons. "He is back, your bastard son."

Thurstan started. "What makes you say that?"

"I saw him going down the stairs."

"Ah." Thurstan sighed. "Few people in Durleigh know of Simon's and my...connection. I would keep it that way." At least until he'd discovered who was poisoning him.

"As if I would want the world to know my brother the bishop did father a son on—"

"Have a care, Odeline, lest your own indiscretions become common knowledge."

"A trade. My silence in exchange for Blackstone Heath."

"Blackstone is Simon's. I'll find another bone for your pup to chew on," Thurstan said nastily.

Her lips curled back in a feral snarl. "You promised *my son* that estate, and he will have it."

"Not without my say so. And I say nay."

"Bastard." She struck him in the chest with both hands. Her shove sent Thurstan backward.

He cried out, reaching for her as he lost his balance. She didn't move. The last thing he saw before his head struck the desk was the smile that spread over her face. Even that winked out in a shower of inky stars.

Chapter Two

Someone was following her.

The realization pierced the fog of misery that had enveloped Linnet Especer since leaving Thurstan.

Night had fallen while she'd been with Thurstan. The lights from the cathedral and the bishop's palace winked back at her, islands of light in the darkness, promising a safe haven. Yet she dared not return. Archdeacon Crispin heartily disapproved of her relationship with Thurstan, and, since the bishop's decline, he had become more vocal in voicing it. Not that she cared what the archdeacon thought of her, but his accusations sullied the good name of a man who was, to her, nearly a saint.

There! A shadow drifted down the path from the palace, cloak billowing in the light evening breeze. One of the archdeacon's spies, she thought in annoyance. Yet he was tall and moved with more purpose than any monk. As his cloak shifted again, she caught the glint of light on metal. A sword.

The sheriff?

The notion that Hamel Roxby might be after her quickened Linnet's pulse and deepened her fear. Her closeness with Thurstan had kept the sheriff from pressing his unwanted attentions on her. But maybe Hamel had noted the bishop's growing weakness and thought to take advantage of her.

Her heart in her throat, Linnet rushed out through the stone gates of the cathedral courtyard and onto the Deangate. The street was nearly deserted, free of the pilgrims and worshipers who flocked to the cathedral by day. The most direct route back to her shop was along Colliergate where the charcoal burners plied their trade and thence across town to Spicier's Lane. But it was also the least trafficked in the evening.

So she darted along Deangate and into the center of Durleigh. The scent of freshly baked bread rolled over her as she rounded the corner onto Blake Street. The narrow thoroughfare was not crowded, but there were enough people hurrying in and out of the bakeshops lining it to make her feel a bit more comfortable. And the light from the open shop doors made her less afraid. Halfway down the street, she glanced back, hoping she had been wrong about her pursuer.

Nay, there he was, just entering Blake, a head taller than those around him, his stride measured but purposeful. The way he moved, seeming to slide from one group of people to the next, sent a shiver of fear down her spine. He used them for cover as a fox might use stands of brush when sneaking up on a rabbit.

Linnet did what any rabbit would do. She jumped down the nearest alleyway. Durleigh had been her home from infancy, and even in the dark she knew every twist and turn that would take her home. The Guildhall sat on the corner of High Gate and New Street, an imposing stone-and-timbered building, testament to the wealth of Durleigh's tradesmen. Day or evening, the hall was usually abustle with activity. Tonight was no exception.

Torches lined the front of the building, flickering in the wind, sending light and shadow over the clerks hurrying home for the day and paunchy merchants arriving for some supper. Many of them were known to her, but none would have aided her against the sheriff, either out of fear or because they believed she was Thurstan's mistress and reviled her for that.

Linnet lingered in the alley long enough to remove her cloak and fashion it into a bundle with the prayer book inside. She loosened her long, tawny braids, shook her hair free and pulled it about her face. As disguises go, it was not much, but if Hamel were indeed following her, he'd be looking for a cloaked woman, not the laundress she hopefully resembled.

Emerging from the alley, Linnet fell into step with a pair of clerks who were heading south on High Gate. She dared not look back to see if Hamel followed for fear of dislodging her flimsy disguise. Her nape prickled, and an icy chill ran down her spine. With every step she took, she expected to be grabbed and spun about to face her longtime nemesis. But she walked on unmolested, past the market square.

When they came abreast of the Royal Oak Inn, Linnet breathed a sigh of relief. Here, at least, she could count on aid. Bidding a silent thanks to the clerks, she slipped around to the kitchen of the tavern. With trembling fingers, she rebraided her hair as best she could, then pushed open the door. Light and the scent of richly spiced food spilled out, welcoming her.

Across the kitchen, Elinore Selwyne looked up from ladling stew into wooden bowls. "Linnet. Whatever are you doing here at this time of night?"

"I—I was passing," Linnet said breathlessly.

Elinore frowned, her sharp eyes scanning Linnet from head to toe. "What is it? What is wrong?"

Conscious of how harried she must look, Linnet opened her mouth to explain, then noticed the maid loitering in the far doorway. Short and curvaceous, Tilly had sly brown eyes and a nose for gossip. Linnet's apprentice, Aiken, fancied Tilly, but the maid had eyes only for the sheriff. It was rumored she'd been seen frequenting his small house near the market square.

"I am hungry is all," Linnet said, biding her time.

"I see." And Elinore likely did. Older than Linnet by a dozen years, she had inherited the inn from her father and now ran it with the help of her husband, Warin. Elinore's tart tongue and keen head for business belied her kind heart. When Linnet's father died the year before, Elinore had taken Linnet under her wing. She had offered comfort, support and advice when Thurstan's intercession with the guild paved the way for Linnet to take over the apothecary. "Aiken has already been here to collect supper for your household, but you'd best stay here and eat. I have no doubt he and Drusa have gobbled down the lot."

Linnet managed a smile. Both her apprentice and her elderly maidservant had prodigious appetites. "I appreciate your offer." Heart in turmoil, she set her cloak down on the floor beside the door and waited while Elinore finished filling the bowls.

The tavern kitchen was small, but neat and efficiently run by the plump, pretty Elinore. A brick hearth tall enough to stand in filled the far end of the room. Inside it, a toothed rack supported two massive cauldrons for cooking. Before it sat the long plank worktable where the food was prepared, flanked by two chests, one for cooking implements, the other for spices. Shelves on the far wall held wooden bowls, horn spoons and platters for serving the broken meats, bread and cheese.

"Serve that quick before it gets cold," Elinore admonished, shooing Tilly out the door. "Now..." She advanced on Linnet, blue eyes steely. "Whatever has happened? You look all afright. Your hair is half undone, your eyes wild as a harried fox's."

"Nothing." Linnet's lips trembled, and tears filled her eyes, making Elinore's lined face blur.

"Come. Sit down." Elinore wrapped an arm around her waist and led her to the bench beside the table.

Linnet sank down. "I—I fear the bishop is dying."

"Dying." Elinore crossed herself. "What is it now?"

Poison. But Linnet dared not voice her suspicions, even to her dearest friend. She did not want anyone to guess, as she had, that the bishop was killing himself out of grief. She, too, had mourned when Simon was reported dead. And Thurstan's grief was all the sharper because he felt he'd failed Simon in life.

Six months had not dulled the anguish of Simon's passing for her, though she had never been his, not really. She had admired him from afar for years, but had only gotten close to him once. The night before the Crusaders left Durleigh. That single, brief encounter had changed her life forever. She mourned him deeply. It seemed impossible that so bright and vibrant a soul as Simon's had been snuffed out.

"The tonic you took the bishop last week did not help?"

Linnet shook her head, fighting back her tears. If she let them fall, she feared she'd never stop crying. For Thurstan. For Simon. And for another life, lost to her, too.

"He has not been well since last autumn when word came that the Crusaders had died." Elinore patted her hand. "One and fifty is not such a great age, but when the heart weakens…"

Or when it ceases to hope. Linnet sighed. "I fear you are right, but it hurts so to see him in such pain and be unable to help." There was no antidote for monkshood, but if she could find his supply and destroy it, perhaps she could save him.

"Your friendship has eased him and brought him joy." Elinore frowned. "But it has sullied your reputation, my dear."

"I do not care what others think of me."

"Not now, but when he is gone," Elinore said delicately,

"those whose tongues were stayed by the bishop's power may speak out against you."

"Their words cannot harm me."

"They might if they cost you custom or your place in the guild," said practical Elinore. "And then there is the matter of Sheriff Hamel's persistent interest in you."

"Aye." Linnet shivered. "Why can he not leave me alone? I have said time and again that I want nothing to do with him."

"Silly girl, you know little of men if you ask that."

Indeed. She had known only one man, and him so briefly.

"Men are hunters who revel in the chase. To Hamel you are a challenge. If he caught you, he might well abandon you the next day and never bother you again."

Elinore's words ripped open an old wound. Simon had taken Linnet's innocence that warm spring night and looked straight through her the next morn when the Crusaders left Durleigh for the East. Nay, he had not done it out of meanness. Logically she knew darkness and drink had likely fogged his memory. After all, Simon had been unaware of her existence, while she had mooned over him for some time. Fate had thrown them together for that brief, passionate interlude in the dark stables. Shame had driven her to creep off while he still slept. So it was her own fault if he did not know with whom he had lain that night.

"Well, I will not give in to Hamel," Linnet said. Though Simon was gone, she could not sully the memory of their loving by giving herself to another. And then there was the other, the greater sin that weighed on her conscience. She had already betrayed Simon once by giving away his most precious gift.

"No woman should be forced to endure someone she dislikes. I am only saying that you must be prepared. If God does see fit to take our good bishop, Hamel may pursue you."

"I fear it has begun already." She told Elinore of the tall man who had trailed her from the cathedral.

"Well, that explains why you looked like a hunted thing when you bounded in the door. Let me give you a room here." Elinore had made a similar offer when Linnet's father died.

"I hate to leave Drusa and Aiken alone."

"Bring them here. He can sleep here in the kitchen, and she can have a pallet in your room."

"I do not know." Linnet twisted her hands together. "To leave the shop and my spices unguarded does not seem wise."

"It is just through the back lane," Elinore said. "I can have one of our serving lads sleep there if it would ease you."

"Thank you, Elinore, you are a dear friend to try to protect me, but, if worse comes to worse, I would not want you to fall afoul of Hamel on my account."

A soft gasp warned they were no longer alone. Tilly stood in the doorway, her eyes alight with speculation.

"What mean you sneaking in here?" Elinore demanded.

Tilly sniffed. "I didn't sneak, mistress. I've come after four more bowls of stew. For the sheriff and his men."

"The sheriff is here?" Linnet cried.

"Aye. He said he likes the food—" Tilly smiled provocatively "—and the service."

Linnet waited to hear no more, but rose and headed for the outside door with Elinore close on her heels.

"Stay. It'll be safer here," Elinore whispered.

"Nay." Linnet grabbed up her bundle. "I had best get back to the shop." She dashed out the door with Elinore's warning to take care ringing in her ears.

Behind the Royal Oak was a modest-size stable and beside it, the privy. A narrow lane cut through the grassy backyard and disappeared into a thick hedge. The lane led clear

through to the back door of the apothecary. Here there were
no lights to guide the way, but Linnet knew it well enough.
She ran, the cloak clutched tight against her chest. Just as
she cleared the hedge, she ran headlong into something warm
and hard as rock.

She bounced off and flew backward, striking her head as
she went down and driving the air from her lungs.

"Are you all right?" inquired a low male voice.

Linnet whimpered, more from fear than pain. She tried to
move, but her limbs only twitched, and a gray mist obscured
her vision.

"Easy." Large hands gripped her shoulders, stilling her
struggles. "Lie still till I make certain nothing is broken."

The voice was hauntingly familiar.

Blinking furiously, Linnet made out a figure hunched over
her. His hair and clothing blended with the gloom so his face
seemed to float above her.

Simon of Blackstone's face.

"Sweet Mary, I have died," Linnet whispered.

A dry chuckle greeted her statement. "I think not, though
doubtless you will be bruised come morn. I am sorry I did
not see you coming." Dimly she was aware of gentle pokes
and prods as he examined her arms and legs. "I do not think
anything is broken." He sat back on his haunches. "Can you
move your limbs?"

"Simon?" Linnet murmured.

He cocked his head. "You know who I am?"

"But…you perished in the Holy Land…."

"Nay, though I came right close on a few occasions."

Joy pulsed through her, so intense it brought fresh tears to
eyes that had cried a river for him.

He leaned closer, his jaw stubbled, his eyes shadowed by
their sockets. "Do I know you?"

A laugh bubbled in her throat, wild and a bit hysterical.
She cut it off with a sob. She had been right. He did not

even remember her or their wondrous moment together. "Nay."

"Curse me for a fool. You've hit your head, and here I leave you lying on the cold ground. Where do you live?"

"Just yonder in the next street."

He nodded, and before she could guess what he planned, scooped her up, bundle and all, and stood.

The feel of his arms around her opened a floodgate of poignant memories. "Please, put me down."

"Nay, it is better I carry you till we can be certain you are not seriously hurt."

So gallant. But his nearness made her weak with longing, and she feared she might say something stupid. "I am not hurt."

"You are dazed and cannot judge."

"I can so. I am an apothecary."

"I see." His teeth flashed white in the gloom as he smiled. Though she couldn't see it, she knew there'd be a dimple in his right cheek. "I should have guessed, for you smell so sweet." He sniffed her hair. "Ah, roses. I thought longingly of them when I was away on Crusade."

She had always worn this scent. "Did they remind you of a girl you had left behind?" she asked softly, hopefully.

"Nay." His eyes took on a faraway look, then he shook his head. "Nothing like that. I have no sweetheart and never have."

Linnet's eyes prickled. "Please put me down."

"You are stubborn into the bargain, my rose-scented apothecary," he teased. "But I am, too. Which way is home?"

Linnet sighed and pointed at her shop. It was heaven to be carried by him, to feel his heart beat against her side. If he had dreamed of roses, she had dreamed of this. She looked up, scarcely able to believe this was not some fevered imagining, but the warmth of his body enveloping her as it had long ago.

All too soon they reached the back of her shop.

"Will someone be within?" he asked.

Shaken from her reverie, Linnet nodded. "My maid."

Simon kicked at the door with his toe.

"Who is there?" Drusa called out.

"It is I, Drusa," Linnet said, but the voice seemed too weak and breathless to be her own.

Nonetheless, the bar scraped as the maid lifted it, then flung open the heavy door.

"Oh, mistress, I was that wor—" Drusa gasped and fell back a step, one hand pressed to her ample bosom, her lined face going white as flour.

"Fear not," said Simon gently, "Your mistress has taken a tumble and hit her head. Where can I lay her down?"

Drusa, not the most nimble-witted soul, goggled at them.

Aiken appeared behind her. "What is this? Mistress Linnet!"

"I…" Linnet's wits seemed to have deserted her.

"Your mistress has hit her head. Direct me to her bedchamber, lad," Simon said firmly but not sharply. "Drusa, we will want water for washing, a cloth and ale if you have it."

Used to following orders, Drusa spun from the door, hurried across the kitchen and began gathering what he'd requested.

Aiken scowled. "Ain't fitting for ye to go above stairs."

"Aiken…" Linnet began, her head pounding in earnest now. "Pray excuse his rudeness, sir. He was Papa's apprentice, and with my father gone, sees himself as protector of our household."

Simon nodded. "Your caution and concern for your lady do you credit, Aiken." His voice held a hint of suppressed amusement. "But these are unusual circumstances and I am no stranger. I am Simon of Blackstone, a Knight of the Black Rose, newly returned from—''

''They said ye all died!'' Aiken exclaimed.

Simon smiled. ''Only six of us survived to return home.'' The smile dimmed, and profound sadness filled his eyes.

Linnet's heart contracted, thinking of the hardships he must have endured. But he was back, alive.

Aiken grunted. ''I suppose it's all right, then.'' He led the way through the kitchen and into the workroom beyond. ''Those stairs go up to the second floor.''

''Will you light the way?'' Simon asked.

Aiken grunted again, seized the thick tallow candle from the worktable and tromped up the stairs.

Simon followed.

''I can walk,'' Linnet whispered.

''Not till we've made certain you are not seriously hurt.'' Simon took the narrow stairs carefully so as not to bump her head. They opened into the room that served her as counting room, withdrawing room and bedchamber. He hesitated a moment, then headed for the big, canopied bed.

''Nay, the chair,'' Linnet murmured. The thought of him laying her down in the bed where she'd woven so many dreams was intolerable. ''Else Aiken will surely think the worst.''

Simon chuckled, a deep rich sound that made her pulse leap, and deposited her in the high-backed chair by the hearth. ''Could you build up the fire and bring more candles, Aiken?'' he asked.

''I'll go down and get more wood directly,'' the boy replied, his expression respectful now instead of wary. Apparently Crusader knights were to be trusted.

''There are candles in that box on the mantel,'' Linnet said as Aiken hurried off.

Simon turned away, selected one and lit it on the tallow.

''I am sorry to be so much trouble,'' Linnet said. ''If I

had been looking where I was going I…'' The words died in her throat as the candle flared, illuminating Simon's face.

His face was leaner than she remembered, the stubble on his cheeks and squared jaw hiding the cleft in his chin. His eyes, too, were changed, the ghosts of turbulent emotions swirling in gray-green pools that had once danced with humor. The mouth that had kissed her with such devastating thoroughness years ago was now drawn in a somber line.

"Who were you running from?" he asked.

Linnet opened her mouth to reply, then recalled the long-ago enmity between Simon and Hamel. That night Simon had come out of the darkness to save her, which had ended in disaster. She was not involving him again. "I was not running, I—"

"You fled as though some evil demon pursued you."

"Nay, I was not." Linnet lifted her chin, but could not meet those piercing green eyes.

Aiken emerged from the stairwell cradling two logs in his arms. He stopped and glanced at them. "What is wrong?"

"Nothing," Linnet said quickly, glaring at Simon.

Aiken shambled over, added the logs to the banked coals and blew them into life. Apparently unaware of the tension between them, he stood. "How is she, Sir Simon?"

"Stubborn," Simon growled.

"She did not break anything, then?"

"Certainly not her spirit."

"I am fine," Linnet grumbled.

"Drusa thinks 'twas hunger made ye fall."

Simon frowned. "You have not eaten?"

"I was just on my way home to sup when we, er, met."

"Hmm." Aiken shuffled his feet. "There is not much left, but I could run down the lane and fetch something from the tavern. The Royal Oak," he added, looking at Simon, "lies just behind us. Their fare's the finest in Durleigh."

Simon nodded, his gaze resting on Linnet's face. "So I recalled. I was on my way to meet friends there."

"Well, we will not detain you longer." Much as she craved his company, Linnet knew it was not wise to be around him. He was alive, and that changed so much. Guilt mingled with her joy.

"I have not eaten, either." Simon stroked his chin, his eyes fixed on her face. "If it would not be trouble to fetch food for two, I will pay for it."

"Nonsense," Linnet exclaimed. "I can pay—"

"I owe you for the fall you took."

Nay, I owe you. But there was no going back. No changing what she had been forced to do. "Very well," Linnet said. *Pray God this is not another mistake.*

"Brother Oliver, if my lord bishop is not well enough to join us, we will certainly understand," said Archdeacon Crispin silkily. He and the prior were seated at the long table in the bishop's great hall, to the right and left of Thurstan's chair.

A chair either man would have sold his soul to occupy, Crispin mused. But when the time came to name Thurstan's successor, Crispin was confident he would be chosen. Walter de Folke was, after all, of inferior stock, being half Saxon. And the prior was nearly as corrupt and manipulative as Bishop Thurstan. What the good folk of Durleigh needed was a stern hand to guide them, a religious leader who thought more of their souls than their trade and prosperity.

"The bishop bade me apologize for his tardiness, but a matter arose that required his immediate attention."

"Indeed?" Crispin sniffed and regarded Brother Oliver with a level gaze that made the little toad squirm beneath his robes. The secretary was cut from the same flawed cloth as the master he served so zealously. When he was bishop, Crispin meant to name Brother Gerard as his assistant. He and

Gerard had been together since entering the priesthood and agreed on the importance of piety, chastity and poverty, three tenets that were totally disregarded at Durleigh Cathedral.

But not for much longer, Crispin thought. The bishop grew weaker by the day. He could not last another month. And then—

"My lords!" Lady Odeline burst into the hall, her face white as new snow, her eyes wide with horror.

Crispin raked his eyes over the lush figure so scandalously displayed by her tight, low-cut gown. Her presence in the bishop's residence was an affront to all that was decent. Since her coming, the confessionals had been crowded with clerics and students tainted with the sin of lust. "What is it?"

"My brother…he…" She clasped a hand to her heaving breasts.

"The bishop is ill?" Crispin was on his feet at once.

Odeline's perfect chin wobbled. "He…he collapsed."

Ah, joy. Crispin schooled his features to reveal none of the excitement that coursed through his veins. "Is he…dead?"

"Nay. He is breathing," Odeline cried. "But so still—"

Brother Oliver exclaimed in dismay, charged across the room and pushed past her. "Fetch Brother Anselme," he shouted.

"Of course." Crispin turned to send Gerard on that errand…slowly, of course. But the spot to his left was empty, and he recalled having set Gerard to watch in case Linnet should defy his orders and try to see the bishop.

"Go for the infirmarer," said Prior Walter to the young cleric who attended him.

"Thank you, brother." Crispin looked into the prior's cold, measuring eyes and felt a chill move down his spine. *He cannot know anything.* But the words brought scant comfort. "Come, we must attend our fallen bishop." Even as he swept from the room, Crispin was conscious of the prior's measured tread at his heels. Drat, what ill luck that the sharp-eyed Walter should be here at this critical moment.

"Take care you do not trip on your hem," Walter said softly as they mounted the steep, winding stairs.

"I am ever cautious," Crispin replied, his agile mind already leaping ahead to the things that must be done. A funeral to arrange, letters to send to the archbishop at York…

Brother Oliver's scream cut off his thoughts.

"Quickly, brother." Walter pushed on his back, urging him up the stairs. Together they burst into the upper corridor and hustled the few steps to the bishop's withdrawing room.

There, on the disgustingly flamboyant carpet sprawled the body of Bishop Thurstan, his limbs flung wide, his mouth contorted in anguish, his head resting in a pool of crimson blood.

Bile rose in Crispin's throat. "Is he dead?"

Walter knelt beside the bishop, felt in the folds of his neck and looked up at Crispin. "Aye, he is." Turning back, Walter began murmuring the prayers that would ease Thurstan's soul into the hereafter.

Crispin sent his own prayer after it. *I was not here and cannot be blamed for this.* The words only marginally eased the burden on his conscience.

Chapter Three

Drusa clomped up the stairs with water and towels. "Let us see where ye are hurt, dearling."

"It is nothing. A bump on the head, a bit of a scrape on my elbow," Linnet insisted. "I can tend my—"

Drusa clucked her tongue. "Always did want to do everything for herself." She smiled wryly at Simon and set to work.

Simon leaned his shoulder against the mantel and watched the woman tend Linnet with the gruff tenderness that bespoke years of caring. The old longing curled in his belly. What would it be like to be loved like that? He shook it off with practiced ease and set his mind on the present, not his troubled past.

Covertly, he studied the woman he had run down. When he'd bent over her on the dark path, something about her had seemed familiar. But now, seeing her in the light, that sense of recognition faded. Perhaps it was the scent of roses she wore that had struck a chord with him. She was certainly beautiful enough to make him *wish* he knew her.

Linnet's delicate profile was so perfect it might have been carved from marble, marred only by the bits of dirt Drusa was gently washing away. The maid had also loosened Lin-

net's braids, so her hair tumbled over her slender shoulders
and down her back in a honey-colored river, glinting like
gold in the firelight.

He guessed her age at twenty or so, which would have
made her ten and six when he left on Crusade. Old enough
to have attracted his eye when he'd been in town on Lord
Edmund's business, comely enough to have merited a second
glance. Her brown eyes were warm and expressive. They
sparkled with two things he valued in men and women: intelligence and wry humor. And when she had smiled, her
whole face had seemed to glow, as though lit from within.

Linnet the Spicier was a woman he would know better.

But that was not the only reason Simon lingered in her
cozy little solar. The vulnerability and the fear she could not
quite hide worried him. She had been fleeing something when
they collided. Or, more likely, someone. The aura of danger
aroused the protective streak his friends had often teased him
about.

You have problems enough of your own.

Simon shoved them aside to be considered later. Part of
him, the soft side few men saw, hoped Thurstan would send
word to him. The tough shell he had developed as an orphaned youth warned him not to care. He had been six when
he arrived at Lord Edmund's household as a page. Though
he had not been abused, neither had he been loved. There
had been no father to shield him when the older pages
taunted and teased him, no mother to dry his tears when he
was hurt in practice. The only true friends he had were the
five knights of the Black Rose.

"There." Drusa set her cloth in the basin. "I've put bet-
ony cream on those scrapes, and the bump does not look
grievous."

"Thank you," Linnet grumbled, obviously irked at the
fuss.

"I am much relieved to hear you have suffered no serious

harm, Mistress Linnet. I feared you might set the sheriff on me," Simon teased.

Linnet shivered. "That is the last thing I would do."

Interesting. Sheriff John Turnebull was a fair man, if Simon recalled correctly. Did she fear the sheriff would ask questions she did not want to answer?

"If ye will sit with her a moment, sir, I will put these things away and fetch some ale."

"You do not have to watch over me," Linnet muttered.

"It is no hardship at all, I assure you. And the ale would be most welcome. You may have recovered, but I still feel a bit shaky," he said dramatically. "In fact, I think I had best sit." Simon pulled over a stool and plopped down at Linnet's feet, stretching his boots toward the fire.

"Just so. I'll be back in two shakes." Drusa hurried off.

Linnet snorted and rolled her eyes. "You, a fearless knight returned from the Crusades, are shaky?"

"The sight of a woman in distress does affect me most severely. And the thought that I might have caused you grievous injury…" He put a hand over his heart and sighed mightily. It was a pose Nicholas struck. It never failed to make women melt.

Linnet laughed. The sound was musical, captivating. The merriment transformed her features from comely to striking. Firelight picked out the gold flecks in her eyes and made her hair shimmer. It was as though the sun had suddenly come out from behind a cloud to shed its radiance on the world, to banish darkness and cold.

Simon had an unexpected urge to pull her onto his lap, to kiss her breathless, wrap them both in her glorious hair and see if she could measure up to his dream. Already he could feel his body responding, his pulse leaping, his loins quickening in prelude to a chase as old as time. But he had never wanted any woman as swiftly or with as much certainty as he did this one.

She felt it, too. He measured her awareness in the widening of her eyes, the soft gasp that seemed to fill the room with possibilities. What would she do? Scream? Faint? Throw herself at him and fulfill their unspoken fantasy?

"Aiken has returned with the food," Drusa called up the stairs. "I'll bring it up directly."

Linnet started, shattering the moment. Her cheeks turned bright red, and her eyes filled with such confusion Simon knew she was new to this. Perhaps even a maiden.

The notion heightened his turmoil, the craving for her warring with the need to protect her. He knew he could not be alone with her in this room and be certain he would not act on the desire that sizzled between them.

"We will come down, Drusa." Simon smiled wryly and climbed to his feet. "There is a time for everything, they say. Our time will come."

She ducked her head. "Perhaps it has come and gone."

What an odd thing to say. Simon extended his arm. "Come, Linnet, we are both in need of food." He started when she laid her hand on his arm, the tingle warming his flesh. How was it that this woman he had only just met excited him so?

Drusa and Aiken were waiting for them in the kitchen. A steaming bowl of stew sat in the middle of the table, flanked by bread, butter and a pitcher of ale.

"Drusa said Elinore would worry if I told her ye'd been hurt, so I said nothing," Aiken remarked.

"Not even to Tilly?" Linnet asked.

Aiken's expression turned sullen. "She was serving the sheriff and didn't even see me."

Linnet let go of Simon's arm and sat on the nearest bench, but not before he had felt her shudder.

What had she done? He wondered again.

Drusa served up three bowls of stew and poured ale for

all of them before joining Aiken across the table from Simon and Linnet. "How does it happen ye survived, Sir Simon?"

"It was God's will, I would guess," Simon replied. God's will, a bit of luck and a lot of hard fighting.

"How did you come to be reported dead?" asked Linnet.

"Eat, and I will tell you." Between bites of stew, Simon related the events leading up to Hugh's capture and eventual transport to Acre, from whose stout prison they'd freed him.

"A miracle." Linnet's eyes shimmered with tears.

How compassionate she was to care so for a stranger, Simon thought, drawn to her even more strongly. Their gazes locked, and he felt the tension stir between them again.

"Did ye kill a host of the fiends?" Aiken asked, his eagerness typical of many who had sailed with Simon to the East.

Simon smiled faintly at Linnet and forced himself to look away. Unfortunately, the Crusade had been not only a dismal failure, but a living hell. Deplorable living conditions, terrible weather, disease, lack of supplies, loneliness. These had taken more of a toll on the Crusaders than the infidels' swords and arrows. "We killed our share," he allowed.

Aiken's lower lip came out. "Wish I could have trained to be a soldier instead of a spicier," he grumbled. "Then Tilly wouldn't look down her nose at me."

"There are other girls in Durleigh," Linnet said gently. "Girls who would realize that a successful apothecary can earn twenty times what a soldier would."

"Lot ye know." Aiken shoved back the bench he shared with Drusa, nearly toppling the woman.

Simon caught hold of Drusa's hand to steady her and glared up at Aiken. "Courtesy to others, especially women, is one of the first duties a knight learns."

Aiken paled. "I didn't mean to hurt her."

"I am sure ye didn't," Drusa said hastily.

"Sit, then, lad, and I will tell you of the wonders I saw while in the Holy Land."

"Tilly would certainly be impressed," said Linnet.

Aiken sat and listened eagerly, but it was to Linnet that Simon spoke as he spun tales of sailing ships and cities with gold-domed buildings, of endless deserts and towering palms, strange people and even stranger animals. Time drifted away until he suddenly realized that Linnet's face had gone pale and dark smudges rimmed her eyes. "You are tired."

"It is fascinating."

"Nonetheless, I should go." He stood slowly, reluctant to leave the cozy kitchen and the woman who intrigued him more with each passing moment.

She rose beside him. "Have you some place to stay?"

"The Royal Oak." He grinned down at her, thinking how small she was—her head came to the center of his chest. And how close, only a foot separating them. His body hummed with the desire to take the single step that would bring them together. He relished the ache, for it had been a long time since he had felt passion stir this sharply, other than in his special dream.

"Sir Nicholas and Sir Guy, two of my fellow Crusaders, went to the inn earlier to reserve a room. They are likely wondering what's become of me." Still he could not look away from her.

"Come, Aiken," said Drusa. "It's time we were settling in, too. Go through to the shop and make certain all is locked."

Linnet nibbled on her lower lip, her eyes eloquent. "Let me give you a torch to light the way, Sir Simon." She lit a pitch-tipped pole in the coals and handed it to him. Stepping outside with him, she pointed the way. "The path is over there and leads through the hedge to the inn's backyard." She sounded as breathless as he felt.

Knowing he should not touch her, but unable to help himself, Simon put his hand under her chin and lifted it. "Linnet. I would like to call upon you again."

"Oh, I would like that above all things." She smiled.

"Tomorrow, then." He lowered his head, just to brush her lips with his, but the moment they touched, he was lost. Her mouth was so soft it seemed to melt beneath his. Groaning, Simon slid his hand into her hair, cupping the back of her neck as he deepened the kiss.

She responded so sweetly, her hands coming up to clutch at his tunic as she followed where he led. Her throaty moans set his blood afire, but when he slipped his tongue inside to explore her more thoroughly, she started and drew back.

"Easy." Simon lifted his head but kept his hand on her nape, soothing her slender neck with his thumb. "I would never hurt or force you."

Her chuckle was unsteady, and she leaned her forehead into his chest. "I am afraid it would not be force."

Simon groaned and closed his eyes, praying for strength. "You should not tell me that."

"Why?"

He looked down to find his features reflected in her wide, passion-hazed eyes.

"Because, I do not trust myself to guard your innocence."

Pain flickered in her eyes. Or was it a trick of the half light? "Perhaps I am not as innocent as you think."

Simon smiled indulgently, pleased that she wanted him enough to lie about her experience. "I will be back tomorrow." He guided her to the door, bade her lock it and stayed until he heard the bar drop. Then he went off to the inn, his step lighter than when he'd left the bishop.

Linnet sagged against the door frame, her knees still weak, her body trembling from the force of her reaction to Simon.

"The Lord does work in miraculous ways," Drusa said as she bustled about putting away the remains of their meal.

Linnet straightened and tried to calm her raging emotions. "Aye, it is a miracle six of Durleigh's Crusaders returned."

"To be sure. I'll give thanks when I go to the cathedral for mass. That *he* should be one of them is the true miracle."

"What do you mean?" Linnet had never discussed Simon with anyone except her mother and Thurstan.

"Yer mama said ye were taken with him."

If you only knew. "He was unaware of my interest in him then," Linnet said primly. Why should he have noticed? They had never met face-to-face or spoken a word until he had stumbled out of the darkness and rescued her from Hamel's unwanted attentions.

Drusa cocked her gray head. "Well, I've seen the way he looks at ye. My Reggie used to watch me so when we were courting, like he couldn't wait to get me off in some shadowy corner and steal a kiss."

"I do not know what you mean," Linnet said airily. But the memory of the kiss made her cheeks burn and her lips tingle.

Drusa chuckled. "Ye cannot fool me, dearling. I've served this house since ye were born, and I know ye inside and out."

Linnet's smile dimmed. There was one thing Drusa did not know. Nor did Simon. She felt something akin to relief wash through her. If he recalled nothing, then perhaps she would not have to confess that their loving had produced consequences.

Consequences. What a cold, inadequate way to describe something at once so terrible and so wonderful it had marked her forever. If only she had been stronger....

Do not think of it, for that way lay madness.

"This was but an accidental meeting. He may not return."

"Oh, he'll be back." Drusa grinned. "Now, off to bed with ye. We cannot have ye all hollow-eyed when he comes calling."

Linnet just shook her head, but she climbed the stairs and readied for bed with a lighter heart than she had in years.

Simon was alive. Simon was back.

Suddenly the future did not seem so bleak and lonely. She was just pulling on her nightshift when she remembered Thurstan. How could she have been so selfish not to have thought of him sooner? He would be overjoyed to discover Simon was alive. First thing tomorrow, she must go to the cathedral and tell him.

That decided, Linnet knelt beside her bed, crossed herself and prayed to a God she had almost ceased to believe in when word of Simon's death had come. She begged forgiveness for that, thanked the Lord most fervently for sparing Simon, and added a plea that the return of his son would lift Thurstan's spirits.

Lastly, she prayed for the well-being of the babe she and Simon had made that long-ago night.

The babe she had given away.

Linnet shuddered as the pain lanced through her, followed by a wave of longing so sharp it made her moan. If only she could hold her baby daughter for just a moment. But she did not even know where the baby was. Thurstan had assured her the babe was not only loved and accepted in the home he had found for her, she would not bear the stain of bastardy. That alone had given Linnet the courage to give her up. But knowing her daughter was better off did not still the ache in her heart.

Or the guilt.

Walter de Folke stood nearby as Brother Anselme knelt over the body of Bishop Thurstan. Around them, the brothers of Durleigh prayed for the soul of their departed bishop. The fervent Latin mixed with Brother Oliver's wrenching sobs and the softer weeping of Lady Odeline. Ensconced in a chair by the fire, she was attended by her son. They made a striking

pair, the beautiful, red-eyed woman and the pretty, sullen
boy. Lady Odeline had wept a river, alternately lamenting
her brother's passing and her own uncertain fate now that he
was gone. Jevan had stood beside her, as emotionless as a
statue.

"To think that while we waited below our beloved brother
collapsed and died," Crispin murmured.

Beloved brother? Walter bit his tongue, knowing the archdeacon had despised Thurstan. For his part, Walter had admired de Lyndhurst's keen intellect but envied his genius for
amassing wealth and power. Now the scramble would be on
to see who succeeded to the rich bishopric Thurstan had built.
That contest pitted Walter and Crispin against each other.
Walter believed he held a slight edge, for he was well-known
to the archbishop and had served His Grace most ably. "Indeed. His Grace will be much saddened to learn that his great
friend has succumbed to this illness," Walter said.

"It was not the ague that took him," growled the portly
Brother Anselme, still on his knees beside the body, eyes
drenched with sadness.

Walter nodded. "The illness caused him to collapse, and
he struck his head on the table as he fell."

"The blow to the head seems too deep for a fall."

"What are you saying?" Crispin demanded with a shrill-
ness that silenced both the praying and the weeping.

"That this may not have been an accident," Brother Anselme replied.

Walter stared into the monk's troubled brown eyes, trying
to read the suspicions that lurked there.

"He was struck down?" the archdeacon barked. He
whirled. "Brother Oliver, did you say a knight burst in upon
his lordship? A crazed man who—"

"I understood he was a Crusader," Walter said calmly.

"He was in an agitated state. It may be that he blamed our
good bishop for sending him on Crusade." Crispin sniffed.

"You do know that Bishop Thurstan coerced some men into going."

Walter inclined his head, fascinated by the play of emotions in Crispin's usually austere features. From the moment Lady Odeline had rushed screaming into the dining room with news of finding the bishop, Crispin's color had been high, his beady eyes unusually bright. "Brother Oliver, what say you?"

Oliver raised his head, eyes so puffy they were mere slits in his wet face. "It is true, I did see the knight leaving this very room as I was coming to ch-check on his lordship."

"Who is this knight?" Crispin demanded.

"I—I think he is called Simon—S-Simon of Blackstone," Oliver stammered, "b-b-but I spoke with the bishop, he was alive and well after the knight left the palace. Si-sitting in this very chair, he was—" Oliver's eyes filled with tears "—talking with Mistress Linnet the—"

"That woman was here tonight?" Crispin shouted.

Brother Oliver cringed and glanced sidelong at Walter before nodding in mute chagrin. "She came to see how he—"

"There is your murderess, Brother Prior," snarled Crispin.

"Why would she wish our bishop ill?"

"She is an evil woman, who did conspire to tempt our bishop to forget his holy vows," said Crispin piously. "Doubtless she killed him out of frustration when her plans failed."

Walter suppressed a snort of derision. Crispin's theory had more holes than new cheese, yet he was clearly anxious to find Thurstan's killer. Doubtless so he could put himself in a favorable light with the archbishop and gain Durleigh for himself. Walter girded himself for battle. "I will question her and this Sir Simon," he said.

"You? By what right do you question anyone?" Crispin cried.

"By the power vested in me by the archbishop." Walter

smiled thinly into Crispin's furious face. "His Grace did send me here to check on his dear friend, and he will expect a full accounting of this sad event when I return to York." *I have you there, you sanctimonious old stick.*

Brother Anselme rose between them. "I do think we should look more closely into this matter, Reverend Father," he said to Crispin. "At the very least, we must know how he d-died."

The color leached from Crispin's face. "Of course. Take the body to the infirmary and see what you can learn."

The monk nodded.

"I would also suggest that the room be sealed and a guard placed on the doors so that nothing is disturbed till we know what is what," said Walter, earning a glare from Crispin.

"Brother Gerard will compile a list of everyone who entered the palace this evening," snapped the archdeacon. "On the morrow, I will personally speak with each one." He left in a swirl of coarse gray robes.

The lady Odeline followed directly, leaning heavily on her son's arm, her face buried in a linen handkerchief. Jevan's expression was as remote as carved marble, but when he reached the door, he turned back, sweeping the room with avid eyes before exiting with his mother.

Curious, that, Walter thought as he moved aside so Thurstan's body could be lifted. Did the boy expect to inherit some of his uncle's fabled wealth? If so…

Walter sighed. *Dieu,* he was as bad as Crispin, seeking to point the finger at everyone he saw. Jevan had been at supper in the dining hall with the others when summoned to hear the dreadful news his uncle had died. And Lady Odeline had no reason to wish her brother ill. Without Thurstan's support, she and her sullen chick would be cast out into the cold.

But the fact was that someone within these very walls might have murdered the bishop.

Chapter Four

A lady cried out.

Simon stopped and turned. Swaying slightly, a wineskin dangling from his hand, he squinted at the shops and homes lining the street.

All were dark and deserted, the owners off at the feast hosted by Bishop Thurstan to celebrate the departure of Durleigh's Crusaders. The roofs of the buildings were silhouetted against the glow of lights from the market square where the festivities were being held. How had he wandered so far away? Dimly Simon could hear the hum of voices raised in song and prayer as the folk of Durleigh bid Godspeed to their Crusader band.

A bubble of drunken pride rose in his chest. Tomorrow he would be leaving with them…a knight bound for the Holy Land. Stumbling slightly, he started back to the fete.

The woman cried out again. "Don't. Please don't!"

"Get back here," roared a male voice.

Simon whirled toward the sounds and caught a flash of white moving in the alley across the way, followed closely by a large, dark shape. "Bastard." Throwing the wineskin away, he drew his sword and staggered after them. Down *the alley, and through it into the next street, he pursued them, driven by the vows he'd sworn earlier in the evening.*

To uphold justice and protect the downtrodden. The oath burned bright in his heart, like a fever driving out the effects of a day spent drinking. He felt strong and powerful.

At last, Simon saw them. The wretch had a small figure in white trapped against the side of a building.

"Unhand her!" Simon roared.

The assailant whirled, his face a pale blur in the gloom, his sword gleaming as it came up to counter Simon's lunge. Steel rang on steel as the blades met.

Simon grunted, pain shuddering up his arm. He had drunk too much. He met his opponent's flurry of blows cleanly, but slowly. Too slowly. He wondered if the girl had gotten away, but could spare no time to look. Then he heard a sound that sent a chill down his sweaty spine.

"To me! Bardolf, Richie, to me!" the assailant cried.

Simon groaned and redoubled his efforts, knowing he'd never survive a trio of swordsmen. Suddenly a length of cloth flew out of the darkness and settled over the man's head. While he flailed and cursed, a hand grabbed Simon's arm.

"Quick, come this way." The speaker was a woman. A small hand grabbed his arm and led him down a side alley. It was so dark he could see nothing except the faint blur of her white gown. A few harried steps later, he ran into a wall.

"Trapped," Simon whispered.

"Nay. There's a door." Hinges creaked, a draft of air eddied around them, smelling strongly of straw and horses.

"Stables?" he muttered.

"Aye. We can hide here."

"Knights do not cower in—"

"Please. You cannot prevail against so many."

"But…"

"I am so afraid."

Simon could hear the terror in her voice and feel her trembling, though he could not see her face. "All right."

Inside the stable it was pitch-dark. "We'll be safer up in the loft," whispered the woman. "There should be a ladder. Ah, here. Let me go first."

Simon followed her up, one hand on the hem of her skirts. He reached the top and fell forward into the loft. His body came up against hers as they hit the straw.

"Thank you. I-if you had not come..." She shuddered.

Simon drew her close. She was small and slender. "You should have run off while we were fighting."

"I could not leave you, not when he was besting you."

"Bah, I could have taken him with a few blows had I not drunk half the ale in Durleigh."

"Aye. You are so strong." Her hands were on his chest, kneading. "Hold me," she whispered.

"I am."

"Tighter. Hold me tighter." She pressed against him, her breasts teasing him through the layers of their clothes.

"I will not let anything happen to you," Simon murmured. Her hair smelled so good, like roses and woman. He buried his face in it and rolled so he covered her with his body. "How perfectly we are matched."

"I knew it would be thus."

Simon nodded, his mind too dizzy with ale and desire. "I have to touch you." Her breasts were small and firm; her sigh when he caressed them tore at his control. He could think of only one thing, being inside her. He tore at the laces of his hose and levered himself over her.

"Simon," she whispered, drawing him to her.

He groaned and sank into the most perfect bliss he had ever known, hot and tight and welcoming, her body closed around his. It was like coming home.

A sharp pounding shattered the dream.

Simon groaned and sat up, his breathing rough, his body hard as tempered stone.

"Open, I say." The coarse voice came from below his window.

It took Simon a moment to recall he was not in the hayloft with his perfect lover, but in the room he'd taken last night at the Royal Oak. Moaning, he flopped back on the pillow and threw an arm over his eyes.

The dream again. He had had it the first time on the night before leaving for the Holy Land, waking hot, sweaty and half-dressed in a stable loft. The dream had reoccurred so many times since, that every aspect of it was engraved on his heart. Yet he could not see the woman's face, or decide whether the encounter had been real or a figment of his ale-soaked brain.

How odd that he, who had ever been cautious in his dealings with women, should dream that he had coupled with her only a short while after meeting her. Odder still, he had spent these past years searching for a flesh and blood woman who matched him as perfectly as his dream lover.

A fist collided with the door below. "Open, I say..."

Hinges creaked in protest. "What the hell is going on?" Simon recognized the voice of Warin Selwyne, the tavern owner.

"I am looking for a knight. Simon of Blackstone, they believe he's called."

"Who believes? And what do ye want him for, Bardolf?"

"None of yer business. My orders are to find him and bring him for questioning."

Simon was already out of bed, his first thought that something had happened to Nicholas or Guy. When he'd arrived at the inn, he'd found a note from Guy saying he had followed Lord Edmund to London. Nicholas had not been at the inn, either, but one of the maids recalled seeing him go off with a comely woman soon after he'd arrived.

"What is this about?" Warin grumbled.

"Sheriff's business. Will ye tell me if he's here, or do I have to come in and look for meself?"

Simon opened the hide shutters and looked down on the confrontation between Warin and a large man with lank brown hair and ill-fitting clothes. Behind him lounged two more thugs.

"I am Simon of Blackstone," Simon called.

Bardolf tilted his head back, displaying an ugly face and close-set eyes. "Ye're to come with me."

"What for?"

"Questioning in the death of Bishop Thurstan. And don't think to try to run out. I've got men watching the front."

"Death?" Simon exclaimed. "He is dead?"

Archdeacon Crispin Norville sat behind Bishop Thurstan's desk, a thin, austere man who managed to look down his beak of a nose at Simon standing before him. Flanking the archdeacon were Brother Oliver Deeks, and Prior Walter de Folke of York.

The archdeacon had already judged him guilty, Simon thought, dread piercing his earlier shock.

"Brother Oliver says you burst in upon the bishop last eve. What business did you have with him?" the archdeacon demanded.

Conscious of Bardolf lurking in the doorway, Simon chose his words with care. "I wanted to tell him that six of his Crusaders had returned." Bardolf had hinted there was something suspicious about Thurstan's death, but the under-sheriff had refused to say what. "Is it true the bishop is dead?"

The archdeacon waved away the question, his long fingers naked of rings. "Why did you not make an appointment?"

Simon's nape prickled. As an orphan bastard, he had learned early on to sense trouble, and this luxurious room fairly reeked of it. "I understood that the bishop was upset by reports we had all died, and I was anxious to alleviate his grief.''

''Hmm.'' The archdeacon steepled his soft, slender hands. He had sharp brown eyes and the manner of one who liked power. He and the manipulative Thurstan must have butted heads. ''You came directly here, then, the moment you arrived.''

''I did.'' Three years Simon had burned to confront Thurstan. He could not have waited a moment more. Now the answers to his questions would forever go unanswered. Thurstan was dead, and he could not begin to say how he felt about that. Later, when this interview was over he would think on it.

''Where are the other five knights?'' asked the prior. He had the smug look of a frog about to snap up a fly, his eyes narrowed, his bald pate shimmering in the early morning light that streamed into the withdrawing room.

''Three returned to their homes. Two of them came as far as Durleigh with me, but they continued on about their business.'' Simon missed them sorely. He would have welcomed Guy's sage counsel, Nicholas's easy charm and strong sword arm.

''Was the bishop pleased to see you?'' the archdeacon asked.

Simon frowned. He had been caught up in his own anger and resentment. Now that he thought on it, Thurstan's initial reaction had been one of astonishment. Followed by joy when he realized Simon was not a spirit, but a real man. It shamed Simon that he had felt no pleasure in seeing Thurstan. ''He was.''

''Oliver says he heard raised voices.''

The secretary hunched his shoulders and looked at the floor. He was short and pudgy, with a round face and eyes red-rimmed from crying. His soft woven robe seemed too fine for a priest, in sharp contrast with the archdeacon's coarse wool and the prior's simple linen. But it was Oliver's reticent expression that piqued Simon's interest.

Had Oliver heard something he should not? Perhaps a woman professing her love for Thurstan? Who was she? Simon wondered, the woman he had lost in the dark last night? "His Lordship cried out in surprise. He did at first think I was a spirit."

Crispin brightened. "In devil's guise?"

Simon saw that trap and sidestepped. "Nay. If I had died on Crusade, I would have been guaranteed entrance into heaven. After a moment the bishop realized I was, indeed, alive. He may have exclaimed again at that."

"He was well when you left him?" asked Prior Walter.

"Well?" Simon felt an unexpected pang of remorse. Nay, the bishop...he could not think of him as his father...had looked sickly and frail. "He seemed to have aged since last I saw him."

"The bishop suffered a seizure when the Crusaders were reported lost," Brother Oliver interjected. "But he insisted on continuing with his many duties."

Simon knew what it was to carry on despite illness, but ignored the unwelcome spurt of sympathy for Thurstan. "How did he die?" he asked again, for this was all passing strange.

"He was struck on the head," said the archdeacon.

Prior Walter shifted. "Brother Anselme, our infirmarer, is examining the bishop's body and will shortly determine the cause of Bishop Thurstan's death."

"I gave orders that Brother Anselme prepare the body for immediate burial." The archdeacon's eyes flashed a warning. "And until the archbishop names a new bishop, I am in charge here."

The prior's smile was thin and deadly as drawn steel. "That is true, but I am here as His Grace's legate. And, if it be determined that someone did kill Bishop Thurstan, His

Grace will want the culprit apprehended, tried and punished.''

"That is why I question this knight," Crispin growled.

Simon tensed, apprehension trickled across his skin. He was glad he had told no one, not even Linnet Especer, of his connection to Thurstan. "When did the bishop die?" he asked calmly.

"His body was found in this very room," said the archdeacon. "Shortly after you departed the palace."

The prickling in Simon's neck increased. He could almost feel the noose tightening about it. If they knew he had spent the past three years hating Thurstan, he would be their prime suspect. "The bishop was alive when I left him."

Crispin frowned. "Did anyone see you go?"

Dieu, he did not know. He had stormed out in a fit of temper, his vision obscured by a red veil of rage. "If Brother Oliver saw me enter, perhaps he saw me go." He looked at the secretary, who had his chin buried in his chest. "The bishop said he was expecting someone, and indeed I heard a woman—"

"We know about that." The archdeacon's face twisted with intense dislike. "I had left orders she was not to be admitted to the palace, but Brother Oliver saw fit to disregard them."

Brother Oliver's eyes filled with tears. "I—I did not."

"It was not Brother Oliver's fault," said a soft voice.

Simon whirled and gaped.

Linnet stood on the threshold, looking vastly neater but no less desirable than she had last night. Her glorious hair was pinned up and covered by a white linen cap. From beneath her gray cloak peeped a murrey-red gown. Her eyes, wide with dismay, were fastened on the archdeacon. She resembled a doe facing down an armed hunter. "Why are you sitting at Bishop Thurstan's writing table, Reverend Father?"

The archdeacon leaped to his feet, his eyes blazing with

hatred. "Harlot! How dare you question me? You will tell truly why you were here last night in defiance of my wishes."

She flinched. "I came last night to see how he fared." She looked about the room. "What has happened? Why are you all...?" Her eyes widened. "Sir Simon, what do you here?"

"You know him?" asked the prior.

"Aye." Her eyes softened, and she smiled tremulously.

A queasy feeling stirred in Simon's gut. His first instinct was to shield her from the rabid archdeacon. But there were dangerous currents here he did not understand. He did not want to be dragged down by them. "We met by chance last night."

One of the priests who'd been huddled in the far end of the room stepped forward. "He followed her when she left."

Followed her when she left. Simon started. *She* had been Thurstan's last visitor?

"So." The archdeacon's eyebrows rose, and his mouth curved into a malicious smile. "Are you accomplices?"

"Accomplices..." Simon sputtered, aghast by the picture of Linnet forming in his mind. Was she the one he had heard profess her love for the bishop last night?

"Accomplices?" Linnet asked. "In what, pray tell?"

"In Bishop Thurstan's death," the archdeacon said bluntly.

"He...he is dead?" Linnet swayed, her eyes rolling back.

Instinct propelled Simon forward to scoop her up before she hit the floor. Cradling her in his arms as he had last night, he carried her to one of the high-backed chairs before the hearth. A vigorous fire crackled there, but the warmth did not penetrate the icy dread that had settled in Simon's gut as he placed her in the chair and knelt beside it. "Linnet?" he murmured.

Her lashed lifted. "Thurstan is dead?" The whispered

query held a wealth of pain. She looked so small and defenseless.

Simon was torn between the urge to comfort her and the need to demand she tell him what she was to Thurstan. Clearly cosseting her could only worsen their plight. Settling back on his heels, he nodded. "I have been told he is dead."

"He had been so sick for so long," she murmured. "But I prayed he would recover. Especially now that you have returned. 'Twas what I came to tell him this morn, that you were alive."

Did she know he was Thurstan's son? A tremor of alarm iced Simon's blood. Precarious as things were, he did not want her blurting it out. "Shh. Stay quiet." He looked over his shoulder and saw the archdeacon lurking there. "She needs wine."

Crispin raised one skeptical brow. "I think this harlot has ensnared you, too, with her wanton wiles."

Too? Simon did not like the sounds of that at all. His skin crawled with apprehension. "We barely know each other."

"You are solicitous for a stranger." The archdeacon tucked his hands into the sleeves of his robe, his expression watchful, vicious. Like a snake with a pair of cornered mice.

Simon stood, enjoying the way he towered over Crispin. "Knights are ever chivalrous of women."

"A woman such as this one can enslave a man with a look."

Oh, Simon knew that firsthand. A few moments in her company last night, and he'd been smitten, had even fancied she might be the woman to equal the one in his dream.

Crispin glanced at Linnet. "Did you tire of the bishop and murder him so you could have this young and comely knight?"

"Murder?" Linnet's face went whiter still.

"He was killed. Struck down," said Crispin.

"We do not know that," Brother Oliver said gently. "It may be he collapsed as he did last autumn and hit his head."

"You think I murdered him?" Linnet said slowly, as though trying to come to grips with it. "Nay, but he was my friend."

"Oh, I think you were more than a friend," the archdeacon said silkily. "You were Bishop Thurstan's mistress."

"Mistress?" Simon was struck with a ridiculous urge to wipe his mouth, to rub away the kiss they had shared.

"It is not true," Linnet whispered, expression anguished.

Simon looked away, unable to bear the sight of her delicate features and beautiful eyes. Lying eyes. To think he had come close to seducing his father's mistress.

"Aye, she was his mistress." Crispin's lip curled with loathing. "But perhaps she fancied a younger protector."

"If so, it was not me," Simon said stonily. "I only returned to Durleigh yesterday."

"Yet Brother Gerard saw you follow her from the palace."

Simon shrugged. "Coincidence. We were here at about the same time, and the Deangate is the quickest route into town."

"You appeared to wait till she left, then pursued her." Brother Gerard had the sharp features of a ferret and the fawning, smug manner of a toady.

Simon despised him on principle. "I lingered in the gardens a moment after leaving the bishop. Which I would not have done were I guilty of murder." A reminder of his service to God could not go amiss, either. "The roses drew me, for I missed their sweet smell while on Crusade in the dry, desolate East."

The archdeacon's scowl eased a bit.

"Bishop Thurstan's death is my fault," whispered Brother Oliver. "If I had been with him when he was stricken, he would not have fallen and struck his head."

"Be at ease, Brother," said the prior. "Whatever happened, it was God's will."

Brother Oliver sighed and bent his head.

Crispin nodded. "Thank you for reminding us of that, Brother Prior. Bishop Thurstan's passing was indeed God's will."

Simon released the breath he had been holding and silently gave thanks for the prior's level head. "I may go, then?"

"For the moment, but do not try to leave Durleigh till this matter is settled. And I would say the same to you, Mistress Linnet." Crispin pinned her with a searing glance.

"I have nothing to hide." Her eyes were haunted, but she held her head up as she turned and walked regally from the room.

The archdeacon stared after her, but his lean face was twisted with loathing. Simon almost pitied her, for she had incurred the enmity of the man who would, if only temporarily, wield much power in Durleigh. It was a fact he would do well to remember if he wanted to remain a free man.

"Come, Brothers, we must go to the chapel and pray for the bishop's soul." Crispin gathered his robes in one hand and swept from the room, followed by the other priests.

Prior Walter remained behind, as did two muscular men Simon had marked as soldiers. When the priests had gone, Walter posted the guards in the hallway, one at the bedchamber door, the other outside the withdrawing room, with orders to let none pass. Then he turned to Simon. "You must have been close to Bishop Thurstan if your first act in Durleigh was to visit him."

Simon hesitated, wondering what to make of this bald little prelate with his sharp eyes and even sharper wit. "We barely knew one another." True enough. "But many of the men in the Black Rose took the cross in response to a penance levied by the bishop. I thought he should know a few of us had survived."

"A noble gesture."

"The archdeacon does not seem to think so."

"Aye, well." Walter shrugged. "Crispin disapproved of everything Bishop Thurstan did and said."

"He covets the bishopric, then?" Simon asked.

"Only because he feels he is better suited to the task."

"What of you?" Simon asked archly.

Walter grinned. "I am not as critical of Thurstan as Crispin, but every man aspires to better himself."

"A clever answer."

"A truthful one. I admired what Thurstan accomplished here, though his methods are not mine. As to taking his place..." Walter shrugged again. "I doubt few men could. I would welcome a chance to try, but I would not kill to get it."

A shrill voice sounded outside in the hallway.

"You have no right to keep me out!" A woman burst into the room. She was not young, but still beautiful. Despite the early hour, her blond hair had been sleeked neatly back, coiled at her nape and encased in a gold wire net. Her fashionable green gown was close-fitting, showing off a slender body.

Close on her heels came the guard. "My lord prior..."

"It is all right." Walter's manner stiffened. "Lady Odeline, is something amiss?"

The lady sniffed and advanced on the prior, followed by a well-dressed youth in his early twenties. "Why have we been refused admittance to Thurstan's chambers?" she demanded.

Her easy use of Thurstan's name piqued Simon's interest. Could this be his mother? If so, she must have been a mere child when she bore him.

"It was by my order, Lady Odeline. We are investigating the circumstances of the bishop's death."

"Surely it was an accident." Tears magnified the eyes she raised to the priest. "Oh, cruel fate to take my brother from me. He was the only one who loved me. The only one who sympathized with my trials.''

"Brother?" Simon whispered. He felt his mouth fall open in astonishment and closed it with a snap. This was Thurstan's sister? His own aunt?

"Whatever will we do?" She clutched at the boy who now stood beside her. "Where will my son and I go? We have nothing. No home, no money. Nothing."

Simon's compassion for her faltered. Clearly she cared more for her welfare than the loss of her brother. But then, her selfishness should not be surprising. Thurstan had cared more for satisfying his pleasures than for his holy vows or for the fate of any child he might sire.

"I am certain the bishop provided for you," said Walter.

"Nay." Lady Odeline was sobbing now. "He always said his money would go to build a chapel for his remains. And to the abbey. We will have nothing."

Walter sighed. "Jevan, take your mother above stairs to her chambers that she may rest."

"Nay, I would remain here and pray for my brother," Lady Odeline said.

"Tomorrow, when the matter of his passing has been settled, you may sit vigil here," said the prior.

Rage dried her eyes, and her cheeks went red as fire. "You would deny me this?" she demanded.

Walter met her glare with coolness. "Regrettably. Nothing must be disturbed till we know what happened."

Simon looked to see how Jevan was taking this and found the boy staring at him. He was a head shorter than Simon with the lean build of a whippet, glossy black hair and pale skin. His eyes were narrowed to angry slits, glinting with blatant hatred. *He knows I am Thurstan's son.* Simon felt the shame burn up his neck to his cheeks.

"Jevan!" the lady cried. "We will take this up with the archdeacon." She swept from the room, her son at her heels.

Walter sighed. "Spoiled and willful. The lady is Thurstan's youngest half sister. Doted on by her mother and always in trouble. A scandal led to her exile from court. Had Thurstan not agreed to let her stay here while Jevan studied at the cathedral school, they would both have been homeless."

"Jevan is studying to be a priest?"

"A clerk. Thurstan feared that without discipline and a trade, he'd turn out like his father." Walter paused. "The man was a drunkard, killed in a back alley brawl. Come," he added. "Let us see if Brother Anselme has learned anything."

"Do you think Thurstan was killed?"

"I do not want to believe it possible, but he had a look of such horror on his face." Walter shuddered. "And Brother Anselme was most insistent upon examining the body."

Simon followed Walter to the door, then turned to scan the room. All was as it had been last night, except for the blood on the corner of the writing table and the dark stain on the carpet before it. What had happened here after he left?

Simon was surprised to find that he cared. For more than three years he had burned with the desire to see Thurstan de Lyndhurst suffer for his crimes, but now…

Regret mingled with the thirst for revenge. Now he would never have the answers he sought. His mother's name. The reason why Thurstan had ignored him.

But if he was not very careful to hide his parentage, he might find himself framed for the bishop's murder.

Chapter Five

Linnet stole silently into the infirmary, a long, gloomy room whose ceiling was supported by huge columns of stone. "Brother Anselme? Are you here?" she called.

The healing brother emerged from behind the screen set up at the far end of his infirmary. "Linnet!" He hurried past the rows of empty cots. "You should not be here."

"I know." Linnet wanted to throw herself at him, but wrapped her arms around herself instead. "Oh, Brother Anselme, the archdeacon thinks I killed Bishop Thurstan."

"Here. Here." Anselme put an arm around her, led her to a bench and sat beside her. "Why would he say such a thing?"

"Because he hates me and would have someone to blame, I suppose." She wiped her face, then looked up into the cherubic face of the healing brother who had become a dear friend. "Is it true? Is Thurstan really gone?"

"Aye." Tears swam in his large brown eyes.

"I hoped it was wishful thinking on the archdeacon's part. He so disapproved of Thurstan's ways."

Anselme nodded. "Did Crispin send for you to arrest you?"

"Nay. Oh, Brother, I came to bring the bishop good news. Simon of Blackstone is alive."

Brother Anselme was one of the few who knew the truth about Simon's parentage. "According to Brother Oliver, Simon visited Thurstan last night. So at least before he departed this life Thurstan had the satisfaction of knowing Simon lived."

Linnet clenched her fists. "Crispin wanted Thurstan gone so he could run Durleigh as he sees fit."

"Shh, daughter, mind what you say." Anselme stood to pace.

"His death was not an accident, then?"

"Nay, it was not."

"What have you found?" she asked shakily.

The good brother paused and looked at her. "It is not a fit subject for you to think on."

Linnet's throat tightened, but she had learned when her parents died, when Simon was reported dead, that grief would not bring back her loved ones. "I must know how this happened."

Brother Anselme nodded grimly, looked skyward, as though for divine guidance, then crossed himself. "There is evidence of foul play." He glanced about the empty chamber, then drew closer to her, lowering his voice as he spoke. "I have only had a short time to examine him, for I first had to master my grief and offer prayers for his soul. There is a wound to the head, which came from striking his table, but that did not kill him. I have also found evidence he was poisoned."

Linnet groaned, his words like a knife to her heart. "Oh, sweet Mary, I hoped I was wrong."

"You knew of this?"

Linnet swallowed, but the lump in her throat did not budge. Even the cup of wine the brother hastily fetched did not ease her dry mouth or her conscience. "These last few days he seemed so much weaker that I got out great-grandfather's herbals, searching frantically for some tonic, some potion.'' She took another sip of the wine. ''I came across an entry Grandpapa had made about a man wasting away from a mysterious illness. He was an older man, wealthy and wed to a young wife. The sons by his first marriage suspected foul play and called upon Grandpapa to examine him ere he was laid out. Grandpapa found evidence the man was being poisoned over time with monkshood. The wife was accused and did confess. Thurstan's symptoms seemed similar.''

''Monkshood.'' Anselme sank down beside her. ''It sounds a slow and painful death, yet it would explain his long illness.''

Linnet bit her lip. She hated lying to Anselme but could not tell him she believed Thurstan had grown despondent and poisoned himself. Suicide was a mortal sin, one that would bar Thurstan from burial in holy ground. ''I came here last night to tell Thurstan what I suspected, but he was agitated and sent me on my way. Now he is dead.''

Anselme sighed. ''Aye, and we will miss him sorely. But it was not monkshood I found in—''

''Brother Anselme, what have you learned?'' Walter called, walking into the infirmary with Simon beside him.

Anselme surged to his feet. ''I have discovered a few things, Brother Prior.'' He looked questioningly at Simon.

''You may speak freely before him,'' said Walter as they drew nearer. ''This is Sir Simon of Blackstone.''

''Ah.'' Anselme inclined his head. ''Linnet said you had miraculously returned. I am glad you had a few moments at least with the bishop. He was greatly troubled by news of your death.''

Simon grunted. ''How did he die?''

Anselme stiffened. ''I assume you mean our beloved bishop.''

Simon grunted again. "Forgive my brusqueness, Brother, but I find myself suspected of murdering a man I scarcely knew and am anxious to clear my name so I may be on my way."

He was leaving? Linnet suppressed a moan.

"You have only just returned to your home," said Anselme.

"It was a mistake to come back. There is nothing here for me." Simon glared at Linnet as he spoke.

She shuddered. *Thurstan was my friend, nothing more.* But perhaps it was better for this to end before it went further. If Simon so easily believed her capable of murder, how great would be his loathing if he learned about the babe.

"I understand Brother Crispin gave instructions that the bishop be prepared for immediate burial," said Walter. "I have convinced him that we must first learn how Thurstan died."

Anselme nodded. "I am glad, for in addition to the blow to the head, I found signs that Thurstan had ingested poison."

"Poison!" exclaimed Walter and Simon in unison.

Linnet groaned and ducked her head to hide her fear.

"Belladonna," said Brother Anselme.

"Belladonna?" Linnet exclaimed in surprise.

"How was it administered, and how long would it take to do its deadly work?" asked Walter.

"I cannot be certain till I have examined the bishop more thoroughly," Anselme said. "Along with the wine, brandy and water kept in his chambers."

Belladonna, not monkshood. Linnet felt weak with relief. Thurstan hadn't been poisoning himself after all.

"God save me," Walter whispered, clutching his throat. "I drank wine with him yesterday."

"If it contained belladonna, you would already know it, Brother Prior," Anselme quickly replied.

Walter swallowed convulsively. "I will go myself and gather the flagons for you to examine."

Anselme sighed. "I cannot believe anyone would kill him."

"Men such as him make enemies," Simon muttered. "I'd not speak ill of the dead, Brother, but the whole town bore the print of Thurstan's heavy hand. Nothing was done but by his leave. He ruled like a king, and grew rich into the bargain."

"He used his power for good," Linnet cried, heartsick that Simon should so revile the man who was his sire. And her dearest friend. If not for the bishop, she would have been ruined, and her babe branded a bastard.

Simon turned on her. "Your staunch defense of him does not surprise me, *mistress*."

His hatred wounded her so deeply she could not reply. And she knew that his would not be the only voice raised against her. Heartsick, she longed to return to her shop, crawl into bed and hide until this was over. "I had best leave."

The door to the infirmary rattled open, and two men hurried in, their spurs grating on the stone floor.

"Brother Anselme, are you within?" called a familiar voice.

Hamel Roxby.

Just when she thought the day could not get any worse. Linnet whimpered and prayed she would sink into the floor.

Hamel Roxby.

Simon's hand fell instinctively to his sword hilt as he watched the man approach.

Hamel had been under-sheriff when Simon left on Crusade, a mean and clever man who subtly abused the power of his position. Pity someone had not ended his career. In appearance, Hamel had changed little, his lean features and long nose giving him a hawkish look. He had yet to notice

Simon, hidden behind a stone pillar, but there, running from Hamel's right temple to the edge of his eyebrow, was the pale scar where Simon's blade had nicked him when they'd crossed swords years ago as youths of six and ten. The rivalry between them was old and bitter. Simon could not abide a bully, and Hamel hated anyone who stood up to him.

"I hear the bishop is dead," Hamel called cheerfully.

Simon's hackles rose. It was one thing for him to decry the man who'd sired him, another for Hamel to find joy in his death.

"Mistress Linnet." Hamel's face lit with the unholy glee of a hunter spying easy prey. "Is it true? Is your bishop dead?"

She shivered. "Aye."

"Well, well." Ignoring the priests, Hamel strolled toward her through the gloom with the easy swagger of a born bully.

Simon stepped into Roxby's path. "Hamel."

Hamel's black eyes widened with surprise, then narrowed. "Simon of Blackstone. I'd heard you were back from the dead."

Simon grinned. "Aye, alive and returned to Durleigh."

"Alive for the moment." Hamel reached for his sword.

Brother Anselme dashed between them. "Hold. We'll have none of that in God's house. Why have you come, Sheriff?"

Hamel was now sheriff? That boded ill, Simon thought.

"I went out late last night hunting wolves and returned to news the bishop had been murdered. I've come to investigate."

"Thank you for your concern, Sheriff," said Prior Walter. "But Brother Anselme will examine the bishop."

Hamel glared at the plump priest. "Who are you?"

"Walter de Folke, Prior of York, come to Durleigh on the archbishop's business. I will investigate this matter and take a full accounting to His Grace."

"If a murder's been committed, it is my duty to—"

"Bishop Thurstan was a priest who died on church lands. His death is church business," Walter said sternly.

Hamel's eyes narrowed. "Not if the culprit was someone from Durleigh. There's some who resented having the bishop's nose in their affairs," he sneered. "Bringing such a person to justice would be *my* business, so see you keep me informed."

"You have not yet been confirmed as sheriff of Durleigh, have you?" Prior Walter asked smoothly.

Hamel grunted, but the heat left his eyes. "I will be. Sheriff Turnebull trained me himself, and my da was his under-sheriff. Archdeacon Crispin has found my work satisfactory."

"He may not be our next bishop," Walter mused. "But we keep you from your work. Good day, *Sheriff.*"

Hamel scowled. "Send word to me when you learn how the bishop died." He spun on his heel and strode out, his spurs grating on the stone floors. And on Simon's nerves.

The moment the door closed, Linnet sank down on the bench and Brother Anselme heaved a sigh of relief.

"Well done, Prior Walter," Simon murmured. He usually found priests annoyingly passive. It was refreshing to meet one who stood up for what he believed in, even to someone like Hamel.

"It was my pleasure. I remember Thurstan saying that Hamel Roxby was not half the man his father was. Thurstan and Lord Edmund had reservations about Hamel being under-sheriff, but could find no grounds for dismissing him."

"Hamel is a clever man who loves power," Simon said. He looked at Linnet's ashen face and felt a wholly unwelcome urge to comfort her. Instead, he looked away. "I would appreciate knowing what you find out, Brother Anselme."

"Of course, but it may take several days—"

"Time is critical," Walter said. "In my years of service to the archbishop, I have regrettably undertaken other such investigations. The more time that passes, the harder it is to discover the murderer, important facts are forgotten, clues disturbed.''

Brother Anselme nodded. ''I will work as quickly as I can.''

''Excellent.'' Walter tucked his pudgy hands into his sleeves. ''And I would ask you report your findings only to me. Now I will go make certain the bishop's chambers are secured and return with those flagons.'' He hurried away.

Linnet stood. ''I had best be getting back to my shop.''

''I do not like you walking back alone with Hamel lurking about. Simon, would you go with her?'' Anselme asked.

Nay. He did not trust himself to be alone with Linnet for fear the contempt he felt for her would erupt.

''It is not necessary. I will be fine.'' She walked away. This time her head was bowed, her shoulders slumped.

He would not care. Simon looked away. ''Perhaps I could help you with your work, Brother.''

''It is not a pleasant task for a relative.''

''Was I the last person in Durleigh to learn the bishop had a bastard son?'' Simon growled.

''No one else knows save myself and Linnet.''

''It does not matter. He was no father to me.''

''He was more of one than you realize.'' The monk sighed. ''But we've no time to argue the point now. I must find out how he died. You can help me by seeing Linnet back to her shop.''

''I am certain she knows the way.''

''And so does Hamel Roxby.''

''What do you mean by that?''

''Our sheriff is interested in Linnet.''

Simon ignored a spurt of alarm. ''She is not my concern.''

''In that, too, you are wrong, my son,'' he said cryptically. ''She does not welcome Hamel's advances.''

The spurt of alarm grew stronger. ''I do not care.''

"You lie to me and to yourself," Anselme snapped, eyes crackling now with anger. "But I have neither the time nor the patience to argue. Linnet has had enough sorrow in her short life. If you will not do this out of the kindness of your heart, then I offer a bribe. Keep Linnet safe and I will share with you what I discover about the bishop's murder."

"You are certain about the poison?"

Brother Anselme nodded grimly. "I do not know exactly how he died, but there are signs he was poisoned, aye."

Simon's throat tightened. He had no alibi, only his word. The word of a man who had hated Bishop Thurstan for four years. "All right. I will see she reaches her shop safely."

"Good." The monk clapped him on the shoulder. "Stay there with her. I will come as soon as I am finished here. Surely no later than vespers."

"But that is hours away. What will I do cooped up with her in that small shop of hers?"

"You know the place, then?"

Simon groaned. *Dieu,* if he did not watch his tongue, he'd condemn himself. "I have never visited a large apothecary."

"Ah." Anselme smiled. "Your wits are as quick as I'd heard. If anyone should ask why you go with her, say I have need of some lavender to sweeten the bishop's shroud."

Simon was only too glad to leave the clever monk to his gruesome task. The path from the infirmary took him past the sweet-scented rose garden. The plants were lush and green, laid out in neat, sweeping beds. Whoever tended them had a knack for nurturing. As he approached the main gate, he met Brother Gerard coming toward him.

"Did Linnet Especer pass this way?" Simon asked.

The ferret stopped, tucked his hands into the sleeves of his robe and glared at Simon in perfect imitation of the archdeacon. "Chasing after her again, sir knight?"

"Brother Anselme bid me ask her for some lavender."

"It is not wise of you to associate with that murderess."

"Why would she want to murder the bishop?"

"Women do not need reasons. They are sly, evil creatures."

Simon's hands clenched. He longed to plow a fist into the ferret's face, but losing his temper would only make matters worse. "I will remember your warning," he said through his teeth and stalked out the gates onto the Deangate. His expression was so fierce that people scrambled to get out of his way.

The street was not overly crowded, and Simon was taller than most folk, but he did not spot Linnet's fair hair up ahead. Had Hamel already snatched her? Fear quickened his stride, until he was fairly running, across Deangate, down Colliergate. The stink of burnt wood and the cries of the charcoal vendors followed him. At each intersection, he paused to look both ways, searching lanes and alleyways for some sign of Linnet.

As he passed the mouth of Hosier Lane, he saw something that stopped him midstride.

Hamel had someone pinned up against the side of a tavern. His hands were braced on the wall, hiding his victim's face, but a cloud of fair hair was visible.

The sight stirred something in Simon's memory…a vague, dreamlike sense of having stood here before.

Ridiculous.

Simon shook it off and plunged into the gloomy lane, his strides eating up the distance. "Mistress Linnet," he called.

Hamel whipped his head around, his eyes narrowed to furious slits. "What are you doing here?"

"Looking for the apothecary."

"Find another. This one is busy," Hamel growled.

Simon peered over Hamel's beefy arm at Linnet. The only color in her white, stricken face was in her eyes, great pools of ginger-brown, terrified, beseeching. No matter how she'd tried to deceive him, he could not leave her here. "I fear no other will do. Brother Anselme sent me to buy from her stock.''

"Buy from someone else.''

"He was most specific that it be Mistress Linnet,'' Simon replied, aware that a man had come out of the tavern. The wool merchant, one of Durleigh's most prosperous citizens.

"Sheriff, what is—?'' Edric Woolmonger's eyes rounded in his fleshy face. "Simon of Blackstone! Aren't ye dead?''

"It seems not, Master Woolmonger. I am pleased you recall me.'' Simon was relieved to see Hamel step back from Linnet.

"Of course I remember ye. Did ye not twice escort my wool to Tynemouth for shipment? And without losing a single wagon. Praise be to God for sparing ye.'' Edric crossed himself. "I would have ye to sup and hear of yer adventures, but—'' his smile faded ''—now I must go to the cathedral and offer prayers for our beloved bishop.'' Edric cocked his head. "Will ye return to Lord Edmund's service now ye're back?''

"I do not know. His lordship is away at present.''

"Well, 'tis good to see ye alive, at any rate.'' Edric turned to Hamel. "What luck did ye have last night catching that wolf?''

"None.'' Hamel's eyes blazed hatred at Simon.

"Well, it must be caught before it devours my whole herd,'' Edric grumbled. "Walk with me apace and tell me what can be done about the wolf.''

Hamel shot one more hot look at Linnet, then fell into step with the merchant.

Linnet whimpered, her head falling forward, her eyes closing. "Thank you,'' she whispered.

"Brother Anselme asked me to come,'' Simon said coldly.

She lifted her head, her gaze haunted. "You wanted to refuse. I am very glad you did not.''

So was he. She looked so fragile, so damned vulnerable,

it was all he could do not to sweep her into his arms and carry her. "I promised him I'd see you to your shop."

"A promise grudgingly given, I'll grant. I wish I were brave enough to refuse your reluctant escort." She looked down the lane in the direction Hamel had taken. "But I am not."

Simon wished it, too. Despite all he'd learned this morning, she still drew him.

"How are we going to find the charter if we cannot enter Thurstan's room to search for it?" Jevan demanded for the dozenth time since he and his mother had retreated to her room.

"We will have to wait." Odeline paced before the empty hearth, kicking her skirts from her path in impotent rage.

"I am tired of waiting," Jevan whined. "Curse the luck, why did Simon of Blackstone have to turn up alive? In another few weeks Thurstan would have died and Blackstone Heath come to me."

Odeline le Coyte stopped and turned to regard her only child. He was so like her, she thought, her heart swelling with love. He had inherited the good looks, quick mind and driving ambition shared by all the de Lyndhursts. From his father, Jevan had unfortunately gotten a black temper. She had tried her best to teach Jevan to control his outbursts, but he always wanted more than he had and lashed out when he could not get it immediately. "How can you know his death was so near?"

"'Twas written on his face, plain to see."

Odeline shuddered. She was not a murderess. She was not. The wee shove she had given Thurstan had not been forceful enough to kill him. He had been alive when she'd gone to fetch help. She knew it, his face and limbs relaxed as in sleep, but when she'd returned with the prior and archdeacon...

Dieu, the torturous twisting of her brother's body, the anguish etched into his features had been terrible to behold. It would haunt her all her days. But she was not responsible. He must have suffered a seizure of some sort.

"We have to find the damned charter," Jevan whined.

Odeline started and shoved her guilt aside. "Just be patient a bit longer, Jevan. The guards will likely be gone from Thurstan's rooms by nightfall. I will go down after everyone is asleep and find the charter."

"I should have made him give it to me first."

"What do you mean?"

Jevan gave her an odd, calculating look and turned toward the window. "Why, before I agreed to attend his school." The slick words, the cocky set of his head, were so like his father's.

Odeline shivered. Jevan was not like his father. He was not. "You were at supper when Thurstan died?" she asked softly.

Jevan turned and smiled. "As any number of good brothers will vouch." The smile turned feral. "I want Blackstone Heath."

"I promise you will have it." No matter what she had to do.

Somehow, Linnet managed the walk to her shop, but she could not have said what route they took or who they passed. What remained of her slim store of energy was devoted to putting one foot in front of the other. Yet she was oddly aware of the man who walked beside her.

This was the second time Simon had saved her from Hamel. But he did not remember that first time. She was glad of it, for if he had, Simon would truly think her a loose woman. The sort who coupled with a man she had only just met.

"Damn, it looks as though you have customers waiting."

Linnet raised her head, surprised to find they had reached

the corner of Spicier's Lane. A small crowd did indeed seem to be gathered in front of her shop. Dread trickled down her spine. "I hope nothing is wrong." She started forward.

"Wait." Simon stepped in front of her, as he had in the infirmary, one hand on his sword hilt. "Stay behind me." He crossed the lane and headed slowly toward the shop.

As they drew near, Linnet saw that Aiken had raised the shutters at the front of the shop. He stood behind the plank that served as a counter, busily dispensing goods. Drusa stood in the street, chatting with two of the women.

"Is business always this brisk?" Simon asked.

"Nay, I cannot think why—"

"There she is. There is Linnet," someone called. As one, the dozen or so customers turned. All were known to her, their expressions ranging from sympathy to curiosity.

"What is going on here?" Simon asked.

"Gawkers." Come to see how she was bearing up under the strain of Thurstan's death. "It was the same when Papa died." Nay, that was not quite true. Then people had looked at her with sympathy. Today, many were curious, a few openly censorious.

Simon sniffed disapprovingly. "I will order them away."

Tempting. Linnet shook her head. "It would only make matters worse. I had best get inside and help Aiken." The crowd parted easily to make way for Linnet. Several of the women were crying, some murmured words of support.

"Is it true the wretch is dead?" asked a querulous voice.

Linnet gasped and spun around to find Old Nelda behind her.

Crazy, some folk called the old woman. She lived down by the river, dabbling in charms and noxious potions. "Is it true?" Her iron-gray hair was pulled back so severely her skin stretched tight as old leather. She stared at Linnet, her yellow eyes as intent as a cat's watching a cornered mouse.

"Bishop Thurstan is dead," Linnet whispered.

"Did he die in yer bed?" Spittle foamed at the edges of Nelda's thin lips. The crowd went deathly silent.

"Of course not," Linnet cried. She started as a warm, wide hand touched her shoulder. Simon's hand.

"Cease this vile gossip, old woman, and be on your way," Simon growled.

Nelda smiled slyly, revealing black stumps. "Gossip's always got a grain of truth. They say she was his mistress. They say she bore him a bastard babe when she was at Blackstone Abbey some years back."

Linnet shuddered. Or was it Simon's hand that shook in the instant before he removed it. Suddenly she felt cold and alone.

"Be gone." Simon's voice was low and hard.

"I'll go, but ye cannot still me tongue." Nelda waggled her bushy brows at Linnet. "Nay, Thurstan's gone. Can't keep me quiet now." She turned and shuffled off, dirty bare feet peering from beneath the hem of her ragged clothes.

Simon muttered an oath, then turned to the rest of the onlookers. "If you have come to buy, do so. If not, get about your business and leave Mistress Linnet to hers." He took her arm with surprising gentleness. Gentle, too, was his voice as he whispered, "Come inside, away from this crowd."

Drusa met them at the door and hustled Linnet toward the kitchen. "Poor lamb. Sit down here. I'll mull ye some wine."

Linnet collapsed onto the bench. Her heart ached, her head pounded. She laid it on the cool wood and wished she could simply melt into the oak, be absorbed by it.

"Are you all right?" Simon asked.

Linnet opened one eye. Up close, she saw what she had missed earlier, the dark shadows under his eyes, the raw emotions in them, a swirl of shock, pain and, aye, fear. "I should learn to ignore her ravings."

"Has this sort of thing happened before?"

"Nelda is always speaking out against the bishop. Earlier

in the year he had her exiled from Durleigh for peddling her purgatives and abortives in the market square.''

''So she has reason to hate him?'' *Was she telling the truth about you and the bishop?* His eyes asked.

''And to spread lies, aye.'' Linnet sat up and scrubbed her hands over her burning eyes. ''I do not care for myself, but to besmirch the name of so fine a man and bishop....''

''She is not the only one who thinks you were his mistress.''

Linnet sighed. ''Bishop Thurstan said it is not in people's nature to think a man—even a man of God—and a woman can be friends. The talk about us began before I went to the abbey.''

''Why were you at the nunnery?''

Linnet looked down at her hands, knotted in her lap, for fear he would see more than she wanted him to. ''To study healing from the sisters. Bishop Thurstan arranged it. Catherine de Lyndhurst, his own sister, is abbess there.'' She heard his indrawn breath. ''She is a full sister and not like Odeline.''

''I see,'' he said slowly. ''And the part about the babe?''

Linnet clenched her hands until the nails bit into her palms. Sweet Mary, how can I bear this? But she must. ''Gossip,'' she murmured. ''Gossip and hurtful lies.''

He said nothing.

The silence stretched and grew around them until Linnet did not think she could last another minute. ''Thank you for coming to my aid and seeing me home.''

He sat down across the table from her. ''I told Brother Anselme I would wait here for him.''

''There is no need,'' she said stiffly.

''He will bring us news of how Thurstan died.''

Linnet lifted her head. ''I thought you did not care.''

''I stand high on the archdeacon's list of suspects. And if Thurstan's death was not natural or accidental...''

"But he was alive when I left him."

"Which was shortly after I left him." He leaned closer. "But we have just our word on that, and if the poison was a slow-acting one, we may yet be charged."

"What motive could either of us have had for killing him?"

Simon sighed. "None as far as anyone knows, but you can be assured Crispin and Hamel will dig furiously to uncover some. It is best they not learn I was in your shop last night."

"What can that matter?" Linnet whispered.

"It matters because we provide an alibi for each other. If we are strangers, we have no reason to lie. If not..."

Linnet's mouth went dry. How many people in Durleigh knew that she and Simon had been lovers long ago?

Chapter Six

He did not want to like her.

Scowling, Simon leaned his shoulder against the far wall of Linnet's shop and tried to ignore his growing fascination with her and his appreciation of what she had created here.

The shop was small but tidy. The walls were lined with cupboards holding clever displays of creams and potions in clay pots, interspersed with bunches of dried flowers. More flower-filled earthen crocks sat on the table in the center of the room, alongside wooden bowls of peppercorns, red, black, green. The whole effect was pleasing to the eye and the nose.

Aiken had been kept busy at the counter, really more like a wide windowsill, over which he dispensed common herbs like sage and rosemary to customers on the street.

Simon had been here all morn, watching Linnet ply a trade at which she obviously excelled. There had been a steady stream of women who had come seeking treatment for everything from the ague to dry skin. Small wonder the apothecary was so busy. Linnet considered each problem, no matter how trivial, as though it mattered to her personally. Her concern was evident in her soft voice as she asked a question, her smile as she hit upon the solution. Only the shadows under her eyes and the faint tension in her expression betrayed the strain she was under.

It bothered him that he noticed these things. It bothered him more that they moved him. Dammit, he did not want to like her. Uncomfortable with his feelings, Simon scowled.

The woman Linnet had been waiting on looked up at him, gasped softly and fumbled with the pennies in her pouch. "Never mind about the cinnamon. I'll get it another time."

"It will take only a moment to grate some," Linnet said.

The woman cast another fearful glance at Simon, shook her head and rushed out, clutching her purchases to her chest.

Linnet bustled around the table and confronted him. "If you do not cease glowering, you will drive away my customers," she hissed under her breath.

"You should be resting."

She sighed, and her eyes filled with bleak despair. "If I lie down, I would not sleep. If I do not have work to keep my mind busy, I would go mad thinking of what has happened."

"My own thoughts have been none too cheery."

"That much I guessed from your black looks." She smiled ruefully. "I thought it was because you are wroth with me."

Simon shrugged, unsure how he felt about her.

"Well, could you not take your scowls elsewhere? Even if Hamel did come here, I should be safe enough in this crowd."

"I doubt these goodwives would stop the sheriff."

She shivered and looked away, but not before he read her fear. "I will be all right."

"As you would have been outside the Hosier Lane tavern had I not found you? I am staying till Brother Anselme comes."

The glance she sent him mingled sorrow and gratitude. "I had forgotten he was the reason you came."

So had he. And that troubled him. "I would not want to

ruin your business,'' he said stiffly. ''I will go into the kitchen. If anything happens, you have only to call out and I will come.''

''I know,'' she said softly. ''You always do.''

''Always?'' Simon asked, but she had turned away to wait on a customer, so he went through the workroom to the kitchen.

Drusa looked up from sweeping the floor and grinned. ''Tossed ye out, did she?''

''Aye. Said I was bad for trade.'' Simon sat at the table where they had eaten last night. *Dieu,* those happy hours now seemed a lifetime ago. From this vantage point he could see through the workroom and into the shop beyond.

''Ye do look intimidating when ye scowl.'' She set a cup of ale before him and sat down across the table. ''Are ye upset because the bishop is dead?''

''He was nothing to me,'' Simon said sharply.

''Bishop Thurstan affected the lives of everyone in Durleigh.'' Drusa sipped her ale.

That Simon could not dispute. ''What of Linnet?''

Drusa regarded him over the rim of her cup. ''If ye are asking was she his mistress, the answer's nay. And ye cannot know her if ye believe the gossip.''

''I do not…know her.'' He drank deep of the ale, letting the coolness soothe his tight throat. ''She is old to be unwed.''

''Twenty's not ancient. She's been busy learning her trade.''

''She said she spent time with the sisters at Blackstone Abbey.'' It gave him an odd jolt to think she had studied in the abbey where he had been born. Were there records of his birth? His mother's name, perhaps? He did not recall the place. His earliest memories were of a manor where he'd been reared by an elderly couple. They had told him he was the bastard son of a young maid and Lord Edmund's distant cousin. The fact that Lord Edmund had fostered him and seen him knighted had seemed to support this.

Lies, all lies.

Above all things, Simon hated lies. He wanted to know who his mother was, whether she was alive or dead and, most important of all, what sort of person she had been.

"We missed Linnet while she was gone." Drusa's expression changed subtly. "But the sisters taught her much. There is not a more capable apothecary in all of Northumbria. It worries me that these vile rumors about her will ruin the business and the reputation she's worked so hard to gain. There's some in the guild who resent her success. Jealous men."

Not only men, Simon mused, thinking about Nelda's vicious accusations. "Why did she not wed another spicier? If she had a husband in the trade, he would protect her interests."

"And claim the proceeds of all her hard work." Drusa snorted. "She's that independent, our Linnet. Besides, there was no man she fancied enough to put up with."

Simon grinned, oddly warmed by Drusa's words. Judging by Linnet's response to him last night, she fancied him.

"And, too, her heart had not mended."

"What?" His smile faded.

"There was someone she loved," Drusa continued. "A Crusader of the Black Rose, he was. She cried herself sick when they left and again when they were reported dead."

Who was it? Two hundred men had left Durleigh with him. Young farmers, jaded tourney fighters, ambitious third and fourth sons eager to make their fortune. Which one had captured Linnet's heart and rode off to his death? It bothered him to think of her pining away for some other man.

"But ye see, the fact that she'd not entertain any suitors made folk suspect there was already someone. When Hamel

Roxby began pestering her, and the bishop warned him off…''

"People jumped to the wrong conclusion." Or had they?

It is because I love you that I am worried, Thurstan.

Linnet's words. If they had been lovers, Linnet might not have admitted it to her faithful maid.

"I have closed for dinner." Linnet entered, followed by a frazzled-looking Aiken.

"Such a morn," the apprentice whined. "My legs and feet ache something fierce."

"And my back." Linnet arched subtly as she crossed the room, seemingly unaware of the tempting way her breasts pushed against the bodice of her gown.

Simon looked away quickly, but not before Drusa caught him staring and grinned. Face heating, he leaped up and offered Linnet his place.

She smiled and brushed past him to sit, the scent of roses teasing his nostrils.

"I'm starved. What's there to eat?" asked Aiken.

"Ye're always hungry." Drusa bustled to the hearth. "Chicken soup." She lifted the cover, and a mouthwatering aroma filled the room. "There's bread and meat pies, too. I figured we'd need a bit more than usual to fill yer belly, Sir Simon, and young Aiken's hollow legs."

Simon frowned. "You fed me last night, as well. Let me pay you for the meal."

"We owe ye, for twice saving Mistress Linnet."

"I was happy to be of service."

"And we are happy to feed you," said Linnet.

"My thanks." Simon sat but did not relax. Whenever he looked up, his vision was filled with Linnet. The mere sight of her face tugged at him.

"After we eat, I'll step across to the Royal Oak and fetch back some more ale," Aiken offered.

Linnet sighed. "Tilly will be busy this time of day."

"I know." Aiken traced a drop of ale with this finger. "But I can see her, at least." His voice was low and mournful.

Linnet understood Aiken's anguish only too well. For years her dreams had been fed by glimpses of Simon. The second and fourth Saturdays of every month she had gone to the field off Stonebow to watch Simon and Lord Edmund's other knights train the menfolk of the town in the use of sword and bow, in case Durleigh was attacked.

"Mind ye don't get in the way," Drusa grumbled. "Don't want Dame Elinore complaining ye're keeping Tilly from her work."

"No need to worry about that. She barely sees me. Especially if Sheriff Hamel is about," he muttered darkly.

Linnet started. "I did not know he was often there." Lurking in her own backyard. It was intolerable, frightening.

"He spreads himself about, does Hamel. Wherever he can get a free meal and a few cups of ale."

Simon accepted the bowl Drusa handed him. "I was surprised to find him sheriff."

"He has been our temporary sheriff since January," said Linnet. "Sheriff Turnebull was killed then, chasing the bandits who've been plaguing the roads to the south."

"If they were the same men who set upon my friends and me, they will not be causing any more trouble...except in hell."

"Ye killed them?" Aiken asked around a mouthful of stew.

"All but one." Simon scowled.

Linnet touched his arm. "Do not feel guilty, they were a bad lot, who robbed and killed many a merchant. Since Allan Turnebull's death, they have grown more bold. Few dare to travel these roads without an armed escort."

"Hamel does nothing to catch them?"

Linnet made a face. "He claims to be trying."

"He spends most of his time swaggering about the town impressing the women," muttered Aiken. "He has a wee house near the market square, and it's said there's a constant stream of women at his door." He sighed enviously.

"Well, the bandits will not be terrorizing anyone else," said Simon. "I am only sorry one got away, wounded but alive. I thought I recognized him from Durleigh Cathedral."

"An outlaw priest?" Drusa exclaimed.

Aiken chuckled. "Fighting's not something they teach."

Teach? Perhaps the brigand had been a student, not a priest. Simon frowned, but could not remember exactly when he'd seen the man. "I'll know him if our paths cross again."

"What of the battle?" Aiken actually set down his spoon as he leaned forward.

"The engagement was short and none too well fought, the thieves being cowards." Simon frowned. "Odd now that I think on it. You say they had robbed all winter, but they were skinny, scruffy creatures, not well armed."

"I want to be a knight," Aiken said suddenly.

Linnet sighed but bit her tongue. She was rewarded by a sidelong glance from Simon. His smile of sympathy warmed her clear to her boots.

"It is a hard life and not so pleasurable as the ballads make out," Simon said to Aiken. "Unless you have land of your own, you are at the beck of others."

"Still, there's nothing so fine as a man in chain mail."

Linnet could almost hear Tilly saying that.

Simon's lips twitched. "Perhaps tomorrow I will let you try mine on and you can see how it sets."

"Really?" Aiken's eyes fairly bugged out. "Can Tilly come?"

"Insolent pup," Drusa chided. "Eat yer supper and leave Sir Simon to his. Tilly, indeed."

The rest of the meal passed in companionable silence, broken only by Drusa's offer of second helpings. Aiken accepted, of course, cleaned his bowl and left for the inn. Drusa went with him. For a spot of air and to see what Elinore was planning for supper, she said.

Linnet was suddenly aware that she and Simon were alone. The room seemed close, the air heavy with possibilities. Nervous, she picked up their bowls and carried them to the wash table. "I am sorry he is such a pest. He does not truly want to be an apothecary."

"A pity," Simon replied from just behind her. "He is too slightly built for soldiering." His arm brushed hers.

Linnet froze, the bowls still in her hand. Her blood warmed and her skin felt all prickly.

"His questions do not bother me. Most lads his age are fascinated with fighting and killing."

Ordinary words. Concentrate on them. Do not let him guess his nearness made her heart race. "You are good with him." She set the bowls down and dried her hands on a linen towel. "It has been difficult with Papa gone." Her hands trembling, her voice shaky, she fought for control. "Aiken does not much like taking orders from a woman only a few years older than he."

"What makes you so nervous?" Simon asked.

"N-nothing." Linnet turned, the rest of her words died.

Simon's eyes were more green than gray now, staring intently into hers. "You are hiding something."

Several somethings. "I do not know what you mean."

His eyes narrowed. "Last night I heard you tell Thurstan that you loved him."

The air left her lungs in a rush of relief. "I do." Tears prickled behind her lids. "He was a dear, dear friend, and I will miss him all the days of my life."

"He was a liar and a fraud."

Linnet gasped, then realized what must have happened. "He told you the truth last night."

"That I am his son, you mean." His expression grew even

grimmer. "Nay, I had that news from a priest who went on Crusade with us. Three years I waited to confront your *dear friend,* to hear from his lips why he—"

"You hated him," Linnet whispered.

"Because of him, my whole life has been a lie. I am not the son of Lord Edmund's cousin, as I was told, but the bastard of a selfish, manipulative priest who betrayed his vows of celibacy to sire me on some poor maid."

"He was not selfish. He was good and kind."

"He broke his covenant with God, violated my mother and did not even have the decency to claim me."

"I am sure he had his reasons."

"Aye. Protecting his reputation," Simon growled.

And yours, Linnet thought, but she saw he was in no mood to listen to anything good about his father. So much anger, and beneath it, pain. How it must have eaten at him while he was away. Festering like an unhealed wound. "When you saw him last night, did you tell him how you despised him?" she demanded.

"I told him that I knew the truth, and I demanded to know about my mother. But he would not answer my questions."

"Likely he was too shocked. We thought you were dead. How he grieved when the news reached us. He collapsed and—"

"Likely he feared I'd ruin his pristine reputation."

"You are wrong about him. He loved you."

"So much so that he ignored me." Simon turned away.

"Fool. You know not how he truly felt." Temper seething, Linnet grabbed his arm to stay him and raised her chin to challenge his dark scowl. Angry words crowded her throat. The pain she glimpsed beneath his rage held back her sharp retort. The silence spun out, growing heavier by the moment. She was acutely aware of how close they stood, of the warmth of his arm seeping through his woolen sleeve and the strength of the sinewy muscles contracting beneath her palm.

His eyes narrowed slightly, the expression in them changing from fury to something even more dangerous. An earthy hunger that reminded her of the kiss they had shared.

A knock at the back door shattered the moment. Brother Anselme stuck his head in. "I have come at a bad time?"

"Nay." Linnet let go of Simon's arm, conscious she had narrowly escaped the trap she'd fallen into last night.

Simon stepped back from her, his expression shuttered. "You have discovered something, Brother?"

"Your servants, are they about?" Brother Anselme's guarded look and low voice were chilling.

Linnet shivered. Something bad had happened. "They have gone to the tavern, but I cannot say how long they will stay."

"Let us walk in the garden, then," said the monk. "I have spent a long day inside."

They fell into step beside her, out through the tiny gate and into the garden that had been started by her mother's father. It took up nearly as much room as the shop, surrounded by a high stone wall her father had put up to keep out the pigs and chickens that roamed free in the yards. A narrow gravel walkway separated the beds from one another laid out in the shape of a wagon wheel, with a rowan tree in the center.

Anselme stooped to pick a sprig of basil. Holding it to his nose, he inhaled deeply.

Simon shifted impatiently. "How did Thurstan die?"

Anselme exhaled and let the herb drop. "I do not know exactly." His voice dripped weariness.

"But you said you'd not come till you knew," said Linnet.

"Oh, his body has told me all it will, but I still am not certain what happened. Three things were done, any of which might have taken his life." Anselme began to pace. "As you suspected, Linnet, he was being poisoned with monkshood."

"Monkshood?" Simon frowned. "I thought it was bella-donna."

"I will get to that," said Anselme. "I found traces of monkshood in the herbal brandy he drank before retiring."

Linnet's belly cramped. Did Anselme suspect Thurstan had done it himself? She sank limply onto the small bench where she'd spent so many happy hours with her plants.

"The monkshood killed him?" Simon asked.

"It weakened him, and it would eventually have killed him," Anselme murmured. "But there is also the wound to the head."

"Oliver thought he'd fallen and hit the desk."

"It is possible, but the cut is deep. More likely he was pushed so he struck with greater force."

"And that killed him?" Linnet asked, relieved.

"It might have. But there is one other bit of evidence. The belladonna that had been forced down his throat."

"Forced?" Linnet shuddered.

"Why not more monkshood?" asked Simon.

"Exactly." Anselme steepled his hands, brow furrowed. "You can see why the manner of his death is so much a mystery."

Simon nodded. "Any of these three things could have killed him. Though the monkshood would have taken more time."

"We have someone who wished Bishop Thurstan to die a slow and painful death," Anselme said grimly. "Then along comes someone who strikes the bishop down. Perhaps in a fit of rage."

Had Simon been angry enough to strike out at his father? Linnet glanced at Simon through her lashes.

He gazed out over her garden, his brow creased in con-centration. There was no hint of the man who had stood in her kitchen a few moments ago, his face suffused with anger, his eyes blazing hatred for the man who had sired him. Nor of the knight who had kissed her so passionately last night.

Simon cocked his head at the monk. "And the belladonna?"

"A complex riddle. It could be that the monkshood poisoner became impatient and resorted to belladonna."

"Or the two could be unrelated," said Linnet.

"What does the archdeacon think?" Simon asked.

"I have not told him about the monkshood. Only we three and the prior know thus far."

Linnet twisted her hands in her lap. Her shop records showed the sale of monkshood to Thurstan. One look at them and she'd be judged guilty. Should she alter the record?

"I could not have given him the monkshood," Simon protested. "I only arrived yesterday."

"True." Anselme sighed. "I fear the archdeacon is already bandying about the theory that you and Linnet acted together."

Linnet just gaped at him, horror-struck at how close Crispin had come to guessing part of the truth. If it came out that she and Simon had been lovers, that she'd borne a child and that Thurstan had found a home for it....

"That is a lie," Simon exclaimed.

"Easy, my son. The prior and I do not share this belief. The archdeacon is anxious to prove himself worthy of assuming the bishop's cap by solving this case quickly. You make handy suspects. You two were the last to see the bishop alive."

"What of Lady Odeline?" Simon asked harshly.

"She says he was already down when she found him," the monk replied. "And she had more reason to want him alive. Linnet is an apothecary with knowledge of herbs and poisons. You are a warrior, Simon, a man trained to use violence to settle your problems, and you are the son he never acknowledged."

"Does Crispin know that?" Simon demanded.

"Nay, but if he should find out—"

"We will be arrested and hanged forthwith." Simon sighed and pinched the bridge of his nose. "A man like Thurstan must have had enemies."

"Not everyone appreciated him," Anselme murmured. "But neither did he quarrel openly with many."

"Brother Oliver said Thurstan had had a trying day," Linnet murmured. "Suppose he had argued with someone earlier and that person came back to confront him."

"An excellent notion," said Anselme. "Prior Walter is going to question all those who live within the cathedral walls to learn if they saw or heard anything. If Allan Turnebull were still with us, he could talk with the townsfolk who visited the bishop. But I fear Hamel Roxby would make a hash of things with his arrogant rudeness."

"If he made the effort at all." Simon grimaced. "Hamel would love to see me hang for this or any other crime."

Linnet's blood ran cold thinking of the archdeacon's virulent hatred and Hamel's ruthlessness. "What can we do?"

Surprisingly, Simon stepped up beside her. "We can help find the murderer. Get me a list of those who held a grudge against the bishop, and I will flush out his killer."

"I believe you would, but the archdeacon would not like it." Anselme paced to the bed of sweet basil and back. "I will ask Prior Walter's advice. With his permission, I will get from Brother Oliver a list of those who visited Thurstan yesterday."

"Thank you, Brother," Simon replied.

"I will get word to you on the morrow. A word of caution, Sir Simon. To the folk of Durleigh, you are an outsider. They may speak more freely if Linnet is with you. And I would feel better if she was not left alone till this matter is settled."

Simon nodded and glanced down at her. "I guess, then,

that we are partners in this dreadful enterprise.''

God help us both, she thought.

''Damn, what are they saying?'' Jevan demanded.

Rob FitzHugh shielded his eyes from the sun and looked out the upstairs window of the Royal Oak at the trio in the apothecary garden. ''Hard to tell from here.'' The especer's shop was a good hundred yards away across a large, weed-choked field. Even from this vantage point, he could see only the tops of their heads over the stone wall that enclosed the garden.

''I have to know what he's doing.''

How the hell should I know? Rob took one look at Jevan's dark scowl and bit back the words. No one threw a fit to equal Jevan's. He raged like a mad dog, all flashing eyes and gnashing teeth. ''Why don't I just creep over there when it gets dark and slip my knife between his ribs?'' Rob offered.

Jevan's smile was nearly as deadly as his scowl. ''A tempting thought, but it needs to be done with delicacy and timing. Aye, the timing's the thing. I want you to keep track of Simon's comings and goings.''

''Hamel's got Ellis watching out front.''

''How clever.''

Rob shrugged, grimacing as the movement pulled on the stitches Old Nelda had set in his shoulder. ''I owe him. Old Nelda says my arm won't work right for a long spell. If ever.''

''He will pay, but it will be done my way, understand?''

Rob sighed. ''I'll watch him close, never fear.''

Chapter Seven

Someone was watching them.

The feeling skittered up Simon's spine. Looking away from Linnet and Anselme, he scanned the garden. Even the taller herbs would provide scant hiding for anything larger than a cat.

"I will ask Brother Oliver to bring the list of Thurstan's visitors," Anselme said. "Just after None at the infirmary."

Midafternoon. "Thank you, Brother." Simon gazed across the weeded lot to the tavern. He studied each blank window in turn. There, in the tiny garret under the eaves, he detected movement. A face, pale in the dark square. It vanished quickly, furtively, as though the person had seen Simon looking and moved back.

Tilly, fetching something from an attic storeroom? Or had Hamel set a watch on them?

"Let us see you to the door." Simon motioned for Linnet and the monk to precede him from the garden. They reached the kitchen door ahead of him and entered. Simon turned back.

There it was again. A face in the attic window.

Simon entered the kitchen, barred the door and hurried through to the front just as Linnet was bidding Anselme goodbye. Traffic on the street was light, a pair of women with laden baskets, a pie man crying his wares, a cart pulled by a donkey. Across the way, a beggar sat cross-legged in front of a rival pepper's shop. At least, he was supposed to be a beggar.

"Thank you for bringing us news. I hope you do not incur the archdeacon's wrath on our account," Linnet said.

"He is busy setting the bishopric to rights," Anselme said unhappily before looking at Simon. "Keep safe, both of you."

"We will." Simon shut the door and set the bar.

"What is wrong?" Her face was ashen in the gloomy entry.

Simon hesitated. It was not his way to frighten women, but Linnet had pluck. Too much, in fact, and was likely to venture out alone and stumble into danger. "We are being watched."

Her eyes widened. "Hamel?"

"I would guess the beggar is Hamel's man. His face is not gaunt enough for a beggar's, and his boots have no holes in the soles." About the tavern, he said nothing, not until he had checked it out. "I need to go to the castle. There is someone I must see there." It felt odd not to have Nicholas, Guy and the others ready to stand beside him in this. He hoped Wolfsmount Castle's captain could spare him a few men to help guard the apothecary in case Hamel tried to force his way inside.

What to do with Linnet? Immediately he thought of Warin Selwyne. They had shared a cup of ale last night, and Simon had found the innkeeper as honest and open as he remembered. Warin would not give the sheriff a room from which to spy on Linnet. It must have been Tilly hoping to pick up a bit of gossip. "I want you to wait for me at the inn with Elinore."

Linnet bristled. "I will be fine here."

Stubborn. "Unless Hamel is waiting for me to leave so he can come and question you."

She shivered, and her shoulders slumped. "Very well."

Nay, it was not. The sharp longing to hold her, to comfort her, swept through him. Simon battled it back and escorted her outside. "Are you certain you will feel safe with the Selwynes?"

"Of course." Linnet stopped. "Will you be all right alone?"

Simon bit back a smile at her concern. "I will."

Elinore was in the kitchen, chatting with Drusa and chopping onions. She dropped her knife. "What is wrong?"

"Nothing." Simon ushered Linnet in and closed the door. "I am going up to Wolfsmount to tell some of my old comrades that I have risen from the dead. And thought it best Linnet wait here."

Elinore's smile faded. "There has been more trouble."

"Nay." Linnet shot Simon a worried look then sighed. "We think Hamel has someone watching the shop."

"You did well to bring her here," Elinore said. "Hamel will not try anything with my Warin about, not if he wants to be confirmed as sheriff. Warin is an alderman."

"So he told me last eve." Simon smiled at Linnet. "I will be back within the hour. But before I go, I will step through and tell Warin you are here."

"It is not necessary," Linnet said gently.

"To me, it is." Their eyes held for a moment, the emotions swirling in hers painful to behold. No matter how he felt about Thurstan, she had lost a friend and stood suspected of murder. The awareness of how alone and frightened she must be knotted his belly. Dimly he realized that for once it was not just his inbred need to protect that made him afraid. He cared about her.

Dieu, but he was a fool.

Turning away in self-disgust, Simon stepped to the door

that led into the tavern room, then recalled another matter and turned back. "Elinore. I would like to keep a closer watch on the apothecary. Could I move from my room to the chamber under the eaves? That one has a better view of the back."

"Oh, I fear it is occupied."

"Who has it?"

"Jevan le Coyte, the bishop's nephew. He is studying to be a clerk, but says he needs to get away from the priests and their strict rules." Elinore winked. "If you know what I mean."

"Indeed." Simon was not surprised that Thurstan's nephew would, like his uncle, bend church rules to suit himself. "A handsome lad like that must be a favorite with the ladies."

"His mother keeps him close by," Linnet said. "I've heard they often take walks by the river together of an evening."

"Have you heard Olf's run off?" Elinore asked.

"He is Old Nelda's son," Linnet explained. "Thurstan employed him to tend the rose gardens."

"Why would he hire the son of a woman who hated him?"

"Out of pity," Linnet said. "He could not turn a blind eye to the abortions Old Nelda performed in the back room of her shop. Especially after one of her patients nearly died. Archdeacon Crispin wanted Nelda hanged. Thurstan spared her life, but said she could not live within the city."

Simon frowned. Such charity did not fit with the image he had of the bishop as a ruthless, grasping man. "I will be back quick as I can." Nodding to Linnet, he stepped into the short, dimly lit passageway that led from the kitchen to the tavern room. It took up the entire front of the building.

Midway down the hallway was a door leading to the outside. Opposite it were the stairs up to the sleeping rooms. When he'd taken a room, Elinore had warned him that the

outside door was locked from dusk to dawn for the guests'
security. Simon considered going up to see if Jevan was in
his room, but he did not yet want to tip his hand and so
continued on.

The tavern's common room was twenty by forty feet, with
whitewashed walls and a worn stone floor. Light streamed in
from the four windows that faced the street and a fire crackled cheerily in the huge hearth along the wall it shared with
the kitchen. It was not crowded at this time of day. Three of
the dozen tables were occupied. A pair of men stood at the
bar across the room, chatting with Warin.

"There he is now," Warin exclaimed.

The two men turned. Simon's hand fell to his sword, then
relaxed, smiling as he recognized them. "Gaspare. Piers."

Gaspare le Vrise launched himself across the room and
engulfed Simon in a rib-cracking hug. "'Tis good to see you
alive, *mon ami!*"

"I'll not be for long," Simon wheezed, winking at Piers.

Taller and slimmer than his bosom companion, Piers du
Bonheur's swarthy face was wreathed in smiles. "It is good
to see you again, my friend."

Simon disentangled himself from Gaspare's beefy arms
and grinned at the two knights who had served with him as
part of Wolfsmount Castle's guard. "It is good to be back."

"Who else returned?" asked Piers.

"None who served with us at the castle," Simon said
sadly. "You might have met Hugh of Halewell or Nicholas
of Hendry." Of Guy, he said nothing. He did not know what
Lord Edmund would make of the son he had not known he'd
fathered.

"Come." Gaspare clapped him on the back. "Let us buy
you an ale. We would hear what befell you in the Holy
Land."

"And I would gladly share the tales, though there was little
glory in the dismal mission. But I am pressed for time."

''What has happened?'' asked Piers.

Simon looked around, then led his friends to the most isolated table. When Warin bustled up with three cups of ale, he asked the man to join them. A tavern keeper was usually aware of everything that went on in town.

''Has trouble followed you from the East?'' Gaspare asked.

Simon shook his head. ''You know that the bishop is dead?'' The men nodded glumly. He noted that all three, men whom he respected, looked genuinely sorrowful.

''William FitzAllen has sent a messenger after Lord Edmund to tell him of the tragedy,'' Piers said. ''But his lordship may not return for the funeral. He has pressing business in Calais.''

A handy excuse, Simon mused. Given the friction that had always existed between the two stern, powerful men, he wondered if Lord Edmund would truly mourn the bishop's passing. ''Is William FitzAllen still master of horse at Wolfsmount?''

''Nay, he is captain of the guard now.'' Gaspare made a rude sound. ''He swaggers about like a king.''

Simon sighed. ''I had hoped to borrow a few men from the castle's garrison, but William will not be disposed to aid me.''

''He still decries the fact you bested him at swordplay during the Christmas tourney five years ago,'' Gaspare replied.

''For what do you need the men?'' asked Piers.

''Guard duty.'' Simon glanced around, saw no one near but leaned closer to his companions. After swearing them to secrecy, he quickly told them that Thurstan had likely been murdered, but none of the particulars. ''Brother Anselme does not yet know how he was killed, but Crispin Norville's suspicion has fallen on myself and Linnet Especer, the apothecary, since we were the last to see the bishop alive.''

Gaspare frowned. "But that is ridiculous. Why would either of you have wished the bishop dead?"

"We did not," Simon murmured, glad no one here was privy to his personal turmoil. "But the archdeacon is apparently anxious to prove himself by solving the crime quickly."

"That one." Gaspare made an even ruder sound. "Sanctimonious idiot. To him, everything but prayer is a sin. If he becomes bishop, there will be much grumbling."

"But Thurstan ruled the diocese like a tyrant," said Simon. "Even Lord Edmund grumbled that Thurstan overstepped himself."

"Granted, the bishop had strong ideas, God grant him peace." Warin crossed himself. "But a cannier man I never met. And most of the burghers, at least, would agree. It was thanks to his strength and foresight that the town has grown so. And, of course, to Lord Edmund's capable garrison."

"Lord Edmund would agree, I am sure," Piers said. "He did complain about the bishop's methods. Called him highhanded, meddlesome and worse, but between them, my lord and the bishop made Durleigh prosperous."

That even Simon could not dispute. The town had grown in the four years he had been gone. "Well, whether the archdeacon becomes the next bishop or not, my immediate problem is to clear my name. Prior Walter is overseeing the investigation for the church, but Hamel Roxby is also casting about for clues."

"Was there not bad blood between you two?" asked Piers.

Simon nodded. "He was not best pleased to see me return."

"And he has been sniffing about Linnet," said Warin.

"I heard she was the bishop's leman," muttered Simon.

"Groundless rumors spread by the archdeacon." Warin scowled. "She has been a good friend to my wife, and I can tell you there was only friendship between Linnet and the bishop."

Simon wished he were as certain as Warin. He wanted to believe Linnet, but sensed she was lying to him. "Do you think FitzAllen would be willing to lend me a few men?"

"Only if he did not know it was you doing the asking," Gaspare replied.

"Alas, we are short of men at the moment," Piers added. "Four knights and fifty men-at-arms accompanied Lord Edmund to London. Yesterday Lady Isabella took a company of twenty men when she and a Sir Guy set out after her father."

Simon sighed. Guy's message had said that he and Lord Edmund's stepdaughter were bound for London. There was no calling Guy back, but he heartily wished Nicholas would finish dallying with his current paramour and return to the inn.

"I could loan you my two men-at-arms." Piers indicated the pair at a table by the door. "They are strong and quick-witted."

They looked to be seasoned fighters, broad of shoulder with weathered faces and watchful eyes. "I thank you, my friend. I will feed them, of course, and pay them two pennies each per day for the few days I should need them."

As he left the inn with his two new guards, Simon looked up and saw a face at Jevan le Coyte's window. He nearly waved at his randy cousin. *Cousin*. Did Jevan and Odeline know they were related to him? Surely not, Simon thought. Thurstan would have kept the sin from his family.

Linnet stood in her workroom, scowling through the open doorway at the two soldiers. Jasper and Miles sat at her kitchen table wolfing down mutton stew. "This is ridiculous."

"I agree. I should never have offered them two pennies *plus* the food," Simon quipped.

"I meant having them here. Where will they sleep?"

"On the floor, one across the back door, the other at the front. Warin loaned them sleeping pallets."

"They will be underfoot all day."

"One will patrol the front, the other the garden."

"They will frighten off my customers."

Simon cocked his head and grinned. "I'd say they are more likely to attract a few new ones...young women, for instance."

"You are as bad as Bishop Thurstan," Linnet snapped. "Always ordering folk around."

Simon stiffened. "I am nothing like him."

Oh, aye, you are. In all her years of studying Simon, why had she not noticed that his eyes, though more green than gray, were the same shape as Thurstan's? And his chin was as square and arrogant. And he had that same annoying air of command.

"Now that I have Jasper and Miles to look after you, I will go alone to meet with Brother Anselme," Simon said.

Wretch. He had Thurstan's compulsion for protecting those he saw as weaker. Well, she was not weak. "I will go, either with you or by myself." To reinforce her point, Linnet grabbed up her cloak, called out to Aiken to lock the door behind them, and headed for the front door with Simon muttering behind her.

The beggar was still across the street. His head came up abruptly as they exited her shop. She caught a brief glimpse of burning eyes set in a dirt-streaked face.

Looking away, she whispered, "I have seen him with Hamel."

Simon nodded grimly, but his touch was gentle as he took her arm to guide her down the street.

The feel of his wide palm on her elbow sent gooseflesh rippling across her skin. Her mouth went dry, her heart galloped. She settled it with the reminder he was only being courteous. Still, as she watched other couples stroll by arm in arm in the gathering dusk, it was impossible not to wish that she and Simon were sweethearts.

"Come, this way, quickly." Simon tugged her down a lane just past the ironworks. The air was thick with the tang of hot metal and smoke from the fires used to bend it to men's will. "Damn," he muttered. "I thought this lane went through to Castle Gate."

"It did. Durleigh has grown so that many of what used to be empty yards behind the buildings have filled with homes and small shops. I think there is a way through." She led him past a bakeshop to an alleyway. "Here."

Simon looked over his shoulder, then followed. "What a noisome place," he grumbled. The alley was muddy from the recent rains, bounded on either side by flimsy wooden homes that leaned wearily against each other. Babies' cries, raised voices and the smells of rotten food seeped out through the cracks.

Linnet pressed a hand to her nose and hurried along. She did not breathe again until they stepped out onto Spurrier Gate. The spur makers had closed their shops for the night, but several had removed to the tavern on the corner. Grimy, barrel-chested men, they sat on benches in the yard, some still in their thick leather aprons, sipping ale and exchanging stories.

"I do not go through those back alleys often, but when I do, I give thanks for being born who and what I am."

Simon nodded and kept them moving down the street. "I saw worse in the East—poverty, sickness, hopelessness—but seeing it here at home is somehow worse." His grip on her arm tightened fractionally. "You should not enter such places. The folk who live there would kill you and sell your clothes for food."

"If they want food, they have only to go to the almshouse. Soup and bread are always available there. Free."

"Whose largess is that?"

She glanced sidelong at him, wanting to see his reaction. "Bishop Thurstan convinced the merchants to pay for renovating the building and keeping it supplied with foodstuffs."

"How did Thurstan manage that?" Simon asked. Was that admiration in his voice?

"I do not know. There was some grumbling at first, I understand, for some of the merchants are close with a penny."

"Might any of them have held that against the bishop?"

"Perhaps, but the almshouse has been open for two years."

"Hmm." Simon suddenly herded her out of the street, tucked her into the doorway of a shut-up shop and blocked her in. His back was to her, his hand on his sword.

"Does the beggar still follow us?" she whispered.

"Nay, we have lost him, I think, but we will wait here a moment to be certain before going on."

"All right." Linnet studied his big body, the width of his shoulders, the muscles bulging beneath the sleeves of his tunic. Like a rock, he appeared, strong, invincible. But she knew that his warrior's facade hid a lonely, wounded soul. He had grown up without the warmth and affection all creatures crave. The longing to wrap her arms around his lean waist and offer the healing balm of her love rose inside her, sharp and poignant. She could almost remember what it felt like to be held by him, to feel this cool, self-contained man surrender to passion. To her.

"Linnet?" He glanced over his shoulder. Some of her turbulent emotions must have showed, for the expression in his eyes shifted suddenly. They filled with a dark, powerful hunger that made her mouth go dry and her heart roll into her throat. Her whole body warmed as a familiar, syrupy heat spilled through it, and with it the memory of how right it had felt to lie in his arms, to join with him as intimately as two people can be.

"We had best go," Simon whispered.

Slowly, regretfully, she nodded and followed him.

The gates to the cathedral enclave were closed, but the porter on duty opened them promptly. "Brother Prior said he was expecting you and bid me direct you to the herbarium."

"I know the way." Grateful they would not need to enter the infirmary, Linnet led Simon around behind the building to the stone hut in the herb garden. The stillness, the familiar scent of herbs washed over her, soothing her tattered nerves.

"It is so peaceful here it makes one forget there is evil in the world," Simon murmured.

"How nearly your thoughts mirror mine."

The hard planes of his face softened briefly. "That seems to happen with increasing regularity."

"Aye, it does." Linnet grinned, pleased by his answering smile. They both sobered when Brother Anselme opened the door.

"Ah, you have come at last."

"I regret we have kept you waiting," Simon said as they were ushered into the hut. At first glance the small room seemed cluttered, with shelves lining the walls and herbs hanging from the open rafters. But all was scrupulously neat, including the worktable that occupied the center of the room.

"Nay, you are prompt. It is just we are all a bit tense." Anselme glanced toward the small corner hearth where Brother Oliver sat hunched on a stool. "Brother, they are here."

Brother Oliver turned, his smooth cheeks wet with tears. "I cannot believe he is gone."

"Aye, I know." Anselme laid a gentle hand on the cleric's shoulder. "It is our duty to catch his murderer. Have you brought the list of those who saw him that day?"

Oliver nodded and reached inside his sleeve for a rolled-up parchment. "I've also brought his notes on the visits."

Anselme carried it to the worktable, unfurled the two

sheaves and anchored the corners with small pots. Everyone gathered round to examine the lists.

"He saw all these people in one day?" Simon asked.

"Aye," said Oliver. "His days were always full."

"My name and that of Mistress Linnet are not on here."

Oliver sniffed. "You did not have appointments."

"Did anyone else intrude upon his day?"

"Lady Odeline came at noon and ate with him."

"Hmm," was all Simon said.

Oliver pursed his lips. "She did not follow the good example of our bishop and Abbess Catherine. The lady has been embroiled in one scandal after another. An elopement with a drunken wastrel who gambled away her inheritance and died when Jevan was young, affairs with married men." He rolled his eyes. "Her last paramour was the king's own uncle, and that got her sent from court in disgrace. Had Bishop Thurstan not taken pity on her, she and the boy would have starved to death."

Simon nodded. "She seemed worried about her future."

"Well she should," Oliver grumbled. "The new bishop will not let her stay at the palace, nor pay for Jevan's schooling."

"She had little reason to wish Thurstan dead, then," Simon said. "Did he see anyone else who is not on the list?"

Oliver frowned. "He spent an hour in the garden with Olf."

"I understand the gardener has disappeared," Simon said.

"He is simpleminded and was disturbed by Brother Crispin's sharp questions," said Anselme. "He would never harm Thurstan."

Simon looked at the prior. "I heard his mother rant against the bishop. She could have used Olf as a tool to kill him."

Oliver sniffed. "Olf has never been allowed inside the palace. The porter on duty would have stopped him."

"I see." But to Simon, Nelda was still a suspect. He

moved through Oliver's list, asking about each person's business with the bishop. He borrowed quill and ink from Anselme and made notes next to some of the names.

So cool and efficient, Linnet thought, admiring his quick, logical mind yet disturbed by his lack of emotion. She very much wanted to make Simon see how wrong he was about his father. Why that should be, she did not know, except perhaps because she knew Thurstan had loved the son he had not acknowledged.

"My thanks, Brothers." Simon tucked the list away. "What luck have you had with the brothers, students and laymen?"

"I have learned nothing," Walter replied.

Simon studied Walter, trying to see beneath his shuttered gaze. "Someone living inside the cathedral walls would have had easy access to the bishop's brandy. Perhaps there was some priest who had a grudge against him or coveted his post." Like Crispin. Or even the prior himself. A chilling thought.

"I cannot imagine a priest committing murder," Walter said. "Most everyone was at supper at the time of the attack."

Simon regarded him coolly, letting no hint of his suspicions show in features long schooled to hide all emotion. "If you learn anything, send word to me at the Royal Oak. On the morrow, I will visit the townfolk who saw the bishop."

"*We* will visit them," Linnet said, lifting her chin.

A pox on independent females, Simon thought. And yet, was that not part of what set her above other women? Staring into her proud gaze, he was struck by the lethal combination of beauty, strength and honor that was Linnet Especer.

His heart cartwheeled in his chest. He fought the sensation as fiercely as he ever had an armed opponent, for her weapons were more deadly than drawn steel. He would not like her, Simon vowed, for that way lay madness.

Chapter Eight

"I have not been able to find the journal," Odeline said.

Jevan looked at her, aghast. "You promised."

"I know. I did go down and look the moment the prior's guards were gone." Odeline paced before the fire in her chamber on the palace's third floor. It was not so fine as the one she had occupied at court. But then she had been the mistress of the king's uncle. Here she was only the sister of a bishop. A nuisance, tolerated by Thurstan. *Dieu,* how she had hated that.

It is over, done. He can never make you feel small or unworthy, she thought staring into the embers. They glowed and twisted, like figures writhing in pain. Souls condemned to hell. Her soul, paying for the sin of murder.

Nay, it had been an accident. She had not killed him. Thurstan had been alive when she left him. A seizure had—

"Perhaps the prior has it."

"What?" Jerked from her anguished thoughts, she turned, absorbing Jevan's words. "I watched from the top of the stairs. His men took only Thurstan's flagons, cups and such," she said quickly, not wanting him to run afoul of the quick-witted prior.

Jevan's eyes widened. "Why? What do they suspect?"

An icy trickle ran down her spine. "There is some question whether Thurstan was attacked or fell and hit his head."

"They think he was killed?" Jevan exclaimed.

"It is not certain it was murder," she said quickly, not daring to confide her secret even to Jevan. "But Mistress Linnet was the last one to see Thurstan alive. If suspicion falls on anyone, it is her." *Not me.* No one had questioned her. She was, after all, the bereaved sister.

Jevan nodded, but his eyes remained hard. He had worn that pinched, desperate look since their dismissal from court. It was her fault they had been cast out from the life of excitement and privilege they both loved. And if a blot on her soul was the cost of putting things right for him, so be it.

"I know he hid the charter in his journal," Jevan growled. "If we do not find it before Thurstan's will is read, Blackstone Heath will go to the church."

"Keep your voice down. We do not want anyone to know that we might profit from Thurstan's death," she whispered, grabbing him by the shoulders. It surprised her to feel muscles fleshing out his bony shoulders, saddened her to think that her little boy was nearly a man in some ways. "We will find it."

"What if we cannot?" Jevan wrenched free and glared at her, nostrils flared with rage. "What if he gave it to Simon?"

Odeline gasped. "I had not thought of that." She frowned, thinking back. Thurstan had been shocked by Simon's arrival. She had heard his shout of surprise as she was coming down the stairs from her room and recognized Simon through the partially open door. The charter had not been mentioned while she stood there, frozen with horror to see Simon risen from the dead. Oliver's sudden appearance at the other end of the corridor had forced her to hide in the stairwell so as not to be caught spying. Had Thurstan given Simon the charter after she left?

"Simon must have taken a room somewhere in town."

"We cannot search his room. I will ask Hamel to find it."

"Hamel." Jevan turned away from her in disgust. "I do not see how you can associate with that crude ruffian."

"Because he is a man of power in these parts." And because Hamel desired her. It salved her ego to control someone when she was nothing, less than nothing, in Thurstan's household. And too, the passionate blood of the de Lyndhursts ran hot in her veins. Hamel satisfied her needs very nicely and very discreetly…for now. When she was installed as chatelaine of Blackstone Heath she would sever her association with Hamel and find another. A man of wealth and power. She would have clothes and jewels and, most important, a home in her own name. Never would she be forced to beg for charity.

Her temper heated as she thought about how Thurstan had looked down his nose at her as he granted her a few crumbs from his bountiful table. Cretin, that he should scorn her so when he had sinned against God by fathering a bastard son.

But Thurstan was dead now.

Odeline's rage drained away as she thought of the way he had looked sprawled on the carpet at her feet.

And the mighty shall be brought low.

"We must find the charter," Jevan growled. "Blackstone Heath is mine, and I want it. I deserve it."

"Aye, you do. You will have it, my son." She had paid too heavy a price to lose all now.

Her skin was as soft and fragrant as rose petals. Her lips tasted of sweet wine and even headier desire as they parted beneath Simon's.

So warm, so welcoming. He let her kisses sweep him away, lowering his normal reserve. With her, there was no need for caution, no need to guard himself against betrayal. She loved him totally, unconditionally. She would never leave him, never hurt him. "I love you, I love you," he whispered, opening his eyes even though he knew it was too dark to see her.

Linnet's face stared up at him.

Simon jerked awake and lay there, his heart stumbling, his breathing raspy in the silent chamber. *He was alone. It was only a dream.* For a moment, he could not remember where he was. Then he recognized the rough walls of his room at the tavern.

Dieu, was it not bad enough that Linnet plagued his waking hours, did she have to invade his dreams, as well? He threw an arm over his eyes, but it did not block out the image of her face and eyes that seemed to see clear through to his soul. But it was her natural warmth that drew him. She glowed like a lantern, lit from within. And he was so cold.

Nay, he was mad. Mad to desire the woman who, if she had not been Thurstan's mistress, was at least hiding something from him. Dark secrets flickered through her soulful eyes like ghosts.

Knowing he'd not sleep, Simon dragged himself out of bed and stumbled to the window. Dawn was still a few hours distant, the air cool and frosty when he exhaled. Waning moonlight shimmered on the slate roofs of Durleigh stretched out below him. His eyes went first across the scraggly field to the apothecary. All was quiet, but he cocked his head, searching the shadows around the building for some sign of movement. He had not wanted to leave her, even with Jasper sleeping fully armed in the front entryway and Miles in the kitchen.

Linnet had been apprehensive, too. "You…you are not staying?" she had asked.

"Nay. It would stain your reputation if I slept here."

"I fear it is already somewhat smudged." Her smile had been both sad and rueful.

He had wanted to hold her, to soothe the worry from her

face. And that had convinced him leaving was best. Quite simply, he did not trust himself to be alone with her.

And now she had invaded his special dream.

Simon scrubbed a hand over his face and turned away from the window before he weakened and went to make certain all was right at the shop. Lighting the candle, he sat at the small table he had borrowed from Elinore. From his pack, he took parchment and began to copy over the list Oliver had given him. He added the notes he'd made earlier and left space for more.

Ten names, more than he could likely visit in one day, but he desperately wanted this business over so he could be on his way. He checked off two: the priest and nun from Blackstone Abbey. According to Oliver, they had left Durleigh before noon, taking with them the daughter of a local merchant.

"Was she taking holy vows?" Simon had asked.

Oliver had shaken his head, glanced at the prior then shaken his head again. "She wants to be an illuminator."

Something in the way he had said that raised Simon's curiosity. He could see no motive for murder in sending a daughter to be taught a craft, but if time permitted, he would stop at the metalworks and speak with the girl's father, Clarence Billeter, a surly brute if Simon recalled correctly.

A knock at the door brought Simon out of the chair. Hefting his sword, he sprinted across the room. "Who is it?"

"Aiken," said a muffled voice. "Mistress Linnet is set on going out alone. Miles thought ye should know."

"Fool woman." Simon pulled on his boots, grabbed up his sword and cloak, and yanked open the door. Furious, he swept out of the tavern and across the yard, reaching the apothecary just as Linnet was leaving by the back door.

"Simon!" she squeaked, one hand fluttering at her throat.

"Where do you think you are going?"

"I—I wanted to get an early start on speaking with the—"

"Without me?"

"Aye, well…" She glanced over her shoulder at their avid audience, the two soldiers from the castle and her servants. "You had no right to tattle on me."

Miles scowled. "I promised Sir Simon I'd look after ye."

"And we are both grateful for that." Simon glared at Linnet. She was too impetuous by half and needed to learn who was in charge of this enterprise. "We will leave together, after we have eaten and decided whom to see first."

She tossed her head. "I have eaten."

"I have not. Drusa…?"

"There's fresh bread, hard cheese and ale on the table," the maid said, her relief obvious.

Linnet sidled like a nervous mare. "Eat, then, Sir Simon. You can catch up with me at—"

Simon grabbed hold of her arm before she could slip by him. "Would it be too much trouble for you to bring me a plate and cup out here, Drusa?" he asked through clenched teeth. "Linnet and I have a few things to discuss. In private."

The onlookers scattered like leaves before an angry wind.

"Let go of my arm," Linnet said tightly.

Simon battled the urge to shake some sense into her. "I will when you tell me which person you did not want me to see."

Her eyes widened. "I…you are mistaken."

"Is one of them your lover?" he growled, alarmed by the sharp sting of jealousy.

"I have no lover."

"Then who are you sneaking off to visit?"

She shivered and closed her eyes. "It is not that, I—"

Drusa bustled out, carrying a covered tray. Aiken hurried after her with a pottery jug. They made a great show of arranging the food on one end of the stone bench.

"My thanks," Simon muttered. "We will serve ourselves." He released Linnet's arm and bowed. "My lady…"

She exhaled heavily and walked to the bench like a prisoner bound for the gallows.

Simon sat and poured them each a cup of ale. "I thought you trusted me."

She whipped her head up, her eyes deep wells of compassion. "Oh, I do. It is just…embarrassing."

"What is?"

"Hana Billeter," she whispered.

"The girl who went to study illumination?"

"Hmm." She knotted her fingers in her lap. "Hana is with child. And unwed."

Bastard. The old taunt rose like bile in his throat. "So they have sent her to the abbey." As they had his mother.

Linnet nodded. "Bishop Thurstan arranged it."

"I am sure he is a practiced hand at that." Simon suddenly wondered if he had a gaggle of half brothers and sisters hanging about somewhere.

"There have been others. Oh, not his, I assure you," she quickly added. "But other girls from the diocese who have found themselves in trouble and in need of aid."

"What happens to the babes?"

She looked down again, but not before he saw the color drain from her face and the light from her eyes. "Good homes are found for them, with parents who have lost little ones to sickness or who cannot have any of their own."

Simon's heart went out to them. Unless they were very lucky, they would grow up as he had, unloved.

"Master Billeter was against this. He paid Old Nelda to abort Hana's baby, but Jean, her mother, confessed it to Thurstan, who took steps to save the babe."

"He violated the sanctity of the confessional?"

"He did what he had to to save a child's life."

"And line his pockets at the same time," Simon muttered. "I daresay this charitable couple will pay dearly for the babe."

"How can you say that?"

"It is likely how Lord Edmund got me. A strapping lad to train, another knight to serve the house of de Meresden."

"Did they abuse you?" she whispered.

He shook his head. "I was punished for my transgressions, but no more than any other fostered there." He hesitated. How could he expect someone who had been raised by a loving mother and father to understand what it was like to have no family, no one who truly cared about you? "I was not abused," he said curtly. "But neither was I truly wanted."

"Oh, Simon…" She stood slowly, reaching for him.

He stepped back. "Save your pity."

"It is not pity. I—"

"We wander from the business at hand." He picked up a cup and drained it. The ale did not wash the bitterness from his mouth. "Do you think the Billeters bore the bishop a grudge?"

"Master Clarence does, I am certain. He is a large man with a temper as hot as his forges. Mistress Jean, however, is a mouse of a thing. I am surprised she stood up to him on this, and do not doubt she was punished for it."

"A man who would beat his wife for loving their daughter might be capable of murder."

"I could see him striking in anger, but poison…" She shook her head. "I doubt he'd know belladonna or monkshood from sage."

"Hmm." Simon sat and motioned for her to do the same. The explanation made sense, but her face was pale and her manner edgy as though she hid something more. "Why go there alone?"

"I thought I could speak with Mistress Jean in private and learn where Clarence had been yesterday."

"Might not this hot-tempered man have taken his fists to you if he caught you whispering in corners with his wife?"

She started. "I—I had not thought about that."

That is what worried him. "And we have no reason to suspect he was at the cathedral yesterday. Still, I will ask Brother Oliver if anyone saw him about."

"Where do we start, then?"

"It would be best if you remain safely here."

"I will go, with you or without you." She folded her arms, molding the wool bodice to her breasts. The sight was not half as provocative as the combative light in her eyes.

"You need me."

You have no idea how much. Indeed, he sensed that was true, a mark of her innocence where men were concerned. She did not play with words to tempt or seduce. She spoke from the heart.

"I know most of the folk on Oliver's list, if not personally, then by reputation."

Simon sighed and gave in to the inevitable. Better to have her beside him where he could protect her than trailing along behind, fair game for Hamel or footpads. "Very well," he growled. "We will visit the grave digger first."

She groaned.

"Change your mind about accompanying me?"

"Nay." She raised one brow. "Do you always get even?"

"Always." He smiled sardonically. "Among my acquaintances, and most especially my enemies, it is well-known that Simon of Blackstone never forgets a slight."

The light in her eyes went out like a snuffed candle, leaving them dark and flat. "I shall remember that."

They found Digger Martin in the cemetery plot behind St. Mary's Church, standing hip-deep in an empty, coffin-size hole.

"Are you Digger Martin?" Simon asked.

Digger glanced up, shielding his grimy face with a filthy hand. "Who wants to know?"

"Simon of Blackstone, a Knight of the Black Rose."

"Ye're the one came back from the dead." Digger grinned, toothlessly. "Bad for business, that." He cackled.

Simon smiled. "But good for me. Would you step out a moment so we could talk?"

"Gotta make my quota or I don't get paid."

Simon took a penny from the pouch at his waist, tossed it into the air and caught it. "For your time."

"Fair enough." Digger hefted himself out of the hole. He was a rough man, of stocky build, his arms and shoulders bulging with muscles. But did that make him a murderer?

"You know the bishop is dead?" Simon asked.

"Aye." Digger chuckled. "Wonder if he'd want me digging up his bones in a year's time and selling 'em?"

Linnet gasped and leaned into Simon.

He wrapped an arm around her. "What sort of vile thing—?"

"That's why ye've come, isn't it? 'Cause someone remembered Old Digger was up to the palace yesterday and thought he might have bashed his lordship over the head."

"Did you?" Simon growled.

"'Course not. Bones. That's what the meet was about. The Stick caught wind of what the bishop were about and called us both to account. Threatened to excommunicate me." Digger sniffed. "Not that I'd care."

"What are you talking about?" Simon demanded.

Digger cocked his head. "Cost ye two pennies."

"Providing I'm convinced you are telling the truth."

"No reason to lie now." Digger sat down on a mound of dirt. "Two years ago, it was. I was earning a bit of extra money by taking out dead apple trees in the church orchard yonder. Unearthed a grave, I did. Ten bodies buried all together."

"Sweet Mary." Linnet crossed herself. "Who were they?"

"Dunno. There was no marker and they were naught but bones wrapped in rags. They'd been there some time. I told Father Stephens, who was priest at St. Mary's then. Right angry he was. Told me to fill the hole in and say nothing of what I'd seen."

"He knew about them?" Linnet whispered, aghast.

"Aye. It didn't sit well with me, but I told no one…except my confessor."

"Bishop Thurstan," Simon growled.

Digger nodded. "He was right furious, especially when he learned the ten were riverfolk swept to their deaths in the spring flooding six years ago. Father Stephens was supposed to have buried them in hallowed ground, at St. Mary's expense."

"He saved himself the expense."

"Aye, but Bishop Thurstan fixed him. Vengeful sort, for a priest. Sent Father Stephens off to a poor church along the Scottish border. Killed in a raid, he was, the next year."

"And the bodies of the riverfolk."

"The bishop said as how it would cast the church in a bad light did we tell folk what had happened, and most of the dead ones didn't have no family to care. So…" His eyes twinkled with wry humor. "He sold them."

"Sold them?" Simon scowled.

"Aye, sold them as holy bones for reliquaries and such."

Linnet was shocked speechless.

"Blasphemy," Simon hissed. "Sacrilege. To think a bishop would do such a deceitful thing."

"Didn't do no harm," Digger grumbled. "The bishop used the money for that almshouse of his. Said it was fitting that the bones of the poor should buy blankets for the living. Besides, everyone knows that most of the bones sold for such things is really the part of some animal, not a saint."

"You said The Stick had found out about this," said Simon.

"Archdeacon Crispin. That's what I calls him. He learned about the bones somehow. Took on something fierce. Thought he was going to take that fancy staff of his to the bishop.... Say, ye dinna suppose he clobbered him after I left?"

"An interesting notion," Simon said softly. He toyed with it as they walked to the ironworks. Logically he agreed with Walter that Nelda and Clarence seemed likely suspects, but his gut told him something else. A churchman would have had easier access to Thurstan's drink, and Archdeacon Crispin did have two reasons for wanting him dead: hatred and hope of personal gain.

"Here we are." Linnet knocked at the front door of a prosperous-looking stone-and-timber home. It was answered promptly by a mouse of a maid, who scurried off and returned with news her mistress would receive them.

Mistress Jean sat before the fire in a small corner chamber, bent over her mending. She lifted her head warily at their approach. Her face was thin and pale, except for her left cheek, which was marred by a violet bruise. The eye above it was swollen nearly shut. "I'm sorry to hear about the bishop," she mumbled through a split lip.

"Aye." Linnet looked as furious and helpless as Simon felt, but she introduced him, and accepted a chair and a cup of ale from the maid. "Your Hana has gone to the abbey?"

"Aye. Yesterday."

"We have heard your husband was not pleased." Simon twisted the cup in his hands and wished he could get them around the neck of the brute.

"Nay, he was not." Jean sighed. "He had plans to wed her to Maurice Larson, but Hana fancied Gib Farmer's youngest son, Alain. Even when we learned she was carrying Alain's babe, Clarence thought to save his plans by getting rid of it." Her voice trembled, and she looked down at her hands. "I'm glad the bishop stopped him, for he was the only one who could have."

"She will still be giving up the child to be raised by strangers," Simon muttered.

Linnet flinched, his contemptuous words cutting deeper than he could possibly know. There were stretches of time, minutes, hours when she nearly forgot about the past and believed they might have a future together. But if he ever found out...

"Much can happen in six months," Jean said. "Hana and Alain might wed and run off...once his broken leg mends." She sighed. "Clarence's doing that was. Might have beaten Alain to death if his pa hadn't heard the fracas and come running."

Simon shot Linnet a meaningful glance. "Do you think Clarence might have decided to punish the bishop, too?"

"Might have liked to after he finished lessoning me." She gingerly touched her cheek. "But first Clarance took two of his lads and rode out to Gib's farm after Alain."

"When was this?"

"Late afternoon yesterday."

"And when did he return?"

"Near nightfall." Jean smiled faintly. "Took him that long to recover from the beating Gib and his sons gave *him*. I dosed him with a cup of wine and put him to bed. He's up there now, battered face to the wall, groaning fit to wake the dead." Her smile became a crooked grin. "It isn't Christian to rejoice in another's pain, I know—"

"I'm sure God would be willing to make an exception in Clarence's case," Simon said savagely.

Linnet echoed his sentiments, but as they took their leave, she wondered if Simon would forgive her her sins. The need for his understanding was like a dull ache, weighing down her heart.

* * *

Hamel straightened as Tilly emerged from the side door of the Royal Oak. "Did you search his room?"

"Aye. But there was no books about."

Hamel frowned. Three possibilities occurred to him. Simon had hidden the journal, taken it with him or given it to someone else. Linnet, perhaps.

She touched his arm. "There's an hour or so before we serve the noon meal. Will ye sit and have an ale wi—"

"I have work to do," Hamel grumbled. His man, Ellis, had lost Simon and Linnet again. Damn, he wished he knew where they kept disappearing to. What were they up to? He could not break into the apothecary and search for the journal Odeline wanted because two men-at-arms were guarding the shop. More of Simon's doing. Curse him. Why could he not have stayed dead?

Of course, there were ways to correct that.

Hamel smiled grimly, but even that hint of pleasure faded as he thought about the confrontation to come. He had promised Odeline he would find the bishop's journal for her, and she would not be pleased when she learned he had failed her. Wanted it for sentimental reasons, she'd said. Odd, he had not thought she was that fond of her iron-fisted brother. But then, a death made folks look at things differently.

And Odeline's request gave him an excuse to go after Simon. Even now, Bardolf and two of his best men were combing the streets, with orders to arrest the knight for questioning.

There were not many men who survived his questioning, Hamel mused. Smiling, he headed away from the tavern.

Chapter Nine

Clouds rolled in to obscure the sun as they left the home of the cloth merchant. Appropriate, Simon thought, glancing sidelong at Linnet. Her expression was as glum as the weather. His own spirits were not much better. More than half the day they had spent speaking with those who had seen the bishop yesterday and they were no closer to solving his murder.

Oh, several of the townspeople had freely admitted that Bishop Thurstan was a man who liked power. A few had even told tales of how the bishop had maneuvered them into doing something against their nature. But none had displayed either fear or animosity. The reason each had given for having seen Thurstan jibed with the information Oliver had provided. The only bit of dissension had occurred during the visit of the four-man delegation who had come to discuss plans for the chapel being built by the town's leading merchants to honor Thurstan.

"He refused to approve the drawings I'd brought of the statue of himself," the master stonemason had grumbled. "He thought it was too grand. Said he wanted something plainer, but the bishop ain't a plain sort of man."

"What was decided?" Simon had asked offhandedly, all

the while staring at the man's strong hands and bulging muscles.

"Oh, I'll be taking off some of the decorative touches," the mason had muttered. "I'd not want to offend the bishop—in case he's at God's feet."

Yesterday, Simon would have curled his lip at such a suggestion, but that was before he had spent a day listening to the tales of Thurstan's good deeds. Not that he was a saint. Far from it, for he had often bent the rules to suit himself. And yet, countless folk in Durleigh were the better for what Thurstan had done. Women saved from abuse. Poor people given food, shelter, work and, most important, a future.

Simon had never believed that the end justified the means, but he had to admit that Thurstan had accomplished more with his unorthodox methods than he could have by adhering to stricture. Did that make it right? *Nay, but am I any better?* he wondered, thinking of the fortune in ransoms he'd brought back from the East. Bah, it was not as though he had sought out men of wealth to capture, as had some of his fellow Crusaders. In battle, it was kill or be killed. Through a combination of luck and skill, Simon had prevailed. When his opponents had laid down their arms and cried quarter, he had granted it.

He was not like the bishop. He was not. But the blood that pounded against his temples mocked him. Thurstan's blood.

"We are done, then," Linnet murmured.

Simon nodded and shook off his dark thoughts. Done except for Old Nelda. But he would speak with her alone, not wanting to expose Linnet to more of the woman's nasty remarks.

The streets were more crowded now with servants out to fetch the day's foodstuffs, vendors crying their wares, clerks in their long brown gowns and laborers grimy with sweat. He took Linnet's arm and drew her closer. At the entrance to the Shambles, the street of the butchers, he paused.

Even from here, he could smell the blood. They did not kill the animals in the Shambles, except for the chickens and ducks, nonetheless the pall of death hung over the place, thick as the black flies buzzing about overhead.

Simon turned away.

"Where are we going?" Linnet asked. "The shortest way home is through here."

"We will go another way."

She looked down the street of open-air stalls adorned with bloody carcasses and winced. As they continued on, she added, "Thank you. It was kind of you to think of my sensibilities when you do not particularly like me."

"What?"

"You do not believe Thurstan was only my friend."

"I believe you...now."

"What has changed?" she asked, hope soaring.

"I know you, where before I did not." He brushed against her as they squeezed by a cart laden with charcoal.

The scent that was uniquely Simon filled her senses, bringing back a flood of memories from that long-ago night. Oh, you know me *very* well, she thought, her blood warming.

"You have too much honor to behave so shamefully."

Guilt swamped her. She stumbled and would have fallen had Simon not caught her arm. She looked back over her shoulder into his ruggedly handsome face and anxious eyes.

"Are you all right?"

Nay, she was not. She was a hoax, a fraud. "Simon, I—"

"Damn! 'Tis Bardolf!" Simon exclaimed softly.

Linnet swiveled her head and spotted the under-sheriff some distance off on the opposite side of the street. He walked slowly, glancing into each shop, looking hard at each passerby. "He seems to be searching for something or someone."

"Us." Simon let her go. His hand fell to his sword.

Terrified he'd be arrested or killed, Linnet spun, looking

for a route of escape. "In here." She tugged Simon through an open doorway into a dim, low-ceilinged room.

Simon paused on the threshold, looking for a place he could leave Linnet while he dealt with Bardolf. The narrow room stank worse than the Shambles. It contained four large wooden troughs. The women standing in them gasped and gawked. They were young, their skirts tied up to leave their legs bare from the knees down while they trod about on the cloth soaking in the troughs.

"This is the fuller's shop I was telling you about," Linnet said brightly. "They produce the finest cloth in the district."

Simon blinked, his mind whirling. Fight had been his first reaction, but alone, with Linnet to guard, flight might better serve. And yet, to run through this shop would be to attract undo attention. "I see."

"I prayed you might." Her eyes eloquent, she drew him farther into the cramped, smelly room. "The raw wool fabric is rubbed with fuller's earth—a noxious mix of sand and urine—then soaked and walked to cleanse and soften it."

"Fascinating," Simon murmured.

"Hardly that."

He leaned down and whispered, "I meant your quick wits."

"I was afraid Bardolf would attack you."

Her protectiveness might have pricked his pride if it had not touched his heart. "Likely I could have bested him."

"I know you are very good with a sword. I used to watch you train on the practice field, but if he had men with him—"

"You used to watch *me?*" Simon asked, recalling what Drusa had said. "Or all of the soldiers?"

Her cheeks turned bright red. "I—"

A middle-aged man bustled in through the back door. "Mistress Linnet. What brings you here? Is someone ailing?"

"Nay, Master Fuller," she said quickly, grateful for the

timely interruption. "I have brought Sir Simon to see your goods. He is one of our Knights of the Black Rose."

"Indeed." The fuller's fleshy face lifted in a joyous smile. "Welcome home."

Simon nodded. "Your shop is as fine as Linnet promised." He glanced about, but Linnet saw him studying the door.

If Bardolf came by and glanced in, he'd see them. She had to get them out into the back.

"I've done well." The fuller patted his expansive belly. "Though who knows if these prosperous times will continue," he added, sobering. "Bishop Thurstan contracted favorable trade agreements. The next bishop may not do the same."

"He will be sorely missed," Linnet murmured.

"Aye, that he will. Bishop Thurstan was not originally destined for the church, ye know," said the fuller. "Trained to be a courtier, was Thurstan de Lyndhurst, God rest his soul. 'Twas his older brother for whom their sire bought the bishopric of Durleigh, only Richard died and Thurstan took his place. Thurstan would have done right well at court."

It was news to Simon that Thurstan hadn't had a true calling for the church, but it didn't surprise him. Nor did it excuse his fathering a child and abandoning it. "I am sure the archdeacon wished Thurstan had gone to court."

The fuller nodded. "Different as day from night, they were. The bishop was flexible in his views of right and wrong. To him, the end result was what mattered. The archdeacon, on the other hand, is rigid as a pike staff. To Crispin, things are either black or white. I've heard they didn't get along at all."

"Hmm." Simon glanced anxiously at the street door.

"Could you show Sir Simon the finished cloth goods?" Linnet asked brightly.

"Happily." The fuller led the way out the back door to a cobbled courtyard enclosed on three sides by high stone walls. Rows of upright wooden frames filled the yard. ''We hang the cloth to dry on the tenters here, stretching it to size with tenterhooks.'' He waved a fat hand at the frames. ''And when the cloth is dry, the nap is cut smooth.'' He beckoned them past the maze of frames to long tables spread with cloth. A half dozen women bent over the fabric, clipping away with huge shears.

Simon grunted, busy scanning the walled courtyard, looking for a way out. He craned his neck to see over the tenter frames. There must be a way out, but where? Had Bardolf come to arrest them, or merely to follow them? Either way, they must escape.

''We are in your debt, Master Fuller.'' Linnet smiled archly at Simon. ''We should be off to look for the gloves you wanted.''

''Gloves?'' Simon exclaimed. ''What we need is to get—''

''Does the Glover's Gil lie just behind here?'' Linnet asked.

''Indeed. If you go through my rear gate, it will save you going all the way round.'' Motioning for them to follow, the fuller waddled around the end row of tenters to an oak-plank door, took a key from the ring at his belt and opened the door.

Simon walked through first, looked around the vacant, weed-choked field to make sure the way was clear, then motioned for Linnet to follow. ''My thanks, Master Fuller.''

The fuller bowed, shut the door and locked it.

''Sweet Mary.'' Linnet swayed where she stood.

Simon caught her close, moved by how delicate she felt, how frantically her heart beat against his side. It seemed the most natural thing in the world to hold her, but the familiar urge to protect something small and vulnerable was overlaid with the memory of how sweet her mouth had tasted. The wanting shivered through him, and it took all his control to remember where they were and why. "That was a masterful piece of playacting."

"I—I wanted to run, but I thought if we did the fuller would think us thieves and raise a cry."

"Bringing Bardolf." Simon held her tighter, burying his nose in the crown of her head. The faint scent of roses washed over him. His heart lurched, and his whole body quickened. He struggled against the longing to shift her so they met more fully. "You are canny and brave," he said hoarsely.

"I do not feel very brave." The hitch in her voice quelled his hunger in an instant. "Do you think Bardolf has orders to arrest us?"

"Perhaps Hamel would make certain we do not evade justice."

"Justice." She trembled again. "Neither of us would get justice from Hamel."

"Or, I think, from Archdeacon Crispin Norville."

Her eyes narrowed. "I think he is the murderer."

"Nay." Simon glanced around the deserted field.

"You are as afraid of Crispin as everyone else." She jerked her arm free, stomped across the field and into the street past stalls hung with belts and leather pouches.

Simon caught up with her at the boot maker's and tugged her out of the street. "Have you forgotten about Bardolf?"

Her eyes widened. "But Crispin is—"

"Later." He had his own suspicions about the archdeacon, but if he admitted that, God alone knew what she would do.

"You do not believe me?"

"I am concerned with saving your neck. We have no proof against Crispin, and if you go about accusing him, you could find yourself in worse trouble than you already are."

"I am right," she said fiercely.

"Not another word till we are private." He gave her the quelling look that had kept many a hardened soldier in line.

She lifted her chin and met his glare without flinching. "I am going to prove he is guilty, with or without your help."

Fear clenched deep in his gut. She would do it. Or try. Simon gripped her shoulders a little tighter, wanting to haul her into his arms and keep her safe. "You are going to keep your mouth shut, or I will gag and bind you," he said, exasperated. She flinched then, and the tiny movement cut straight through him. Growling a curse, he dragged her against his chest and held her there with both hands.

"Simon, what are you doing?" she mumbled into his tunic.

"I wish I knew." She turned him inside out, brought all his carefully guarded feelings too close to the surface for comfort. He felt raw, yet curiously alive when he was with her. He was not certain he liked that, but he could not seem to ignore her, either. Like a man addicted to drink, he kept going back for another sip. One day soon, he'd need the whole bottle.

As though sensing his precarious mood, she put her arms around his waist and squeezed. "I am sorry I made you angry."

"I am not angry," he said softly. "I am afraid for you."

"Oh, Simon." She lifted her face, lips already parting for the kiss they both craved.

Simon groaned. Desire ripped through him, a fierce, hungry beast straining on its leash. Because he didn't think he could control it, he reined it in. "Not here," he murmured while his body ached in protest. "We must leave."

Ignoring her hurt expression, he took her arm and hurried her down High Dur Gate. The tension between them was palpable as they crossed the bridge to the other side of the river that separated Durleigh into two parts. She walked meekly at his side. Too meekly, but Simon kept going until they came to the narrow street dotted with shops and taverns that ran along the river. By then Linnet's steps were flagging.

Concerned, Simon stopped at the first clean-looking tavern. He scanned the room quickly, spotted a side door and led Linnet to a table near it. If Bardolf did come in, they would have a means of escape.

He seated her on a stool and took the one that put his back to the wall, giving him a clear view of the main door. The noon meal had already been served, but the maid, a plump, comely girl, promised them bread, cheese and cold meat.

"I am sorry I accused you of fearing Crispin Norville," Linnet muttered as soon as the serving wench had bustled away.

Simon groaned, but knew he'd not delay this longer. "In a way, I am afraid—afraid of what he might do to you."

"He can do nothing. I am innocent. He is guilty."

"You have no proof."

"True, but I have—"

"A feeling?" he challenged.

"Slightly more than that." She leaned forward, eyes gleaming. "I recalled something about the herbal brandy."

"Crispin gave it to Thurstan?" Simon asked eagerly.

"Nay, Thurstan bought it himself from an Italian merchant. Thurstan first broached the cask while I was visiting. We shared a cup in his chamber." She hesitated, a dull flush staining her cheeks. "Crispin burst in and accused us of improper behavior." She reached a hand to Simon. "But I swear we were just sitting and talking."

"I have said I believe you."

A look of pure anguish flitted across her face. Or was it a shadow cast by torches along the wall? "Crispin said that the brandy was a witch's brew. He said that I was trying to enslave Thurstan's soul with it."

"And then the brew turns out to be poisoned."

"Exactly. Too much of a coincidence, I'd say."

Simon sighed and scrubbed a hand over his face. "Slim evidence on which to accuse a priest of murder."

Inside Linnet something snapped. "How can you be so cool and calm about this?"

Simon leaned back, his expression remote. "It is my way, or so I have been told. Some men say I have ice in my veins."

Linnet glanced at him through her lashes. "Having kissed you, I'd say your blood runs as hot as fire."

"Linnet!" he exclaimed, his cheeks flushing.

Intrigued, Linnet arched one brow. "Of course, your men have doubtless not seen that side of you."

"Nay." His grin eased the years and the cares from his face. This was the man he should have been had he been raised with the nurturing love all things crave.

"Simon—" She broke off as the maid returned to set down a platter of food, two cups and an ale pitcher. By the time the woman left, Linnet's thoughts had traveled further down that road. "You owe it to Thurstan to find his killer."

The light in his eyes went out. "I owe him nothing, but I do admit," he said grudgingly, "that speaking with these folk today has shown me things I did not know about Thurstan."

Linnet sighed. So much pain, and seemingly no way to ease it. "Good thing, I think. If only Thurstan had lived long enough to explain—"

"There is no excusing what he did," Simon muttered, his gaze carefully blank. It was as though shutters had been drawn to shield his gaze from hers. "We'd best eat and be on our way." He bent to the task of demolishing bread and cheese.

Linnet stared at the top of his glossy black head and cursed her hasty tongue. A few ill-chosen words had shattered the closeness they had built up over the past few days. Damn. How could she have been so careless?

Thurstan himself had told her that Simon's reserved air hid deep scars. *I thought I'd done well to have him trained to be a knight like my older brothers. Too late I realized he had his mother's loving nature and was hurt by that cold, tough life.*

Aye, his upbringing had forced him to become self-reliant, to count on no one but himself. Discovering that the life he had so painstakingly built for himself was a lie had made Simon even more wary of trusting others. But he had come to trust her and to care for her. She had seen the tenderness mingled with the desire that flared in his eyes. She had felt the quickening of his body when he held her. Bad enough she did not truly deserve the respect he had accorded her, but to rip at his wounds...

She exhaled. "Forgive me," she said cautiously. "Mama used to say I had an unfortunate habit of blurting out things better left unsaid." Picking up her cup, she extended it to him. "Peace?" she asked, smiling faintly.

"Peace." Simon turned the word over as he stared at her mouth, the full lower lip, the tilted corners. It was a mouth made for smiling...and for passion. She was a woman who felt keenly and showed her emotions openly. He envied her that, the ease with which she lived in her own skin, for his had never fit quite right. Always he strove to be better, to prove himself. Somehow, despite all his accomplishments, it was never enough.

"I would have us be friends, Simon," she said.

The huskiness in her voice slid down his spine like warm honey, igniting possibilities he dared not explore. But he wanted to. *Dieu,* he dreamed about her—even when he was awake—of kissing her, of exploring the tempting curves beneath her plain gown. Lust, he thought. It was understandable, given the fact he had lived like a monk since leaving Acre. And yet, she was different from other women he'd met. That terrified him. He did not want to need her. "There are reasons why we cannot afford to become involved."

"You are right. More right than you can know."

Simon wanted to ask what she had meant, then decided to

let well enough alone. "Best eat. We've much to do before evening."

They ate in silence. Every time Simon looked up, her head was bent over her plate. He regretted the loss of the easy camaraderie they'd enjoyed earlier. But better to make things plain from the start. He liked her and did not want to hurt her when it came time for him to leave Durleigh. He did not yet know where he would go. Perhaps he would go home with Nicholas and from there visit the other knights to see how they fared.

Linnet sighed and pushed her plate away. "I am done." In truth, it appeared she had eaten little.

Simon stood and fished a few pennies from his pouch.

"I can pay my way." She stood also.

"Nay, I owe you for supper last night." He was troubled by her slumped shoulders. "I will take you home and then go up to the cathedral and speak with Brother Anselme."

That brought her head up. "About the archdeacon?"

"Linnèt, Crispin is a priest," Simon reminded her as he escorted her to the door.

"Perhaps he thought to save the church from Thurstan."

"The same might be said of Prior Walter," Simon muttered. "He, too, covets Durleigh. And being the archbishop's man, might stand a better chance of being named to the post."

She hesitated, then shook her head. "It does not fit."

"Because you like Walter and do not like Crispin."

"Crispin is guilty. I feel it," she taunted.

"Shh." He took hold of her shoulders, sighed and leaned his forehead against hers. "What am I going to do with you?"

"Help me find Thurstan's killer."

"I thought that was what I was doing."

"Aye." She reached up and stroked his cheek. Her touch

crackled across his skin like heat lightning. "I do not know what I would have done without you today."

Her soft gaze made him uncomfortable because he wanted to offer more yet knew he could not afford to. "Well, we'd best be getting back to the shop before dark," he muttered.

She smiled knowingly. "All right."

Feeling as though he had lost an important battle, Simon peered outside. The gloom had deepened, lengthening the shadows cast over the river walk by the buildings. Foot traffic was sparse. The two boats tied up alongside the walk had been emptied of their cargo and now bobbed forlornly on the choppy water. Of Bardolf, there was no sign.

"The way is clear." He took Linnet's arm as they started south toward the Dur Bridge.

"Did you see the new bridge?"

Simon moved to the edge of the walk and looked upstream. The river was high this time of year, swollen by heavy spring rains. A fine stone bridge had replaced the old timber one. "It is indeed a grand structure."

"Tolls from the river bar paid for it. Normally they go into the bishopric's coffers, but Thurstan remitted one half of his rents toward the building, and the town matched the amount."

"A good and just arrangement." Simon half turned. Out of the corner of his eye, he saw someone move up behind them.

The man had wild, angry eyes. His cheeks were stubbled with a brown beard, but Simon recognized him instantly.

The bandit who'd ambushed him and his companions near York.

"What the hell!" Simon spun, but even as he reached for his sword, the bandit lunged with a knife.

"Nay!" Linnet grabbed the assailant's arm. The fiend shook her off with a shouted curse and shoved her back.

Simon watched in horror as she went over the low stone wall and into the swiftly moving river.

"Bless me, Father, for I have sinned."

Crispin Norville scarcely felt the cold that seeped from the chapel's stone floor and through his coarse robe to chill his bony body. His heart was already an icy lump, weighing down his soul.

"I did not mean for him to die." Crispin clutched his rosary beads so hard his knuckles ached. He welcomed the pain.

"But you know that," Crispin murmured. "For I told you that Brother Thurstan was not pure, and you did put in my path the foreign brandy and the monkshood. You did show me the way to save Durleigh from the bishop's evil ministrations."

He worried the plain wooden beads with his fingers. "I did not kill him," Crispin whispered. But was it his fault that Thurstan had been too weak to fight off his attacker?

Crispin shuddered and closed his eyes, wracked by the memory of Thurstan's pain-twisted features. Even an enemy did not deserve such a death. "The woman is to blame." He would prove Linnet guilty and see her punished. Her death was the only thing that could clear the stain from his own immortal soul.

Chapter Ten

The icy water closed over Linnet's head with terrible finality, clogging her nose and mouth, blinding her in murky gloom. For an instant, she lay passive as the current sucked her along. Then the burning in her lungs penetrated her shock.

Struggling against the force of rushing water, she fought her way toward the light above. She popped free, gasping for breath, clawing to keep her head above water. Already the riverbank lay twenty yards or so away, and the gap was widening. Her papa had taught her the rudiments of swimming, but her gown and cloak weighed her down. She would never make it so far.

"Linnet! Hang on!"

She turned and saw Simon cutting toward her through the choppy water. "Go back!" she cried, fearing he would drown, too. The words ended in a gurgle as her head slipped under again. Something snagged her hair and pulled her up. She surfaced, choking and wheezing for air.

"Easy, I have you." He had an arm around her waist, his thick muscles straining as he fought the tumultuous river.

"My clothes...pull us down...." she rasped. "Let me go." But her fingers instinctively clutched at his tunic. She could feel his heart thudding, his legs milling to keep them afloat.

"I'll get you out. Stay calm." Still treading water, he ripped the broach that held her cloak on. The river immediately claimed the heavy garment. Only Simon's grip kept her from being sucked after it. "We'll be frozen stiff if we don't get out soon. Hang on to the back of my tunic, kick if you can." He shifted her to his back and struck out toward the bank.

She ordered her legs to move, but they were numb and unresponsive. It seemed to take hours. The water was so cold, the current so strong it carried them farther and farther downstream. She could sense him tiring, feel the strain as he called on his body's last reserves to carry them to safety.

We will not make it, she thought. *I am slowing him down.* Everything inside her rebelled at that. She would not be the death of him. Shuddering, she loosened her hold on his tunic.

"Nay." He cursed and reached back, catching her arm with one hand in the instant she let go. "We will make it." He clamped an arm around her waist and stroked toward shore, his long legs scissoring out behind them.

"Grab the rope!" a voice called, and something struck the water in front of them.

Simon lunged for it, wrapping the thick hemp around his forearm. "Pull!" he shouted.

Linnet lifted her eyes to the shore, to the ragged line of figures bent to the task of wresting them from the river's icy maw. She could see their faces, men, women and even children hauling them in.

Hands reached for her, hauling her up on the bank. She lay there on her belly, coughing and gasping like a beached fish.

"Linnet." Simon turned her over and crushed her to him. "*Dieu,* I thought I'd lost you. Why did you let go?"

Because I love you. Too shocked and weary for words, Linnet lay passive in his arms.

"Linnet. Are you all right?" Simon moved back so he could see her. His hand trembled as he stroked her wet hair from her face. Her eyes stood out black against her ashen skin, haunted by the fear that still knotted in his own belly. But she was alive. Alive. How much more precious she seemed, more delicate and more vulnerable. "Why did you do it?"

"So I would not pull you down."

"Linnet," he whispered, eyes squeezing shut. "I could have lost you."

"But you did not. You saved me." She raised one hand to stroke his cheek. "I owe you my life."

His eyes opened slowly, filled with emotions so raw and tangled they stole her breath anew. "Linnet, I never thought—"

"Come," interrupted a new voice. "Let us get you inside and dry before you both catch the ague." A priest hovered over them.

Simon looked up, but did not release her, his expression neutral once again. "Our thanks for the timely rescue, Brother..."

"Brother John Gibson, the almoner."

Linnet could cheerfully have kicked the almoner for his untimely interruption. What had Simon been about to tell her? *That he loved her?* Ah, well, she did not deserve his love, even if he had been willing to bestow it. Sighing, she managed a watery chuckle. "I had intended to show Simon the almshouse, but this was not the way I'd hoped to arrive."

"Quickly, Brother, we must get her inside and out of these wet things ere she catches the ague." Simon's scowl as he scooped her off the ground was darker than the water that had nearly claimed them both.

"Of course." Brother John hustled them toward the brightly lit almshouse.

Linnet huddled into Simon's embrace. Thinking she had never felt safer or more secure, she stared up at his stark profile. Once she might have mistaken his expression for anger. Now she saw the fear he sought to hide and a concern that warmed her despite the icy wool clinging to her. It was almost worth the dunking to discover he was not immune to her, after all.

"Dead, are you certain?" Jevan demanded.

Rob FitzHugh nodded. "She fell into the river, and he jumped in to save her."

"Idiot." Jevan cuffed him in the head. "You were supposed to take him prisoner, get the journal and bring it to me."

Rob fell back against the wall, both arms upraised to ward off the next blow. "It weren't my fault. I came at him, ye see, thinking I could take him prisoner. That fool woman grabbed my arm. Look here." He pulled back his sleeve, displaying the long scratches where her nails had raked him. "I pushed...she fell."

Jevan sneered and turned away to pace the tiny garret atop the inn. He'd sneaked away from class to wait for Rob. The chancellor of the school had already warned Jevan he'd be whipped if he missed any more lessons, but things were in an uproar over the bishop's death, and he'd likely not be missed. Any more than he'd been missed from supper two nights ago.

The important thing was finding the charter. It was an amendment to Thurstan's will. In it the bishop granted Blackstone Heath to Simon, but he had changed the charter after Simon's death, leaving the manor to Jevan instead. *Dieu,* what if Simon had had the journal on his person when he went into the river? "Have the bodies been found?" Jevan asked, turning on Rob.

"Nay." Rob straightened, eager to please as a cur. "The sheriff's men are searching along the river. But the current is so swift, who knows where they'll end up. Want I should go and help them look?"

"All right, but this time do not make a hash of it. Find Simon's body and search it for the journal."

"Ye can count on me." Rob dashed off.

Jevan waited until Rob's footsteps had died away, then went down to search Simon's room for himself.

Night was fast approaching by the time Simon and Linnet left the almshouse. It had rained during the time they were inside recovering from their ordeal. The dusky sky was cloudless now, the air filled with dewy freshness. Appropriate, Simon thought, for in a sense, he felt reborn.

"Thank you for all you did, Brother," Simon said.

"That is why we are here," replied the almoner. "To help those in need."

Brother John had done more than that. He and the tenants of the poorhouse had saved their lives. John was a round little man whose soft eyes belied his boundless energy. He had insisted they remove their wet clothes and wrap up in thick blankets while the garments were dried before a cheery fire in the common room. The cook had offered hot soup to warm their insides. The women, many of them widows with small children, had pitched in, chafing Simon and Linnet's numb feet.

Simon had been glad of the crowd and their distracting activity, for they kept him from dwelling on what had happened. Near brushes with death were not a novelty to him. But his reaction to Linnet's involvement was. He kept reliving the moment when he'd felt her fingers slipping away.

She had courted death to save him.

It was not unheard of in the heat of battle for a soldier to risk his life to aid a comrade. But that was a matter of training and of honor, and few expected to die. They expected to prevail. Linnet could have had no such hope.

She had been willing to die to save him.

The realization was both moving and humbling. It changed things in ways he feared to examine.

"Thank you again, Brother John," Linnet said. Her voice was still hoarse, and she trembled as she spoke.

That little tremor cut through a lifetime of defenses like a dagger through cheese. Simon put an arm around her slender waist and drew her closer. The feel of staunchly independent Linnet leaning into his embrace made his heart roll over in his chest. She needed him. He was used to that, had committed himself to helping people in need. The fact that he needed her was novel and unsettling.

Simon shrugged the feeling aside. "I am much impressed with your almshouse." When he could send to London, Simon meant to donate a large share of his fortune to the almshouse.

"The credit goes to God and to Bishop Thurstan." John crossed himself. "Pray we will be allowed to continue our work."

"Who would stop you?" Simon demanded.

Brother John sighed. "I fear the archdeacon does not approve of the way this house was conceived and may close it."

"But the poor would starve," cried Linnet.

"True." Brother John's lips thinned. "Brother Crispin is one who believes in following each stricture to the letter. I first met him at Wells, where he was a canon and I a young novice. A fellow novice sneaked away without permission to visit his ill father. A storm came up, forcing the boy back to the cathedral after the gates were closed for the night. Crispin decreed that according to our rules the gates could not be opened again till the morn. By then, the boy had frozen to death.''

"He let him die?" Linnet exclaimed.

"Crispin believed it was God's will, a punishment for disobedience, and the dean of Wells did not dispute him."

Linnet inhaled sharply. "But—"

Simon gave her a quick warning squeeze. Appalling as this was, much as it added to their suspicions about Crispin, silence was essential. "Come. Drusa and Aiken will be worried."

"I will send two of the lay brothers along to make certain you reach home safely."

"Thank you," Simon murmured. Already dusk was deepening the shadows that hugged the buildings. By the time they reached the apothecary it would be full dark. And somewhere out in the dark, the brigand waited. If he'd had only himself to think of, Simon might have chanced it. Nay, he would certainly have gone alone, hoping the man would give him another chance to finish this. But he had Linnet's welfare to consider.

Simon set out with one hand on his sword and the other around Linnet, the two strapping lay brothers close behind. The journey through the center of Durleigh to the apothecary was tense and silent, but uneventful. Most folk were home supping, and many of the shops were closed.

As they turned down Spicier's Lane, Simon noted that the beggar was not at his post across the street from the apothecary. Was he out looking for them? If so, they might get inside without the sheriff's man being any the wiser.

Simon turned to the brothers and pressed two coins into the older one's hand. "I noticed a bakeshop near the almshouse. On your way back, perhaps you would buy cakes for the children."

"It is kind of you to think of them, sir. Coin for treats is scarce."

"I know." The folk who had raised Simon had not been nearly as loving as Brother John.

"Thank Brother John again for us," Linnet said.

Aiken answered the door at the first knock. "Mistress, Sir Simon. We were beginning to worry."

"No need." Simon rushed Linnet inside, closed the door and set the bar across it. "We were buying clothes and lost track of time. Did you notice when the beggar left his post?"

Aiken frowned. "An hour or so ago. I was weighing peppercorns for a customer. Why?"

"Did he leave of his own accord?"

"Well." Aiken scratched at the few hairs on his chin. "Bardolf walked by, and then the beggar left."

"Excellent." Hamel obviously believed them dead. "Where are the men-at-arms?"

"In the kitchen, we were just sitting down to sup," Aiken added. "Shall I fetch them for ye?"

"Nay." He'd speak with them later and make plans for the watch this evening. "If you would tell Drusa we have returned and ask if she could attend her mistress. We've had a—"

"I can see to myself," Linnet muttered as the lad hurried through to the kitchens.

"You have had a shock. You need rest and quiet."

"Please, say nothing to them of…of what happened at the river. I do not want to alarm Aiken and Drusa."

Simon scowled. "I will not lie to them on two accounts. I hate lies." And with good reason, for his whole life had been one. "And if the bandit's attack was planned, we need to take precautions against his trying again."

"I thought he was a footpad."

Drusa bustled into the entryway. "Aiken says ye need my help. Has something happened?" Her sharp eyes searched each of their faces in turn.

"She fell in the river," Simon said bluntly.

"And he jumped in after me."

Drusa gasped. "Ye could both have drowned."

"Sir Simon is a strong swimmer," Linnet said, cleverly downplaying the incident without lying. "And we are fine, as you can see. The almoner took us in. That is where we have been so long. He insisted on drying us out."

"My poor lamb." Drusa enfolded Linnet in her ample bosom. "Come upstairs straight away, and I'll warm the bed for—"

"I am not tired." Linnet gently disengaged herself from the maid's arms. "But some food would be most welcome."

"Of course. Aiken stepped over to the inn and brought back a mutton pie. But it is not fitting that ye should eat in the kitchen with those rough soldiers," Drusa said. "I'll have Aiken bring a tray up to yer room."

"And something for Sir Simon, as well," Linnet said.

Drusa gave him a measuring glance, then hurried away.

"Linnet. It is not proper for us to be alone in your chamber." It was damned dangerous, in fact.

"We need to speak of what we have learned today and what we will do next. I would prefer discussing it in private."

Simon sighed. She was right. Drusa could be counted on to keep silent about anything she heard, but Aiken was young and flighty. And the soldiers did not owe any particular allegiance to Simon. "Lead on," he muttered grudgingly.

Linnet's smile teased. "I will behave myself."

Simon wished he could promise the same with some certainty. He trooped up the stairs after her. To keep his hands busy, he bent to rebuild the fire in the hearth. As a precaution, he kept his sword on when he was done. *Difficult to seduce a woman with a broadsword in the way.* "Where shall we begin?"

"You could start by not glowering at me." She had shed her borrowed cloak and draped it over the bed. "Sweet Mary, but it seems a hundred years ago I left this room."

"Aye. Much has happened in a short time." He felt raw, as though he'd been turned inside out and stood before her, totally defenseless. At her mercy.

"Too much." She joined him at the hearth and stood looking into the flames. "My whole world has been turned inside out. Thurstan's death, your return, the threat to us…"

Simon nodded and glanced sidelong at her profile. It was not the bishop's death or even the current danger that caused his turmoil. His father had been dead to him for years and danger a constant companion for the past four. It was Linnet who disturbed the inner peace Simon had struggled to create for himself. He stared at her features, gilded by the firelight, the wide, intelligent eyes, the high cheekbones and the soft mouth.

Aiken clomped up the stairs. His eyes alive with curiosity, he set down the covered tray. "Drusa said ye saved Linnet's life, Sir Simon. We're grateful."

Simon shrugged. "It was nothing."

"Not to me." Linnet smiled ruefully at him.

"What happened?" Aiken asked avidly.

"My rashness landed me in trouble as usual," Linnet said.

Simon glowered at her. "Run along and have your supper, lad, while I speak with your mistress about her…rashness."

The boy left, feet scuffing.

"You know the man who attacked us?" Linnet asked.

"What makes you think I do?"

She just stared at him.

Simon refused to be intimidated. "Let us eat." He stalked to the table, pulled out the two stools and sat on one.

She folded her arms and waited. Just waited.

"Oh, very well," Simon grumbled. "Come here."

There was no smugness in her expression as she took the other stool. Merely patient curiosity.

Loath as he was to speak of this and worry her, he could

not lie. "He was the leader of the group of bandits who ambushed us on the road from York."

"Ah." Linnet slid into her stool. "The one who escaped?"

"Aye. God rot him." Simon took his eating knife, cut the mutton pie into pieces and put the choicest slice into her bowl before filling his own. He picked up a spoon and began to eat, more for something to do than out of hunger. His belly was still too tight for that. "I could swear I'd seen him in Durleigh. At the cathedral. Did he look familiar to you?"

"Nay, but then my eyes were on his knife."

Simon shuddered. He had come so close to losing her.

"Curious he should search you out."

Simon raised his head. She was not eating, but staring at him with that level gaze. Why had he admired her cleverness? "Likely he spotted me and thought to avenge his cohorts."

"Why did he not wait till you were alone?"

"Obviously he was not very wise."

"Yet you said he led this band of brigands, and I do assure you they must have been clever, for they eluded both Sheriff Turnebull and then Hamel when he became temporary sheriff."

Simon blinked. "In truth, my mind was so filled with reaching Durleigh—" *and confronting Thurstan* "—I had not given the bandits another thought. Likely they were in league with someone, a corrupt baron, perhaps, who gave them protection in exchange for a share of their plunder."

"Then why come all the way to Durleigh?"

"Perhaps he feared the baron would punish him."

"Or he needed to have his wound tended and had heard that Old Nelda would see to him with no questions asked."

Simon frowned. "My wits must be scattered, for I'd not thought of that, either. I will question her and see if she knows where he is."

"She is not one to answer questions."

"A piece of silver may loosen her tongue."

"I am sure it would." Linnet picked up her spoon and toyed with the pie. "Do you think I am wrong to suspect Crispin?"

"I do not like him. But murder..." Simon shook his head.

"What of the tale Brother John told. If Crispin could leave a novice outside to freeze for running away, might he not be capable of punishing Thurstan for his transgressions?"

"I suppose. One hears tales every day of priests who have sinned to gain what they wanted, be it wealth, power or a woman." He thought of his mother and wondered if she had lain willingly with Thurstan or if he had taken a fancy to her and forced her into his bed.

"I fear we will never solve this." Linnet stood abruptly and walked away, but not before he saw her anguished expression.

"Do not lose heart." Simon followed her to the hearth.

A slight tremor shook her, and she wrapped her arms about her waist as though to still it. "I had not realized till this afternoon how close is the margin between life and death."

Simon shuddered himself, thinking how nearly he had lost her. "Ah, Linnet." He opened his arms to her. She came to him, and it seemed as natural as breathing to clasp her close.

Never had he been as conscious of the contrast between his maleness and a woman's soft fragility as he was now. Perhaps because he had never spent this much time with any one woman. Parents kept their marriageable daughters well away from penniless bastard knights like himself, and he had never been tempted to linger with the whores he had sought out to ease his lust.

He had no ties other than the oath of fealty he'd sworn to Lord Edmund and few friendships, except those he'd formed with the other five knights of the Black Rose. But Linnet was different. Lively and compassionate, strong yet vulnerable, she awakened something in him he had not known existed.

He tried to will it away. She was not for him. No woman was. Long ago he had vowed that he would not wed nor sire a child. And now that he knew whose blood flowed in his veins, he was more determined than ever.

"I needed this," she whispered, burrowing into his embrace, ripping at his control. "All the while dear Brother John was trying to help, all I wanted was for you to hold me."

"I know." God help him, he knew. Simon gritted his teeth and fought the urge to crush her to him, to rip away the layers of wool separating them and bury himself in her welcoming heat. "I was afraid I would not reach you in time."

"But you did." She raised wet, shiny eyes to him. "You risked your life to save me."

"How could I not?" Tears magnified the size of her eyes. Reflected in them he saw his own dazed image. Drowning, he thought, he was drowning in her. It was his last conscious thought before he lowered his head and kissed her.

A low sigh broke from her as she opened to him, her arms sliding around his neck, her body melting into his. Lush and pliant, she responded to him with an urgency that matched the fire in Simon's belly. He had never wanted anyone this hotly, this desperately. He swept his hands down her supple back and lifted her, fitting them together.

Perfect. The soft hills and valleys of her body fit the hard angles of his perfectly. Like a dream. His dream.

Simon groaned and deepened the kiss, stunned by the overwhelming sense of rightness, the sense of belonging.

"Sir Simon! Sir Simon!"

Simon jerked his head up, looked into Linnet's dazed, startled eyes, then realized the shout had come from below.

The guards!

"Stay here." Simon set her from him and sprinted for the stairwell. Miles waited at the bottom. "What is it?"

"There's a man at the back door."

"At this time of night? Something must be amiss." Simon started toward the kitchen, wondering what fresh ills had befallen them.

Chapter Eleven

"Simon!" Brother Anselme swayed in the doorway of the shop, one hand clutched to his heart.

"Easy, Brother." Simon took hold of the infirmarer and half carried him to the bench by the hearth.

"You are alive!" Brother Anselme's face was pale, his red-rimmed eyes filled with hope. "What of Linnet?"

"She is above stairs, resting." Simon glanced up to find them encircled by an audience: the worried Drusa, avid Aiken and two curious soldiers. "Drusa, I think the good brother is in need of a drink."

"I will fetch some whiskey and assure the mistress all is well." She departed in a flurry of russet skirts.

Simon sent Miles and Jasper to search the garden and Aiken to look out the front, then sat beside the monk. "Who told you we were dead?" Simon asked. "And when?"

"It was late afternoon, hours past None. I had gone to tell Brother Crispin of my findings. Sheriff Hamel and Lady Odeline were with him, celebrating the demise of Thurstan's killers."

"Meaning Linnet and myself." Simon stroked his chin.

"Aye. Crispin is determined you two are guilty. But what happened? How came you to be reported dead?"

"Later," he murmured as Drusa rushed in bearing a flask.

Linnet followed close behind. Rising, he gave way for Linnet to sit by the monk and stood back watching the tearful reunion. The closeness between Linnet and Anselme was as obvious as the hovering Drusa's concern. The outpouring of genuine affection stirred something in Simon's gut. Envy, he thought and tried, unsuccessfully, to will it away.

A commotion at the rear door signaled the return of the soldiers just as Aiken clumped in through the workroom. All three reported nothing was amiss.

Simon welcomed the interruption. Briskly he sent the soldiers back to their posts and considered how best to handle this. He had questions to ask of the monk and no desire to be overheard, even by Linnet. Especially by her. "Brother Anselme, I will walk you back to the cathedral."

Linnet whipped her head up. Shock and exhaustion had dulled the golden lights in her eyes, but they brightened briefly with suspicion. "I will come with you."

"Ye'll do no such thing," Drusa cried. "It's off to bed with ye, miss, and I'll be sitting with ye till ye sleep."

Linnet glared at Simon. He smiled benignly back. Careful to keep his smugness hidden, he borrowed a coarse cloak from Jasper and hustled Anselme from the shop. Once outside, with the door barred behind them, Simon heaved a sigh of relief.

"What is going on?" Anselme hissed.

"I will tell you while we walk." Simon pulled the cowl up to shield his face and set out via the back streets. The night was nippy and there were few folks abroad, but he kept his voice low as he retold the day's events.

"Thanks be to God you are safe." Anselme crossed himself. "But why would this brigand seek you out?"

"I think our assailant is the sheriff's man."

"The sheriff in league with outlaws?" Anselme shook his head. "I can scarcely credit it."

"That is because few people know what Hamel is really like," Simon muttered. "He is greedy, ruthless and cunning."

"It would explain why the bandits have been so successful in avoiding capture."

"Aye, it would. The man looked familiar to me." Simon described him as best he could. "Have you seen such a man in town or at the cathedral?"

"Alas, I cannot tell. I am not often in town, and the cathedral is a busy place. Students, pilgrims and even brothers from other orders are constantly visiting us."

"Well, the important thing is that we are safe."

"Aye, but there is evil gossip abroad." Anselme waited until they had crossed busy High Dur Street and entered another side street to explain. "The archdeacon put forth the theory that, unable to live with her guilt, Linnet threw herself into the river, and you died trying to save your lover."

"A neat, tidy package," Simon muttered. The two people Crispin had accused of the crime were unable to defend themselves. It made Crispin seem more and more guilty. "Are the sheriff's men still looking for us?"

"As far as I know. The river is wild this time of year, and I gathered the search has moved out beyond the town walls."

"What of the prior? Was he in the hall, too?"

"Nay, I've not seen Prior Walter all day."

Simon's sixth sense prickled. He had first suspected Crispin because of things Walter had said. Was the prior trying to divert suspicion from himself? "He has not left Durleigh?"

"Nay. I've been busy in the infirmary is all."

"Have you found out anything else?"

Anselme's sigh seemed to fill the night. "I have confirmed my earlier theory. Thurstan was being poisoned. Slowly."

"For how long?" Simon asked, stopping midstride.

"He first took ill five months ago."

"December. Did anything unusual happen then?"

"He collapsed in November, at the mass said for the souls of our Crusaders." Anselme smiled faintly. "Prayers that were answered by your return. But he had begun to recover by December and was well enough to conduct the Christmas services."

"When was Old Nelda exiled?"

"The first complaint was lodged against her after the new year," Anselme said. "By the archdeacon. But the hearing was not held for some weeks. Even after she had been found guilty, Thurstan refused to turn her out till the weather warmed."

Simon tucked the information about Nelda away. She might well be the murderer, but she did not have easy access to the bishop. "I would imagine he and Crispin argued about that."

"That they did."

"And then there was the matter of the bones." Simon told Anselme about their visit with Digger.

"I have heard no mention of this."

"Digger said that on the day Thurstan died, he was called to the cathedral by the archdeacon—to bear witness against the bishop. According to Digger, Crispin was furious with Thurstan."

"What do you mean?" Anselme's troubled features were illuminated by light spilling from a tavern doorway.

"Just that the archdeacon hated the bishop."

"What you suggest is impossible," the monk exclaimed. "Unthinkable. Master Billeter hated Thurstan most fiercely."

"Aye, so I have heard." Simon related Jean Billeter's tale. Anselme smiled. "The Lord works in mysterious ways."

"Aye, he got what he deserved." Simon sighed. "But Clarence could not have attacked the bishop two nights past, nor does he seem the sort to patiently poison someone."

"Nay. But Brother Crispin?" Anselme crossed himself and shook his head. "He is the most pious among us."

"Zealously so." Simon waited a moment, then told the monk about the novice who had been shut out of Wells Cathedral and froze to death. "Perhaps the archdeacon is another who believes that the end justifies the means."

Anselme bowed his head. "All you say is true, my son."

"And Crispin would have had easy access to the bishop's rooms and his things."

"Aye." Anselme halted across the street from the cathedral enclave and stared at the walls, his eyes sad. "But murder..." He shook his head again. "I cannot credit it."

Nor would anyone else, Simon thought grimly. Not without solid proof. "If I could search his things, I might find—"

Anselme stared at him aghast. "Brother Crispin would never give permission for such a thing."

"Nor would I ask...for fear of alerting him. It is possible he has already gotten rid of the poisons."

Anselme scowled. "Crispin could not have hit him on the head or doused him with the belladonna. He was in the great hall with Prior Walter, waiting to dine with Thurstan."

"I know. Perhaps Crispin was in league with someone."

"Lady Odeline?" Anselme asked, voicing Simon's thoughts.

"Perhaps," Simon said carefully. "You did say they were sitting together a short time ago. Is that not odd?"

"Aye. And she found Thurstan," the monk murmured. "Though she said he was alive, and she did look most genuinely horrified when we reached his chamber and discovered him dead."

"Perhaps she is a skilled mummer."

"Holy Mary." Anselme wiped a hand over his face. "I do not know which is worse, accusing a priest or Thurstan's blood kin. In any event, the crime was a vile one indeed and would have taken some strength. I have learned Thurstan was alive when the belladonna was forced on him.''

"Forced?" Simon felt his own throat close.

Anselme explained that had Thurstan been dead, he'd not have been able to swallow, and a large dose of the poison had lain in Thurstan's stomach. "There were bruises on his jaw where it was pried open."

"Would he have been in pain?" Simon whispered.

"Some." Anselme's mouth worked. "Belladonna paralyzes before it kills, but they say the mind remains clear."

"Damn." Simon closed his eyes against the horror. It was one thing to wish dead the man who had ignored him, quite another to think of him dying by degrees, unable to call out, aware his life was ebbing away. Bile rose in his throat, bitter and edged with guilt. If he had not torn away in such a blind, hate-filled hurry, he might have seen something. He might have been there to thwart the murderer.

"It was over quickly. A few moments at most."

A few moments of sheer hell. Simon wondered if Lady Odeline had knowledge of herbs.

"It was the belladonna that distorted his features and made us think he'd had a seizure."

"I would prefer that Linnet not learn of this," Simon said.

"I plan to tell few people besides yourself and the prior. As you can see, Thurstan's death was so heinous I am loath to believe either Crispin or Odeline responsible."

Simon looked up, gut churning, and found the sky filled with stars. He had a brief, dizzying image of Thurstan gazing down, waiting for justice. *Who killed you?* There was no answer except the whisper of the night wind. Snorting, Simon shook the bit of whimsy aside. "But someone was, and I must find out who, lest Linnet and I are framed for the crime. Could the monkshood and belladonna have come from your infirmary stock?"

"I thought of that. Our noxious medicines are kept in a

locked cupboard, and I have the only key. I took a thorough inventory last night. Everything is as it should be. Not so much as a grain or drop is missing.''

Simon studied the monk's open, honest face and believed him. ''All of the containers hold what they should? Nothing has been substituted?''

''I checked that, of course,'' Anselme said sharply.

Simon held up a hand. ''I know you think I am grasping at straws, Brother, but I am desperate to free Linnet.''

''I know.'' The monk laid a hand on Simon's arm. ''Thank you for saving her from the river.''

Simon shrugged, uncomfortable with the light shining in the monk's eyes, but in his heart he knew he had never been more grateful than when he pulled her out of the water. Alive.

''What will you do next?''

''Next?'' Simon swallowed hard. Shoving the latent guilt aside was tougher, but he was used to pushing unwanted bits of life into a corner of his mind and ignoring them. ''Tomorrow we will come to the palace and show the archdeacon we are very much alive.'' His mouth twitched. ''I want to watch his face.''

The compline bell rang out over the city, its solemn notes echoing off old stone.

''I must go,'' Anselme said. ''Again my thanks for saving Linnet. She was as dear to Thurstan as a daughter. He would be pleased to see you together.''

''We are not *together*,'' Simon snapped.

''Indeed.'' Anselme's brows rose, his eyes dancing. ''You know best what is in your heart, my son.'' With that, he left.

Nay, Simon did not know what was in his heart. He had sworn it was as empty and cold as the grave…until he'd met Linnet.

''To you, my lady.'' Hamel lifted his cup and touched it lightly to Odeline's. They were seated in the bedchamber of his little house off the market square.

Odeline sipped and gauged how best to bend him to her will. Perhaps with a bit of the truth, for Hamel was a greedy man. "Oh, Hamel, with Thurstan gone, I fear Jevan and I will be tossed into the streets."

"Nay, I will take care of you." Hamel set down the cup and took her hands in his great paw. "And Jevan has a place at the cathedral school."

"Only because Thurstan paid his way." The thought of living in this tiny house, in this remote town, with only the dullard Hamel for company, made tears well. "Thurstan did intend for us to have a small estate when he died. He showed me the charter, but now it is missing. Stolen by Simon." *Stupid. Stupid that she had not asked Thurstan for it days ago.*

"An estate?" Hamel's eyes brightened.

"Small, but prosperous." A tear slid down her cheek as she thought of that rich estate with its beautiful manor going to the church. She could have sold it for a tidy sum and returned to London to live in style. "The charter is in the journal I had asked you to find."

"Do not cry." Hamel patted her hands. "I will get it."

"How?" Odeline sobbed. "Jevan searched Simon's room and could not find Thurstan's book."

"I will search again. Now that he is dead, I can take his possessions, slit open his mattress, shred his clothes—"

"It could be he had it on his person when he drowned."

"Hmm. My men have had no luck in finding the body, but when they do, I swear I will tear it limb from—"

"Spare me the details," Odeline murmured.

"I am sorry, my dear. I forget you are so delicate." He patted her arm. "Could the bishop have entrusted another copy of this charter to someone else? The archdeacon, may-hap?"

Odeline rolled her eyes. "Thurstan would dance with the devil before he entrusted anything to Crispin Norville." It was her fondest hope her brother *was* dancing with the devil. It would serve him right for having looked down upon her and for teasing her with that charter.

If you avoid scandal while you are here, I will gift Blackstone Heath to Jevan when he completes his studies, Thurstan had promised.

She had lived like a nun. Or at least she had until Thurstan was taken ill, then she had done as she pleased...with Hamel.

"Besides," Odeline added. "There is only one copy. Now it is missing. I suppose I should have told the archdeacon about this, but he does not approve of me. I fear he might try to seize the estate for the church."

Hamel snorted. "That pious prig would insist it go to the church. Nay, it is better if we find it."

Oh, far better. Odeline smiled up at Hamel through her lashes. Men were such stupid, predictable beasts. She let her gaze wander over his muscular body and wide hands, thinking how strong and ruthless a lover he was. She looked up to find him watching her through lowered lids, eyes glittering with sensual heat. "Promise to say nothing of the charter," she purred.

His wicked lips parted in a smug smile. "Nothing."

Odeline let the tension crackle between them for a moment, gauging his lust by the rasp of his breathing. Just as he leaned forward to take her mouth, she stood. "It is possible that Simon left it in the apothecary shop for safekeeping." She walked to the window, knowing he would follow. Like a trained dog.

"I will search there, too, then."

"How? On what pretext?"

Hamel spun her around. "I'll find an excuse." He took her lips in a bruising kiss. "Just trust me."

Odeline trusted no man. Jevan was the only one she could

count on to support her. And she him. "All right, but we must have the charter before Thurstan's funeral."

"It will be done." He carried her to the bed and fell on her like a starving animal. His passion fired her own, and they rolled across the coverlet, tearing and scratching in their haste to satisfy their urgent craving.

Wherever you are now, Thurstan, I hope you can see me, she thought as Hamel mounted her and drove her up the final peak.

A short time later, Odeline washed, tidied her clothes and slipped out of the room, leaving Hamel snoring.

Jevan roused from his post by the back gate. "Well?"

"He will look for the charter."

"Good. Though I little like him, the sheriff can search with impunity in places where I cannot. I will not lose Blackstone Heath after all I've gone through to get it."

Odeline nodded, pulled up the hood of her cloak and the two of them walked slowly toward Petergate and the cathedral.

"I should have made him give me the charter first," Jevan grumbled, kicking stones from his path.

A shiver of unease skittered down her spine. "What do you mean, first?"

Jevan glanced sidelong at her and shrugged. "Before I agreed to stay here." He curled his lower lip. "I cannot abide this school a day longer. Me, a clerk." He made a rude noise. "I would rather die."

"So your uncle said when our brother, Richard, died and father informed Thurstan he was to take poor Richard's place as bishop, but that worked out right well for him." She looked ahead to the bishop's palace, the gray stone bleached white by the torches rimming it.

Power. Wealth. Prestige.

Aye, her half brother had done well, the ruthless bastard.

Until the end, that is.

Odeline smiled into the darkness.

* * *

Simon circled the apothecary once to make certain no one was lurking about, then rapped at the back door.

Miles opened it at once. "Any trouble, Sir Simon?"

"Nay, all is quiet."

Drusa rose from the kitchen table. Her gray braids were down and she wore a thick bed robe, but her expression was troubled. "She would not lie down till you returned."

Nightmares, Simon thought, certain he'd have them himself. He would have given anything to go to her, to hold her through the night, but it was not only comfort he wanted to offer. "What if you were to sleep in the room?"

"I offered. She said she wants to be alone." Drusa wiped her eyes on her sleeve. "She just sits there, holding the prayer book and rocking."

"Prayer book?"

"Aye. The bishop gave it to her—" Drusa's mouth trembled "—that last night."

Simon felt his gut tighten. It was irrational to be jealous of a dead man, but where she was concerned, he did not seem to be rational at all. "I will go up and speak with her."

He found Linnet sitting in a chair before the dying fire, her eyes glazed but dry, a small, leather-bound book clasped to her breast like a beloved child. "Linnet, you will make yourself sick with this."

"I should have stayed," she whispered. "I was angry with him, and I left. If I had stayed, whoever killed him might—"

"Stop." Simon knelt down and took hold of her shoulders. Frustration made him want to shake her, but she needed all the gentleness he could muster. "I was there, too. Do you think I have not flayed myself with that same whip?" he asked softly.

"But...but you do not care that he is dead."

"A few days ago, that was true, but now...?" He sighed

and kneaded her shoulders, marveling that such a slender body could contain such strength. "He was no father to me, but I have come to see that he was a good man in many other ways. A capable, caring shepherd to his flock."

Linnet smiled faintly. "Aye, he was that. I am glad you have come to care for him, at least a little. But I keep thinking that if I had not left him alone…"

"Shh. You might have put the murderer off that night, but he would have found another time."

"I suppose." She hugged the book a little tighter, her grief-ravaged gaze searching his for answers.

Simon hesitated. He'd seen such anguish in others, fellow knights who had lost a friend in battle, innocent peasants whose whole lives had been destroyed by war. There were no answers to such deep pain, but he wanted desperately to ease her suffering. "Shall I read to you from the prayer book?"

She thought that over for a moment, then shook her head. "My heart is not yet ready to accept the healing words."

Simon nodded. "Let Drusa come up and sleep on a pallet."

"Nay, but I would like it if you stayed."

His blood heated. His heart raced. "You are tired, distraught, you cannot know what you are saying."

"But I do." Her eyes were softer now, filled with a longing he understood only too well.

Simon trembled, poised on the brink of giving in to the desire that had raged between them from that first moment in the garden. He wanted her, and Linnet wanted him. Her skin was flushed, her eyes were hazed with passion, but beneath the fire lurked a vulnerability that tempered his needs as nothing else could have. "I will stay," he whispered, lifting a hand to stroke her cheek.

She murmured his name and turned to kiss his palm. The

gesture tugged at his heart, yet made him more certain than ever of what he must do.

"Linnet." Simon stood and lifted her from the chair, prayer book and all. With her eyes locked on his, filled with silent need, he carried her to the bed. As he laid her down, the scent of her skin filled his nostrils. *Dieu*, but it reminded him of his dream, teased him with the urge to see if she alone could match it. "Linnet," he murmured again, releasing her and straightening before he gave in to insanity.

"Simon?" She frowned, clearly baffled by his withdrawal.

"Sleep. I will stay with you…in yon chair."

"But I thought…" Her eyes filled with tears. "I wanted…"

"As do I." He smiled gently, despite the war going on inside himself. "But not tonight when we are both weary from our struggles and worried over what tomorrow may bring." He touched her hair briefly, then walked away before he could change his mind, snuffing out the candles on the mantel to cast the room in near darkness.

"Simon?"

He started, overwhelmed by a sense of having been here before. Her voice, coming out of the night, reminded him so forcefully of his dream. "What is it?"

"Thank you for staying. I feel safe with you near."

Simon groaned. She should not, for his control was perilously close to shredding. "Sleep," he murmured, doubting he would, for if he dreamed he might seek her out.

Chapter Twelve

Archdeacon Crispin hurried down the cathedral steps, barely conscious of the other brothers and students filing out behind him. He was weary, and he had much to do on the morrow, changes to make in the way Durleigh Cathedral was run. But it had occurred to him, as he listened to Gerard natter on about his efforts to determine where the residents of the cathedral had been when the bishop was assaulted, that there was something he'd neglected to do. One bit of evidence that could link him to Thurstan's illness.

The crock of monkshood powder.

"God knows I did not mean for him to die," Crispin whispered. He had only wanted the bishop to sicken and be removed from his post so another, more worthy man might take his place. Someone like himself, though he would have accepted another had he been godly and pure of purpose.

"It was God's will," said Brother Gerard, appearing suddenly at Crispin's side.

"What?" Crispin exclaimed, aghast he'd been overheard.

"It was God's will *that woman* and the knight drowned for killing our bishop," Brother Gerard said primly. "They were lovers before Simon of Blackstone took the cross."

"Aye. Sheriff Hamel told me he caught them together on the night before the Crusaders left for the East."

"Doubtless the knight was furious to discover that the bishop had been poaching in his territory."

Crispin nodded, his heart jumping like a rabbit making good its escape from a trap. There would be no messy investigation, no need to fear that someone would discover what he had done. All that remained was to dispose of the monkshood, write to the archbishop and pray he'd be named bishop of Durleigh. "It *was* God's will," he said.

"Most assuredly. Will you need me this evening?"

"Nay," Crispin replied, thinking of what must be done, then seeing Gerard's shocked expression, he added, "I will pray in my cell tonight. On the morrow we will take up our work."

Gerard nodded but kept pace with Crispin to the bishop's residence. Crispin began to fear the cleric meant to follow him to his rooms. But at the steps, Gerard bade him good sleep and continued across the cloisters toward the chapter house.

Crispin let go the breath he'd been holding and scurried into the palace. The entryway was draped in shadows cast by a pair of torches set in rings on the wall. Out of the gloom a figure materialized, making Crispin gasp and retreat.

"'Tis just me, Reverend Father," said a youthful voice.

"Ah, good eve to you." Nerves ajangle, Crispin nodded to the cleric serving as door porter this evening and headed into the stairwell to the right. Here, more torches cast meager light into the circular staircase. Out of habit, Crispin looked up toward the bishop's chambers. They were far too grand for a man of God, he thought as he headed down into the cellar with its storage rooms and simple cells for visiting monks.

Though he had been offered a suite of rooms in the chapter house, Crispin had preferred the damp cold of these narrow rooms. Stopping to pick up a candle from the basket on the floor, he lit it on the torch, then proceeded past locked storerooms and doorless cells to his own. The tiny room was just large enough to contain the thin pallet on which he slept and the chest that held Crispin's few possessions: parchment rolls with prayers he'd written, a coarse cloak and an old robe and, beneath it, wrapped in a length of linen, the jar of monkshood.

Crispin glanced at the chest, then back over his shoulder, regretting the lack of privacy. But the need to rid himself of this last link with the vile deed burned in his gut. Setting the candle on the floor, Crispin slowly raised the lid.

"Ah, Brother Crispin," hissed a low, sly voice.

Crispin spun on his heels, lost his balance and landed hard on the packed earthen floor. Through the stars dancing in his head, he made out a figure filling the doorway.

Walter de Folke.

"B-brother Prior," Crispin stammered, barely resisting the urge to throw himself in front of the chest. "What do you here?"

"I am sleeping in the next cell."

"But…but you have rooms above."

"Fine rooms." Walter's smile had an edge to it that grated on Crispin's raw nerves. "But I have taken a vow to renounce all such luxuries till Thurstan's murderer is caught."

Crispin scrambled to his feet, heart racing. "She…they… are dead. Drowned in the river. God's will," he blurted out.

"Indeed?" Something cold and suspicious flickered in Walter's eyes. "They may be dead, but I am not certain we have learned the whole truth of the matter. Till I have it, I will fast and live as simply as St. Benedictine. To that end, I have taken the cell next to yours, where I will spend the night in prayerful contemplation. I bid you good sleep, Brother." Walter inclined his head and slipped away.

Crispin groaned and fell to his knees. The cold of the earth was nothing to his chilled flesh. Did Walter suspect something? Or was he merely trying to thwart Crispin's advancement by solving this himself?

Either way, Walter must learn nothing.

Crispin glanced at the chest. He dared not move the monkshood now. He must bide his time, as he had for these past few months, and pray that all would work out.

Simon lay before the door on the pallet Linnet had insisted he pull from under the bed. The thin layer of straw did little to mask the floor's hardness nor did the accompanying blanket ward off the chill that had crept into the room as the fire died down. He had not slept much, either, but discomfort and sleeplessness had become old companions while he was on Crusade.

What was different was the longing in his gut.

The sounds of her even breathing, the rustle of straw as she turned in her sleep had teased him all night. Knowing she would have welcomed him if he'd crawled into her bed had sharpened his desire.

Honor was a vastly overrated commodity, Simon decided as dawn sent pale fingers sliding in through the thin hide that covered the window. But he could no more change that about himself than he could change the blood in his veins.

Did he want to?

The question had haunted him all night, but the ghosts were different from the ones that had plagued him after he'd learned Thurstan de Lyndhurst was his father.

His father.

Simon shifted. He had avoided even thinking those words, but meeting Linnet and listening to the folk of Durleigh had changed his perception. Nothing, of course, could ease the pain of having been ignored all his life, but now he wondered why a man who championed orphans had abandoned his own son.

Bah. Simon sat up, wincing as his stiff muscles protested. Nothing could change what Thurstan had done. There was no excuse for abandoning your own child, he thought, slowly rotating his shoulders until the ache in them, at least, eased. The emptiness in his heart was something that would never go away.

Casting aside the blankets, Simon stood and glanced at the bed. Linnet was turned toward him, her hands tucked under her chin, her face vulnerable to the pale light. It was that vulnerability, as much as frustrated desire, that had kept him awake and tossing all night. If he did not find out who had killed Thurstan, the murder might be pinned on her. Gut tight with dread, he eased open the door and crept down the stairs.

Drusa was already up and stirring a pot of porridge in a black pot slung over the fire. "How is she?"

"Sleeping."

Her eyes searched his with piercing intensity. What she found there must have reassured her because she smiled. "Ye're a good man, Simon of Blackstone. Come break yer fast."

Simon settled for a hunk of cheese and bread. He took them with him as he slipped into the crisp morning. He waited until Miles barred the door before setting off. All the way through town, he hoped the brigand would jump out from some alleyway and give him a chance to repay his treachery with cold steel.

Alas, he reached the Red Tower Gate without incident. The guard at the gate gave him directions to Old Nelda's hut. It was a surprisingly sturdy structure of wood and wattle huddled in the lee of the town walls. The old woman sat before the hut on a three-legged stool, stirring a cooking pot in the dawn gloom. She did not look up at Simon's approach, but when he was a few feet away, said, "I heard ye were dead, Simon of Blackstone."

"Indeed?" Simon crossed his arms over his chest. "Good news travels quickly, I see."

"Good?" She glanced up. "Who would rejoice at yer passing?"

"Bishop Thurstan's murderer."

Her expression didn't change. "Is that why ye've come, with fire in yer eyes, to accuse Nelda of killing the bishop?"

"Or Olf."

She snorted. "Ye think my lad killed his lordship for forcing me to live here?" She waved a stained hand at the hut and the rocky bank that spilled down to the edge of the river. Though the water ran swiftly, it stank of the filth it carried away from Durleigh.

"You had it better when you lived inside the town."

"Not much, and it cost me, too. Here I live free."

Simon glanced at the closed door of the hut. "Is Olf within? He has not been seen since the bishop died."

"What if he is?"

"I have a few questions I would ask him."

"He knows nothing."

"I'm told he worked late in the gardens. It is possible he saw or heard something that night."

"I would doubt it." Nelda looked out over the river. "Olf's mind is slow. A curse laid upon him for my sins. Isn't much he knows, but Thurstan taught him to care for those roses." She turned troubled eyes on Simon. "What'll happen to them and him?"

"Hard to say until they name a new bishop."

"If Archdeacon Crispin has his way, the roses will be pulled up by their roots. That one has a mean soul."

Simon smiled. "On that we agree."

"Is he trying to say my Olf killed the bishop? I thought he was keen to hang Mistress Linnet for it."

Simon's throat tightened. "He is keen to settle the matter quickly so he can boast of his prowess to the archbishop."

"Hmm. Crispin Norville as bishop?" She shook her greasy gray head. "That don't bode well for Durleigh. Say what ye will about Thurstan, he did right by the town."

"I expected you would hate him."

Nelda shrugged. "He did what he thought was right. Can't say I agree with his decision, but there was folks who wanted me hanged over the matter. Himself stopped them." She grinned, revealing broken teeth. "Hard to hate a man for that."

"But you speak ill of him."

"'Tis expected. If I praised him, there'd be folk who'd say Old Nelda got off too easy and seek to punish me or Olf."

Simon looked past her to the hut, catching what he'd missed at first glance. The wood was weathered gray, but the wattle was uncracked and the door new. "He paid for this, didn't he?"

Her smile broadened. "Ye're quick, there's not many who'd guess he'd help sinful Nelda."

"Why would he?" Simon asked bluntly. "What you were doing went against all the tenets of the church."

"Thurstan and I wanted the same thing—to help any lasses who found themselves in the family way with no husband." She shrugged. "We just went about it different, that's all."

It was Simon's turn to look into the impersonal swirls of the river. "At least your way left no innocent bastard babes to pay for the sins of their parents."

"Ye cannot forgive Thurstan, even now?" she asked.

Simon whipped his head back around. "What do you mean?"

"Nelda knows much, but she also knows how to mind her tongue." She smiled smugly. "Ye'd be surprised what secrets Nelda keeps. Even fine ladies come here for potions they cannot buy from *decent* apothecaries like yer pretty Linnet.''

"She is not mine," Simon grumbled, upset by the notion that Nelda knew he was Thurstan's son.

"So ye say, but Nelda knows different." She gave the pot a stir and changed subjects. "Ye must have gone straight to the bishop when ye reached town."

"Aye." Remorse churned in his gut. He'd have done things differently if he had known it would be the last time he'd see Thurstan alive.

"Angry words were spoken, I'd reckon. Ye are a hard, unbending man, Simon of Blackstone."

"What he did was inexcusable."

"Would ye have been happier raised in the shadow of the man many feared and some hated?" She sighed. "Better to cast yer own shadow, I'm thinking."

"I would have survived."

"Likely. Ye are strong and stalwart, but a parent cannot always know how a babe will turn out, and so must guard it as best she can." She tilted her head, expression crafty. "Odd how history do oft repeat itself, ain't it?"

Simon straightened. "Does he have other bastards?"

"None I know of." Her eyes were shifty, filled with secrets and secret amusement. "But don't they teach us that no one is without sin, even good folk such as yerself? Interesting thing, sin. Folks will go to great lengths to cover theirs up. Or to defend them…pretty them up. Thurstan knew that well, ye ken?"

"What did he know?"

"A great many secrets." She cackled. "He had a gift for using what he knew to bend folk to his will."

Like the men Thurstan had sent on Crusade as a penance for their sins, he thought. "Manipulating people is not a gift."

"A talent, then. Ye've got it, too." She laughed when he

tried to deny it. ''All leaders have a *gift* for getting other folk to do their will. It's the use they put that *gift* to that separates the good ones from the evil. And ye can bet Nelda has seen plenty of evil in her day.''

Simon nodded, hesitated but a moment, then told her about the monkshood in the brandy. ''Olf used that in the gardens.''

Her mouth tightened. ''Are ye accusing my lad?''

''Whoever did this was clever and calculating.'' Olf was neither. ''He also had access to Thurstan's rooms.''

''Crispin is all those things.''

''We can hardly accuse him of murder without proof. I was hoping Olf might remember having seen someone around his shed.''

''We can ask.'' She cocked her head again like an inquisitive sparrow. ''Ye said the archdeacon was set on accusing Mistress Linnet. Are ye championing her cause again?''

''Again?''

''I saw ye help her get away from Hamel Roxby the night before the Crusaders left Durleigh.''

Simon frowned, trying to see through the haze that obscured most of that night. ''It was not I. You must be mistaken.''

''It's possible. Everyone had had a bit too much ale that night. Meself included.''

''Likely,'' Simon muttered. It bothered him that he could not remember exactly what had happened. ''We stray from the matter at hand. Will you let me speak with Olf?''

Nelda called the lad, who came out blinking and rubbing the sleep from his eyes. Only a mother could love his wide face with its bulging eyes, flattened nose and slack lips. When Olf saw Simon, he gasped and retreated.

Simon extended his empty hands. ''I only wanted to talk about the roses.''

''Tell Sir Simon about the bishop's roses,'' Nelda said gently.

Olf looked at Simon. "Himself didn't come to see the roses yesterday." His brow scrunched with worry. "Do ye think he's wroth with me?"

Simon closed his eyes briefly, his heart contracted. No one had told Olf that Thurstan was dead.

"Olf, ye recall we talked about the bishop going to see God," Nelda murmured.

"Aye, but he should be back." A line of drool seeped from Olf's lips. "I stayed up for two moons. Caught me this many moles." He held up three filthy fingers.

"That is good." Simon's will quailed. "They have been harming the roses, haven't they?"

Olf nodded. "They eat the roots. Roses die. The bishop got monkshood from Mistress Linnet."

From Linnet. Dread trickled down Simon's spine, bringing with it old suspicions. Why had Linnet not told him she'd given Thurstan monkshood? "When was that?"

"Dunno."

"February, I think," Nelda said.

"Did that kill the moles?"

"For a time. Then not." Olf frowned. "They eat the grain Olf puts out, but they don't die."

Because someone had replaced the monkshood with harmless powder? "Did you tell the bishop?"

"Aye. Tolt him someone had been in my shed, too."

"Who was?"

"Dunno." He looked at his mother. "Tricksters."

Nelda sighed. "The village louts sometimes play tricks on Olf, taking his things and mocking him when he tries to get them back. Did ye recognize any of them?"

"Didn't see anybody. Things was moved. I didn't do it." His chin wobbled. "Does he stay away 'cause he's angry with me?"

"Nay." Simon put a gentle hand on Olf's shoulder. He could not bear to give him the news his mentor was gone.

"Two nights ago, did you see anyone leaving the bishop's palace?"

"Saw ye, standing in the yews."

Simon brightened. "Did you see anyone else?"

"Mistress Linnet. She came out after. In a hurry."

"How did you know it was her?"

"She walks just so…" Olf took a few short, quick steps, his hips swaying from side to side, his back straight and his head held high in a fair imitation of Linnet.

Simon laughed. "That is very good, Olf."

"Good." Olf nodded and traipsed back and forth a few more times, chuckling to himself. Then he imitated Crispin's economical stride and Brother Anselme's brisk gait. "Other lady like this…" He thrust out his chest and glided along. "Like a snake," he added.

"Who is that?" Simon asked.

Olf shrugged. "Other lady. I see her at night."

Thurstan's current mistress? "Did she visit the bishop?"

"Aye." Olf bobbed his head. "She kissed him."

Disgust warred with curiosity. Could this woman be his mother? Simon wondered. "Was she young or old?"

Olf frowned.

"Did she have gray hair?" Nelda asked.

"Nay. Black…and the lad, too. Him that's at the school. He seed the bishop, too."

Odeline and Jevan. Simon sighed. "Where does Odeline go at night?"

"Out. She wears a priest robe, but I know her walk." Olf frowned. "I have to go back. Wait for the bishop."

Simon looked at Nelda, who shook her head. She was right. What good could come of forcing the boy to face the truth? "Thank you for talking to me, Olf. I think your roses are beautiful, and I am sure the bishop does, too."

Olf beamed. "I'm hungry."

"Go down to the river and wash up, then we'll eat."

Simon kept a smile on his face until the boy had turned and tromped down to the water's edge. "On the way to Durleigh, my companions and I were set upon by brigands. We killed all save the leader, a wiry man with dark hair, a lean face and sly black eyes. He took a sword cut to the left shoulder. Have you been asked to treat such a wound?"

"Perhaps."

"Do you know where he might be staying?"

Nelda grunted and squatted over her pot. "He didn't say and I didn't ask. It's why folk come to me."

"Did Hamel bring him to you?"

She straightened. "Nay, but there was someone with him. Kept to the shadows, he did, so I never saw his face."

"It was a man, then?"

"Aye, but not near as big a one as Hamel."

"It could have been one of his men."

Nelda shrugged. "Hamel might be in league with the brigands. He has a craving for power. Thurstan curbed it while he was well."

"Could Hamel have killed Thurstan to clear the field?"

"Nay, for all his scheming, Hamel is not clever enough. But I do know where the lady Odeline goes of a night. To see Hamel."

"Hamel and Lady Odeline?" Simon exclaimed.

"Don't be fooled by her pretty face and fine manners. She's a lusty one and canny as a fox. But I'd venture to say she's just amusing herself with Hamel. The one person she cares about, excepting her pampered self, is that sly son of hers."

"How did she feel about Thurstan?"

"Grateful, I'd guess, seeing as he took them in."

Or resentful. And her rooms were just above Thurstan's.

"Oh, and the brigand's name is Rob FitzHugh," Nelda added. "He's a mean one...carries a knife in his boot top."

Simon inclined his head in appreciation. "I thought I had recognized him from Durleigh Cathedral, but—"

"Ye did, right enough. Five years back. He was one of the men who laid out the bishop's gardens. Drifted about working at this and that, I'd guess, till he turned outlaw."

"Thank you, Dame Nelda." Simon reached into his pouch and handed her a silver penny.

"Guard yer back, Simon of Blackstone. I've a feeling a few folk will be displeased to find Bishop Thurstan had a son."

A bastard. Simon's belly filled with that old, sick feeling that had tainted his youth. He shoved it away, older now, and stronger than he'd been. "They can ignore me. Just as he did."

"Ignored ye? That he did not. Aware of everything ye did." Nelda barked out a laugh. "Wealthy man like him, I'm betting he left ye something in his will." She ducked inside her hut and left him standing there, wondering.

Chapter Thirteen

The moment Simon walked in through the back door, Linnet leaped up from the stool where she had been sitting vigil for hours. "You toad!" she cried.

"Toad?" He stopped on the threshold, one brow rising.

"How dare you go off by yourself?"

"I—I thought you needed sleep—" he stammered.

"Sleep?" Ignoring the soldiers and servants lurking in the kitchen, she glared at Simon. "How could I sleep when I was worried sick that…that fiend had attacked you again?"

"I—" His gaze moved past her, doubtless hoping for rescue from the avid onlookers.

Linnet had had her fill of them, too, with their clumsy attempts to excuse Simon's absence. "Out!" she cried, whirling to point an imperious finger toward the shop door. Not waiting to watch them slink away, she spun on Simon. "Lout! You think because you are big and strong that you are invincible."

"I think no such thing," Simon said carefully.

"Aye, you do." She advanced and poked a finger into his rock-hard chest. "You worry about protecting others and give not a thought to your own safety."

"Linnet, you are being foolish. I can—"

''You are the one who is foolish, dammit. And I am so furious with you I could…could…'' Her lower lip wobbled. ''I could quash you over the head.'' She hugged him about the waist.

A chuckle rumbled through his chest, and his hand gently stroked her back. ''I am sorry you were worried, but I am fine.''

He felt fine, more than fine, the heat from his strong body seeping through the layers of clothing to drive out the chill that had lodged inside her. ''I lost you once, I could not bear—''

''Shh.'' His arms went tight around her. His breath was warm on her temple, ruffling the fine hairs and making her senses tingle with possibilities.

Soon. If I do not have him soon, I will die of longing, she thought as she melted into his embrace.

''It is the same for me,'' he whispered, making her aware that she'd spoken her deepest desire aloud.

Linnet tipped her head back and studied his face. Fire from the hearth sent shadows dancing over his features. The gloom could not hide the tenderness in his expression. His eyes were soft and dark with a yearning she understood, for it filled her, body and soul. *I love you. Even more than I did four years ago.* The words sang in her heart and hovered just behind her lips, but an inbred caution kept them prisoner.

Despite all they had been through these past few days, despite the desire that sizzled between them, Linnet feared he was not ready to accept her love. And might never be. The signs were there, in the slight stiffness of his chin, as though braced to take a punch, and in the coolness that eddied beneath the smoky passion hazing his eyes. He was not a man who trusted easily.

He wanted, but could he love? Could he love her?

Linnet lowered her gaze lest he read her thoughts. She was not deserving of his love or his trust.

A sigh rippled through Simon, and his grasp on her eased. "I could stand here all day," he whispered. "But we'd best go up to the cathedral. Loath as I am to see him, I want to be the first to let the archdeacon know we are alive."

Actually, the thought of confronting Crispin was preferable to the thought of ever telling Simon about their babe. Anything, even death, was preferable to that. Aching inside, Linnet forced herself to step free of Simon's embrace.

"Is aught wrong?" he asked softly.

Linnet shook her head, marshaled every ounce of self-will she possessed and met his gaze with one she hoped hid her tattered soul. "I am none too anxious to see him, either, and listen to more accusations."

"Stay here, then."

That put the steel back into her spine. "You'll not be leaving me behind." Whirling, she took her cloak from the peg by the door and tied it on. The flurry of leave-taking, Simon's orders to Miles and Jasper, her own instructions for Aiken, gave Linnet time to settle her nerves. By the time they stepped outside, she had herself under control.

The sun was high above the town wall, and traffic on the streets was brisk. She glanced sidelong at Simon. His eyes darted about in the shadows cast by his cowl, appraising each person they passed as though he or she might be about to attack.

"What is it?" he growled, taking his eyes off the street just long enough to rake them over her face.

"Where did you go this morn?"

"To speak with Old Nelda."

"Did you learn anything from her?" she exclaimed.

"Aye." He returned his attention to the crowd.

Linnet ground her teeth over an oath. "What?"

"Nothing of import."

Lout! Let me decide that. Linnet opened her mouth to chide him, then shut it again. She was no better. She should at least have told him they had lain together his last night in Durleigh. But she had not for fear that once begun, she would spill the whole tale and tell him they had created a life. Simon would hate her if he learned she had given up their child. He would not see she had been trying to give the babe a chance at an untainted life. He would see it as a betrayal. Another betrayal.

What was she to do? Linnet wondered, torn between the need to tell the truth and the certain knowledge that to do so would doom whatever future they might have together.

"Well, here we are," Simon muttered.

Linnet shoved her dark thoughts aside and gazed up at the gates to the cathedral grounds.

"Ready to beard Crispin in his den?" he asked.

"He will doubtless be disappointed to see us again."

"I hope so." Simon's lips quirked up, his eyes sparkling with wry good humor.

Linnet tucked her hand in the crook of his arm and grinned, feeling a sort of special magic move between them.

"Stay close by me in case there is trouble."

"I will, if you will be careful."

"I am used to looking after myself."

So strong, yet so vulnerable. "I worry because I care about you," she murmured.

His eyes widened, his features softened. "Linnet, I—"

Brother Anselme came around the corner of the bishop's palace, his face tense. "You are prompt. All is well?"

"As well as can be," Simon replied. "I went this morn to visit Nelda. I do not think either she or Olf is guilty. The boy did say that someone had been in his shed, and the monkshood had stopped killing off the vermin in the garden."

Linnet frowned, annoyed that Simon would confide in Anselme but not her. Men stuck too much together.

"Do you think someone took the poison?" the monk asked.

Simon nodded. "We must search the shed."

"To what purpose if it is gone?" Anselme asked.

"To see if the monkshood has been returned," Simon said. "If it is not there, I want to search the archdeacon's room."

"Ah," Linnet exclaimed.

Simon frowned at her. "You must say nothing of this till we have proof in hand. Is that understood?"

"I am capable of keeping a secret." *Too capable.*

Simon looked back at Anselme. "Does Crispin have rooms in the bishop's palace?"

"Aye, a small cell in the lower level."

"Where is Crispin now?"

"He and Prior Walter are in the hall composing a letter to the archbishop."

"You told Walter we were alive?" Simon asked.

"As you asked. He was most glad and vowed to say nothing. But he thought it a good idea to keep an eye on Crispin."

As they stepped into the entryway, they were met by Brother Oliver coming down the stairs. "You are alive!" He rushed to them. Tears slid down his wrinkled cheeks as he listened to their tale of being rescued by Brother John. "'Tis a miracle."

"I doubt the archdeacon will think so," Simon said wryly.

"Indeed not." Oliver wiped his cheeks. "He is in the great hall composing a missive to the archbishop crowing over his success in solving the murder. He barely hides his relief that our bishop is dead. 'Tis a sad day indeed for Durleigh."

Linnet looked at Simon, expecting his customary snort of disdain, but he merely appeared thoughtful.

"Did the bishop keep a journal?" Simon asked.

"Aye, he did. *My confessional,* he called it."

"Where is it now?"

Oliver frowned. "I do not know. He usually kept it locked

in the chest beside his bed, but when Brother Prior opened the chest, I did not see the journal within.''

"His will was there?" Anselme asked.

"Aye. 'Twill be read after Reverend Mother Catherine of Blackstone Abbey arrives. 'Tis well-known the abbey will receive a large bequest, including the manor of Blackstone Heath.''

"Poor lady," Linnet whispered, recalling how kind the abbess had been to her. "She was very close to the bishop.''

"Aye, she was," Oliver said.

"Could you bring us to the archdeacon, and then look for that journal of the bishop's?" Simon asked.

"Indeed." Oliver led them down a short corridor lit by torches. He paused before a set of double doors made of carved oak. "In here." He eased the doors open.

The great hall was a long, magnificent room, illuminated by torches set in wall brackets, the whitewashed walls enlivened by tapestries, the floor covered by mats of woven rushes. A fire crackled in the hearth at the far end. Around a table set before it were Prior Walter and the archdeacon. Crispin's plain robes contrasted mightily with the richly carved bishop's chair.

Behind the seat of power lurked Brother Gerard. He looked toward the door. His sly, ferret's eyes widened. "God save us!"

Crispin turned, then lunged to his feet, wide-eyed, mouth agape like a beached fish's.

Simon smiled. "I am sorry for the intrusion, Archdeacon. I feared you might be overset by rumors of our demise.''

"Rumors?" Crispin fell back into the chair, his face the same gray-white as the walls.

"Rumors." Simon took Linnet's hand and drew her into the room beside him. "As you can see, we are both whole and hale.''

Linnet ducked her head to hide the smile she could not

quite contain. It was almost worth a dunking in the river to
see the stern archdeacon so discomforted.

"But...but the sheriff assured me you had drowned."

"As you can see, he was mistaken," Simon said lightly
as he drew Linnet across the hall to the hearth.

She peered up through her lashes and caught the fury that
invaded Crispin's face. The hatred glittering in the dark
glance he sent her way made her belly tighten.

"How did you survive?" Crispin demanded.

"I am a strong swimmer. I managed to reach Mistress
Linnet and pull us both from the water, though it was far
downstream from where we went in." Simon paused.
"Doubtless that is what gave rise to the fear we had
drowned."

Crispin's face was so red he looked ready to explode.

"Let us give thanks for this miracle, then." Prior Walter
rose and came around the table. Speaking in Latin, he
touched first Linnet's shoulder, then Simon's. His tone was
somber, his face, hidden from the view of Crispin and Gerard, held a smug, conspiratorial grin. It vanished as he turned
back to the archdeacon. "We should hold a special mass of
thanks—"

"What we will hold is an inquiry," Crispin snapped.

"Oh, there is no need," Simon said smoothly. "I am sure
the man who jostled Mistress Linnet did not mean for her to
fall—"

"An inquiry into the bishop's death," Crispin said through
bared teeth. "She killed him, and I mean to prove it."

Linnet shivered.

Simon's hand clasped her arm a little tighter. "It could not
have been either of us. Brother Oliver spoke with the bishop
after we were seen leaving the palace."

"She was poisoning him," Crispin said. "After you left,
the bishop collapsed and died of the poison."

"She had no reason to want him dead."

An ugly smile lifted the corners of Crispin's mouth. "I think she had a good reason to kill him. She wanted to be rid of the bishop because her lover had returned from the Crusades."

"Me?" Simon exclaimed. "I assure you I have never—"

"The two of you were seen together the night before the Crusaders left Durleigh. By the sheriff," Crispin added.

Linnet felt the tremor that shook Simon and knew that if he hadn't had a strong grip on her arm she would have fled. Do not let it all come out here and now, she prayed.

The answer to her prayers came swiftly and unexpectedly.

"A word, Archdeacon," called an imperious female voice. Lady Odeline advanced in a flurry of dark, rich skirts. Midway into the room, she stopped and cried out, "Demons! Ghosts!"

"I assure you, we are quite real," Simon called.

Odeline started screaming. "Spirits! Evil spirits risen from the dead!" Her high-pitched shrieks rolled through the hall, echoing off the timbered ceiling.

"My lady!" Prior Walter hurried over, grabbed her shoulders and gave them a little shake, which stifled her cries. "Mistress Linnet and Sir Simon are not demons."

"That remains to be seen," Archdeacon Crispin muttered.

Walter supported Odeline over to the chair he had vacated and offered her his cup of wine.

"You are supposed to be dead." Odeline glared at Simon over the rim of the cup.

Linnet glanced surreptitiously at Simon. If he found the lady's behavior odd, it did not show in his face as he repeated the abbreviated tale of their rescue.

"It is a miracle, is it not?" Walter remarked.

Odeline kept her hate-filled glance on Simon. "I will have Hamel arrest you for my brother's murder," she snapped.

"This is church business, my lady," Walter said. "It will be tried before the canon court."

"I assure you, we are even more anxious than you are to learn who so foully killed Bishop Thurstan," Simon said stiffly.

Linnet thought that Crispin flinched.

"I have decided that Bishop Thurstan's funeral will take place on the morrow, at first light," Crispin said. "When he has been decently sped on his way we will conduct an inquest into—"

He was cut off by a chorus of protests.

"That is scarcely enough time to inform the townsfolk and arrange a suitable ceremony," Brother Oliver exclaimed.

"I must agree this haste is unseemly," said the prior. "The archbishop will surely want to attend."

"And Reverend Mother Catherine must be here. What if she has not arrived by then?" Linnet cried.

Crispin held up a hand for silence. "The decision is mine, and I say that if we delay further, the bishop will become—" he sniffed significantly "—offensive."

"What say you, Lady Odeline?" asked Prior Walter. "As the bishop's blood kin, your wishes should be considered."

Lady Odeline said nothing, just continued to stare at Simon through narrowed eyes.

"But—" Linnet began, only to be silenced by Simon's firm grip on her arm.

"When will you hold the funeral?" Simon asked.

"At terce, I think. Eight in the morn is not too early nor too late." Crispin turned to Gerard. "Fetch me fresh parchment. We must compose a new message for the archbishop."

Thus dismissed, Linnet left with the three men. It was not until they were in the corridor with the door firmly shut behind them that Brother Oliver spoke. "This is an outrage!" he protested.

"Calm yourself," whispered the prior.

"But how dare he bury our bishop with so little thought and no ceremony? The archbishop himself should be here."

Prior Walter nodded, his face a mask of controlled anger. "I am sure His Grace will not be pleased by this unseemly haste, but I do not even know if my message found him at York. It may be he is traveling and could not get here in any case."

"Why?" Oliver muttered. "Why is he doing this?"

Guilt, Linnet thought.

"It is not our place to question, Brother Oliver," said Anselme stiffly. "Why do you not send word to the mayor and the guilds that the funeral will be tomorrow? Let them ready delegations to attend." As Brother Oliver glumly walked away, the monk turned to Linnet. "Have a care what you say. Brother Oliver's heart is good, but he speaks before he thinks."

"As do I." Linnet sighed and looked up at Simon, drawing strength from his solid presence. "What can we do?"

"Work to prove your innocence," Simon said quietly.

Fear shivered down her spine. She had been too busy being angry at Crispin over the funeral to recall her own danger.

Anselme frowned. "He thinks to bury the evidence with Thurstan. I must finish my notes."

"Come with us first, if you will," said Simon. "I mean to search Olf's potting shed and could use a pair of eyes expert in herbs and such."

Simon of Blackstone was alive.

Long after he had left the room, Odeline continued to stare at the door, her mind in turmoil, her heart filled with rage.

Life was so unfair. They did not have the charter, and Simon was still alive. What was she going to do?

Gradually she became aware of the two clerics arguing over their next course of action. It was clear they thought Linnet Especer was the murderess but lacked proof.

"She is a spicier. She has access to these poisons," Crispin exclaimed.

"So, likely, does every other apothecary in Durleigh." Gerard shook his head. "It is not enough."

"She was his mistress," Crispin hissed.

Odeline's lip curled. Thurstan had been quick to censure her for her affairs yet he, a priest, had had a mistress.

"There is no proof of that, either, though I listened at the door whenever she came to visit," Gerard muttered. "And even if there were, we need more." His glittering eyes narrowed. "If we searched her shop, we might find something."

"Proof of what?" Odeline asked.

The two priests started and turned as though they'd forgotten she was there.

Gerard looked down his nose at her. "Brother Anselme believes the bishop was being poisoned with monkshood."

Odeline gasped. Jevan had some small knowledge of poisons learned from her mother. Had he been desperate enough to murder for the estate? She thought about the way Thurstan had looked when she returned with the priests. His body had been twisted, his face contorted in pain. "H-how?"

"Our brother infirmarer believes it was being administered in small doses over several months," said Gerard.

"Several months," Odeline repeated, somewhat reassured. Jevan would not have the skill or patience for that.

"Brother Anselme thinks—"

"That will do, Brother Gerard," Crispin snapped. "You are upsetting the lady with such talk," he added, though his own face had gone pasty white.

Far from being upset, Odeline was relieved. 'Twas not her puny shove that had killed Thurstan but the monkshood. "Mistress Linnet was fond of my brother. Why would she kill him?"

"So that she could be with Sir Simon," Crispin replied. His lip curled. "They were lovers of long standing."

"Ah." Odeline's agile mind darted through this reasoning

and found it full of holes. "So she knew Simon had not died on Crusades and was on his way home?"

Gerard nodded. "I saw Sir Simon leave the palace that night, wait for Mistress Linnet and follow after her."

That did not explain why Linnet would have slowly poisoned Thurstan. Bah, what did it matter so long as someone else was charged with her brother's murder? Odeline thought. And better still if that someone was Simon. "Might not the knight have discovered Linnet's affair with the bishop and killed him?"

"I fear not," Crispin said with a hint of regret. "Brother Oliver spoke with the bishop after the knight left. And Sir Simon had only just returned to Durleigh."

Odeline sighed. She would have to find another way to be rid of Simon. Which brought them back to the matter of Linnet. "Might the sheriff be able to find proof of her guilt?"

"This is a church matter," Crispin grumbled. "Brother Gerard will search her shop."

Men, Odeline thought, even men of God, guarded their territory as fiercely as wild dogs. "But what would the good folk of Durleigh think if they saw their priests ransacking a merchant's shop?" She let that sink in, pleased by their shocked expressions. "On the other hand, the sheriff is paid to capture and punish wrongdoers…by whatever means necessary." And it would give Hamel license to look for the charter.

"That is true," Crispin said. "But the sheriff would have to be willing to turn over his evidence to me."

"Oh, I am sure he would be," Odeline murmured.

A dozen questions gnawed at Simon as they left the bishop's residence, chief among them having nothing to do with finding Thurstan's murderer.

Had he and Linnet been together during the farewell for the Crusaders? He remembered little of the latter part of the evening, when speeches and prayers had given way to drinking and merrymaking. Sometime in the heart of the night he had awakened in a stable near the Red Tower Gate, a foul taste in his mouth, his mind still muzzy from drink. What he did recall was the dream he had had. The dream of perfect love.

What if it had not been a dream? What if he had not been alone in the stable?

Simon glanced at Linnet's profile, so pure in the soft spring light. Nay, he could not imagine her lying with a man she did not know. And yet she had admitted watching him on the practice field. Drusa said she had loved one of the Crusaders. Could it have been him? The question hovered on his tongue. Knowing it must wait until they were alone, he trailed Linnet and the priests along the path that wound through the rose garden.

"I love these gardens," Linnet said softly, wistfully.

"Aye." Putting aside his personal mystery, Simon scanned the neat beds, laid out in the form of a wheel with a round stone bench in the center and hedged at the outer edge by thick yews. The roses' sweet scent hung rich and vibrant in the warm air. "It was one of the things I missed most while I was away."

"Visitors to Durleigh claim they are the finest roses in all England," she said, looking at the garden.

Simon gave up on this personal mystery. "Can we enter the garden shed without being seen from the residence?"

Anselme nodded and led them off the path, around behind the infirmary to a small shed at the back of the grounds set along the wall. The wooden door creaked as he opened it. The scent of dirt and sweat wafted out. The inside was surprisingly tidy. Shelves held pots, thick leather gloves and tools. Larger tools hung on the walls alongside a worn tunic, likely Olf's. In one corner lay his straw pallet and a blanket ^y folded at the end.

Simon poked at a sack of seed.

"Careful with that," Anselme warned. "I helped Olf mix a bit of monkshood into that as bait for the vermin."

"The monkshood came from your shop?" Simon asked.

Linnet nodded. "I gave the bishop a small jar of ground herb. It was well-stoppered, labeled with the word *Monkshood* and a large black *X*." She turned, scanning the shelves.

Anselme joined in the search. "The crock was half-full, and I bade Olf store it high up, out of the way."

Simon upended a crate used to store tools and stood on it to search the highest shelf, but did not find the crock of monkshood.

"Someone must have taken it away," Walter said at last.

"Aye, but I think he left something behind." Simon pointed to the bit of cloth caught on the edge of the rough shelf.

"Could it be Olf's?" Walter asked, craning to see.

"This cloth is gray. That tunic by the door is russet wool, as was the garment Olf was wearing today." Simon plucked the fabric from the splinter and climbed down. While the others examined it, he explained about his visit to Old Nelda.

"Perhaps Bishop Thurstan took the monkshood away with him," Linnet said.

"My assistant and I searched his rooms thoroughly after he died," Walter said slowly. "We took three flagons containing wine and all the cups to test them for the poison. Of the crock, there was no sign."

"This bit of cloth is coarse, such as a laborer might wear," Simon said. "Or a priest."

"It is too rough for a priest," Walter commented. His own robes were of finely woven wool bleached the color of new cream.

"The lads at the cathedral school wear brown," Anselme said. "As do myself and most of the brothers. But this—" he fingered the swatch again "—is the sort of thing the archdeacon favors.'' He looked up at Simon. ''I recall Thurstan saying Crispin's robes were a near cousin to a hair shirt.''

''That is what I thought,'' Simon murmured.

''But how can we accuse the archdeacon of murder based on this?'' Walter asked, shaking his head. ''Though I find his sanctimonious nature grating, Crispin is a goodly man.''

Which was why he detested Thurstan so, because the bishop had been flexible in upholding church tenets. ''You are right,'' Simon replied. ''We must have more proof.''

''Where will you find it?'' Walter asked.

''I do not know, but find it I will.'' He had to, Simon thought, gazing at Linnet's pale face. Not only because it went against the grain to let the murderer of his sire unpunished, but because Linnet's whole life hung in the balance.

Somehow, in the span of a few short days, protecting her had become vital to him.

Chapter Fourteen

"Simon of Blackstone is alive!" Odeline shouted at Hamel.

"Alive?" he repeated.

"Aye." Teeth bared, she glared at him across the cozy first-floor chamber of his little house. She had waited all day for nightfall so she might come here and confront him.

"But they were swept downstream by the river. No one could have survived in that swift, icy water."

"Well, Simon of Blackstone did."

"Pity." Hamel rubbed at his sleepy eyes, poured two cups of wine and handed one to Odeline.

She hissed a most unladylike curse and hurled the cup to the floor. "You promised to get rid of him."

Hamel frowned and bent to mop up the stain rapidly spreading across the carpet. "I will."

A buzzing filled Odeline's head. *Idiot, did he not realize that time was of the essence?* Nay, of course he did not. She wrapped her arms around her waist and struggled for calm, trying to think how much to tell him. Not the truth, surely. If he knew that Thurstan had intended to give Blackstone Heath to Simon, it might seem Jevan had reason to kill Thurstan. The charter must be found before Catherine arrived and the will was read.

"Do not worry. I will take care of everything." Hamel approached and put his arms around her.

"Not now," she grumbled, wriggling free to pace the shabby little room.

"What would you have me do?" Hamel whined. "Much as I would like to, I can hardly arrest him for no reason and torture him till he gives over this journal."

"I must have it," she added, growing desperate. "If we do not find the charter, Jevan will be cheated of his rightful inheritance." She batted her lashes at Hamel. "I cannot think of our future till my son's is settled."

Hamel smiled. "Ah, I see now why you were so anxious to have this book...so that we may wed." He gave her a hard, wet kiss. "You are certain Simon has it? I searched his room myself and found not a single book."

And she had searched Thurstan's chambers. As the youngest in a brood of greedy, ambitious children, she had learned how to ferret out hidden treasure. The journal was not there. "Perhaps Simon has given it to another...say Linnet Espercer."

"Linnet?" His eyes narrowed. "Aye, he's spent considerable time in her company. But I have no reason to search her shop."

So, he did have a care for the little spicer. Any sympathy Odeline had had for Linnet vanished in a wave of jealousy. Hamel was hers for as long as she wanted him. "Why do you need a reason? You are the sheriff."

"I've not been confirmed in the post, and I will not be if I am seen to abuse my authority," Hamel said primly.

"The archdeacon thinks she poisoned my brother."

"Poisoned? But I thought he'd been bludgeoned over the—"

"She killed him with monkshood. Archdeacon Crispin wants the records from Linnet's shop to prove it."

Hamel blinked. "But I do not think she would—"

Odeline cursed and poked a finger in Hamel's chest. "Do you want to be confirmed as sheriff of Durleigh? If so, you had best not run afoul of Crispin, who will likely be the next bishop."

"I just do not see why she would kill Thurstan."

"Perhaps she tired of having an older lover," Odeline said harshly. "Or, perhaps she found out that Simon was alive and returning to Durleigh."

"I suppose that could be," he said grudgingly.

"We are agreed, then. Tonight your men and one that I have hired will enter the shop, take the ledger and search for the journal." And Jevan's man would kill Simon during the search.

A sound jerked Linnet from a restless sleep. She opened her eyes to total darkness. The night candle on the bedside table had gone out. She judged it was still night, for the room was as black as the inside of a pocket.

What had awakened her?

She opened her ears, straining to hear. Memories of yesterday flooded back: the confrontation with Archdeacon Crispin, the search of Olf's garden shed with its slim store of clues. Frustration clawed at her, the gut instinct that Crispin was guilty butting against reality. They simply did not have proof to accuse him. And Simon…

Simon.

Linnet shivered. She had managed to avoid being alone with Simon, except for their quick walk back to her shop, but all day she had seen the questions bubbling behind his sharp gaze. Questions about that long-ago night of the Crusaders' fete.

A moan broke the silence, scattering her thoughts.

Fear pounding in her veins, she sat up and turned toward the sound. There, on the floor before the door, lay a body.

Drusa.

Tears of gratitude welled. The old woman had bedded down on the floor to be nearby in case Linnet had need of her.

Drusa moaned again, thrashing about in her blanketed nest.

Smiling fondly, Linnet tossed back the covers and crept across the cold floor. "Drusa, I..." Linnet gasped.

It was not Drusa who lay there, but Simon, his sword on the floor beside him, the blankets in a tangle about his waist, leaving his chest bare. He had one arm thrown over his face. Below it, his jaw was dark with whiskers, his mouth drawn into a grim line. It parted on a sigh. "Linnet..." he whispered.

"I am here." She knelt beside him, the chill seeping through her thin shift, and put a hand on his arm. Hard as stone, it was, and just as cold. Poor thing, no wonder he was restless. He should not be sleeping here on the icy floor, her champion, the man who had thrice saved her life. "Simon, come with me." She took his hand and tugged gently. "Come..."

Come. The voice shimmered through Simon's dream, inviting, bewitching him, as it had so many, many times. Yet this time his lover's voice seemed so near, so real. And the hand clasping his was warm where he was cold. So cold. He reached for her, sighing as her heat enveloped him.

Blindly he searched for her mouth. She smelled of roses and tasted even sweeter, her lips parting eagerly. The groan that rumbled through him was answered by her moan of surrender as he deepened the kiss, exploring her with a hunger that grew with each touch, each sigh. The dream was different tonight, more urgent, more vivid. Tightening his embrace, he clung to her, afraid to open his eyes and find the bed empty beside him.

Never had he wanted her this fiercely, his dream lover. He swore he could feel her breasts swelling beneath her clothing, the nipples hardening against his chest as she wriggled closer. Heat shuddered through him, and with it the primitive need to conquer. He dragged her head back, his mouth skimming down her slender neck.

"Simon," she whispered. "Oh, Simon..."

Shock held him immobile. The vision never spoke. Slowly he opened his eyes. The room was not pitch-black, as it always was in his dream, but pale gray, the soft light caressing the face so close to his.

"Linnet?" he gasped.

"Aye." She framed his face with her hands and smiled. "Come to bed with me. The floor is hard and cold."

Simon blinked, his mind grappling with the pieces of a puzzle. The dream. Nelda's revelation that she had seen them together on his final night in Durleigh. Confirmed, it seemed, by Hamel Roxby. "My dream," Simon murmured.

"You were dreaming of me?" Her smile turned sweeter still.

"It is an old dream—from the night before we left. Or at least I thought it was a dream. Now, I wonder..."

She moaned softly and closed her eyes.

"They were right. We were together all those years ago."

"Oh, Simon..." She tried to move away.

Simon rolled, half trapping her beneath him, a dozen questions tangling in his mind. "Look at me."

The eyes she opened to him were drenched in tears.

"Why did you not tell me?"

"You did not remember me." She blinked, dislodging one tear to slide down her cheek. It was more moving than a flood.

He had been drunk that night. Blind, staggering drunk. But it hardly flattered either of them to admit it. "It was dark."

She nodded, looking more miserable. "And you were drunk."

He let that pass. "You were so young," he whispered. "And you knew I was leaving. Why? Why did you lie with me?"

"I was foolish."

"Nay, you were—" he shied away from one word and chose another, safer one "—taken with me."

She shivered and turned her head away.

Simon caught her chin and gently brought it back so their gazes met, locked. "I know you. You would not have given yourself to me unless you cared, Linnet."

Her lower lip trembled, then firmed. "I loved you."

Inside Simon, something colder and harder than the floor beneath them seemed to ease. All these years, when he had been alone, so alone, she had loved him. "I wish I had known."

Her eyes widened, filled with hope. "You do?"

"I would have given much to know someone cared." But Simon wondered if he would have valued her enough back then. He had been young himself and full of bitterness. And he had no experience at loving or being loved. He still did not, but she was teaching him. Little by little, she was healing the scars.

"I still care." She slid her arms around his neck and drew his head down. The softness of her lips opening to his was like a healing balm.

He basked in it, gorged on it. When he finally broke the kiss, they were both breathless. "Linnet." With one finger, he touched her cheek, the shell of her ear. "I want you."

"And I you." Her voice was shaky, her eyes skittish.

An agonizing thought intruded. "Did I hurt you then?"

"Only...only a little."

Dieu. Simon laid his forehead against hers. "I am sorry."

"It was only a little hurt, over quickly."

"Did I please you?"

"I wanted to be with you."

It was not an answer, but it told him what he needed to know. It hurt him immeasurably to hear that he, who had never been unkind to a woman in his life, had failed her. Reining in his own passions, he set himself to rectify his error. "I would make it up to you if you would let me."

"Oh, aye." She offered him her mouth again.

Simon brushed it lightly. "Not here." He stood, helped her to her feet, then swept her off them and carried her the few steps to the bed. Gently he laid her down on the tumbled sheets, evading her hands when she reached for him. "A moment. There is something I must do first."

He collected all the candles he could find, a dozen in all, lit them on the coals in the hearth, then set them about the bed, bathing it in golden light.

"What are you doing?" she asked nervously.

Simon smiled and sat down beside her. "The first time, we loved in darkness. This time we will have light. Nothing will be hidden. We will see, and remember, everything."

"Oh, Simon." Her lashes were wet, her eyes shining.

"Linnet." He undid her braids, then spread her hair on the pillow, sifting the thick strands through his fingers. "I have wanted to do this since I met you in the garden my first night back. Like golden silk, it is."

He was touching her hair, nothing more, yet imagining how it would feel to have those long, clever fingers on her skin sent a ripple of awareness through Linnet. Her body seemed to hum and vibrate.

Simon watched her eyes darken, her lips part on a sensual sigh, and a jolt of pure desire arrowed through his already heated body. The urge to tear aside her flimsy robe and bury himself in her liquid heat ripped at his control. But he had done that once already, and the deed shamed him. She deserved better, and if holding back until she got it made him ache and burn, it was no more than he deserved.

"You are so beautiful," he whispered, toeing off his boots and stretching out beside her. The way she braced, as though expecting him to jump on her, confirmed his worst fears. "Did I attack you like a starving wolf that first time?"

She smiled. "I was flattered that you wanted me so."

"Tonight, I will savor you."

"Savor? What do you mean?"

"Only good things, I promise." He grazed her cheek with the backs of his fingers, then stroked them down her neck, leaving tingling flesh in their wake. "Tell me what happened that night. How did we come to be together?"

"We were at the feast, the one Thurstan hosted in the market square for all of Durleigh."

"That much I recall. There was food and music and drink. Too much drink. The thought of leaving home for a far-off, dangerous land, perhaps never to return, makes a man reckless."

Linnet doubted he did many reckless things. "Most everyone had drunk too much, myself included. It made me weepy, thinking of you going off, so I left my parents and neighbors to walk along the river."

"A dangerous thing on such a night."

"Aye, it was. Unbeknownst to me, Hamel followed. He caught up with me near where the almshouse is now. I screamed and fought, but he was so strong." She shivered. "And then, just when my strength was giving out, you came." She smiled, remembering the way her heart had soared when he'd charged out of the darkness, sword aloft. "Like an avenging angel."

"Drunk as I was, it's a wonder I could walk."

"You knocked Hamel down, grabbed my hand and we ran."

''That was in my dream,'' Simon murmured. ''Only it was a dragon I was fleeing.''

''Hamel did roar like one,'' she said, and they both laughed.

''And then where did we go?''

''We hid in the stables.'' Linnet felt her cheeks burn.

''Tell me.'' His fingers toyed with the laces on her shift.

''You touched me.''

''Where?'' He was loosening them, one by one.

Her breathing quickened. ''My…my breasts.''

''Ah.'' He worked the laces with maddening slowness.

Anticipation coiled tighter. Four years she had lain in bed, reliving those few moments in the hayloft. Months of being tormented by memories of his touch. She sighed as the last lace was pulled free. Now. Now, she thought, trembling with need.

He stroked a finger down the valley between her breasts, his gaze reverent. ''How could I have forgotten such softness?''

''We…we did not take off our clothes.''

He raised troubled eyes to her. ''Did I do nothing right? Did I give you only pain and sorrow?''

Linnet froze, thinking of the child. Pain and sorrow aplenty. *Nay, do not think of that now.* ''The past is gone,'' she murmured. ''Let us look to the future.'' And if he gave her another babe this night, that child would be part of their future, for she knew he would not desert her.

''Was there ever a woman more forgiving?'' Simon brushed featherlight kisses over her cheeks, her eyes, her nose, watching the way she nibbled on her lip with tiny, nervous teeth. So precious, so wary. And who could blame her after the way he had apparently attacked her the first time? Though he did not recall that night in detail, he was certain he wanted her no less than he had then. More fiercely perhaps, for he knew her worth, her kindness, her unswerving loyalty. Did he have the patience to seduce her as carefully as she deserved?

He must. "I will make it up to you."

"You have. You are. To be with you like this is wonderful."

"Not yet, but it will be." Simon kissed her with infinite tenderness, soothing his tongue over her lower lip, then dipping it into the corner of her mouth. She opened to him like a flower, so fresh and sweet, tempting him to plunder.

Gentleness. She had not known he was capable of such gentleness, nor that it would set her blood to boiling. His tongue dueled with hers, parrying, then darting away, coaxing her to follow. It was a lure she could not resist. The heat building in her belly, she tunneled her hands into his thick hair, slanted her mouth across his and took and took.

Simon shuddered beneath the onslaught. He had known he could make her want him, but not that with a simple kiss she could send his passions spiraling out of control. Groaning, he tore his mouth free and stared down into her flushed face.

"Simon," she whispered, voice full of wonder. Her lashes lifted slowly, her eyes smoky with desire. "I never knew a kiss could make me feel so…so dizzy."

Had he not even kissed her properly? Simon ground his teeth over an oath. There was no going back. She had taught him that. "Everything about this time will be different." He trailed a finger down her neck, delighting in the way she shivered. "Did I touch you like this?" He slipped one finger into the vee of her bed robe and brushed the upper swell of her breast.

She shook her head, breath quickening in anticipation.

Simon bent his head and kissed the vulnerable hollow of her throat, smiling as her pulse leaped. "Did I kiss you here?" He nibbled his way across her collarbone. "Or here?" Down the valley between her breasts, he went, where her heart pounded to the same erratic rhythm as his own. The scent of roses and woman teased him. He wanted to rip aside the robe and gorge himself on the taste of her, but held himself in check. "I want to feel your skin against mine," he whispered.

"Aye." Linnet shivered as he eased her robe open, feeling vulnerable and exposed. Yet she wanted this. She craved his touch, her body tense, her breathing suspended as her tingling flesh awaited his next gentle caress. This tenderness was the last thing she had expected in one so aloof and remote.

"Beautiful," he murmured. His callused palm glided up her ribs to rest below her breast. "Did I touch you here?"

"Nay, I...oh..." She sighed as his hand closed over her breast, warm and possessive. Pleasure spiraled through her as he flexed his hand, kneading gently. Groaning his name, she arched into his caress, pleading for more. He obliged her by catching the sensitive peak in his clever fingers and tugging with such delicacy she was lost in a rush of glittering sensations.

Simon lowered his head and drank the whimpers of ecstasy that fell from her lips. When he could stand it no longer, he slid his mouth down to the small, proud swells. "Did I kiss you here?" he whispered, blowing on the berry-hard nipple.

Linnet could only groan, waiting in a fever of impatience for what she knew must be coming, but knowing and feeling were two different things. She shuddered when the velvet edge of his tongue laved one sensitized peak.

"Do you like that?" he asked in a heated whisper.

"Aye. More," she demanded, drawing his head down.

"Wanton," he teased and then proceeded to turn her inside out. He did not just kiss her, he feasted on her, nipping at her taut nipples, then drawing one into his mouth, savoring it with aching thoroughness.

Linnet cried out in delight, sinking her hands into his hair and clinging to him, her anchor in a spinning world. "Do not leave me," she said when he raised his head.

"Never, never again." He transferred his attentions to her other breast, sucking with a satisfying greed that sent little licks of fire cascading through her. "So beautiful. So responsive," he murmured against her heated flesh. His hands moved down, stroking over the curve of her hip to her belly, leaving a trail of fire in their wake.

Deep inside her, the coil tightened, arrowing down to the hidden cleft between her thighs. She shifted her legs, seeking to ease the ache, but it grew and grew until she feared she would fly apart.

The feel of Linnet twisting in his arms fueled Simon's desire as dry wood did a firestorm. He wanted her with a fierceness that made a mockery of his much valued coolness and control. But he wanted this moment to last, wanted to bring her to such heights it would wipe out that first disastrous time. "Shh, love. Easy, let me pleasure you."

"Hurry, hurry," she demanded, pleaded.

Simon smiled, beguiled by his imperious, impetuous darling. "Nay, I will not hurry. Not this time." He stroked a hand down the center of her body, relishing the way she quivered with anticipation. "I want you to take all I have to give."

Linnet moaned softly as his fingers tangled in the nest of curls that guarded her innermost secrets. Instinctively she parted her thighs and was rewarded by his touch, there, where she needed it most. She arched up, body straining to the rhythm set by those long fingers. The core tightened, then splintered in a rush of pleasure so sweet and sharp it sent her flying.

Listening to her sob his name, watching her eyes darken with haze, Simon felt a satisfaction unlike any he'd experienced. Oh, his body was aroused to the point of pain, but his soul was sated on her joy. For her sake, and his own, he kissed her hungrily and took her up again, relishing the way her nails bit into his shoulders as her body convulsed a second time.

"Simon," Linnet whispered, stunned by the depth of her response to him.

"Aye." His eyes were dark, glittering with sensual triumph. And there, behind the banked flames was the love he concealed, even from himself.

It warmed her nonetheless and gave her courage. One day, he would admit what he felt. Until then...she opened her arms to him. "Come to me, love," she whispered. "I have tasted pleasure such as I never knew existed, but inside I am empty."

"Not yet, you need—"

"You, to fill me...complete me."

Groaning, Simon ripped aside the hose he still wore, giving her a heart-stopping glimpse of the rampant passion he had held carefully in check. For her sake. Then he was stretched out beside her again, pulling her close, matching the cradle of her hips to the power of his. "I will try to be gentle, but I want you more than I thought it was possible to want anyone."

"Then come to me." Emboldened by the needs shimmering in his eyes, she reached down to touch him, glorying in the way he shuddered when she traced the length of him, steel sheathed in velvet. "I need you. Now."

"And I, you." The words came out a groan as he levered himself over her, parting her thighs with hands that shook. He filled her in one smooth, erotic plunge.

Linnet gasped, shocked by the size and power of him. But there was no pain, no feeling of being invaded, only a deep and abiding sense of rightness.

"Are you all right?" He hovered over her, his hair a wild tangle, his features fierce in the candlelight. He would not be an easy man to love, this complex, soul-weary knight who had captured her heart so long ago. But love him she did.

"More than all right. Welcome home, Simon." She twined her arms around his neck and canted her hips, opening herself to him, drawing him in until they were as close as two people can be.

"Home." Aye, joining with her was like coming home. Her body enveloped his like a silken glove, hot and tight, as though she would never let him go. Deep inside him, the cold, hard kernel of pain he had carried with him forever seemed to ease. "Let me show you how much you mean to me." Cradling her hips in his hands, he took her on a journey as old as time, but with her it became a voyage of renewal.

Linnet clung to him, drowning in the sensations they evoked in each other, the give and take. His increasingly urgent strokes made the fire inside her burn hotter and hotter, until suddenly the molten core shattered. Crying his name, she took him with her, out of the darkness and into the light.

Chapter Fifteen

Sometime later, a moment, an hour, he was not certain, Simon's mind cleared enough for him to think of something besides the passion that had burned him to a cinder. Linnet was tucked close to his side, her head pillowed on his chest, her breath stirring the hair over his heart. He could lay here forever, contentment spiraling through him like warm honey.

Making love with Linnet had surpassed his dream on every level, he mused. Her warmth, her openness, her capacity for giving both humbled and moved him. Being with her was like awakening after a long, deep sleep.

He needed her. In ways that went far, far beyond the desire that sparked between them. He would not, could not, call it love. Passion, caring, respect, all those he felt for her and more. But love…? Instinctively he shied away from the word. Love was for fools who believed the nonsense spouted by troubadours. The feelings that welled inside him were concern, nothing more.

Simon's arm tightened fractionally around her. How small and vulnerable she was, he thought, his fear growing. What if Crispin somehow found a way to frame her for murder?

He lay there, battling the urge to crush her to him, to somehow absorb her into himself and keep her safe.

In the distance, the cathedral bells tolled for matins. Just past three in the morning. The heart of the night, really. Yet he guessed that the archdeacon would be up and on his way to say the first mass of the day. Then prepare to officiate at Thurstan's funeral.

Which meant his room would be vacant, his secrets vulnerable to any who came searching.

Simon eased free of Linnet's embrace and out of the bed, reluctant to leave her, yet prodded by duty. He stood a moment beside it, drinking in her beauty, her serene face framed by the honey-colored hair that tumbled across the pillow they'd shared. When she woke and found him gone, she'd doubtless worry again, but this was something he must see to alone.

She whimpered and burrowed into the hollow he had vacated, as though searching for him even in sleep. As he tucked the blankets under her chin, his hand lingered on her hair, his heart so full it beat painfully against his ribs. What would it be like to have the right to share this bed with her each night? Such permanence was not something he'd ever thought he wanted. Now he yearned for it.

Dieu, he was a sorry case, mooning when there was work to be done. Quickly, silently, he slipped back into the hose, tunic and boots he had ripped off in an ardent fury hours ago. With the skill of long practice, Simon stole from the room and down the stairs. Everyone was yet asleep, the house dark except for the night candle burning on the kitchen table. By its faint light he made out Miles on a pallet before the door.

"Miles?"

It was heartening to see the soldier pop up, instantly alert, sword in hand. "Oh, 'tis ye, my lord."

"Aye. Thought I'd take a turn in the garden." No need to say it was the cathedral gardens he intended to visit. "Keep an eye on things here till I return."

Simon waited outside the back door until he heard the bar

drop into place, then he moved along the rear of the building, keeping to the shadows. The streets were deserted, the buildings shut up and dark. He reached the cathedral walls without incident and moved around to the backside where they met the town walls. From beneath his cloak he took the slim scaling rope. At the first try, the hook at one end of it caught on the top of the wall. In moments, he was up and over.

Across the grassy courtyard, he saw a line of dark-clad figures converge on the massive doors of the cathedral. The priests and students arriving for their devotions.

Simon hung back until the last of them had filed inside and the great doors had clanged shut behind them. Then he moved, keeping to a half crouch as he trotted across the open field to the palace. He had planned to go in through the kitchen door, but the scent of fresh bread in the crisp air warned him the cook staff was up and working. Instead, he went to one of the rear windows. Taking a knife from his belt, he slipped it between the two halves of the wooden shutters and flipped open the metal clasp that held them. In a twinkle, he was over the sill and inside the great hall.

Tension sizzled down his spine as he scanned the room and found it empty, lit only by a dim glow from the banked embers in the hearth. It was enough to guide him safely around the furniture to the door. The hall beyond was black as pitch. Which suited his purpose exactly. Down the corridor and across the entryway he went in a soundless rush, making for the square of light that marked the stairwell. He ducked into it, cursing the torches that flickered at every bend in the stairs.

He paused only long enough to make certain there was no one about, then moved down toward the cellars. This foray was no different from dozens of others he had made when the Crusaders had been invading the city of Damietta. But then he'd had comrades to guard his back. What he would not have given for Hugh's strong arm or Guy's sharp ears.

Or even the help of feckless Nicholas. Damn the man for choosing this particular time to go wandering off with a woman!

The sound of Simon's breathing was harsh in the narrow space, but his feet made scarcely a whisper as he glided down the worn steps. Taking the torch from the wall, he moved slowly along a narrow corridor. Off of it opened a number of storerooms and rough chambers barely large enough to hold a pallet and stool. Cells for visiting clerics, by the look. All appeared to be uninhabited except the last one.

Crispin's, he guessed, though the room looked as spartan as the others. A gray robe hung from a nail at the foot of the pallet, and a small chest had been positioned near the stool. On it sat a candle and writing implements.

Simon glanced about, then entered, wishing for a door to close while he searched. A quick examination of the robe showed a small rent in the sleeve. Scarcely daring to hope they might match the ones found in Olf's shed, he pulled off a few threads and stuck them into the pouch at his belt. He patted down the straw-filled pallet, but did not find the missing crock of monkshood. It took only moments to search the rest of the room.

The chest was locked, but opened to the tip of his knife. Inside were a few bits of thick winter clothing and scrolls of parchment, some blank, most covered with a neat, cramped script. All were written in Latin.

Simon sighed and wished he had not been such a poor student. Linnet could read and write the language, he knew from watching her in the shop, but he could hardly steal all these on the slim hope that there was some scrap of information. As he moved to replace the other papers, the light caught on something white in the bottom of the chest.

Simon leaned closer, his fingers hovering over a small mound of powder too white to be dust.

Monkshood?

Anselme and Linnet had both warned that the poison could be absorbed through the skin. He seized a scrap of parchment, fashioned a packet and, using another bit of paper, gathered up some of the powder. Gingerly, he folded the makeshift pack into a tight square and put it into the scrip on his belt.

The muffled tolling of the bell drove Simon to his feet. Quickly he put everything back where he'd found it, closed the chest and stole to the door. Senses alert, nerves tingling with equal parts apprehension and cautious triumph, he retraced his steps and exited the palace. Hiding in the yews at the corner of the building, he watched the priests, novices and students stream from the cathedral. Some had obviously stayed inside, likely to pray at Thurstan's bier. But he recognized Crispin's brisk stride and gray robes.

"Murderer," Simon growled under his breath. The hatred that coiled tight in his gut caught him by surprise because it felt...personal. Thurstan de Lyndhurst might have ignored him while he lived, but he had given Simon life, and there was a part of him that mourned the loss of the sire he had not known.

Through narrowed eyes, Simon tracked the archdeacon's swaying gray robe across the dark expanse of lawn. How easy it would be to slip up behind the prelate and extract revenge. His hand tightened on the hasp of the knife at his belt. He started to withdraw it from the scabbard, then shoved it back in again. Killing Crispin would avenge Thurstan and save Linnet from harm, but it was not his way.

A few yards from the palace, the archdeacon turned and took the path that led into the rose gardens.

"What the...?" Simon crouched down, scuttled across the lawn and hunkered down behind the yew hedge framing the gardens. Instincts on alert, he parted the prickly bush and watched.

Crispin marched to the center of the garden, stopped and

looked about. His demeanor, his actions, fairly screamed intrigue, and when he bent to dig in the dirt, Simon was certain he knew what Crispin was about. Burying the monkshood.

Elation roared through Simon. *Dieu,* he wished Prior Walter or Brother Anselme were with him to witness this.

Crispin stood, looked about, then moved briskly down the garden path toward the bishop's palace. The moment Crispin was out of sight, Simon hurried to the center of the garden and knelt. Despite the darkness, he saw a patch of earth that was rough, recently disturbed. Probing with the tip of his blade, he struck something solid a few inches down.

Simon rocked back on his heels, mind whirling. Tempted as he was to dig it might be better to secure a witness first.

Linnet awoke in slow stages, like a swimmer emerging from warm water, feeling boneless and content. As she stretched, her hand strayed across the bed and encountered empty space.

"Simon?" She sat up, more hurt than she could say when a brief glance about the room revealed he had not only left the bed but her room as well.

He went to spare your reputation, chided her mind.

He could have kissed me ere he left, her heart replied.

Likely he had not wanted to wake her. Consideration was sometimes overrated, she thought frowning as she lay back down. It was early yet, judging by the darkness beyond her window. She should sleep, for the day promised to be a trying one.

But thoughts of what lay ahead—Thurstan's funeral and a confrontation with Archdeacon Crispin—made sleep impossible.

Sighing, she pushed back the covers and reached for her bed robe. The wee sensual ache in private places made her sigh again, with longing this time. She had not guessed that Simon's resolute—and sometimes fierce—exterior hid such tenderness, such a capacity for giving. His care of her gave Linnet faith they would have a future together. And children. She wanted them, needed them, to heal the empty place in her heart.

The candle by the bed was nearly gutting in its wax. She lit a fresh one and crossed to her writing table. To one side were tally sticks waiting to be notched with the sums of customers' purchases. Lists of the exotic spices she needed in London were jumbled in with notes on those herbs she planned to plant in her garden next year. Quills in need of sharpening were piled helter-skelter beside a pot of ink.

Scowling, she set down the candle and began to restore order. With all that had happened, she was behind in her accounts. As she moved the scrolls into a tidy pile, she came across a small black book.

Thurstan's prayer book.

Linnet sat, eyes filling with tears as her fingers trailed over the precious volume. Reverently, she opened to the first page and saw the book had been a gift from his sister, Catherine, long before she became abbess of Blackstone Abbey.

May you find a measure of peace, if not the happiness that was stolen from you, Catherine had written.

The inside of the front cover was buckled, as though the sheet of parchment that covered the edges of the book's leather covering had come loose and been poorly repaired. Perhaps she could restore it, she mused, turning pages, scanning the familiar Latin of Thurstan's favorite prayers. But when she opened to the fourth page, she stopped and stared.

Here was no ancient prayer, but a listing set out in four columns. Frowning, she bent closer and translated from the Latin: dates and names, many of them folk from Durleigh. Next to the names were brief notes, some no more than a word or two. They were dark, powerful words, representing all the classic sins: theft, usury, avarice and adultery. The final column listed the penances Thurstan had levied on the sinners, from sums of money donated to the church to small acts of charity.

Trembling, Linnet sat back. She had found Thurstan's journal. Why had he kept a record of the sins confessed to him? What would happen if it fell into the wrong hands? And then an even more terrible thought struck her. Frantically she thumbed through the pages until she came to that day when she had confessed her deepest secret to Thurstan.

Linnet Especer, unwed and carrying the child of Simon of Blackstone, she read. *She will go to Blackstone and bear—*

Linnet tore her gaze from the page before she could read the words that exposed the terrible price she'd paid. How could Thurstan have written it all down for anyone to read? Sweet Mary, what was she to do with it?

Hide it. Burn it. But what if the journal contained some clue to Thurstan's murder? Tentatively she reached out to turn the pages—

"Hello inside," called a voice from outside the shop.

Linnet shoved the book aside and hurried to the window that faced the front. It was still dark, but there, in the shadows by the front door a shape moved. She could not see who it was, but heard one of Simon's men call out a question from inside.

The would-be customer's reply was muffled, except for one word. Sickness.

Instantly Linnet turned from the window, grabbed the candle and headed for the stairs. She reached the entryway just as Jasper informed the customer that he'd have to come back.

"Wait," Linnet commanded. "It may be serious."

Jasper's face was a mask of wariness in the flickering light. "Simon said no one was to come in whilst he was gone."

"He's gone?" Linnet felt cold and weak.

"Aye. Out the back some time ago," muttered Miles, joining them in the corridor, his blade out.

Linnet looked from their fierce expressions to the door,

torn between caution and duty. "A customer came by earlier to get a tonic for her sick babe. I said she should come back if the child did not improve. Let me see if this is her husband."

Jasper scowled at Miles, then shrugged. "See who it is."

"Is that you, Master Carpenter? Is the babe worse?"

"Aye," came the gruff reply. "She's taken bad."

"Oh, dear." Immediately Linnet's thoughts flew to cures for the colic. Obviously the asparagus buds boiled in broth were not strong enough. A decoction of lavender to drink and garden rue boiled in oil to rub on the belly. "Let Master Carpenter in, please, whilst I get what is needful."

Linnet entered the shop to find Drusa and Aiken huddled together, eyes wide with fright. "It is all right. Just Master Carpenter come to get some medicines for—"

A cry from the entryway cut her off, followed by sounds of a scuffle. "'Ware, Mistress Linnet!" Jasper shouted. "Brigands." His warning was drowned out by hoarse grunts and clashing steel.

Drusa screamed and collapsed onto a bench.

"Quick, out the back!" Aiken exclaimed.

Linnet took one step in that direction, then reconsidered. "Nay, there may be more of them waiting to take us."

"Where, then?" Aiken cried.

"I do not—"

Four men catapulted out of the hallway and into the shop. They were big and brawny, their expression fierce, their swords red with blood.

Linnet froze, heart racing like a trapped doe's. In that instant, she realized it was the brigand, Rob FitzHugh.

"Where's Simon of Blackstone?" Rob demanded, raking the room with malicious intent.

Drusa screamed again and toppled to the floor, breaking the deadly tableau. Aiken seized an iron poker from the hearth and whipped it up like a sword. The attack lasted only a second, for Rob backhanded the boy into the wall. Aiken's head hit with a crack. He slid down into a lifeless heap.

"Nay!" Linnet started toward her stricken apprentice, only to be caught fast and shoved against the same wall.

"Where's Blackstone?" Rob's breath was hot and rank.

"O-out," Linnet stammered. "But he'll be back in—"

"Give me yer shop ledger and any other books ye've got."

Linnet gaped at him. Rape or money she could understand, but why would he want books? "My ledger?"

"The book where ye record what's sold to who. Hurry up! Hand it over!" He punctuated the words with vicious shakes, bouncing her head off the wall.

Black stars danced before Linnet's eyes. "P-please, I..."

"Is it worth yer life?" The edge of his sword pressed against her throat.

"N-nay." Linnet swallowed. "The...the ledger is in my workroom. My...my other books and papers are above stairs." She gestured limply with her left hand.

"The ledger first." He lowered the blade and grabbed hold of her shoulder, his filthy fingers biting into her flesh.

Linnet stumbled across the room, her legs so weak she feared they would not hold her. At the door he stopped her. It was dark within, but she knew every inch of her small domain.

"Bring a light," Rob called over his shoulder.

Linnet stood there, shivering in his grasp. Her heart was galloping fit to burst from her body. Survival was uppermost in her mind. But in the few moments it took for the other brigand to find a torch and light it, a new fear intruded. Once he had the ledger, would he leave, or kill them?

The queasy knot in Linnet's belly rose into her throat. It went against her grain to simply give up, but what could she do? She had no weapon, nothing except her herbs and spices.

"Here," growled a coarse voice. Light bloomed behind her.

He released his grip on her shoulder to take the torch. "Get the ledger, and no tricks, mind." He shoved her ahead of him into the wee room where she mixed her potions. Light swung over neat shelves of crockery, bunches of dried herbs and vessels filled with everything from goose grease to rose-water.

Perhaps she could bash him over the head with a crock, she thought on a bubble of hysterical laughter. The ledger lay open in the center of the worktable, between a heap of fresh nettles and the pot she'd intended to boil them in.

"Is this it?"

Linnet nodded, her head jerking like a puppet's.

He seized the ledger and examined it with the glazed look of one who cannot read. "This better be what he wants." Rob growled. He thrust the ledger at his cohort. "Take this, Ranulf, and mind it doesn't get dirty."

Ranulf grunted in assent and hurried away.

"Upstairs...we'll get yer books," Rob ordered.

"Why?" Linnet squeaked. "They are of little val—"

"Sheriff wants 'em."

If Linnet had been cold before, now she was frozen. Escape was her first, her only, thought. But how?

"Come on. Ain't got all night." Rob snagged her right arm in his punishing grip and jerked her toward the door.

Instinct had Linnet grabbing the first thing that came to hand. The nettles. She had wrapped the stems in a bit of linen to protect her skin. Now she hid the bundle in the folds of her bed robe and stumbled along beside her captor.

Out in the shop, Ranulf was gone, but the other two thugs were pawing through her baskets and chests, doubtless looking for money. Drusa lay on the floor, moaning softly, her eyelids fluttering. Aiken lolled against the wall, head cocked to one side, blood trickling from his mouth.

Linnet stopped. "Let me see to my apprentice."

"Nay. We'll go up and get the other books." Rob shouted for the others to leave their pillaging.

Linnet's hand tightened on the nettles. Now? Or later? Desperate and so afraid her teeth were chattering, she weighed her chances as Rob dragged her toward the stairs.

Simon stepped out from the kitchen, his sword out, his expression so hard and ruthless she scarcely recognized him. "Let her go, FitzHugh," he growled.

Rob swore, dragged Linnet in front of him and brought up his blade. "Drop yer sword, or I'll run her through."

"Easy." Simon's eyes flicked to hers. The anguish in them mirrored his inner struggle, his determination to save her overriding the instinct to fight.

Linnet watched in horror as Simon lowered his weapon. "Nay!" She brought the nettles up and raked the side of Rob's face with the stinging plant. When he screamed and loosened his hold on her, she jerked free.

"Run, Linnet!" Simon shouted, bringing his sword up. He had only a fraction of a second to applaud her courageous move and no time to see if she had fled to safety. The clash of steel on steel drowned out Rob's curse as he met Simon's blade. The blow numbed Simon's arm to the shoulder. Gritting his teeth, he shook off the pain even as the other two thugs rushed into the fray. Together, the trio backed Simon across the room, blades flashing silver in the torchlight.

Rob's face was a mask of fury in the flickering light, his eyes smug. "Not so sure of yerself now, are ye?"

"We'll see." Marshaling his strength, Simon parried and thrust, catching the man on the left across the ribs. The wretch screamed and went down, but the respite was short-lived. Rob and his cohort took up the battle in earnest. What the brigands lacked in skill they made up for in numbers. It would be a miracle if he survived, Simon thought. Out of the corner of his eye, he saw Linnet and his fear doubled. "Flee!" he cried.

She did not, his brave, impetuous darling. She darted forward and stuffed the nettles down the other man's tunic. Her victim dropped his sword, screaming and clawing at his back.

The momentary distraction was all Simon needed. He slipped his blade under Rob's guard and drove it home. Rob's eyes rounded in surprise. He stared down at the blood on his chest, then slowly slid to the floor.

Simon felt for a pulse, but Rob was gone, taking with him the answers to Simon's questions. "Damn." Simon looked up to check on the others. Linnet had roused Drusa. Between them, they were tending to Aiken. Miles stood over the body of the nettle-ridden brigand. Blood dripped from the soldier's arm, but his gaze met Simon's steadily. "Jasper?" Simon asked.

"Knocked around a bit, but like to live." Miles toed the thief. "This one's alive."

Simon crossed to them and knelt. It was the beggar who'd sat outside the shop. "Call the watch." As Miles stalked away, Simon shook the brigand. "Who sent you here? Was it Hamel?"

The man grunted, his body twisting in pain.

"What did he want?" Simon pressed.

"My ledger," Linnet whispered from beside Simon.

"And...and the bishop's charter." The man looked at Simon. "The one you stole from the...the bishop the night he died."

"I took nothing of him," Simon growled.

"Hamel said...it was...hers."

Simon frowned. "Linnet's?"

"Nay, Hamel's mistress." He gasped hoarsely. His eyes widened then fluttered shut, and his head lolled to one side.

"Damn," Simon whispered. "I needed him alive."

Linnet crossed herself. "Do you think he meant Tilly?"

"Odeline, I'd guess. Nelda said she was Hamel's mistress."

"Odeline and Hamel?" Linnet gaped at him.

"An unlikely pair." Simon rocked back on his heels and looked over at Rob FitzHugh. "It makes me wonder what was in this charter and why Odeline was so eager to have it."

Linnet gasped softly. "Anselme's theory that there might have been two murderers."

"And her chambers are just above Thurstan's."

"She would have had access to the brandy," Linnet added, her eyes bright with hope.

"I do not think she was responsible for that." Keeping his voice low, Simon told her what he'd found in Crispin's trunk. "I did not dig it up myself lest it be said I'd fabricated the story. Prior Walter said he'd see to it as soon as he could."

"Oh, Simon…" Tears of relief and gratitude glistened in her eyes. "Thank you for all you've done to aid me."

"It is not over yet," he cautioned. "Our proof is by no means ironclad." He prayed it was enough to frighten Crispin into making a confession.

"What of this business with the charter?"

Simon raked a hand through his hair. "I do not know. We have only the word of this scum that it even exists." He shuddered, still trembling from the shock of finding Linnet in mortal danger. "*Dieu,* if I had not returned when I did…"

"You came in time." She smiled cheekily. "You always do."

Simon grunted, but she could see the guilt in his eyes.

Little did he know that her guilt outweighed any he could amass. She thought about the journal upstairs on her table— as potentially dangerous as Pandora's box—and wondered what she was going to do with it.

Someone had been searching his things.

Crispin knew it the moment he opened his chest, for the scrolls on top were not precisely as he'd left them.

"Curse you, Walter de Folke," Crispin muttered as he burrowed through his clothes to the bottom of the chest. There, gleaming ominously in the candlelight, lay a tiny pile of monkshood that had spilled from the crock. He had meant to steal Olf's garden gloves and clean it up. Now it was too late.

Air hissing between his teeth, Crispin sat back. *Walter knew. Walter knew.* The words rang over and over in his brain like the tolling of a bell. What would Walter do?

Tell the archbishop.

Crispin groaned, seeing a lifetime of devotion to God and good shattered because of the prior's snooping. Nay, he could not lose all now. If he cleaned the chest, it would be his word against Walter's. He could make it seem the prior defamed him in hopes of advancing himself. But what of the crock?

What if Walter had followed him to the garden? Nearly gagging on his fear, Crispin dashed from his cell. Once outside, he checked his headlong flight. It was still dark, but the brothers were up and busy preparing for the funeral. Haste would attract undo attention.

Feigning a calm that mocked his panic, Crispin forced himself to stroll into the garden. A few interminable minutes brought him to the crock's resting place. It appeared undisturbed. Under cover of examining the roses, he unearthed the crock with the edge of his sandal, bent and retrieved it. Tucking it into the sleeve of his robe, he retraced his steps. When he reached the deep shadows around the palace, he looked over his shoulder and spied Walter entering the garden from the other side.

Crispin watched as Walter approached the spot where the crock had been and bent to dig. *It was God's will that I arrived first,* Crispin thought. Just as surely it was God's will that Walter be kept from reporting his suspicions to the archbishop.

Chapter Sixteen

Durleigh Cathedral was a stone monument to the power Bishop Thurstan had amassed on earth, Simon thought as the funeral commenced. The giant columns of the nave and choir speared skyward to the soaring vaults high above, giving the impression of uncompromising strength and authority. Torches on the walls, candles at the altar, cast subdued light over the somber gathering while the air ripened with incense and the sound of heartfelt weeping.

In the choir, the canons chanted while Archdeacon Crispin and Prior Walter mounted the high altar. Below them, the townsfolk in their feast day best packed the nave like herring in a barrel, sitting cheek by jowl with farmers from the outlying crofts and mailed knights from the castle.

Outside, rain beat a mournful tattoo against the rare window of painted glass bought with Thurstan's bridge tolls. *It was as though heaven, too, cried at his passing,* said more than one red-eyed parishioner.

Simon was only concerned with the feelings of one.

Linnet knelt beside him, her body shaking inside a modest gown of cream-colored wool covered by a sleeveless tunic of rich dark-green. Her hair had been drawn back in a single braid, coiled atop her head and covered by a veil that fell to her shoulders. The fabric was so fine he could see through it to the tears on her cheeks.

A few days ago, her outpouring of grief for the man who had sired him would have angered Simon. Now, though his own reaction was tempered by all they had *not* shared as father and son, Simon's heart was heavy. It had struck him as the monks carried Thurstan's silk-draped coffin into the cathedral that he would never have a chance to ask all the questions that ate at him. He would never learn whether lust or love had caused Thurstan to cast aside his priestly vows. Never know why he had failed to acknowledge Simon, or who his mother was or if she yet lived.

"Repent your sins!" Crispin's voice rang off the stone. He had been ranting on in much the same vein for some time. Though he did not vilify the bishop, he took the occasion to deliver a diatribe on sin in all its guises. He waxed especially virulent on the subject of man's greatest weakness: women. And when he spoke, his searing, almost maniacal gaze fell on Linnet.

Instinctively, Simon moved closer to her, a wealth of emotion welling from deep inside him. She was his, and he would protect her with his last breath. Last night she had opened herself to him, body and soul. Their joining had linked them. Forever. He felt it to the marrow of his bones, to the depths of his being. He did not know what the future might hold, but he would not let Crispin or anyone harm this precious woman.

Simon glared at the archdeacon, letting all he felt burn in his eyes. *Hypocrite. Murdering hypocrite.* Hatred rose to drown his sorrow. *I know you killed Thurstan, and I'll see you pay!*

Crispin stumbled over his words, flushed and looked away, his voice a little less steady as he rambled on.

Satisfied, Simon sought out Prior Walter and Brother Anselme in the crowd. But they were consumed by their prayers for Thurstan and did not look his way. Still, he had to believe that they had succeeded in getting the crock and establishing that it contained monkshood. This afternoon, when Crispin held his inquest, they'd confront him, accuse him of murder.

Walter had been less confident. "Even if he had the monkshood, it is not proof positive he poisoned Thurstan."

"And there is the matter of who struck the bishop over the head and doused him with the belladonna," Anselme had added.

"Crispin could not have done it," said Walter. "He and I were in the hall together at the time the foul deed was done."

Thanks in part to Rob, Simon had an idea who might have been responsible for that second attack. But he had even less proof against Odeline than he had against Crispin. He could hardly accuse Thurstan's sister of murder based on a thief's tale about a missing charter. Perhaps if he could search her rooms he might find some reference to the charter. Or, if he was very lucky, the vial of belladonna. But he was being closely watched. When he and Linnet left the apothecary, Bardolf and another thug had followed them all the way to the cathedral.

Damn, if ever there was a time when he needed the help of his comrades, it was now. He could not fault Guy for having dashed off after Lord Edmund, but Nicholas…

Under his breath, Simon cursed Nick's lack of restraint. Barely a week back in England and the charming rogue had returned to his lustful ways. Doubtless he was too caught up in savoring his latest paramour to consider that Simon might need his help or be worried about his absence.

Simon stopped a moment, wondering if *he* should be concerned. While Nick had often spoken about the wild philandering that had enraged his sire, Simon had not known him to be gone for so long. *Dieu*, it had been four days. Simon's gut knotted. When the mass was over, he'd ask Warin about sending someone to look for Nicholas.

"Amen," the crowd chorused as they surged gratefully to their feet. Many grimaced, stretching stiff muscles and rubbing at benumbed knees as they tottered from the cathedral.

"What now?" Simon asked, taking Linnet's arm and guarding her from the press of people.

"There will be food and drink at the Guildhall and in the market square," she replied in a wooden whisper.

Simon nodded, sensing she was as loath to go as he. Though it was the custom to drink to the departed, his concern was for the living. Specifically with protecting Linnet. "I think we should return to your shop and talk about what has happened."

"You mean the stolen ledger?" she asked anxiously.

He had meant to discuss all he'd learned from Old Nelda and his discovery of the monkshood in Crispin's chest. Between seeing to her wounded servants and preparing to attend the funeral, there had been little time. "Have you thought of some reason why the thieves would take it?"

"N-nay," she said quickly. Too quickly.

Simon stared into her pale face, troubled by her lack of curiosity over the incident. Though they had been together only a few short days, he knew she was as tenacious as a fox when it came to solving a riddle, yet she had seemed not to care why it had been taken. Or perhaps she knew why.

Had she lied to him about that?

Simon's hackles rose. There was nothing he hated more, and to think that Linnet, whom he had come to trust, could lie to him burned like acid in his gut. But now was not the time or place to press her. "We must plan what we will say to Crispin."

She stopped in the aisle, shut her eyes. When she opened them again, the fear had become panic. "Will he question us?"

"He will."

"I see." She glanced at Thurstan's bier. The priests,

monks and clerical students had surrounded it to say a final prayer before he was interred in the vault below. "Archdeacon Crispin has already made up his mind I am guilty."

"It does not matter, for he has no proof against you."

One of the men around the coffin lifted his head. It was Jevan le Coyte, his stare nearly as piercing as Crispin's had been. He looked not at Linnet but at Simon. The boy caught Simon looking back, but instead of lowering his gaze, he curled his lip. His face filled with such malevolence it sent a chill down Simon's spine.

Life had forced Simon to inure himself to what others thought about him, but Jevan's hatred went beyond anything he'd felt before. Curious that a youth who had only met him once should so despise him. Unless...

What if Jevan knew Simon was Thurstan's son? What if Nelda was right and Thurstan had bequeathed something to Simon? Something that was mentioned in this charter. Where the hell was the charter? Odeline did not have it. And it must not be in Thurstan's chamber, for she'd have searched there before asking Hamel's men to look for it at Linnet's shop.

"When a man is as determined as the archdeacon, he may be willing to bend the truth to accomplish his ends," Linnet said.

Simon jerked his gaze back to Linnet. He would have to deal with the charter and Jevan later. Linnet's safety took priority. "Do not fret. Prior Walter and Brother Anselme will stand firm in your defense. And I will not let any harm come to you, that I vow." He put his arm around her waist and led her into the open.

The storm had passed while Crispin vented his fury, and now the sun peered through the scattering clouds.

"How fresh everything smells and looks," Linnet murmured as they walked toward the gate. "If only the rain could wash away all our problems and give us a fresh beginning."

The poignancy in her tone struck him even more forcefully than her words.

"I think we have already made a new beginning," he said softly, thinking of last night.

She smiled for the first time that day, and it was almost as miraculous as the sun's reappearance. "I, too." But beneath the smile there was vulnerability.

Simon slipped his arm around her waist. "It occurs to me that Drusa and her patients will be waiting for us at the shop." Still shaky from the attack, the maid had offered to stay and tend to the injured men. "I still have my room at the inn. Let us go there. We can talk in private of—"

"Talk?" Her brow arched, her smile deepened.

For the first time in many a year, Simon felt his face heat. "Talk," he said firmly.

"I would like that," she murmured.

An hour alone with Simon.

Linnet clung to that like a lost soul spotting the light at the end of a dark tunnel. He had been her anchor all during the long, hideous funeral. When Archdeacon Crispin's hate-filled rampage had chilled her to the bone, she had leaned on Simon, drawing strength from his solid, muscular body, letting its heat seep in to warm her icy flesh as surely as his loving had restored the hope in her heart.

"Here we are," Simon muttered.

Linnet looked up, surprised to realize she had no memory of having walked through Durleigh to the inn. It was closed and shuttered. Elinore, Warin and the staff were most likely at the wake.

Simon stepped to the side door, rattled the latch and cursed. "I should have realized it would be locked."

Linnet reached into the scrip at her belt and produced a key. "Elinore entrusted me with this after Papa died in case I had need of her." She felt tense, slipping into the dark, quiet inn and up the stairs. Even the warmth of Simon's hand riding protectively on her waist as he followed did not ease the knots in her muscles. Like strands in a rope, they coiled and tightened. Partly it was weariness, the strain of the past few days, the uncertainty of the next few hours. Partly it was dread over the questions he was bound to ask. She had seen his skepticism when she'd claimed not to know why Hamel would want the ledger. Should she lie to him, or trust him with her suspicions about Thurstan?

Simon stopped halfway down the gloomy corridor. "Wait here a moment," he whispered. His feet made scarcely any noise as he moved to the next door. One hand on his sword, he unlocked the oak door, pushed it open and stepped inside. He was gone only a moment, yet it seemed an eternity until he reappeared and motioned for her to join him.

"You thought someone might be in here?" The possibility of another assault terrified her.

"I've learned a man cannot be too careful." In his eyes flickered the ghosts of dozens of dangerous events. Battles and sorties that had shaped him into the sort of man who watched out for himself and for those he'd taken under his wing.

Linnet went to him, wrapped her arms around his lean waist and buried her face in his chest.

He started. "Linnet…we have much we need to talk—"

"I need this," she murmured, touched by the way his heart leaped beneath her ear. He needed this, too, a moment's respite before they took up the struggle again.

"We must talk. There are things you are keeping from me."

The babe, was her first thought. Her soul contracted painfully. She could not tell him about the child. It was over and done. The babe had a happy home, free from all taint. Even if she could somehow make him understand why she had given the child up, there were other dangers. Years ago she had admired Simon from afar, not knowing what sort of person he was beyond the courteousness and honor with which he comported himself. Now she knew how drastically his bastardy had scarred him. If he knew he had a daughter, he might try to claim her.

Pain twisted deep inside Linnet, like ripping open a wound that had never healed. She could still remember the stormy night when her labors had brought forth a daughter. The agony of childbirth was nothing to the soul-rending anguish of giving up the life that had dwelt beneath her heart for nine months. The child created of her love for Simon. That she'd believed him dead had made the decision all the harder, for the wee babe was all she'd ever have of Simon.

Putting the child's welfare, her future, above her own wants was the hardest thing Linnet had ever done. Until now... Keeping that life a secret from Simon nearly drove her mad. But she would do anything, even endanger her own soul, to safeguard the only gift she had given her daughter. Legitimacy.

"I would know about the ledger," Simon muttered.

The ledger. She nearly wept with relief. "In a moment." She wriggled closer, needing his warmth and support.

"Linnet, we've no time for this." But his body had other ideas. It quickened, hard and insistent against her belly.

She felt an answering heat kindle deep inside her. It ran like fire through her veins, making her breasts tingle, her womanhood weep with longing. Their time together seemed so short, measured out in precious drops. If something happened this afternoon and Crispin prevailed, these few hours might be all they had left. "Simon, please..." She ran her hands up his chest, glorying in the moan that rumbled through him.

"Linnet. You are overwrought. You need—"

"You. I need you." She wrapped her arms around his neck and tugged his head down for a blistering kiss. Like a flame set to dry tinder, the magic flared between them. Mouths fused together, they tore at each other's clothes. Naked, they tumbled onto the narrow cot.

His breathing was harsh in the silent chamber. His eyes glittered with a hunger that bordered on the violent, but his hands were gentle as he swept them up her rib cage and filled the palms with her breasts. "And I need you, Linnet." He lowered his head and suckled her nipples until she was blind and deaf to everything except the passion he roused in her.

"Now," she whispered, head tossing on the pillow, hands reaching for him.

"Aye." He rose above her, his body tense with an urgency that mirrored her own desperation. A shuddering gasp escaped him as he slowly entered her. It was echoed by her own cry of pleasure as she lifted her hips to meet his.

The feel of his rigid heat filling her, completing her, shattered the last of Linnet's restraint. Wrapping her legs around his lean waist, she gave herself over to the greedy desperation that splintered through her.

"Linnet," Simon groaned, momentarily surprised by her wild abandon. Gallantly, he set himself to fulfill her needs, matching his sure, deep strokes to the powerful hunger he felt building inside her, inside him. How naturally they fit together, how perfectly matched they were, he thought. He gazed down at her flushed face and found her looking up at him. Her eyes, dark with passion, reflected back his own dazed features.

"I love you," she cried, body tensed, poised on the brink of the high precipice.

Simon felt something stir in his heart, but before he could grasp hold of it, the storm broke. Her body tightened around his, demanding surrender. Gladly he followed her, groaning her name as he poured himself into her, body and soul.

"Hmm," Linnet purred, cradled close against him as they drifted down from the heights.

"Aye." He rolled them onto their sides. His hands stroked down her back, tender, gentle, soothing without words.

She was reminded of the way he had touched her last night, sometimes patient, sometimes with fiery haste but always with the respect due spun glass. Would he treat her so if he knew how she had betrayed him? Linnet shivered. Even if they managed to outwit Crispin, how could she live with her secrets?

"What is it?" Simon asked, eyes still hazy with passion.

"Nothing." *Everything*. She wanted to weep.

He must have sensed it. His brows slammed together. "I knew that was not what you needed."

"But it was." She dredged up a smile. "This—you—are the only good thing that has happened in the past few days."

He grunted, but his frown eased. "I think there is some wine hereabouts. It will restore you."

Nothing short of a miracle could do that. She wanted to cling when he gently disengaged himself, but didn't.

"We have little time and much to do." He stood and padded across the room, supremely unconcerned with his nudity. Down on his haunches, he went to root through a pile of clothing, muscles cording and flexing beneath sun-kissed skin.

Dieu, he was magnificent. Linnet lifted herself up on one elbow, tucking the blanket over her breasts, and admired the view. It was thrilling and a little humbling to think that such a beautiful man desired her.

He looked up and caught her gaze. "What makes you smile?"

You do, she mused, taking in the sensual curve of the lips that had kissed her senseless. Even more remarkable was the intelligence glinting in his gray-green eyes. He was the man who had won her bruised heart in only a few short days. But his own heart was even more deeply scarred and more closely guarded.

He had not replied to her declaration of love. If the stark terror in his eyes was anything to go by, it would be a long time before he admitted he loved her. If ever.

"This room. It is surprisingly untidy for a man as precise and controlled as you, Simon Blackstone. It pleases me to see you are not perfect after all."

"This chaos is not my doing," he grumbled as he crossed to her. "My room has been searched."

"By Hamel?"

"Likely."

"Is anything missing?"

"I had little of value here." He shook the fall of black hair from his face, sat on the bed and handed her a wineskin.

Linnet frowned. "Is there a cup?" When he shook his head she sighed, pulled the stopper from the wineskin and peered into the narrow opening.

"Wait!" Simon's thumb flew over the end just in time to prevent the wine from gushing out. "You'll spill it."

"I've never drunk from a skin before."

"Let me help." He encircled her with one massive arm and held the skin up to her mouth. "Tip your head back and open."

Linnet sprang her jaws as wide as a hungry trout's.

Simon chuckled. "Close up some, or we'll have this on you instead of in you." When she complied, he put the nozzle to her lips and squirted a bit of liquid inside.

"Argh." Linnet started, swallowed and choked on the flood of red wine. It was strong, exploding like fire in her belly.

Grinning, he tipped his head back, squirted some into his own mouth and drank a goodly quantity. Without spilling a drop.

"Pleased with yourself, are you not?" she grumbled.

"Aye." Light kindled in his eyes. "And with you."

Linnet felt a blush creep up into her cheeks.

"Are you ashamed of what we did?" he asked, low and tight.

"Nay," she said quickly, truthfully. "I am new to this, and you are so...so beautiful." Her gesture took in his body, magnificently naked in the sunlit chamber.

"You are the beautiful one." He bent to kiss her shoulder and whisper in her ear, "I would like to keep you here, naked in my bed, till you no longer felt shy, but I fear we've much to do." All business now, he restoppered the wineskin and set it aside, then sorted out their scattered clothing.

Loath as she was to discuss the ledger, she'd feel less vulnerable clothed. She was touched by the way he turned aside while she struggled into her shift and under-tunic, rounding only when she asked for help with the laces.

"You are keeping something from me," Simon said without preamble as he tied the last lace.

Linnet jerked, barely resisting the urge to wrench away, to hide her face from his knowing gaze. "I think Hamel wanted my ledger because it shows that I gave Thurstan the monkshood."

"What?" Simon's eyes fairly bugged out.

Linnet flinched. "There is no need to shout at me."

"No need!" he exclaimed, face red.

"I did not poison him, if that's what you are thinking," she said in a small voice.

"Of course I do not think that. Damn..." He shoved both hands into his hair, the struggle for calm twisting his mouth into a thin line. "But how could you not have told me this?"

"I..." Linnet wrapped her arms about her shivering body.

"Easy. Come sit." He led her to the only chair and leaned his hip on the corner of the nearby table. "I did not mean to frighten you, but—" he exhaled sharply "—how could you have kept something this dangerous from me?"

"I was afraid," she whispered, then seeing his brows raise

in alarm, added, "Not that I'd be accused, but that some would think Thurstan had poisoned himself."

"Poison himself?" Simon echoed incredulously.

Linnet nodded and explained how upset Thurstan had been when news came that Simon and the others were dead. "He seemed to lose all interest in life. It was only a few days ago that it occurred to me Thurstan was possibly being poisoned. I was reading some papers on healing and came across great-grandfather's notes on a poisoning case he had been called in to solve. The symptoms sounded so similar to Thurstan's that I feared he was not just ill. 'Twas then I recalled the monkshood Thurstan had bought from me and became concerned he was killing himself. That is why I went there that fateful night—to confront him and beg him to give up the mad notion."

"What did he say to that?"

"I never got the chance to speak about that. He was so overset, he would not answer my questions."

"Why was he upset?"

"Now I know it was because you had returned." She cast her mind back, trying to recall details lost in the subsequent shocks of Simon's reappearance and Thurstan's death. "But he was anxious about something, too. He spoke about everything having changed. There was something he had to see to. Something he had to change." Her eyes widened. "Could it have been the charter?" She seized his arm, voice breathless. "Suppose he had left you some property, then you died, so he deeded it to someone else."

"To Blackstone Abbey along with the rest of his estate?"

Linnet bristled. "Abbess Catherine would not harm him."

"You know her well?"

"Of course, I lived there when—" Linnet broke off, remembering why she'd gone to stay at Blackstone.

"What of Odeline? Would he have bequeathed coin or manor house to her?"

"It is possible. Thurstan had little respect for her and her son Jevan, but he did pity them."

Simon nodded slowly, grinding his teeth. "If we could find the charter, we might prove they had reason to wish him dead." Frustration built inside him, roiling with the anger and the fear. Fear that for all his strength, training and prowess in battle, he would not be able to save Linnet from being framed for Thurstan's murder.

"Let us leave Durleigh," he said suddenly, urgently.

"Leave?" Hope flickered in her eyes, then dulled. "Even were this not my home, I could not run away."

A pox on honor, he thought. "We'd best get ready then." Mentally he girded himself for the most important struggle of his life. "I promise, I will not let them harm you."

She smiled at him as though she believed he could do that.

He only wished he knew how.

"I have Linnet's shop record," Hamel whispered, coming up beside Odeline.

"Excellent." Odeline checked her step, then slowed until they were at the end of the line of mourners snaking toward the Guildhall. "And the charter?" she murmured.

"Nay, there was not time."

Odeline gritted her teeth. "Why?"

Hamel raked his greasy hair back. "Simon returned. He killed Ellis and the man you had hired."

"So they did not search," she grumbled.

"Jesu, Ranulf was lucky to come away with the ledger."

Idiot! Odeline's fingers curled until the nails bit into her palms. Striking out at Hamel would accomplish nothing and paint her as a violent woman. "It is something, I suppose."

Hamel exhaled sharply. "I still do not believe Linnet would kill the bishop."

Nor did she, but it was imperative that a culprit be found.

"The archdeacon is certain she did," Odeline said absently. "Simon must have the charter on his person."

"Well, the only way I'd get it is if he's dead."

"Precisely." Odeline glanced at him through her lashes.

"He is a hard man to kill," Hamel grumbled. "And I cannot just walk up to him and plunge a blade into his heart."

"Nay, but he is fond of Linnet. When she is found guilty of murder, he will most certainly try to protect her." Odeline smiled faintly. "He is a warrior, after all, a man of violence. If you can goad him into a fight, it will give you an excuse to eliminate him."

"Aye." Hamel grinned, obviously pleased with the notion. "I'd best him in a battle."

"I am sure you would," Odeline soothed. He outweighed Simon by several stone, and she did not doubt that a man such as Hamel knew tricks that a Crusader knight might quail from using. Still an incentive would not hurt. "Get the charter for me, Hamel, and I will wed you."

"Odeline." Hamel's muddy brown eyes glittered. For an instant she feared he might kiss her, here on the busy street.

"Go on ahead, Hamel, I must speak with Jevan." Another difficult male to be coerced into line. But her son would not be so easily fobbed off. It was he who had insisted that Rob help Hamel's men search for the charter. Now Rob was dead, and they were no closer to finding the charter. Jevan would be furious. Of late, he had been impossible to reason with, his moods swinging sharply between petulance and violence. There were times when he'd get that odd look in his eyes and she'd wonder…

Nay! She jerked her mind back before it could even start down that path. Jevan was still her special, loving boy. He was frustrated, that was all. Thurstan could have given the estate to Jevan outright...no strings attached. It was Thurstan's fault Jevan was behaving so oddly.

She clung to that as she walked to the Guildhall and Thurstan's wake.

Chapter Seventeen

"Nelda knew you and I had been together the night of the Crusaders' fete?" Linnet whispered. Simon had finished telling her all he'd learned from the herb woman and they were preparing to leave for the cathedral.

"She claimed to be privy to that and a great many other secrets," Simon replied as he belted on his sword.

Linnet stared at him, aghast. What else did Nelda know? Linnet thought back to the terrible day when she had confessed to her mother that she was pregnant. Her mama had been saddened but not surprised, for she claimed Linnet had "the look" about her. Had Nelda noticed it, too? She was, after all, a skilled midwife, trained to see such signs as glowing skin and thickening waistlines. What if she said something?

"Come, we'd best be leaving."

Linnet forced herself to take the hand Simon held out. "Do you think Nelda will be at the canon court?"

"I do not see why. Crispin has little use for her."

"But if she is and if she says she saw us, shall we lie about being together that night?"

"Certainly not," he said gruffly. "Lies always make matters worse. Do not forget that I rescued you from Hamel. If he remembers it, we will be exposed as liars. To some, it might seem a short step from that lie to one about Thurstan's murder.''

"I suppose." Heart in turmoil, Linnet followed him down the stairs. This morn, before leaving for the funeral, she had considered destroying Thurstan's journal lest her secret, and countless others, fell into the wrong hands. But Thurstan had given her the book and asked her—nay, begged her—to keep it safe. Why had he entrusted her with such a burden?

The sound of the door opening below stopped Simon midway down the stairs. "Shh," he cautioned.

"I wish someone other than Crispin had conducted the funeral mass. Bishop Thurstan deserved a more fitting send-off than a sermon on sin," grumbled a woman.

"Aye. The archdeacon grows odder by the day."

"It is Elinore and Warin," Linnet whispered.

Simon nodded. "Let us go down, then. I must speak with Warin ere we go up to the cathedral." They traced the pair into the tavern's main room.

"Linnet...Simon, what do you here?" Warin asked, turning with a mug of ale in his hand. "I thought you'd be at the cathedral."

Linnet looked down and fought the urge to blush.

"I had something I needed to fetch," Simon replied. "Only I found that my room had been ransacked."

"'Twas not us, I assure you." Warin scowled. "And I gave no one leave to search, though Bardolf did come sniffing around."

"I'll wager it was Tilly," Elinore said. "Is aught gone?"

Simon shook his head. "Everything of value is with me." He put a hand on Linnet's waist.

Elinore smiled. "So I see. And right glad I am of it, Sir Simon. Would you like a cup of ale?"

"Just a small one." Simon drew Linnet with him to the oak-planked serving bar and accepted a crockery mug.

"Warin, do you recall the two knights who arrived the same day I did?"

"Indeed. The darker one seemed agitated and stayed only a moment before going off on an errand."

"When I returned that same evening I found a note from Sir Guy saying he'd been called away. One of your maids said the other knight had left with a woman. Do you know who that was?"

Warin scratched his chin. "Can't say I do. He sat in the corner, had a cup or two of my finest ale. Caused no trouble—"

"No trouble," Elinore scoffed. "Him with his handsome face and wicked eyes. He had my maids so aflutter I barely got a moment's work out of them while he was here."

"Do you know where he might have gone?" Simon pressed.

"Has there been trouble?" Warin asked.

"I'm just concerned that I've had no word from him. On the other hand..." Simon grinned. "Nicholas has been known to forget time when he's with a lovely lady."

Elinore smiled suddenly and turned to Warin. "Was the widow Marietta not here that very same day?"

"Could have been. I try to steer clear when she's about."

"She's got her eye on my Warin," Elinore teased.

"And every other man for miles about."

"That's true enough. Linnet. You'll remember the scandal she caused last winter when she took up with Master Baker's youngest son, and him only ten and seven."

Linnet chuckled. "Indeed. The baker gathered his friends and went out to bodily remove his son from her clutches."

"They said the top of her bed canopy was made of polished metal." Elinore waggled her brows. "Like a mirror, ye see."

Warin snorted, but his eyes danced with fascination.

"She sounds like she's cut from the same cloth as Nicholas. He swore he had reformed, but I can see he has not,'' Simon grumbled. "Does the lady live far from Durleigh?"

"Two hours' ride or so," Warin replied. "Would you like me to have someone carry a message to him?"

"Aye. Tell him that I have need of him."

Warin stiffened. "Do you expect trouble?"

"'Tis a foolish man who does not prepare just in case."

"You can count on my support," Warin said at once.

"My thanks." Simon's hand tightened on Linnet's waist. "I think I have the means to prove Linnet's innocence, but it never hurts to plan for the worst."

Her arrest. Linnet fought a shiver of foreboding.

"We've been summoned to the canon court," Warin said.

Simon started. "By whom."

"Hamel Roxby."

"Why is he doing this?" Linnet exclaimed.

"It does not matter." Simon stroked her back. "It is good we will have friends in attendance. Now we had best go."

Elinore nodded, but her troubled gaze mirrored Linnet's own fears. "Warin and I will be along in a moment."

Linnet tried to take comfort in that and in Simon's murmured reassurances, but her heart was heavy. It had begun to drizzle again, and a bank of fog had crept up from the river to eddy about the cathedral grounds. The bishop's palace seemed to rise out of the mist like an ancient dragon, staring down at her from dark, malevolent eyes. A shiver raced down her spine.

"We can still leave," Simon said softly.

It was tempting, so tempting. Linnet shook her head. "Nay, running away would solve nothing, and it would seem like an admission of guilt." She squared her shoulders.

"You are a brave woman." He kissed her brow.

"It comes of having a knight such as you by my side."

"I am sworn to protect you, my lady."

Linnet supposed it was as close to a declaration of love as Simon could come. "Let us go within, then."

Brother Gerard answered the door. "This way." Without relieving them of their wet cloaks, he bustled ahead to the great hall and threw the doors open so forcefully they banged against the wall. The sound echoed through the cavernous room like a clap of thunder, drawing every eye to the door.

Linnet stopped on the threshold, surprised to find rows of benches filling the hall. She had expected to face a sea of hostile priests, but found many townspeople, including Drusa and Aiken. Mayor Edric Woolmonger had a seat near the front row, while Nelda and Olf stood at the back, apart as always.

"I do not understand," Linnet whispered to Simon. "Why are they all here? Did you ask them to come and support me?"

Simon shook his head. "Morelike they were called from the bishop's wake to stand witness."

"Some of them look too drunk to stand," she murmured.

"Aye." Simon did not even smile at her small jest. "I am right glad to see a few friendly faces amongst *them*."

Linnet followed his gaze to the far end of the hall where the archdeacon sat behind a carved table, eyeing them as a scrawny cat might two fat mice. Stern-faced Prior Walter sat to his right and Brother Anselme hovered anxiously in the background. Seated in the front row, Odeline and Jevan wore matching hostile expressions. Hamel and Bardolf lounged against the wall to the left of the door like spiders waiting to pounce.

"Oh, dear," Linnet murmured, shaken.

"Easy," Simon murmured. "Do not let them see your fear. Remember you have friends here. We will not fail you."

Linnet nodded, his support giving her strength to survive what was to come. She was innocent. Everyone would see that. Lifting her head, she walked slowly down the aisle between the benches, grateful for Simon's hand on her elbow.

"Stand here," Gerard commanded, pointing to a spot directly before the archdeacon.

Simon glared at him. He released her long enough to seize a chair from against the wall and place it at the end of the table, so she might see both her accuser and the witnesses.

"Thank you." Linnet sat with as much dignity as her wobbly legs would allow and looked at Anselme and Walter. Both prelates regarded her with deep concern, which did not ease her fears.

"We are come here to investigate the matter of Bishop Thurstan's murder," Crispin said, loud and firm. "To the bishop's soul." He raised a heavy silver chalice toward the heavens. Prior Walter, the only other person who had been provided with a cup, lifted it in silent salute, then drank.

Crispin sipped, fastidiously wiped the wine from his lips with a linen cloth and placed it over the cup. As he turned to the assembly, his eyes passed over Linnet.

The vicious triumph glittering there hit her like a slap. Only Simon's hand, warm and firm on her shoulder, kept her from bolting. What was Crispin going to do?

"Brother Anselme has determined our beloved bishop was being poisoned. Is that not so?" Crispin demanded.

Anselme stepped from the shadows to the other end of the table, his gaze on Crispin. "Aye, someone was feeding him monkshood these past several months. The amounts were small. He did not die at once, but grew ill and weak and suffered much—"

"There is no need to subject us to the sordid details," Crispin snapped, growing paler himself. "Have a care for the tender feelings of Lady Odeline and young Jevan."

And for your own guilty conscience, Linnet thought. Nor did Odeline or Jevan look exactly grief-stricken.

"Suffice to say, he was dying by slow, painful degrees," said Brother Anselme.

A muscle ticked in Crispin's cheek. His head whipped toward Linnet, eyes hot with hatred. "I accuse you, Linnet Especer, of this heinous crime."

A shocked gasp moved through the crowd, accompanied by more than a few murmurs of denial.

Linnet stiffened. "I did no such thing. He was my friend."

"You were his lover, you mean," Crispin said.

"Lover?" The word caused a stir in the crowd.

"She was not!" exclaimed Drusa and Elinore together.

Linnet's gaze skimmed the sea of faces, some taut with ugly speculation. "Nay, I most certainly was not."

"What proof do you have to offer?" Simon demanded.

Crispin shot him a deadly glare and snapped his fingers. Gerard scurried forward to place a ledger before the archdeacon.

Her shop ledger.

Linnet's blood ran a little colder.

"It is noted here, in her own hand, that she did give Bishop Thurstan a crock of monkshood in February," said Crispin.

Simon snorted. "She would hardly have written that down for anyone to read if she had, in fact, been poisoning him. Indeed, the bishop purchased the monkshood to free his rose garden from vermin. As Olf the gardener will attest."

"Aye, he will," Nelda called out.

"Bah!" Crispin waved a dismissive hand in their direction. "Who would take the word of a witless—"

"Simple he may be," Nelda exclaimed. "But my Olf knows right from wrong. The bishop gave him the monkshood."

"I was present at the time," said Brother Anselme. "I instructed the boy in how to handle the poison."

"And did it eliminate these rodents?" Crispin asked.

"Unfortunately it did not," Anselme replied. "Because someone stole the monkshood from Olf's potting shed."

"She did it so she could kill Thurstan," Crispin snapped, his fingers white where they gripped the edge of the table.

"What need had Linnet to take it when she had a ready supply in her shop?" Simon countered.

Crispin scowled at him.

"Nay, I found the monkshood. It was not among Mistress Linnet's things," Simon said. "Was it, Prior Walter?"

This was the point Simon, Walter and Anselme had been angling for, Linnet thought, heart soaring on a bubble of hope.

The prior lurched to his feet. His face was unnaturally pale and running with sweat. He opened his mouth, but the only sound that came out was an agonized gurgle.

"Walter!" Anselme leaped to the prior, catching him just as he fell back into the chair and began to twitch.

Pandemonium erupted. Men shouting, women screaming, Anselme issuing orders that sent his assistants scrambling.

"Poison! The prior has been poisoned!" someone cried over the din. It sounded like Crispin.

"Sit still," Simon hissed in Linnet's ear. "Let Anselme and his monks deal with this." He tried to keep the panic from his voice, but it hammered violently through his body. In numbed horror he waited while Anselme rid the prior's body of all he'd ingested. A tonic was brought, forced down Walter's throat and he was carried, still thrashing and moaning softly, from the great hall. With him went Simon's best hope of saving Linnet. As Anselme made to follow the procession, Simon caught hold of his sleeve. "What did Walter find in the garden?"

"Nothing." Anselme's face was gray. "The earth had been disturbed, but there was nothing there."

Simon's heart stumbled. "Was Walter poisoned?"

"Monkshood, I'd guess," Anselme whispered.

"Will he live?" Linnet asked in an agonized whisper.

Anselme sighed. "I do not know."

"Brother Anselme, see to Brother Prior, then return to us when you can with news of him," Crispin ordered.

The monk nodded and hurried off.

Crispin had poisoned the prior. Simon knew it, but he could not understand why. Unless he hoped to pin it on Linnet.

If Crispin had been smug before, now he positively glowed with triumph. "Much as it pains me to continue in the face of our brother's collapse, we must settle this." He looked at Linnet. "I accuse you of Brother Prior's murder."

The remaining folk gasped and shouted, some repeating the archdeacon's accusation, others denying it could be true.

"She is not guilty," Simon roared. He thought about the chest with its telltale grains of poison, likely gone. Had Crispin seen Walter digging in the garden? "The person who stole the monkshood from Olf's shed left behind threads from his clothing...a robe such as yours, Archdeacon."

Crispin started. "You accuse me?"

"We could see if the fibers match," Simon said silkily.

"How does that prove I killed Prior Walter?"

"The prior is not dead...yet. Whoever wished him eliminated feared he had evidence to give."

Crispin snorted. "You would say anything to free her because she is your mistress."

"First you accuse her of being Thurstan's mistress, now mine," Simon said in a low, tight voice. "I think your mind runs in impure channels, Reverend Father."

Crispin leaped from his chair, nostrils flaring. "My mind has seized upon the truth." An ugly smile twisted his lips. "There is a witness to the fact that you two lay together years ago, on the night before the Crusaders left Durleigh." He stared at Linnet, his face a mask of hatred. "When she learned you were returning, she sought to break off her illicit affair with the bishop. When he refused to let her go, she killed him.''

"That is a lie," Linnet cried, surging to her feet.

"No one knew I had survived," Simon said.

"So you say, but events prove otherwise." Crispin looked to the assembly. "Drusa, on the night our bishop died, did your mistress enter the shop late and in the company of this knight?"

"Aye," Drusa said grudgingly. "But—"

"Describe her state to us," said Crispin.

"Well, she were a mite bedraggled because she'd fallen in the garden on her way from the inn," Drusa said defensively.

"Or mayhap she'd tumbled in the garden with Sir Simon."

Linnet's gasp of outrage and Simon's growl were cut short by Crispin's next questions.

One by one he called upon those who had seen her that night: Warin, Elinore and Aiken, twisting innocent events into seemingly suspicious ones. How could Crispin possibly know what had happened at the inn? Linnet wondered.

"She left the inn in a right hurry when she heard Sheriff Hamel was in the common room," Tilly reported from her place along the wall near Hamel.

"The sheriff had been bothering me with unwelcome advances," Linnet said primly.

"Had he?" Crispin steepled his hands. "It seems that every male in Durleigh wanted to get under your skirts."

A hushed silence fell over the hall. Her friends wore stunned, fearful expressions. Others sat on the edge of their seats, waiting for the next scandalous development.

"It seems my brother and Sir Simon were the only ones who succeeded," Lady Odeline said tartly.

One look at the lady's knowing eyes and smug mouth and dread crept down Linnet's spine. Here was the author of Crispin's accusations. But why should the lady wish her ill?

"Is it not a sin for father and son to share the same woman?" Odeline asked waspishly.

Behind Linnet, Simon groaned softly. She ached with the need to offer him comfort, but things were so precarious, she dared not make a move that might worsen their situation.

"Father and son?" Crispin blinked, then his eyes widened and he speared Simon with a look of shocked loathing. "You…you are the bishop's son?"

For a long moment, Simon said nothing, but a tremor shook the hand that clasped her arm. "He never acknowledged me."

"Alas, it is the truth," Odeline said. "A blot on our family name that haunted our father to his grave."

"Blasphemy," someone cried, and others took up the cry until the hall rang with curses heaped on Thurstan's head.

Linnet risked a glance back at Simon and found her outrage mirrored in his dark, furious expression. "She did that apurpose to turn things away from the archdeacon," she whispered.

"Aye," he replied in kind. "But why? To bare the secret casts shame on her and Jevan."

"The charter," she said under her breath. "What if Thurstan deeded property to Jevan after you were reported dead?"

"Aye." A ray of hope kindled in Simon's eyes. "I wonder when Jevan learned I had returned?" he murmured.

Linnet clutched at his hand. "If it was that first night you were back…"

"Then we may have found our murderer," he said softly. "Rob FitzHugh knew I was alive. He recognized me on the road, and he came to Durleigh. But why would he tell Jevan unless—?"

"They murdered the bishop to hide their incestuous crime!" Crispin shouted, stilling the babble of voices.

Simon lifted his head and his voice. "If you seek one with a grudge against the bishop, you need look no further than the archdeacon. It was in his clothes chest that I found traces of monkshood, and himself I did watch while he buried it in—"

"Liar! Devil's spawn!" Crispin launched himself around the end of the table, fingers curved like talons. "Seize them!"

Hamel and Bardolf came away from the wall, swords sliding from their scabbards. But Simon was quicker. In one lithe movement, he drew his sword and pointed it at the archdeacon's bony chest. "No one move, or he will pay," Simon cautioned.

"Do as he says," Crispin shrieked.

Hamel and Bardolf stopped in their tracks, but their swords still glittered menacingly in the light.

Warin scuttled through the crowd to stand at Simon's side, his long dagger out.

"Put up your weapons," Brother Gerard pleaded.

Oliver wrung his hands. "My son, this is not the way."

"It's the only way we will get a fair hearing," Simon said.

"Fair hearing?" Crispin snorted. "You have shown us all that violence is in your blood."

"As stealth and treachery are in yours," Simon replied in a low voice. "We are none of us leaving till we have the truth."

Crispin's eyes widened. "You cannot prove your—"

"And neither can you. There seems only one solution."

"Simon," Linnet said hesitantly, alarmed by his fierce expression. "What do you intend?"

"Trial by combat," Simon replied. His words set off a wave of shouts and comments. "It is our right to be judged by God," he added, quieting the crowd.

"That is so," said Brother Oliver.

"Combat?" Crispin shrieked. "I'm no warrior."

"I will serve as your champion." Hamel stepped forward, his face flushed with blood lust.

"Agreed," Simon said at once.

"You must not risk your life to save me," Linnet whispered.

"Aye, I must," he said quietly but firmly, his eyes shining with tenderness before he turned them on Crispin. "And when I am triumphant, you will surrender yourself for punishment."

"Me? But she…she did it," Crispin sputtered.

"God knows where the blame lies." Simon kept his hard, searing gaze locked on Crispin's pallid features for an instant before letting it slide to the first row.

Odeline and Jevan stood side by side, their beautiful faces suffused with identical expressions of sly triumph.

"They wanted this to happen," Linnet whispered.

"Aye, but so did I," Simon said, low and tight.

"Simon, I am afraid. You've not seen Hamel fight. He is big and strong and…and he does not fight fairly."

Simon grinned. "Hamel may outweigh me, but I did learn a few tricks from the Saracens." Raising his voice, he said, "It is agreed, then. We will let God decide the matter."

"God's will be done," Crispin said primly.

"Aye." Simon's gaze and his thoughts were on Odeline and Jevan. Dear God, how was he going to find proof against them?

"'Tis settled, then," Hamel growled into the appalled silence. "We will meet on the training fields at noon on the morrow. Meanwhile, I will lock her in the cells beneath my house." He grabbed hold of Linnet's arm.

Linnet cried out and struggled to free herself.

"Nay!" Simon cried, starting toward her.

Crispin barred his path. "You are right to be cautious, Sheriff, lest they run off in the night."

"If you let the sheriff take her, she will be tortured or worse!" Simon cried.

"I am sure Hamel would treat her with the respect she deserves," Crispin said cuttingly.

''Wretch!'' Simon hefted his sword.

''We can settle it here and now,'' Hamel taunted.

''Aye.'' Simon braced himself.

''What passes here?'' cried a high, imperious voice.

Linnet knew that dear voice well. She turned toward the door, and beheld the most welcome of sights.

Reverend Mother Catherine de Lyndhurst, Abbess of Blackstone, stood on the threshold, regal as a queen in her white robes and flowing headdress.

''Reverend Mother!'' Linnet lifted a hand to her mentor. ''Thank God you've come.''

''Linnet? What is going on here?'' The abbess started down the aisle between the benches and then stopped. Her mouth fell open and her eyes rounded. ''Simon? Simon of Blackstone?''

Simon inclined his head curtly, hackles already rising. Though short and slender, Abbess Catherine was a female replica of Bishop Thurstan, right to the tightly controlled mouth and cool gray eyes.

He disliked her on sight.

''Simon!'' The abbess bustled forward, tears trickling down her cheeks. ''This is wonderful.''

Simon grunted and looked away, ignoring the abbess's hurt expression. She had presided at his birth…and that of countless other bastards. She had sent him into the world to be raised alone, in shame, without love. Aye, and did he hate her for it! ''Some other place must be found to confine Linnet.''

''Confine? Why is she being confined?'' Catherine demanded.

Crispin, Hamel and Odeline angrily vied to retell their version of the bishop's murder. When Linnet tried to counter, they shouted her down.

Simon waited until the story ground to a halt. ''There's

not a shred of truth to it. On the morrow, Sheriff Hamel and I meet in battle. God will decide.''

"Till that time, she'll be held in my custody," said Hamel.

Linnet whimpered softly, the sound cutting into Simon.

"I do not agree," Simon growled.

Crispin snapped, "You have no say."

"It is not fitting she be housed there, amongst men," said Catherine in that clipped, authoritative voice of hers.

"She is no innocent," Hamel replied stonily.

"That is for God to decide...on the morrow," the abbess said. "She will remain here, watched over by my nuns."

Hamel, Crispin and Odeline all objected, saying that Linnet and Simon would flee if not locked up. The abbess stood firm. Short of throttling her—which Hamel looked tempted to try—there was no swaying her from her decision.

"You have no authority here," Crispin grumbled.

"Nor do you, but I understand you have buried my brother without waiting either for myself or the archbishop."

Crispin flushed. "I—"

"No excuse would be a good one in my eyes." The abbess turned her back on him, ordered the hall cleared of gawkers, summoned her nuns and began making arrangements to house them in the guest chambers.

"Thank you, Reverend Mother," Linnet murmured. "Simon and I are grateful for your intervention."

Simon grunted. Words of gratitude stuck in his throat, and he would not utter them. Even for Linnet.

Chapter Eighteen

"Simon hates me," murmured Catherine de Lyndhurst. "I know it must have come as a shock to learn he is Thurstan's son, but his bitterness is unexpected. And hurtful."

Linnet sighed and joined the abbess at the window. Several hours had passed since the confrontation in the hall. The palace inhabitants had more or less settled into their rooms. Her nerves had yet to settle. Her thoughts were on Simon, housed in the bishop's rooms below. She wished she could go to him, but Hamel's men stood guard in the corridors with orders to keep her in this room until tomorrow.

The guest chamber to which Linnet had been consigned was on the upper story of the palace, affording a view of the gardens. As she looked down and weighed her words, she spied the roses Thurstan had lavished with the love he could not show his son. "If Simon is angry, it is because he felt abandoned and abused."

"Was he beaten by the couple Thurstan hired to care for him when he was young? Or by Lord Edmund of Wolfsmount?"

"Nay, he says not." Linnet struggled to put feelings into words. "But for all Simon seems aloof and independent, I think he missed being part of a family. Being loved."

"Men are such stoic creatures, we do not realize their needs are not so different from our own." Catherine glanced at Linnet and smiled. "He is most protective of you."

"Aye. We...we have grown close these past few days." A yearning rose inside Linnet, sharp, sweet and oddly painful. "I love him, Mother Catherine, and I think he cares for me. If only it were not for—for—" She choked on the words.

"For the babe?" Catherine asked softly.

Linnet nodded, tears crowding her throat and spilling down her cheeks. "I should tell him, but I cannot."

"Surely he would understand you sought to give the child a home and a life free from the taint that burdened him."

"Nay, he would not." Linnet caught back a sob. "He was angry when he learned Thurstan had sent Hana Billeter to you."

The abbess smiled softly. "I do not think Hana will be with us for long. Young Alain sent word he will come for her as soon as he can sit in a saddle." She glanced at Linnet. "Simon would have come for you, too, had he not been away on Crusade."

"Simon did not remember our...our time together."

"Thurstan would have set things to rights."

This Linnet could not dispute. "I wonder if Thurstan placed the babe nearby, as he did Simon, so he could watch over it."

"My dear." Catherine laid a hand on her arm.

"It—it is just that I have wondered where she is and how she fares." Tears prickled. Linnet fought them back. "I know I vowed I would never seek her out myself, but did Thurstan not at least tell you where he had placed her?"

"Nay, but he did say she would be raised by loving hands and dowered as befitted the daughter of a noble house."

"I should tell Simon," Linnet whispered.

"I do not think that is wise."

"But how can I live with the lie between us?" Linnet asked, the agony cutting deep inside her.

Catherine sighed and stroked Linnet's hair. "In the few months you lived at the abbey, you became as dear to me as the daughter I will never have. I would see you happy, and Simon, too. If the price of that happiness is one small omission—"

"Small omission!"

"Would Simon be happier if he knew that he had a daughter who had, for the babe's good, been adopted by another?"

"Nay. He would be furious and frustrated and—"

"There you have it, then," Catherine said with her usual brisk efficiency. "He should not be told."

"But it is dishonest. Surely he has a right to know."

"It would only bring him greater anguish, and, perhaps, endanger the child. What if he sought to reclaim her?"

"Aye, that could be disastrous," Linnet said miserably. She felt as though her heart were being torn in two. She desperately wanted Simon's love, yet she did not deserve it. And on the morrow, he would risk his life to save her.

How could she let him do that?

Linnet left the window and groped her way back to the hearth. There, on the stool, lay the journal. She had requested Aiken fetch it along with a change of clothes for tomorrow.

"Why, it is Thurstan's prayer book," Catherine said.

"It is far more than that." Linnet hesitated only a moment before telling the abbess what she'd found within the pages. "I think I should burn it," Linnet added at the end.

Catherine traced a finger over the cover. "He could have destroyed it. Instead he gave it to you. For some purpose."

"What purpose?"

"I do not know. Perhaps the answer lies in the journal. Have you translated all the passages?"

"Nay, it would take days."

"Perhaps there is something here he wished passed on. A section for Simon explaining...things."

"His mother's name," Linnet said. "Do you know who she is?"

"I do, but I am bound by the same oath that prevented Thurstan from speaking of her. While he lived."

Linnet picked up the book. "I could show it to Simon, but he may not read Latin." If he did, her secret would be revealed.

"Why do you not look through it yourself? It would give your mind something to dwell on during this difficult night."

"Aye," Linnet said slowly. "I will not be able to sleep for thinking of what Simon must face on the morrow."

"He will prevail," said Catherine, catching Linnet close in a brief hug. "He will not fail you."

"I know." But was she failing him with her silence?

Restless as a caged cat, Simon paced the confines of his prison. Night was fast approaching and shadows gathered in the corners, but he had not bothered to light any candles. The darkness suited his mood. Ironic that they had shut him up in the bishop's suite of rooms.

Crispin had been outraged, but Abbess Catherine had stood firm. For all she barely topped five feet, the abbess flattened opposition faster than a rock rolling downhill. It was by her will that Linnet was safe from Hamel. For one more night. And after that...if he did not prevail...

Simon cursed and shoved the fear aside. If he let it take root, he'd not best Hamel on the morrow. Instead, he turned his energies to the coming battle. Warin had promised to bring his chain mail from the apothecary and watch over his horse to make certain it was not tampered with by Hamel's minions.

A knock on the door scattered his thoughts. "Enter," he called, hoping it was Warin with news of Nicholas.

The door opened and Brother Anselme stuck his balding head inside. "Simon, are you here?"

"Brother, you are well come." Simon rushed to light a candle as the monk stepped within. "Walter?" he asked as the door closed, shutting out the hard-faced guards.

Anselme sighed, his face grayer than his robes. "He lives, but he is still unconscious."

"Was it monkshood?" Simon fetched two cups of ale.

"Aye." Anselme collapsed into one of the chairs by the hearth, downed the ale and sighed again.

Simon took the stool at his feet. "Crispin, do you think?"

"It seems likely. Perhaps he thought Walter had evidence against him, had perhaps seen him bury the crock in the garden. That is why he dug it up again and poisoned the prior."

"Or Crispin wanted to eliminate another rival for the bishopric," Simon muttered.

"I can scarcely believe he would do such a thing. To murder two fellow brothers and attempt to blame Linnet for the crimes…" Anselme shook his head. "If not for Abbess Catherine, things could have been far worse for you and Linnet."

"Aye," Simon grumbled, not pleased to be in her debt. "Do you know if Linnet is all right? Have you seen her?"

"She is lodged above, Brother Oliver tells me, with the abbess and her flock of nuns for company. Linnet will be at ease with them, for she lived half a year at the abbey."

"I had forgotten." Something niggled at Simon's brain. "It is odd she studied with them when her mother and father were both master apothecaries."

"A healer benefits from diverse opinions."

Simon shrugged and returned to the business at hand. "I wonder what Crispin has done with the crock?"

"Do you want me to poke about?"

"Nay. I already have Walter's well-being on my conscience."

"Crispin must be mad indeed to do such a thing."

"And desperate. Be careful what you eat or drink."

"And you, also, my son," Anselme said. "But Crispin cannot have given Thurstan the belladonna."

"I think I know who did." Simon quickly outlined his theory regarding Odeline and Jevan.

"Mon Dieu." Anselme crossed himself. "First the archdeacon, now Thurstan's own kin. Is there no end to this evil?"

"The thirst for wealth and power brought out the worst in all three. I need to search Odeline's and Jevan's belongings."

"Jevan was at supper when Thurstan died."

"Are you certain? Could you question those who saw him that evening? I'll search Odeline's things."

"How will you get into—?"

A commotion at the door interrupted. "See here, ye can't be going in there," growled one of the guards.

"We've brought his battle gear," Warin replied.

Simon bounded to the door, threw it open and gaped at the disheveled figure with Warin. "Nick?" he asked hesitantly.

"Aye." Nicholas's clothes were rumpled, his hair greasy and disordered. His scowl was as dark as the stubble growing thick on his cheeks, and his usually merry eyes were bloodshot.

"You look like hell," Simon growled.

"'Tis exactly where I've been." Nicholas clumped in and dropped his swordbelt onto the nearest chair. *"Dieu,* but I need a drink, a bath and a long sleep."

"But not a woman, I'd wager," Simon snapped.

"Nay, I've sworn off them...for good." Nicholas headed for the ale flagon on the table.

"Low, the prodigal returns." Grinning, Warin entered with Simon's belongings and kicked the door shut after him.

"The least you could have done is sent word where you were so I would not worry," Simon grumbled.

"Send word! I've been a bloody prisoner. Be there still if Master Warin's man hadn't insisted on speaking with me." Nicholas upended the flagon of ale and drank greedily.

"Locked in Widow Marietta's bedchamber, he was," Warin said, eyes twinkling. "Naked as the day he was born."

"She took my clothes. Even stripped the linens and hangings off the bed to thwart escape," Nicholas huffed.

Simon smiled. "I am sure it was terrible."

"It was. She asked me to escort her home. Said the roads were dangerous, and I thought, why not? You and Guy were busy, she was…persuasive." Nicholas snarled a hand in his hair. "I got her home without incident, but she turned prickly when I tried to leave and drugged my wine. It's been a hellish few days."

"Oh, aye, it has," Simon said with feeling.

Nicholas straightened. "Curse me for going on about my paltry troubles. Warin's told me about the bishop and the mess you're in. What do you need me to do?"

"Seduce some information from my aunt," Simon said.

'Twas the heart of the night. The moon rode high in a starlight sky. The bishop's palace slept.

Linnet could not.

Her mind refused to rest. Instead it ran in tight little circles, treading over and over again upon the same problems. Beset by fears for Simon's safety, torn by guilt, she huddled under a thick blanket but could not get warm.

What if something happened to him? What if Hamel—

A scraping sound from the direction of the window scattered her morbid thoughts. Heart racing, she slowly sat up, just as the two halves of the window eased open.

Hamel!

"Go away, or I'll scream for the abbess," she hissed.

"Linnet, 'tis Simon."

"Simon." Before Linnet could free herself from the tangled bed linens, he was beside her. She whimpered his name as he swept her into an embrace so satisfyingly tight her ribs creaked. "You should not be here," she whispered, clinging for all she was worth.

"I know." His grip eased. His hands stroked down her back as he dropped kisses on her hair, her temples. "But I could not stay away for worrying about you."

"Me?" She looked up into his moonlit face. "You are the one who put himself at risk."

"It is worth it to save you."

"Oh, Simon, there is something I must tell you." Though it would surely shatter any hope of a future with him.

"I know." He cupped her cheek, his eyes shining with emotions so pure they stole her breath. "I feel the same."

"You do? But…"

"I—I love you." He blinked, then smiled ruefully. "I never thought to say that to anyone, but you have somehow managed to steal into my heart and heal the—"

Linnet burst into tears.

"Linnet, my sweet Linn." Simon gathered her close, moved by the tremors that shook her slender body. "Shh. It will be all right. I will be victorious tomorrow, and we can be together."

She cried harder.

Poor mite, he thought as he cradled her in his arms. She has been through so much, had met so many obstacles with wit and bravery. But she was done in. "When this is settled, we will go away for a time. Just the two of us. To London, mayhap. Or to visit one of my fellow knights."

She sobbed even louder.

Simon despaired. He had little experience with women, especially crying women. Nick, on the other hand… "That reminds me," he whispered. "Nicholas has returned."

Chuckling softly, he told her what had befallen his roguish comrade-in-arms.

Linnet sniffed and raised tear-drenched eyes to his. "You sent him to seduce Odeline?"

"Well…" Simon smiled ruefully, glad the foolish subject had stemmed her tears. "Nick refused to seduce her—he claims to have renounced women. But he has gone to search her room."

"What of the guards in the hallway?"

"He's gone up the wall with a scaling rope and in through her window…same as I came here to you. Nicholas is adroit at getting in and out of ladies' bedchambers unseen. He will be fine. Besides, Brother Anselme learned Odeline has gone into town…to visit a sick friend."

"To plot with Hamel, morelike," Linnet muttered. "You must be on your guard for trickery."

"'Twill be easier now, with Nick here to watch my back."

Linnet nodded but did not relax. "Even if you find the belladonna, it will not prove them guilty."

"Nay, for that we need the charter."

"Abbess Catherine said that Thurstan had deeded an estate to you. Blackstone Heath, to be exact."

"Blackstone Heath!" Simon spat the name like a curse. "I do not want it." He left the bed to pace. "I was raised there, by the caretaker and his wife. 'Tis a bleak and cheerless place."

Together we could make it a home, she thought. But she had no right to dream such impossible dreams. "If we are correct, it would seem Jevan and Odeline do not share your low opinion."

"It is a large manor, if memory serves. Doubtless the revenues would be good." He padded back to the bed and sat beside her again. "But I do not want it. *He* cannot buy my forgiveness with such a gift. It comes too late."

"Do you hate him still?" she whispered.

"Hate?" He shook his head. "Nay, but neither can I forget what he did to me and my mother."

Linnet ducked her head, seeing in her mind's eye the words she had but an hour past read in Thurstan's journal.

I will love her always, above kith, kin and even God.

Rosalynd le Beckele.

Simon's mother.

Not a simple maid seduced by a cleric, but a great lady, wed to another.

She cannot keep the babe, so I have taken her to Blackstone Abbey on the pretext that she is grieving for her mother, who died the day Rosalynd learned she was pregnant with our child.

It is the blackest day of our lives.

"Linnet…?"

She raised her head and stared into Simon's anxious eyes. His heart was finally healing, but learning that his mother had given him up might deal it a fatal blow. She could no more utter those cruel words than she could bare her own dark secret. How terribly history does repeat itself, she thought, and spoke the only words she could. "I love you, Simon."

His smile was as dazzling as the sun, a balm to her guilty conscience. "Thank God for that. When you burst into tears, I feared you did not return my regard."

"I have loved you forever…from the moment I first saw you."

"It has taken me a little longer to open my eyes, but now that I have—" He took her mouth in a kiss so tender and sweet it made her want to cry again.

Instead, she clung to him, her blood heating, her mind hazing with passion. This was what she needed, to steep herself in him, in them, to forget, even for a few moments, the heavy burdens weighing down on her soul. All too soon, he raised his head. "Simon. Oh, Simon, I want you so…"

"And I you. But not like this, in the bishop's house with the guards outside." Simon gave her a last, hard kiss and reluctantly stood. "Till tomorrow, my love. Sleep well."

"I doubt I will sleep at all," she said tartly.

Simon smiled, ruffled her hair and crossed the room. It took all his willpower to leave her there, warm and soft and all the more desirable for the love they bore each other. But if he stayed they'd neither one get the sleep they needed.

He swung down the scaling rope and in through the window of the bishop's quarters to find Nicholas pacing.

"'Bout time you returned."

"Were you caught in Odeline's room?" Simon asked, hauling in the rope with the ease of long practice.

"Nay. I was concerned you'd gotten, er, caught up."

Simon grinned. "Nearly."

"Hmph. I've never seen you act like this over a woman."

"She is not just any woman, oaf, she is my intended wife."

"Wife." Nicholas shivered. "Perish the thought."

"I no longer find it repugnant in the least. The moment this business is settled, we will be wed. Now, did you find anything in Odeline's room?"

"Aye, though it took some time. The woman has enough clothes, shoes and such to outfit ten jaded court ladies. Stacks of trunks and chests, each one filled with tidily folded garments arranged by color. 'Tis like a portable tailor's shop." Nick threw a blanket and pillow on the floor before the hearth. "I found her stash of cosmetics and false hair rolls all neatly placed in a sack under the bed. It was dusty, so I'd say she'd not been painting herself up while here at the cathedral."

"Did you find belladonna?"

"Nay. She had arsenic powder, rouge pots, even a pot of kohl for darkening the lashes. Women who use such things usually employ belladonna for brightening the eyes," added

Nick, who knew much about such matters. "Perhaps she threw it away."

"Or am I chasing an impossible dream and we will never have a chance to avenge Bishop Thurstan's murder?"

"I am surprised you care after the way he abandoned you."

"So am I." It was Linnet's insistence on showing him the bishop's good side that had eased his bitterness, Simon thought as he wandered off to seek his bed. Meeting her and falling in love with her had changed so much in his life.

One battle left to fight, and then they would have a lifetime together.

He would prevail on the morrow. He had to.

"I want Simon dead," Odeline muttered.

"So you've said…a dozen times." Stripped to the waist before the fire in his kitchen, Hamel worked his sword along the grinding wheel, honing the edge to bite through steel and bone. "I'll kill him for you," he added with relish.

"Hmph." Odeline cast her eyes over the hard muscles bunching beneath his sweaty skin. He was a magnificent animal, strong, sleek, skilled. But in battle, the unexpected did happen, and Simon had survived the Saracen hordes. "I still think we should drug his horse."

"I sent a man round to check. It's under guard."

"We could drug Simon, then."

Hamel lifted the blade from the wheel and stared at her. "You have so little faith in my abilities?"

"Of course not," she said quickly and soothed over the matter by clucking about his safety. "I had best return to the cathedral before they shut the gates." She pecked his salty, whiskery cheek and left. But the idea of drugging Simon stuck in her brain. It might be the only way to assure his death.

She told Jevan so as they walked back to the cathedral.

"Do not worry, Mama. One way or another, Simon of Blackstone will not live out today." His face was set into a fierce scowl, his voice as hard as flint.

Alarmed, Odeline clutched at his arm. "Jevan, promise me you will do nothing rash and endanger yourself."

"Me?" His laugh was high and shrill. "Save your concern for Thurstan's bastard."

"What are you going to do?"

"Make certain I get what was promised to me. Now come along, I have much to do before the contest is waged."

Chapter Nineteen

Overnight, Durleigh's training field had taken on the festive air of a holiday market fair. Hastily erected booths were selling everything from pins and cloth to pottery crocks. The crowd from the ale tent spilled out in all directions, raucous laughter vying with the shouts of vendors hawking hot meat pies and wine.

"This is disgusting," Linnet muttered, glaring so fiercely that two men stepped from her path. She brushed past them, clasping Thurstan's prayer book over her heart.

"People are not always as good as we wish they were," said Abbess Catherine as she led the way to a tiered section of benches shaded by a tent canopy.

Elinore, Drusa and the flock of nuns fanned out to fill the first row. The benches above them were packed with Durleigh's leading townsfolk. All stared avidly at Linnet, some whispered behind their hands. A few of the more sympathetic called greetings and words of support.

Linnet could not reply. Her nerves were strung as taut as the ropes that marked off the large square where the battle would be joined. Behind it, a sea of avid onlookers jostled for position, some holding children on their shoulders.

"Disgusting," Linnet said again. As she turned away, her eyes fell on an even more disgusting sight.

Odeline approached the bleachers from the right, dressed in a lavish gown of berry-red wool, her hair coiled in wheels above her ears and covered with gold netting. Poised as a queen, she was, her sly smile grating on Linnet's brittle nerves.

Alarmed, Linnet turned away. "Where is Simon?"

"There, with my Warin and Sir Nicholas." Elinore pointed to a cluster of figures at the left end of the field.

Linnet instantly picked Simon out of the crowd. Over his gleaming mail, he wore the silver tabard of the Black Rose. She wondered if there was anyone else in the crowd who knew the significance of the emblem Thurstan had chosen for his band of Crusader knights.

A black rose for the rose I lost, Thurstan had written.

Linnet could not bear it if she lost Simon again. "Please, please keep him safe," she whispered.

A stir in the crowd heralded the arrival of Hamel Roxby. Surrounded by his band of thugs, he cantered onto the field like a conquering hero. But his appearance was greeted with more than a few hisses and curses. He drew rein and glared the onlookers into silence. A formidable sight he was, too, burly body encased in chain mail, a sword and brace of long knives at his waist.

"He is so big," Drusa whispered fearfully.

"Aye." Shivering, Linnet hunched her shoulders and watched in growing dread as Simon rode onto the field.

He wore his helmet, but the visor was up, his eyes searching the stands. The moment they met hers, he smiled. His right hand came up to touch the rose embroidered over his heart.

A silent pledge of love.

It reminded Linnet too forcefully of Thurstan and Rosalynd's star-crossed love. Were she and Simon destined to be parted? Somehow she managed a wan smile. "God be with you."

Simon inclined his head and rode on, taking Linnet's hopes and her heart with him.

A priest walked out onto the field, dispensing streams of fragrant incense from a metal burner on a chain. Archdeacon Crispin strode through the smoke, followed by a line of chanting priests and novices. When he reached the knights, he stopped.

"We are come here to settle the matter of Mistress Linnet Especer's guilt in the death of Bishop Thurstan of Durleigh," Crispin intoned. "Who stands for the law and the church?"

"I, Hamel, Sheriff of Durleigh."

"Temporary sheriff," Elinore muttered.

Simon straightened in the saddle. "And I, Simon of Blackstone, champion the lady."

Tears sprang into Linnet's eyes. He had ever been her champion. Never had she felt more in need of one. She clasped the journal tighter and prayed Thurstan would watch over him.

"Let God's will be done," said Crispin. Turning, he led the priestly procession off the field of battle. Barely had they cleared the ropes when Hamel drew his sword and attacked.

"Foul!" Nicholas sprinted down the field. "Foul! You must wait for the signal to—"

His objections were lost in the clash of steel as Simon brought his blade up to counter Hamel's heinous stroke.

Simon shuddered as the impact jarred down the length of his sword, numbing his hand and arm. Though nearly matched in height, Hamel had the advantage in weight and reach. Which meant he would have to be quicker and smarter if he wanted to win. Simon not only wanted to win. He had to win.

But Hamel would not make it easy. Nor, it seemed, would

he fight fairly. He came at Simon with a furious hail of blows designed to crush and maim.

Simon gritted his teeth and gave ground to buy time. The pressure from his knees forced his stallion to dance away. The shouts of dismay from the crowd rose over the thundering of blood against his ears. Simon spared a thought for his terrified Linnet, then closed his mind to everything except the man he must defeat. Hamel might be bigger, but Simon had had the benefit of fighting alongside Hugh, a master swordsman. He could almost hear Hugh whispering in his ear. *Watch him. Look for a weakness. Wait till the time is right, then exploit his flaw.*

Simon watched and waited and endured blow after bruising blow. They tested each other with deadly steel as they had as youths with clenched fists and wooden weapons. Their harsh breathing filled the near silence that had fallen over the field, punctuated only by grunts and the clash of metal on metal. Simon ducked and parried and retreated. He refused to go on the attack, but maintained a stout defense, probing Hamel's fighting style for the flaw that would gain him a victory.

Hamel's eyes glowed in the sockets of his helmet, burning with fury and frustration. "Stand still. Stand and fight, dammit." He went in low, aiming for Simon's mount.

Cursing, Simon drew back sharply on the reins. The stallion reared, screaming in rage. Its hooves slipped on the slick grass. *They were going down.* Instinctively Simon kicked his feet free of the stirrups and jumped. He landed on his back with enough force to drive the air from his lungs and make his vision swim. Vaguely he was aware of the taste of blood in his mouth and of Linnet's screams rising about the roar of the crowd. Marshaling his reserves, Simon rolled onto his knees and came up in a crouch.

None too soon, for Hamel bore down on him, sword aloft, eyes glittering with malicious triumph.

Winded, aching in more places than he could count, Simon lowered his sword and forced himself to wait. It was a game the Saracen youth had played in their camp across the river from the Crusaders'. He'd watched them often enough to admire their horsemanship and understand the value of timing.

Hamel pounded closer...closer...so close Simon could see the triumphant gleam in his enemy's eyes. As Hamel brought his sword in for the coup de grace, Simon ducked under the blade, spun and came up in time to grab Hamel by the back of his tabard. The momentum that nearly pulled Simon's arms from their sockets jerked Hamel from the saddle.

The sheriff landed with a *thud* that made the ground shake, but he was on his feet quicker than a scalded cat and looking just as mean. "Bastard," Hamel screamed and came at Simon, beating him back with a flurry of blows.

Simon could feel himself faltering, the sleepless nights taking their toll in weakening limbs and sluggish responses. He countered the exhaustion by reminding himself what was at stake. Linnet's freedom. Her life.

"I've got ye now," Hamel crowed, moving in for the kill. As he raised his sword, Hamel committed the greatest sin. He overextended, assuming Simon would not attack.

It was the opening Simon had prayed for. He slipped in under Hamel's lax guard. Steel screamed on steel as his blade slid down Hamel's sword, aiming for the shoulder.

Take Hamel prisoner. Find out what he knows.

In the last instant, Hamel twisted. The blade glanced off his shoulder and bit into the side of his neck, drawing a gush of blood. He grunted and looked at Simon, his wide face contorted with pain and shock. The weapon slipped from his hand and onto the ground. Hamel groaned; his eyes fluttered shut, and he followed his sword down.

"Simon! Simon!"

He turned to see Linnet dashing across the trampled grass,

followed by the abbess, a flock of nuns and half of Durleigh. They were chanting his name and hers.

It was over.

Exhausted, bruised, Simon sank down on one knee and waited.

It was over, and they had won.

Standing at the verge of the battlefield, Crispin stared in mute horror at the fallen sheriff and listened in stunned disbelief to the jubilant shouts of the townsfolk as they gathered around the triumphant knight.

The bishop's bastard and his leman had won.

God had chosen them over himself.

The enormity of his loss weighed heavy on Crispin's soul, sin piling upon sin. He had poisoned not one but two of his fellow priests. That neither had died at his hand was a moot point. He had sought their deaths.

It mattered little that he had believed his cause was just, for that holy cause now lay like ashes at his feet.

What did he do now? How could he live with the knowledge that God had not sanctioned his acts?

Crispin buried his face in his hands. Death would be preferable to that living purgatory, but he could not compound the sins he had already committed with that most heinous of—

"It is not over!" cried a female voice.

Crispin lowered his hands in time to see the lady Odeline step from the shadow of the bleachers and onto the field.

"Bastard, you will not take what is rightfully my son's!" Something glittered in her upraised hand as she dashed toward the gathering a few feet from Crispin.

She meant to kill Simon of Blackstone.

Crispin knew it as surely as he knew that his burdened soul would never see heaven. One last act, he thought. One good act to wipe away the sins of the past.

Crossing himself, he stepped into Odeline's path.

* * *

A scream of mortal pain shattered the celebration.

Linnet turned in the circle of Simon's arms and saw the archdeacon go down, blood on his breast, Lady Odeline sprawled on top of him in a welter of crimson skirts. "What...?"

"She's stabbed the archdeacon!" Simon ran to the fallen pair with Linnet hard on his heels. Cursing, he pulled Odeline off the prelate and shoved her at Nicholas. "Hold her fast," he commanded before turning to Linnet. "What can we do?"

Linnet knelt beside her enemy and shook her head. The welling blood told an ominous tale.

"Brother Crispin." Anselme knelt at his side, hands hovering over the jeweled hilt. "I dare not pull it. Get me clean linens and a litter."

Crispin's eyes opened. "Do not trouble yourself, Brother. I am dying." His lips lifted in a half smile. "Blessed death."

"He is mad!" Odeline cried. "He threw himself on my knife."

"Come away, my lady." Nicholas carried her to the benches.

Crispin turned his head, his eyes cloudy with pain, dark with purpose. "I never meant for Thurstan to die, only sicken."

"So you could be bishop?" Linnet asked.

He nodded, his eyes drifting closed again. "Forgive me," he whispered, "for God never will."

"Let me shrive you, Reverend Father." Brother Gerard knelt at the archdeacon's head.

Linnet turned away and was welcomed into Simon's embrace. "He put the monkshood in the brandy," she whispered.

"Aye. Odeline was right, Crispin is mad. Come." Simon took her to the benches where Nicholas and the lady sat. His aunt looked half mad herself, her hair disheveled, her eyes wild. "Did you give Thurstan the belladonna, Odeline?"

"It's finished. Done." Odeline slumped against Nicholas. "All for nothing. Nothing without the charter."

"The charter for Blackstone Heath?" Simon asked.

An eerie smile crossed Odeline's face. "Blackstone Heath...we will be happy there, Jevan. No more living on the scraps of others. I told you I would secure it for you."

Linnet shivered. "Oh, Simon..."

"Did you kill Thurstan?" Simon asked gently.

Odeline stared through him, her eyes distant, unfocused.

Brother Anselme joined them. "I do not think she is capable of answering."

Simon sighed. "Crispin?"

"Is with God." Anselme crossed himself. "And we must look to the living. Sir Nicholas, if you will carry Lady Odeline to the infirmary, I will give her a sleeping potion. Mayhap when she wakens she will be able to tell us more." He looked around the field. "'Tis odd Jevan is not here with her."

"Perhaps Jevan knew what she had done and feared he would be brought down with her," Simon murmured.

"But he is her son," Linnet said angrily. "No matter her crime, he should stand by her out of love."

"Jevan is not molded from such fine cloth, I fear," said Anselme. "Simon, come to the infirmary, and I will tend your hurts." He motioned for Nicholas to follow him.

"In a moment." Simon sat still, suddenly drained both in body and mind. He ached in a dozen places but none of the cuts and bruises were serious. Mostly what he felt was relief. "It is over," he whispered watching the nuns and priests compose Crispin's body on a litter. "It is over, and you are safe."

"Thanks to you. But I was so afraid. If anything had happened to you, I would not have wanted to live." She shivered and burrowed deeper into his embrace.

"I know what you mean." He savored the feel of her warm, slender body. An overwhelming sense of rightness rose inside him, so powerful, so moving that he knew the rest of his life would be empty and meaningless if she was not beside him. "Marry me, Linnet," he murmured, kissing the top of her head.

Marry me. The words she had so longed to hear now cut her like a blade. Sweet Mary, she wanted to wed him, but she could feel the journal wedged between them. A tangible symbol of an insurmountable barrier. "I cannot," she said, low and anguished.

"Why?" Simon cupped her chin and raised it, troubled green eyes searching tormented brown. "Do you not love me?"

"With all my heart, I do." A single tear trailed down her cheek. "But I cannot wed you."

"I can support you. I have money from ransom—"

"Oh, Simon." Unable to bear the bewildered hurt in his dear face, she tried to wrench free. He would not let her go. Her own pain twisted deeper. "Simon..." She looked up, expecting to see the wariness that had edged his voice, instead she saw a love that humbled her. *Tell him. He loves you, he will understand.* "Simon, I..." Where to start? "I bore a child."

His hands tightened on her shoulders, his eyes took on their old coldness. "Whose?"

"'Twas born nine months after you left."

"Mine? Mine!" A fierce joy gleamed briefly, then went out. "The child is not with you. Did it...did it die, then?"

The tears she had held back filled her eyes, blurring his image. She was glad she could not see his face. "I—I gave her up for adoption."

"Gave her up?" Simon let go of her and leaped from the

bench. "You gave our child away?" He stared at her as though she had turned into a depraved monster.

"I did not want her to suffer the stain of bastardy. Thurstan arranged for her to be adopted by a loving—"

"Thurstan!" If anything, Simon's expression grew more fierce. His face was red, his eyes blazed with hatred.

Linnet's heart fell. He was not going to forgive her. Dying inside, she stood and thrust the journal at him. "It is all in here…including the name of your mother. He wrote everything down…except the name of the family to whom he gave our daughter." Unable to bear his scathing glance another minute, she stumbled away.

Linnet had given away his child.

Simon stood still, head bowed beneath the enormous weight of her betrayal. The blow had been so swift, so unexpected. He had loved her, trusted her in ways he had never trusted another, and all the while, she had harbored this dark, heinous secret.

"It was the hardest thing she has ever done," Abbess Catherine said softly.

"Go away."

"After I have said my piece. Linnet loved you, even then, and wanted to raise the babe herself, no matter that she would not have been able to hold her head up in Durleigh. Nor would the Spiciers' Guild have allowed a fallen woman to run a shop. Her parents would have supported her, but once they were gone, she and the babe would likely have ended up in the almshouse."

"So, she abandoned my child for her own selfish—"

"If you must blame someone, blame Thurstan and me. He knew from observing you over the years that the taint of bastardy had embittered you. We encouraged Linnet to give the child up that it might be raised by a loving family with a proper name."

Simon looked up. "Yet he never acknowledged me."

"It was the price he paid for your life."

"What do you mean?" he asked warily.

"Our father, Baron Robert de Lyndhurst, was a powerful, autocratic man. 'Twas he who decided Thurstan would be bishop after our older brother died. The fact that Thurstan was more suited to court life and was in love with a woman mattered not to the Baron. When Father discovered you had been conceived, he ordered the pregnancy terminated. Thurstan declared he would only enter the church if you were allowed to live. So it was agreed, but Thurstan was forced to swear, on your mother's immortal soul, that he would never acknowledge you."

The anger that had filled Simon's heart for the past three years eased a bit. "And my mother?"

"Later she wed another. Only a few of us knew her identity, and we were sworn never to reveal it." Catherine looked at the journal he held. "Linnet says the name is in there. If you do not read Latin, she will translate for you, I am sure."

"You could do it," Simon said, the part of his heart he had given to Linnet still aching and bruised.

"Can you not forgive her?"

"I do not know. I—"

"Simon of Blackstone!" Jevan edged around the bleachers, Linnet held securely in front of him, a knife at her throat.

"What are you doing?" Simon demanded, his gaze focused on Linnet's terrified face. She looked so small and vulnerable.

"Reclaiming what should have been mine, the charter to Blackstone Heath."

"I do not know where it is."

"You have it in your hand. Uncle hid it in the journal."

Simon held the journal out. "Release Linnet and take it."

"I fear the charter is no good to me if you are alive." Jevan smiled faintly. "Uncle worded it that way."

"I will deed the property to you."

Jevan's expression hardened. "So you say now, while I hold your lover at knifepoint, but later you will change your mind."

"Nay, I will not. The manor is nothing to me." Simon looked into Linnet's pale, frightened face and felt something shift inside him. She was the warmest, most loving of women. Giving up their child must have been, as Abbess Catherine said, the hardest thing Linnet had ever done. Yet she had made the sacrifice so the babe might have a better life. He could not fault her for that. The sense of betrayal fell away, leaving in its place a deep sadness, for Linnet, for himself and for the child they would never have a chance to raise. "I will gladly give you—"

"You will do as I say," Jevan cried. With his free hand, he reached into the scrip at his waist and withdrew a small vial. "You will drink this."

Gooseflesh prickled on Simon's body. "The belladonna."

Jevan grinned. "There is plenty left for you."

"You took it from your mother's room and killed Bishop Thurstan," Simon said.

"I had to after Rob FitzHugh told me you were alive. Uncle would have changed the charter in your favor, you see," Jevan said in that calmly insane voice of his. "And I fear you must die, too, so I can have the manor."

"Nay," Catherine and Linnet cried in unison.

"Shut up," Jevan shouted. "Do not move, Aunt Catherine, or I will kill your precious Linnet."

"Jevan…surely there is another way," Catherine pleaded.

"Alas, there is not. Rob, Hamel and even my mother failed me. It is up to Simon, now. If he fails, Linnet dies. You do not want that, do you, Simon?" he asked silkily.

"I do not." Simon looked deep into Linnet's frantic eyes and let all he felt for her…the—love, the respect, and aye, even the forgiveness—show in a tender smile. "She has endured too much for me to fail her now.'' He held out his hand.

"Simon, nay!" Linnet cried. She tried to wriggle free, but the sting of Jevan's blade at her throat stopped her.

"Don't move, wench." Jevan leaned out and placed the vial on the bench. "If you drop it, Simon, I will kill her."

"I understand." Simon scooped up the vial, flicked at the cork stopper and upended the vial into his mouth.

Linnet watched in horror as Simon drank the poison. Her heart seemed to stop in the second he stood there. Then he stiffened, cried out and fell to the ground. His body twitched and jerked convulsively.

"Simon! Simon!" Linnet rammed her elbow into Jevan's soft middle, loosening his grip enough to squirm free. She dashed to Simon, but as she fell onto her knees beside his heaving body, Abbess Catherine grabbed hold of her.

"Nay, love. Do not look." The abbess pulled her back firmly but gently. "There is nothing we can do for him."

Linnet sobbed and clung helplessly to the abbess.

"Just like Uncle Thurstan," Jevan muttered, walking over to survey his handiwork. "Fitting."

Linnet was filled with such loathing it nearly drove out her anguish. "You did not have to kill him," she sobbed.

"But I wanted to." Jevan sheathed his knife and bent over the writhing Simon to pick up the journal. Smiling, he ripped off the cover sheet and extracted the parchment inside. "Mine, now, all—"

His triumphant words ended on a garbled scream as Simon surged up from the ground and planted a fist in Jevan's belly, folding him neatly. The second blow caught Jevan in the chin, lifted him, then sent him sprawling on the ground in a heap.

"Simon?" Linnet flew out of Catherine's arms. "You are alive." She touched his face, grimy but warm with life. "How…?"

"I did not take the cork out." He opened his left hand, displaying the stoppered vial. "Neat bit of playacting, eh?"

"Sweet Mary, I thought you'd drunk it. I have never been so frightened in all my days. 'Tis a miracle. A miracle." Abbess Catherine laughed unsteadily, then sobered and looked down at Jevan. "What of him?"

"We should bind him before he awakens," said Simon. "And turn him over to the authorities for trial."

"Along with his mother." Catherine tisked. "She was always a wild, greedy girl, but to think she would come to this...."

"With Hamel gone, who is the law in Durleigh?" asked Simon.

"The sheriff will likely come from York till a new one can be appointed here." Catherine lifted her skirts. "Stay with Jevan, I will summon the brothers to take charge of him."

Linnet clung to Simon, unable to believe he was really alive. "I was afraid you had drunk it."

"I would have," Simon said. "For you."

"Oh, Simon..." Linnet looked up and found his gaze full on her, stripped bare of bitterness and regret.

"I love you, Linnet," he murmured. "Wed me. Together we will put the past behind us and look to the future."

She wanted to. Sweet Mary, she wanted that with all her heart. But would their love be enough to keep the ghosts of the past at bay?

Epilogue

Oxford, June 10, 1222

Lady Rosalynd's house drowsed in the noonday sun, a warm breeze tugging playfully at the flowers that bloomed beside the door. Built of mellow gray stone, the three-story structure lorded over the simpler timber buildings that flanked it on either side. Even the windows, their shutters thrown open to the summer air, seemed to gaze haughtily down on passersby.

Seated atop his horse, Simon studied the home where his mother reportedly lived and felt a chill creep down his spine.

"I can go to the door if you like," Linnet murmured.

Simon smiled ruefully at his wife of two weeks. "If Nicholas could see me trembling like this he'd call me the veriest of cowards." Just ten days ago Nicholas had gathered his own courage and set out to confront his formidable sire.

"You are no coward, and facing a mother you've never met is far different from Nicholas proving himself to his father."

"Still, I have never quailed from a fight before."

"'Tis not a battle," Linnet said softly.

"Tell that to my belly," he grumbled. "There's a war

going on inside." And there had been since he'd decided to come here.

Linnet smiled gently. "We can go home if you'd rather."

It was tempting, though it had taken them four days to ride here from Durleigh. But he yearned for just a glimpse of his mother. "What would the men say?" he asked, thinking of the guardsmen who'd accompanied them and waited in a nearby inn.

"It does seem like conduct unbecoming the new sheriff of Durleigh," she said, grinning. "If the king gets word of it, you may not be confirmed in your post...no matter that the mayor and half the merchants begged you to take on the responsibility."

Simon nodded, touched anew by the townsfolks' faith in him. He welcomed the challenge of keeping order in Durleigh. "Lady Rosalynd may not want to see the child she gave up."

"I would," Linnet whispered. For an instant, her eyes lost that special glow, and he was reminded of the times he'd awakened in the night to the sound of her muffled weeping. No matter how many times he assured her he understood and forgave her, Linnet was not at peace, for she could not forgive herself. Her unhappiness was the one blot on the life they were building for themselves, the one stain on their perfect love.

He had to do this for Linnet as much as for himself, Simon thought. And he could hardly return to Durleigh and tell Bishop Walter that he'd not seen the lady Rosalynd.

Walter de Folke had not only recovered from the monkshood but had been named Bishop of Durleigh. He had used his connections to learn that Rosalynd le Beckele had wed Baron William de la Hewaite, and was widowed and living in this fine house in Oxford. According to Walter, Lady Rosalynd had spent many years at court. Simon pictured her wearing silk, costly gems and a haughty expression, yet could not shake the urge to see her.

"Let us go in, then," Simon murmured. "We will return to her the letters we found in Thurstan's trunk." Ones she had written long ago when Thurstan was a student. "And let her know of his passing, in case she had not heard. But I will not say that we are related till I am assured it would not cause trouble."

"Would you rather I waited here?"

"Nay!" he exclaimed. "You are my strength. I am going nowhere without you, ever again." He dismounted, lifted Linnet from the saddle and escorted her toward the house. "Perhaps no one is at home," he said hopefully.

Linnet chuckled. "The shutters are open, my love, so—"

A shriek came from around the side of the house.

Simon glanced at Linnet. "Stay here." Drawing his sword, he charged down the path beside the house just as another scream rent the air. Vaulting the low stone wall that blocked his way, he hustled around the side of the building and into a garden. It was an exact duplicate of the one at Durleigh, even to the yew hedges bordering row after row of fragrant roses.

Plumb in the middle of the garden stood a wooden tub containing a large, wet dog. Holding the beast there was a slender woman, her gown drenched in soapy water.

"Mistress, do you require aid?" Simon called out.

She looked up, a woman of middle years, but beautiful still, tendrils of fair, wet hair clinging to her flushed cheeks. "Aye, Bernard hates to be bathed, but he and Rosie got into the mud, and—"

Bernard chose that moment to make a desperate bid for freedom. Woofing, he gathered himself and leaped.

"Get him," the woman shouted.

Simon dropped his sword, lunged and caught the dog just as its front paws cleared the rim of the tub. Both arms wrapped around the beast's slippery neck, he sought to push the dog back, but his feet slid. Simon went under, but came up holding the dog with both arms. "Do not fear, I have him."

The woman laughed. "'Twould seem Bernard has you."

"Simon?" Linnet bustled into the garden. "Are you all right?" She stopped, gaped and burst out laughing.

Simon glared at the two chortling women. A fine impression he was going to make on his mother, soaking wet and smelling of dog. But he would see this through. "If you two can stop laughing long enough you might as well hand me the soap, I will wash Bernard while I'm in here."

"Of course." The woman bustled about, applying strong lye soap to the dog while Simon grimly held on to the indignant beast. Between them, Linnet and the woman poured buckets of water over the dog until the soap was rinsed out.

"Stand back. I'm going to let him loose," said Simon.

The moment he was free, Bernard catapulted from the tub, spraying water in all directions and barking joyously. Despite her ruined gown and disheveled hair, the woman began to laugh again like a young lass.

At least the staff at Lady Rosalynd's was not stiff and proper, Simon thought as he waded into the chaos to grab hold of Bernard's collar. "Have you rope to tie him while he dries?"

"Aye, just there on yon tree."

By the time Simon had secured the animal, Linnet and the woman were back with linen towels. Sitting down on one of the stone benches, he tugged off his wet tunic and dried his hair.

"I am sorry I have no dry clothes to offer you, sir...?"

"Simon of Blackstone."

The woman gasped softly and sank onto the bench.

"The name has meaning to you?" Simon asked, surprised his lady mother would have confided in her maidservants.

"Aye." Tears filled her eyes, magnifying their grassy green color. "*Mon Dieu*, I never thought to see you again, my love."

My love. Simon stared at her, his heart thudding so loudly he barely heard his own voice. "*You* are Lady Rosalynd?"

She nodded, a single tear trickling down her cheek. The faint lines around her eyes and mouth, the few gray hairs among the golden ones, were the only signs she was old enough to be his mother. "How…how did you know to come here?"

Simon stiffened. "I regret intruding upon you."

"Simon," Linnet murmured, laying a hand on his arm. "Your name was in Bishop Thurstan's journal. He…he is dead."

"Aye." Rosalynd sighed heavily. "The news reached me two weeks ago, but I was not surprised. On that very night he died, I awoke with a feeling of such loss that I feared something had happened to him. 'Twas a foul crime indeed."

"We have caught the murderers." His voice gruff with emotion, Simon related the twisted tale. "Jevan hanged himself before he could be brought to trial. His death shattered the last of Odeline's sanity. Reverend Mother Catherine has taken her to the abbey, but Odeline believes she is living at court awaiting Jevan's return."

"A sad business," Rosalynd murmured. "I will mourn Thurstan all my life, but that sorrow is tempered by your return. I am glad he did know you lived ere he was taken from us." She smiled faintly. "It is a joy to look upon your dear face and see you smile back at me. I feared you would hate me for giving you up."

"I did…once." Simon linked his fingers with Linnet's. "But Catherine told me that Baron Robert's hunger for power was responsible for parting you and my father. And Linnet, my wife, has taught me that love sometimes means letting go."

Rosalynd started. "You are Linnet Especer?"

"Until a few weeks ago, I was." Linnet snuggled closer to Simon. "Now I am Linnet of Blackstone."

"Sweet Mary," the lady whispered, her eyes swimming with tears though she smiled broadly. "God does work in mysterious—"

"Nanna! Nanna, I'm clean." A small child trotted down the garden path, pink cheeks glistening, damp blond curls gleaming in the sunlight. Her eyes, a paler green than Rosalynd's, danced in time with her busy feet.

The lady's granddaughter, Linnet thought, speared by a sharp, painful reminder of her own daughter.

Rosalynd scooped the child up and kissed her. Then looked over at Linnet. "I wonder if Thurstan knew, when he first hatched this scheme, how it would all turn out."

"What do you mean?" Linnet asked.

Instead of replying, Rosalynd turned to the child cuddling contentedly in her arms. "Rosie, you remember I told you someday you might meet your mama? Well, this is that day."

Linnet heard her own gasp of surprise echoed by Simon's. "She...she is our daughter?" Linnet asked, scarcely daring to hope.

"Aye." Rosalynd's smile grew to encompass them all. "Thurstan thought it fitting that I should raise her, for he knew I would love her nearly as much as you do."

Linnet stared at her baby girl, her heart so filled with love it was a wonder it didn't burst.

"I don't remember you," Rosie said around her thumb.

Linnet knelt, her shaky insides steadied by the feel of Simon's arm coming around her as he sank down beside her. "I remember you," she whispered, her eyes drinking in every inch of the sturdy little girl with her hair and Simon's eyes. "Though you were much smaller than you are now."

"I'm a big girl," Rosie replied.

"Why do you not show your mama your room and your toys?"

Rosie cast a canny, rebellious eye at her grandmother. "She wants to see the kittens."

"They are too young for you to play with," Rosalynd said.

"We will just look." Rosie slid off her grandmother's lap, and held out a pudgy hand to Linnet. "They are in the stables."

The feel of that small hand slipping so trustingly into hers warmed Linnet clear through, healing her battered soul. Heart so full she could scarcely breathe, she stood and looked at Simon. His eyes glittered with joyful tears. "Can he come, too?"

Rosie tilted her head at him and frowned doubtfully. "He's too big. He might squash the kittens."

"Nay, he is gentle," Linnet said. "He is your papa."

"My papa is an angel. Nanna said so."

"I would not go quite that far," Linnet said, tongue in cheek. "But he is the most wonderful of men."

"Very well, but you must promise to be quiet," Rosie said sternly. She held out her other hand.

Simon took it, and felt a sense of wonder fill him. The three of them were together…a family. His family. It was what he had wished for all his life, and now he had it. Thanks to his father. And mother. He turned back to the lady who sat on the bench, her expression mingling happiness and sorrow; happiness for gaining a son and sadness for…? Surely she didn't think they would leave her out? "Come, Mama, I would not be parted from you, or part you from Rosie."

Lady Rosalynd stood, smiling, and took the hand he held out. "Nor do I want to be apart from you…ever again."

"Are we all going together?" Rosie asked, bright eyes scanning the beaming adults.

"Forever and always," Simon said.

* * *

Later that night, Simon stood over the sleeping child, both of his arms wrapped securely around Linnet. This had surely been the best day of his life. "Happy, love?" he whispered.

"Aye." Linnet leaned into his embrace. "If only Thurstan could be here with us, my joy would be complete."

"He is with us, in our hearts. Always."

Linnet nodded. "I think he would approve of your plans to make Blackstone Heath a home for orphaned babes."

"So do I, but perhaps we'd best wait a bit. If today is anything to judge by, we will have our hands full with Rosie."

Linnet glanced at him over her shoulder and grinned. "Is that your way of saying our daughter is willful?"

"And stubborn. We have much to learn about raising her."

"Then it is well that your mother is coming back to Durleigh with us."

Your mother. Simon liked the sound of that. Better still, he liked *her*. She was warm, caring and witty. And he did relish the notion of spending more time with her, but... "It will be confusing for Rosie to have three parents to order her about."

"Rosie is not much one to be ordered, I think. And it will ease her to have Rosalynd nearby in her new home."

"You do not mind, then?"

"Nay. Never. I am hoping to coax Rosalynd into helping get Blackstone ready to receive its first children. And too..." Linnet stroked Simon's chin. "We are all four a family at last, but the adults, at least, have wounds that are not yet fully healed. They will mend quicker if we are together."

He kissed the tip of Linnet's nose. "Is it any reason why I love you? Even though I do foresee being hard-pressed to keep you and our equally impetuous daughter out of trouble."

Linnet wound her arms around his neck and drew his

mouth down for a blistering kiss. "I can think of no man better suited to the task, my love. My champion."

Simon smiled, a deep and abiding love reflected in his soft gray-green eyes. "It will be my pleasure to champion you all the days of our lives," he whispered.

* * * * *

Women found Nicholas of Hendry irresistible.
All except one. And *she* was the one this
reformed rogue was determined to have....
Be sure to look for

THE ROGUE

by

Ana Seymour

the next book in the exciting
KNIGHTS OF THE BLACK ROSE
miniseries!
Available in February 2000
from Harlequin Historicals

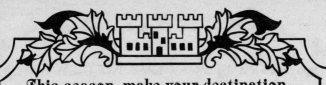

This season, make your destination
England with four exciting stories from
Harlequin Historicals

On sale in December 1999,

THE CHAMPION,
The first book of *KNIGHTS OF THE BLACK ROSE*
by **Suzanne Barclay**
(England, 1222)

BY QUEEN'S GRACE
by **Shari Anton**
(England, 1109)

On sale in January 2000,

THE GENTLEMAN THIEF
by **Deborah Simmons**
(England, 1818)

MY LADY RELUCTANT
by **Laurie Grant**
(England, 1141)

Harlequin Historicals
Have a blast in the past!

Available at your favorite retail outlet.

HARLEQUIN®
Makes any time special ™

Visit us at www.romance.net

HHMED10

3 Stories of Holiday Romance from three bestselling Harlequin® authors

Valentine Babies

by ANNE STUART

TARA TAYLOR QUINN
JULE McBRIDE

Goddess in Waiting by Anne Stuart
Edward walks into Marika's funky maternity shop to pick up some things for his sister. He doesn't expect to assist in the delivery of a baby and fall for outrageous Marika.

Gabe's Special Delivery by Tara Taylor Quinn
On February 14, Gabe Stone finds a living, breathing valentine on his doorstep—his daughter. Her mother has given Gabe four hours to adjust to fatherhood, resolve custody and win back his ex-wife?

My Man Valentine by Jule McBride
Everyone knows Eloise Hunter and C. D. Valentine are in love. Except Eloise and C. D. Then, one of Eloise's baby-sitting clients leaves her with a baby to mind, and C. D. swings into protector mode.

VALENTINE BABIES

On sale January 2000 at your favorite retail outlet.

HARLEQUIN®
Makes any time special ™

Come escape with Harlequin's new

Series Sampler

**Four great full-length Harlequin novels
bound together in one fabulous volume
and at an unbelievable price.**

Be transported back
in time with a
Harlequin Historical®
novel, get caught up
in a mystery with **Intrigue®**,
be tempted by a hot, sizzling romance
with **Harlequin Temptation®**,
or just enjoy a down-home
all-American read with
American Romance®.

You won't be able to put this collection down!

On sale February 2000 at your favorite retail outlet.

HARLEQUIN®
Makes any time special ™

Visit us at www.romance.net   PHESC

Start the year right with
Harlequin Historicals' first
multi-author miniseries,

KNIGHTS OF THE BLACK ROSE

Three warriors bound by one event,
each destined to find true love....

THE CHAMPION, by **Suzanne Barclay**
On sale December 1999

THE ROGUE, by **Ana Seymour**
On sale February 2000

THE CONQUEROR, by **Shari Anton**
On sale April 2000

Available at your favorite retail outlet.

HARLEQUIN®
Makes any time special ™

Harlequin® Historical

is proud to offer four very different
Western romances that will
warm your hearts....

On sale in December 1999,
SHAWNEE BRIDE
by **Elizabeth Lane**
and
THE LADY AND THE OUTLAW
by **DeLoras Scott**

On sale in January 2000,
THE BACHELOR TAX
by **Carolyn Davidson**
and
THE OUTLAW'S BRIDE
by **Liz Ireland**

Harlequin Historicals
The way the past *should* have been.

Available at your favorite retail outlet.

HARLEQUIN®
Makes any time special ™

Visit us at www.romance.net

HHWEST5